"Now you will see just how badly I managed in cotillion
clas

l to

coti ."

ck,
low her
spir gh
he nd
dow her
pal his
shir as
he t

l nd
shou gh
and It
env he
stra

he
had od
help s a
gin

"Full of small-town charm and southern heat...humorous, heartwarming, and sexy. I couldn't put it down!"
—Robin Wells, author of *Still the One*

"A sweet confection...This first of a projected series about the Rhodes brothers offers up Southern hospitality with a bit of grit. Romance readers will be delighted."
—*Library Journal*

"Hope Ramsay delivers with this sweet and sassy story of small-town love, friendship, and the ties that bind."
—Lisa Dale, author of *Simple Wishes*

"Ramsay has created a great new series...Not only are the two main characters compelling and fun, but as you read, the entire town of kooky but very real people become part of your life...I can hardly wait until I visit Last Chance again."
—FreshFiction.com

"Touching...funny...Ramsay's characters were endearing and lovable, and I eagerly look forward to the rest of [the series]."
—NovelReaction.com

"A sweet romance...sassy and fun characters."
—Book Hounds (maryinhb.blogspot.com)

"Captivating...great characterization, amusing dialogue...I am glad that the universe sent *Welcome to Last Chance* my way, and I am going to make sure that it does the same with Hope Ramsay's future books."
—LikesBooks.com

~LAST~ CHANCE
Beauty Queen

HOPE RAMSAY

FOREVER

NEW YORK   BOSTON

Forever
Hachette Book Group
237 Park Avenue
New York, NY 10017

www.HachetteBookGroup.com

Printed in the United States of America

First Edition: February 2012
10 9 8 7 6 5 4 3 2 1

Forever is an imprint of Grand Central Publishing.
The Forever name and logo are trademarks of Hachette Book Group, Inc.

The publisher is not responsible for websites (or their content) that are not owned by the publisher.

For Caroline

Acknowledgments

I would like to thank my wonderful critique partners: Robin Kaye and Carla Kempert for their friendship and guidance on all things romance. I would also like to give a shout out to the wonderful Ruby Slippered Sisterhood—especially the historical writers—who helped me figure out the core qualities of a regency hero so I could create a modern version of one and set him adrift in swampland. Also, many thanks to my wonderful editor, Alex Logan, for helping me to find the best way to tell this story. Thank you, Elaine English, for all your help and support. And finally, my eternal gratitude to my husband, Bryan. I love many things about you, sweetie, but it's your kindness that I love best.

~LAST~ CHANCE

Beauty Queen

CHAPTER 1

Mirrors never lie.

Caroline Rhodes caught the fleeting spark of surprise in her own eyes as she studied her reflection in her Camry's rearview. Despite her professional wardrobe and flawless makeup, the mirror still reflected an image of the small-town Watermelon Queen she had once been. She touched up her lipstick and gave herself one last implacable stare. As usual, the humidity had gotten to her hair. She sleeked it back into its ponytail, but a few stray curls refused to be tamed. It was hopeless.

She snatched her black Coach briefcase from the passenger seat and covered the distance over the blazing blacktop to the front doors of the Columbia Hilton in less than a minute. Icy air greeted her as she passed through the glass doors and headed toward the steakhouse restaurant in the lobby. The heels of her pumps clicked over the marble floor like hammer blows. With each heel strike, the tension coiled inside her.

She was here to meet Hugh deBracy, the umpteenth

baron of somewhere in England, who probably looked down his nose at people who came from small rural towns in the middle of nowhere.

DeBracy had come to these shores to buy up a little bit of that rural land so he could put up a textile machinery factory. Caroline's boss, Senator Rupert Warren, wanted to make that happen. There was the matter of two hundred new jobs at stake.

But there was a teeny-tiny problem. The land Lord deBracy wanted wasn't for sale. Caroline's job was to make this problem disappear—a feat that would take a miracle.

She stepped into the dark, cold environment of the steakhouse and scanned the sparse luncheon crowd. She had never seen a photo of Hugh deBracy, but she found him without any trouble.

He was in his mid-thirties and wore a Savile Row suit and a slightly loosened regimental tie. Except for his curly Byronic hair, the man looked like the dictionary definition of an uptight English aristocrat. He sat at a booth halfway down a long row, and he looked up from the menu he'd been perusing as if he could sense her studying him.

The man's gaze widened as if in recognition. He stood, dropping the menu and nervously tightening his tie.

His glance dropped to her ankles and then rose in a slow circuit that moved up her bare, suntanned legs and the professional silhouette of her business suit. The gaze stopped when it reached the hint of lace at the V of her jacket where, predictably, it stuck.

As an ex–beauty queen with a bustline to match, Caroline was used to this, even if she hated it. It was tough to be taken seriously when people discovered that you once wore a ridiculous pink and green dress accessorized by a rhinestone tiara and a sash across your breasts.

Caroline squared her worsted-clad shoulders and walked forward. His gaze rose to meet hers. The corner of his mouth twitched, and his eyes—the color of scotch whiskey—softened.

"Miss Rhodes?" he asked.

The sound of her name spoken with those clipped British vowels did something totally inappropriate to her insides. Boy, she really needed to find a meaningful love life, one of these days—after the election. In the meantime, she'd continue to find escape in those romance books featuring suave English heroes.

No doubt this secret addiction to historical romances was the reason her girl parts got hot and bothered by Lord deBracy's accent. She had to remember that this guy had the ability to royally screw up her life and her career.

She reached for a cool nonchalance that she didn't for one instant really feel. "Lord deBracy?"

"Um, that would be Lord Woolham. The title applies to the peerage, not the surname. I am delighted to meet you." He nodded his head but didn't extend his hand in greeting, which kind of belied his words.

Crap. She had screwed up, and she really hated doing that. She should have researched English titles before she set one foot in this restaurant or opened her mouth. Despite her gaff, she gritted her teeth, gave him a professional smile that was not too big and not too small, and took her seat in the booth facing him.

"I want to thank you for meeting me here," he said as

he took his seat. He turned and nodded at the waiter in true aristocratic fashion.

"It's not a problem. Senator Warren wants me to help you in any way I can," Caroline said. Her words were misleading. Being here with him *was* a problem. She had everything at stake: her career and her family. His Lordship had nothing at risk, except a potential factory.

The waiter came along, and they ordered: roast beef for him and a small house salad for her. When the waiter left, his Lordship opened the business conversation.

"So," he said, leaning forward slightly. "According to the senator, you're the woman who can help me solve my real estate problem."

She looked him straight in the eye. And his eyes were so warm and brown they didn't seem to match his stiff formality. She wasn't going to let him see how badly she felt outclassed here. So she forced herself not to look away. "I'm good at what I do. But Senator Warren has given you assurances that might be unjustified. There are serious complications."

"I see. Would you care to elaborate?"

No. She wouldn't. If given her druthers, Caroline would get up and run like a greyhound to the nearest exit. But she was stuck. The senator really, really wanted this factory built.

"I'm afraid this is a *very* difficult case," she said, trying to quell the butterflies in her midsection. The waiter came back with deBracy's house salad before she could say anything more.

His Lordship put his napkin in his lap and began cutting the lettuce with a single-minded purpose that verged on obsession. "How so?" he asked. "According to my partner, who was assembling the land for the factory until his untimely death, the parcel of land in question is not being used productively."

Wow. How totally smug of him. No doubt Lord *Woolham* thought that the only productive use of land was in supporting the lifestyles of the rich and aristocratic. "How much do you know about the parcel in question?" she asked.

"Not very much, except that the fellow who owns it won't sell. It's a very small piece of land, too, which makes it even more irritating. I have offered quite a bit of money for that small piece of land."

Like he couldn't actually pay more if he wanted to—not that more money would solve this particular problem. "Do you *need* this particular piece of land for the factory project? Couldn't you—"

"Without it, I won't have access to the rail line or the main highway. I need to acquire it or there will be no factory."

The waiter returned and placed a huge portion of roast beef in front of his Lordship and an itty-bitty salad in front of Caroline.

"Is that all you're going to eat?" deBracy asked, frowning down at her tiny plate.

She ignored his question. She was not about to discuss her struggle with her weight with a member of the English aristocracy.

She picked up her fork and speared a piece of romaine. "Lord Woolham," she said, "I'm just so sorry, but there is nothing I can do to help you get that land."

He looked up as he cut his beef. A little half smile

played at the corner of his lips. Was he satisfied that she'd gotten his title right? The cad.

"The senator told me that you could fix anything."

The senator had asked too much of her this time. "I'm not a miracle worker."

"So tell me why you think it will take a miracle, then." DeBracy conveyed the meat to his mouth and chewed. The muscles worked in his cheeks, and he managed to look debonair, even with his mouth full.

She leaned forward. "The man who owns the land isn't going to change his mind. Trust me on this."

"Is that because he's an eccentric? I've heard he's a bit 'round the bend."

Caroline laid her silverware across her plate and dropped her hands to her lap. She intertwined her fingers and squeezed. She wanted to be anywhere but there, having this conversation. Senator Warren shouldn't have asked her to do this. But if Caroline could find a solution to Lord Woolham's problem, she might just get the promotion she'd been working for—and that job in Washington, DC. So she sucked in a deep breath and said, "The man who owns the land speaks with angels."

"Really? How remarkable. What do they say?"

For the first time, Hugh deBracy had surprised her. "You *did* hear me, didn't you?" she asked.

"I'm not deaf. What do the angels say?"

"They're opposed to selling the land."

"Well, that's predictable. We'll just have to convince the angels otherwise, won't we?"

"Um, I don't think we can do that. You see, there are additional complications."

"Aren't there always?" His voice was laced with impatient arrogance.

"Yes, but these are really big complications."

"How so?"

"There's an eighteen-hole miniature golf course on the land."

"Mini-golf?" DeBracy had stopped chewing. It was hard to tell if he was shocked, amused, or surprised.

"Yes, miniature golf. You know, small holes, putting only, lots of fiberglass hazards and obstacles."

His Lordship nodded, one cheek still filled with unchewed beef.

"Only in this case," Caroline continued rapidly, determined to get the truth out quickly, "there are eighteen holes each depicting either an Old Testament Bible story or a chapter in the life of our Lord Jesus Christ. The place is a bit notorious, actually. It was featured last year in the online guide *Bizarre America: The Ultimate Guide to Tasteless Tourist Traps.*"

His Lordship choked on the steak he had neglected to chew. His face turned red, and for a moment, Caroline thought she might have to perform the Heimlich maneuver. She couldn't live with herself if Golfing for God were the cause of his untimely demise. That might solve one problem for her, but it would certainly annoy the senator.

Luckily, first aid was not required. His Lordship cleared the obstruction and reached for his water glass. His Adam's apple danced as he swallowed. The motion was almost hypnotic.

Caroline pulled her gaze away. "I guess your late partner didn't tell you about Golfing for God, huh?" she said once deBracy had finished his water.

He laid down his silverware and then wiped his lips with his napkin. "No, George didn't provide those details. I did hear from the real estate chap that the owner of the land in question is a complete nutter. But I was given to understand that the business on the property is no longer in operation. Is that not correct?"

Nutter. UK vernacular for crazy as a loon. Great, just great. "Golfing for God was hit by a hurricane and a lightning storm last fall. It's not currently in operation, but there is a movement to—"

"Good, then I should be able to negotiate with the man who owns it. I'm planning to pop 'round to have a look tomorrow."

It was her moment to choke. Luckily she didn't have any food in her mouth. "You can't do that."

"Why not?"

"I don't know who you've been dealing with in South Carolina, but anyone in Last Chance will tell you that trying to get Elbert Rhodes to sell his property would take a miracle. Literally."

"Elbert *Rhodes*?" His eyebrow curled upward. The man ought to have a quizzing glass.

Her face burned with embarrassment. She had managed to tell the truth, and now she would have to endure his snotty, snide, superior laughter. He was not going to take her seriously.

"That's right, Lord Woolham, Elbert Rhodes, the owner of Golfing for God, is my father."

Hugh looked down at Caroline with some surprise. The wanker who owned the land was her father? That wasn't good. What had the senator been thinking?

He studied Caroline for a long moment. She didn't look like the daughter of a wanker. At first glance, she looked the very model of a professional woman, but there was something not quite right about that. Her face was fey and otherworldly, and she looked rather like an Arthur Rackham illustration of the Queen of Faerie, with slashing eyebrows, pale skin, and unruly hair as dark as the ravens in the Tower of London.

She tilted her head, exposing a long, swan-like neck set off by a little gold necklace with a small crucifix. Their eyes met and connected. His cheeks heated.

He had not counted on Miss Rhodes being so dishy. He had expected an older and rather ordinary woman, given what Senator Warren had said about her. He forcibly relaxed his shoulders. He needed to keep his mind on business.

"Well then," he said, his voice sounding thin. "Does Senator Warren know this?"

"He does."

"And he sent you here anyway?"

"He did."

"And you're here, aren't you? You haven't come to sabotage me."

"No, Lord Woolham, I've come to try to talk reason to you. My father is eccentric, and he's never going to sell out, so the best thing all the way around is to avoid a confrontation and look for another site for your factory." She pulled a folder from her briefcase and handed it to him. "I took the liberty of asking the South Carolina Department of Commerce to give me some suggested alternate sites."

Hugh took the folder but didn't bother reading it. "I already have this report."

"You do?"

"Yes. And it's no use, really. You see, my late partner, George Penn, already purchased the land adjacent to Golfing for God, and the man who sold it is not interested in having it back and returning the money I spent on it. So I intend to build my factory right there, in Last Chance. I will have your father's land, one way or another."

Or he would lose his shirt and Woolham House in the bargain. He was mortgaged up to his neck, and he had only one chance to tap into the lucrative U.S. market for textile machinery. But he wasn't about to tell her that. She was, for the moment, as much an adversary as a friend.

He watched her for a moment, halfway expecting her to get her back up. After all, he did sound like a melodramatic villain in a set piece.

Instead she smiled. "Good luck with that. Believe me, you would solve any number of family problems if you could convince Daddy to part with Golfing for God."

"Not very loyal, are you?"

She let go of a nervous laugh. "Don't assume that I'm opposed to your project because it's my father's land that's in question. I'm not against building new factories in South Carolina. Factories create jobs and economic growth that our state badly needs. I don't think I'd shed any tears if Golfing for God was bulldozed. You have no idea what it's like to grow up having a father who speaks with angels and runs a putt-putt place dedicated to the Almighty. But it's Daddy's land and his decision, and his decision is unshakable."

"Are you refusing to help me?" He wouldn't blame her.

Her smile faded. "No. The senator wants me to help you, and I want to please him. But to solve this problem, we're going to have to find an alternate site for your factory. Building it on Daddy's land isn't going to happen."

"Look, Miss Rhodes, I think I've made it clear that I'm not interested in starting over somewhere else. I need to go down to Last Chance and speak with the leaders of the town council and with your father, and maybe even his angels, if I can get them to play along with me. I'd like you to help me arrange some meetings tomorrow, if you'd be so kind."

Miss Rhodes closed her eyes and leaned back against the banquette. She looked miserable and lovely. He sympathized with her plight, but he was in his own tight spot, too.

And failure wasn't an option.

"I'm not good at scheduling meetings with angels," she said.

He had to stifle a little laugh. "The town council will be good enough."

She opened her eyes and gave him a frank and direct stare. She had lovely green eyes. "This would be a terrible time to visit Last Chance," she said.

"Why?"

"Because it's Watermelon Festival time."

"Watermelon Festival?"

"Yes, it's a big deal in Last Chance. Allenberg County devotes a full week to extolling the virtues of the melon. It's also an excuse for a bunch of activities that would bore you."

"What kind of activities?"

"Oh, you know, the usual Watermelon Festival kinds of things—demolition derbies, seed-spitting contests, country music sing-alongs, pie-baking contests, carnival rides, and the official kickoff parade this Saturday, followed by a barbecue where they smoke two pigs."

The smile he'd been fighting suddenly won. "That's brilliant."

"Brilliant? What's brilliant?" She seemed genuinely surprised by his reaction.

"A country fair such as the one you've described would be perfect. It's just the sort of occasion that brings out all the local politicians. I could save a great deal of time. Everyone will be in one place."

"Well that's true, but—"

"Senator Warren put you at *my* disposal until this issue is resolved. I perfectly understand your conflict, Miss Rhodes, but your local knowledge will be invaluable. So I would like you to make arrangements for us to go to Last Chance for this festival. I'd like to be invited to the reviewing stand for the parade on Saturday. Perhaps we can drive down tomorrow afternoon, and have a few meetings on Friday, and then I can do my politicking during the festival over the weekend. I'd like you to arrange a few personal meetings between myself and the various officials, not to mention introducing me to your father."

"I don't think you understand," Miss Rhodes said in a strident tone. "Last Chance is in the middle of nowhere. It's near a swamp. And it's hot. Much hotter than England. And we have snakes and alligators living in the

Edisto River, which runs right nearby. And most important of all, there aren't any fancy hotels there, where a person such as yourself might stay overnight."

Hugh had already read several South Carolina tourist guides on the flight over from the UK. He was well aware of the swampland. And now that he knew, Hugh fervently hoped that George hadn't purchased any of it, although from the looks of it, George was so incompetent he just might have.

Hugh had only himself to blame for trusting George with his money. He could almost hear Granddad's voice in his head pointing out every single one of Hugh's shortcomings. Telling him, in no uncertain terms, that he would never be a success at anything important.

But he would make a success of this. And this beautiful woman in the dark gray business suit might be the only person who could help him achieve that success.

He had to be strong, assertive, and arrogant if he was going to get the job done. He gave her an imperious stare and said, "Miss Rhodes, I intend to build my factory in Last Chance, South Carolina. If I have to go on safari to get there, I will. So, I would appreciate it if you would arrange accommodations for me, and schedule some appointments."

She stared up at him for a long moment as emotions from indignation through acquiescence played across her features. And then something changed in her mien. A mischievous spark ignited in the depths of her green eyes that was neither anger nor submission. She was up to something the way the pixies always got up to trouble in the childhood stories Aunt Petal had told him.

Caroline gave him a big American smile. "Well, I

guess I could ask Miriam Randall to put you up. She lives in a large Victorian house that used to be a hotel a hundred years ago. She sometimes takes in boarders."

He had no idea who Miriam Randall might be, but by the twinkle in Caroline's eyes, he had a feeling he might have just made a terrible mistake.

CHAPTER 2

Caroline slammed her briefcase down on the threadbare carpet in her office cubicle. The senator's Columbia office was in a tired old building not far from the state capitol. The traditional-style mahogany furniture had scars marring every surface, and the standard-issue blue leather chairs looked like they had been in use during the Wilson Administration.

She loved her office just the same. Having this semi-private cubby was a sign of her rank, as well as all of her hours of dedicated service since her graduation summa cum laude from the University of South Carolina.

She'd landed the job with Senator Warren right out of college and had started her career as a caseworker, helping people with their Social Security Disability issues. In just a few years, she'd made herself indispensable. Two years ago, she'd become the administrator of the senator's main state office. When the election was over this November, she hoped to land a job in the senator's office on Capitol Hill in Washington, DC.

But the election was going to be tight. The senator faced two challengers—a Democrat and a populist Independent. So landing a new factory for South Carolina would be of significant political benefit. If she could clear the obstacles for Lord Woolham's factory, the promotion she coveted would be hers.

Caroline fell into her squeaky office chair and rested her head on her desk for a long moment.

Clearing the obstacles for this factory to be built in Last Chance would be impossible. Even worse, this assignment had the potential to blow up in her face and undermine the senator's trust in her.

Senator Warren knew she came from a small town. And he knew Daddy's land was at stake. But she had worked hard to keep the most embarrassing details of her background quiet.

She'd gotten rid of her small town wardrobe. She had learned, through painful experience, to keep her mouth shut and think before she said anything stupid. She was circumspect and professional in everything she did. She didn't want to embarrass Senator Warren. And she certainly didn't want to embarrass herself or her family.

But Lord Woolham was going to blow her cover. And her attempt to talk him out of building in Last Chance had fallen on deaf ears.

DeBracy was going to visit Last Chance, and Caroline couldn't stop it from happening. Given the situation, it was probably better for her to accompany him. At least that way, she might be able to control the damage to her career.

But before she arrived in Last Chance with his Lordship in tow, she needed to issue a general warning to the folks back home.

She picked up the telephone and dialed.

"Rocky, darlin', what a surprise," Ruby Rhodes, Caroline's mother, said on the other end of the line.

Momma and everyone in Last Chance had always called Caroline Rocky because her first name was Sirocco and she had three brothers named Stone, Clay, and Tulane. Losing her quirky name was part of Caroline's makeover. A senator's aide didn't need a name like Rocky Rhodes. A senator's aide wanted a plain name that was easy to spell. Of course, no one in Last Chance ever called her Caroline.

She clutched the phone and squeezed her eyes shut. "Momma, I have some news."

The silence on the other end of the line seemed to last for hours. "Bad news? Are you all right, sweetie?" Momma asked.

"I'm okay. But I have a huge problem. I've been asked to help the man who wants to buy Golfing for God." Caroline said it really fast on the theory that news like this was better delivered rapidly, in the same way that it was better to rip off a Band-Aid quick.

"By who?"

"The senator, who else?"

"And you said yes to this?" Momma apparently had heard every word despite Caroline's delivery. The headache Caroline had been fighting finally blossomed into a throbbing cluster of pain over her right eye.

"Uh, no, I didn't say yes," Caroline countered. "I told Senator Warren that it was impossible. But you know how he doesn't listen." Caroline massaged her eye socket, smearing her eyeliner.

"His inability to listen is one of the reasons I've never voted for him," Momma said.

Caroline didn't respond. Momma was a Democrat. Senator Warren was a Republican. Enough said about that.

Caroline snagged her purse off the floor and tipped it over on her desk searching for the little green bottle of aspirin she always carried. "Look, Momma, I don't want to help this man get Daddy's land." She found the green bottle, and cradled the phone against her shoulder.

"Then why did you call?"

The adult-proof cap finally gave way, and Caroline popped two of those babies into her mouth without any water. She fell into her chair, closed her eyes, and let her head drop back against the high back. "Because," she said, "the stuck-up English lord who wants to buy Daddy's land just told me that he wants to pop 'round for a visit during the Watermelon Festival."

"Pop 'round? Really?"

"Those were his exact words. He's like one of the dukes in those romance books you like so much. He's arrogant and uppity and wants to get his way. He's asked me to make accommodations for him and to schedule meetings with members of the town council."

"You ought to put him up at the Peach Blossom Motor Court just for spite," Momma said.

"I can't believe you just said that."

"I can't believe I said it either. Maybe we could send him into the swamp in a canoe without a paddle or mosquito spray."

Caroline would have laughed if her head didn't feel like it was exploding. "If I do that, Senator Warren will find out, and that would make the boss cranky."

"Honey, you should quit."

Caroline ignored that familiar refrain. "It gets worse. The senator wants to come and hang out with his Lordship in the reviewing stand for the Watermelon Festival parade. He's going to bring his daughter, and you know what a snob Cissy is. Although to tell you the truth, Lord Woolham might give her a run for the money."

Momma snorted.

"You're not helping." Caroline's voice sounded whiny.

"Did you want my help?"

Caroline gritted her teeth. "Momma, I don't really have a choice. The man's going to come to Last Chance whether I bring him or not. So I figure the best thing is to bring him there, let him see the situation, and then convince him to relocate his factory someplace else. I was calling to let you know the situation."

"I see."

"And to ask for your advice. I really do need to find a decent place to stash the baron for the duration. It can't be the Peach Blossom Motor Court. I was just thinking that maybe Miriam Randall could—"

"Oh, that's perfect," Momma interrupted before Caroline could finish her sentence. "You know," Momma continued, "if anyone can beat that English devil, it would be Miriam Randall. You sit tight and let me make a few phone calls. I'll get back to you. And I'll put fresh sheets on your bed. Are you planning to stay through the Watermelon Festival? Or is this another one of your quick trips?"

Just thinking about coming home during the Allenberg County Watermelon Festival made the pain in Caroline's head redouble. Coming home meant running into Bubba Lockheart.

"I'll be there over the weekend, at least, maybe a few days more. It depends on Lord Woolham and whether I can get him to see reason."

"Really? Well, that's something, isn't it? It's been a long time since you attended a Watermelon Festival."

Caroline consciously unclenched her teeth and tried to relax. It was almost impossible. Coming home for the festival was the last thing she wanted to do. She had bad memories of her last Watermelon Festival, twelve years ago, when Bubba had proposed to her in front of everyone in the town.

She'd been all dressed up in her Watermelon Queen dress, with her hair all poufy and a tiara on her head. She'd been having a great time, until Bubba destroyed it.

She hadn't handled the situation well. She'd opened her mouth and spoken in anger. She didn't want to marry Bubba, but she sure wished she could take back the ugly things she'd said.

That moment with Bubba had changed her. And she'd learned her lesson. Now she held her tongue and tried very hard to always keep her cool.

But she had also avoided coming home during the festival. She may have learned from her mistake, but she didn't want to come home every year and relive it.

Caroline pushed the awful memories out of her mind. "Momma, I really appreciate your help and understanding."

There was a slight pause on the other end of the line and then Momma said, "So I reckon I'll tell Dale Pontius to count you in for the parade float."

Caroline sat up in her squeaky chair. Dale, a member of the Last Chance Town Council, had directed the arrangements for the Watermelon Festival parade since cat was a kitten. "What float?" Caroline asked.

"The seventy-fifth anniversary float," Momma said, confirming every single one of Caroline's sudden fears. "Dale came up with this wonderful idea about inviting all the old Watermelon Queens who still live in the county to ride on it. Miriam and I are so excited about it. I even found my old costume, and would you believe it, it still fits. Rachel and Millie are making a pink and green pantsuit for Miriam. She's the oldest living Watermelon Queen, did you know that?"

"No, I didn't." Stark, naked terror made Caroline's hands go clammy.

Momma continued speaking. "I know exactly where your dress is. I'll get it out and run it right down to the cleaners."

"Momma, I can't—"

"Oh, I'm pretty sure you can." Momma always said stuff like that. She didn't believe anyone *couldn't* do anything if they put their mind to it.

"Okay, Momma, I won't. Besides, I have to be—"

"Honey, if you come to the festival and you don't ride on Dale's float, folks around here will talk. I don't think you want that, do you? Especially after what happened the last time you wore that dress."

"Momma, I have moved on in my life. Now, if only Bubba could do the same."

"I'm not so sure you *have* moved on."

Caroline was not about to rehash the Bubba situation. So she took a deep breath and said, "Look, I'm coming home to do a job. I'm not going to put on that dress. You know good and well that it won't help Bubba or me to move on with our lives if I dress up like a Watermelon Queen again. And besides, how is Lord Woolham going to take me seriously if he sees me in a dress like that? Really, Momma, I need to convince him to give up on Daddy's land. For that I need to be professional, you know?"

"Well, I suppose there is some truth in that," Momma admitted. "But you know how Dale gets this time of year. Once he hears you're going to be in town, he's going to want you riding on that float in your old dress."

"Well, he can't make me do it."

"All right, sugar. I understand. So when can I expect you?"

"Tomorrow, late afternoon. His Lordship wants me to drive down with him so I can give him the whole briefing on the town. And I'm so *not* looking forward to that."

"You know, sweetie, we're not all that bad."

"Momma, that's not what I meant. What I meant was that Lord Woolham is going to look down on all of us. I hate people who do that."

"So do I." Momma paused a moment. "Well, I'm sure we can figure out some way to run him off. Believe you me, I can think of all kinds of ways to run off an Englishman. After all, my forebears did a real good job of running the British ragged in the swamps during the Revolution."

Caroline made no comment. Momma, despite her liberal leanings, was eligible to join the DAR. Not even Hettie Marshall, the Queen Bee of Last Chance, could do that. Momma was sweet, but she sure did keep score when it counted.

• • •

The next morning, Haley Rhodes leaned on the table in Granny's kitchen and peered under the lid of the cardboard box. Granny shooed her away. But then Granny lifted up the box lid and a big heap of fluffy green and pink material popped out. Granny pulled out the dress and gave it a shake.

It was the most beautifulest thing Haley had ever seen. It was pink on the top and had a whole bunch of skirts in fluffy layers, each of them a different color of green. In the bottom of the box sat a glittery tiara.

It was a Watermelon Queen dress, and when Haley grew up, she was going to be a Watermelon Queen. Being a queen ran in the family. Granny had been one. Aunt Rocky had been one. And Momma, who Haley couldn't remember, had been a Watermelon Queen, too.

Lizzy, Haley's big sister, said being a Watermelon Queen was dumb. She said it was demeaning to women. Haley didn't know what the word "demeaning" meant, and she didn't care. She was going to be queen one day.

"Isn't that pretty?" Granny asked.

"Oh, yes," said the Sorrowful Angel with a yearning that made something hitch in Haley's chest.

Haley turned around and stared at the angel who was hovering in her usual space right by the broom closet in Granny's kitchen. The Sorrowful Angel had been with Haley for a long, long time. In all that time, she had never said a single word before. Mostly she wailed and wept, especially at night.

"Sugar, what's the matter?" Granny asked.

"The angel just talked to me. She's never done that before."

Granny looked down at Haley with that look grown-ups

sometimes got whenever the angel was mentioned. Like a lot of grown-ups, Granny was starting to lose her faith in the Sorrowful Angel. Haley knew it was hard to believe in something that you couldn't see.

Most folks thought there was something wrong about seeing angels, even though the people in the Bible saw angels all the time. Even Haley's daddy thought it was bad to see angels. Daddy made Haley visit a special doctor two times a week—even in the summertime—all because she could see the angel.

Dr. Newsome was supposed to fix people who saw things that weren't really there. But Dr. Newsome would never fix Haley because her angel was real. Just 'cause no one but Haley could see the angel didn't mean the angel wasn't real.

And that meant that Haley was going to have to go see Dr. Newsome for the rest of her life, if she couldn't figure out a way to get the angel to go back to Heaven.

"What did the angel say?" Granny asked.

"She said the dress was pretty." Haley tilted her head and squinted up at the angel. "Granny, I don't think the angel agrees with Lizzy."

Granny chuckled. "Honey, I don't think many folks in this town agree with Lizzy."

"Well, when I grow up, I'm going to be a Watermelon Queen, just like my momma was, even if Lizzy thinks it's stupid."

Grown-ups got a look on their face whenever Haley talked about Momma, too. Momma was with Jesus and had been ever since Haley was two years old. Momma and Haley had been in a big car wreck, but only Momma went to be with Jesus.

"Granny, do you still have my momma's dress?" Haley asked.

"I don't know, honey. She was living with her own momma when she was a queen. Your daddy might have the dress up in his attic, though. Oh my, but she was so beautiful." Granny ran her hands down over the top of Haley's head. "With honey blond hair, just like yours. I declare your daddy was so smitten with her the day of the parade. He was just eighteen."

"And he stole her away in the night, after the barbecue, didn't he?"

"Yes, he did."

"And she got married wearing her dress, didn't she?"

"Yes, she did. Nearly 'bout surprised everyone in town when those two came back in the morning."

"I want to be a Watermelon Queen and get married in my pretty pink and green dress."

"Well, we'll just have to see how you feel about it when you're older."

"You mean I have to decide if being a queen is demeaning." Haley frowned. "What does that mean anyway?"

Granny laughed. "I have no idea."

"Momma didn't think she was being demeaning, did she? I mean when Daddy ran off with her."

"No, sugar, I don't think so. I'm pretty sure she loved your daddy like life itself. As far as I know, your momma was the only Watermelon Queen who ever got married in her queen dress."

"But Bubba Lockheart asked Aunt Rocky to marry him the night of the watermelon parade, didn't he?"

Granny shook her head. "I do declare, Haley Ann Rhodes, you know the story better than I do."

"And Aunt Rocky was ugly to him and that's why Bubba spends too much time at Dot's Spot, right?"

"Who did you hear that from, young lady?"

"Miz Bray says that all the time. I know you've heard her say it."

"Yes, I have. But it's not something you should repeat, do you understand?"

"But Bubba loved Aunt Rocky."

"Not like your momma and daddy," said the angel.

Haley turned again toward the broom closet. The Sorrowful Angel was looking sad again. Tears ran down her cheeks.

"Did she speak again?" Granny asked.

"Yes, ma'am."

"What did she say?"

"That Bubba and Aunt Rocky weren't like my momma and daddy."

Granny chuckled a little. "Well, then, she's a well-informed angel in addition to being a sorrowful one."

Rachel Polk closed the file she'd been reading. Sick worry nestled down in her gut as she got up from her desk and hurried into the workroom. She quickly photocopied the entire contents of the file and then returned it to Mr. Marshall's desk, where the darned fool had left it, right out in the open.

The file detailed how Country Pride Chicken was not fully compliant with the state's health and safety codes.

Rachel had suspected that her employer was cutting corners. But it was infuriating to see it written down that way and left out, while her idiot boss went off to play golf with his country club friends—something he did at least three times a week.

If Mr. Marshall didn't do something quick to fix these problems, the state might close the plant down. And then Rachel would be out of a job. Heck, half the town would be out of a job.

Rachel sat there staring at the papers on her desk, paralyzed by fear and indecision. What was she going to do? She ought to blow the whistle. But if she did that, everyone might have to go on unemployment.

Just then, her cell phone rang. She checked the caller ID. It was Rocky. Rachel thanked the Almighty for the diversion.

"Hey, what's up?" Rachel said.

"I'm coming home for a few days," Rocky replied.

"During the Watermelon Festival? Really?"

Rachel knew good and well that if Rocky came home at festival time, Bubba would go into a tailspin. Not that it would be Rocky's fault if that happened, but everyone would blame her. And Rachel would be caught right in the middle.

Like she always was.

Like she was caught in the middle of her life.

"Yeah, can you believe it? I haven't been home for a Watermelon Festival since I was eighteen. But I don't have a choice. This snotty English baron wants to buy Daddy's golf course so he can put up a textile machinery factory. The senator wants me to show him around town."

"Wow. Does your momma know this?"

"Yeah, she does. Momma's ready to organize a canoe trip for his Lordship right into gator-infested swampland."

Rachel laughed. "That sounds like your mother."

"Well, it's not a bad idea, you know. I'm thinking once the snooty baron actually sees rural South Carolina up close and personal, he'll go rushing back to civilization. Then maybe I can convince him to build his factory upstate."

"What's wrong with rural South Carolina?"

"Nothing, honey. You know that. I know that. But trust me, this uppity English baron will not love our town the way we do."

"Do you actually love Last Chance?" Rachel asked.

"Sure, why do you ask?"

"I don't know, Rocky. You don't come home much."

There was a long pause on the other end of the phone before Rocky said, "I'm really busy with my job, Rachel. I don't have that much time to come home. And besides, I'm not the one who moved back to Last Chance. We'd see a lot more of each other if you'd stayed in Columbia."

Rocky and Rachel were practically like sisters. They had grown up together, gone to college together, and started careers in Columbia together. But three years ago, Rachel had decided to move back to Last Chance.

Rachel had only one regret about that decision—her best friend didn't understand, and probably never would. Rachel decided not to poke that wound again. She was happy Rocky was coming home. It had been a long time since they'd seen one another.

"So when are you coming?" Rachel asked.

"I'm driving down with the baron this afternoon, late. I thought you and I could have dinner at the Pig Place and catch up on things. And then maybe you can help me brainstorm a few ideas for how to scare his Lordship away from Last Chance and my daddy's land."

"Uh, maybe you don't want to scare him away."

"What? Of course I do."

"Well, maybe that's a dumb idea. I'm just saying. The economy around here kind of sucks. We could use some foreign investment."

"Not if it means bulldozing Golfing for God."

"I realize that. But what about someplace else in Allenberg County?"

"Rachel, is something wrong?"

Rachel hauled in a big breath. "Yeah, but I can't talk about it now. I'll see you tonight."

CHAPTER 3

Hugh deBracy wore one of those Irish tweed caps that made him look utterly exotic in the land of ball-cap good ol' boys. He also looked right at home behind the wheel of the silver Mustang convertible. Somehow Caroline should have known his Lordship would show up driving something like this.

He might even have succeeded in conveying a certain savoir faire, except for the fact that the South Carolina humidity had turned his hair into an unruly mass of curls that his oh-so-cool tweed cap couldn't constrain. He was cute, in a shy, sexy, duke-ish kind of way—exactly like Mr. Darcy.

And he maneuvered that Mustang with all the cool skill of Darcy on horseback, too. Quite impressive.

But he was still a big problem.

And her best idea for solving this problem was to hope that he'd take one look at her hometown and see it as a big joke.

And that bothered her. A lot.

She may have kept her background a secret from her Columbia friends and work associates, but she didn't see her town as a joke.

Baron Woolham would, of course, snob that he was. And she would use his snobbery to help him see reason and save her daddy's land.

So she played up the quirkiness of her hometown during her briefing, giving him an uncensored description of the tangled web of relationships between the members of the Committee to Resurrect Golfing for God, the Ladies Auxiliary, the Garden Club, and Nita Wills's Book Club.

Halfway through her discussion of the enmity between Lillian Bray, chair of the Auxiliary, and Hettie Marshall, chair of the Committee to Resurrect Golfing for God, it occurred to her that she might have a fighting chance to make him see reason if she could get the Last Chance church ladies to collectively scare the bejesus out of him.

Maybe Miriam Randall would come up with some kind of matrimonial fortune for him that would send him packing. His Lordship would not be amused by Miriam Randall. Caroline was sure of it.

And even if Miriam failed to scare him, Caroline could always count on the greased watermelon race, or the seed-spitting contest, or the demolition derby. Those events were a whole heap of fun, but she doubted that his high and mightiness would see it that way. He'd be shocked and awed and appalled.

"Crikey, that's different," his Lordship said when Last Chance's water tower finally came into view on the horizon.

Oh good. Caroline could hardly contain her joy. She was sure Hugh deBracy was getting the message loud and clear, with just one gander at the water tower's striped watermelon paint job.

"I see your town takes watermelons seriously," deBracy said.

"Watermelons are important to our town," Caroline replied in her best straight man voice.

"I would have thought soybeans were more important, judging by the acres of them we've passed."

Caroline cast her gaze over the endless fields of beans on either side of the road. He recognized soybeans when he saw them? That was a surprise. Most city folk wouldn't know a soybean from a corn stalk.

"Well, it's true," she said, "soybeans are the cash crop around here, but they aren't nearly as colorful or flavorful as watermelons. And besides, no one ever took a soybean to Washington and made history."

"Sorry?"

"In 1933, Josiah Rhodes, one of my distant cousins, took a two-hundred-and-ten-pound watermelon up to Washington and presented it to President Roosevelt himself, in person. Had his picture taken with the president and everything. Since that was one of the most historic things ever to happen to our town, our leaders commemorated the event with a parade. And before anyone could say 'Jack Robinson,' the parade became a week-long celebration of pink and green. The water tower wasn't repainted that way until the 1950s."

"Oh, I see. It's all rather like the Harvest Festival in Woolham. Only in that case, it was a very large turnip, and the king in question was Henry the Seventh. We haven't painted our water tower like a turnip, though, I must say."

"Henry the Seventh?" Holy smokes, he wasn't even fazed for one second by the water tower or the watermelon story.

"Hm. Yes, I believe it was Henry the Seventh. It was centuries ago. We Brits have very long memories."

"I guess. Do you have turnip queens?" She couldn't resist asking.

He played it utterly straight and answered her. "No, we usually trot out the old Celtic gods, I'm afraid. It gets the vicar into a right grumpy mood. And since my Aunt Petunia helps organize the annual celebration, I'm afraid I get an earful every Sunday in October until Samhain comes and goes."

Caroline stared at him for a long moment. He didn't exactly fit the stereotype, did he? What would happen if he wasn't put off by the town's quirkiness?

Of course he was going to be put off. Once he met Daddy and visited Golfing for God, he would realize just exactly what he was up against. He looked like a rational kind of guy. He would come around—eventually.

And if Golfing for God didn't do the trick, she would have to put Momma's plan into action and organize an expedition to the mosquito-and-gator-ridden parts of the swamp. Maybe he would tip the canoe, and there would be a feeding frenzy.

The soybean fields gave way to sixties-style ranch houses built back into stands of tall pines. Eventually the pines thinned, and the speed limit plummeted. The houses started to sprout porches and yards with old shade trees. Then, almost without warning, the speed limit hit fifteen, and they motored into the incorporated town of Last Chance, South Carolina, its two city blocks decorated end to end in pink and green.

On the right stood Bill's Grease Pit, the local auto repair place sporting a vinyl banner welcoming tourists to the festival. Down the street on the left, the front windows of Lovett's Hardware had been draped with watermelon bunting. Across the street, the Cut 'n Curl had a hand-appliquéd watermelon flag flying. Of course, the Cut 'n Curl was permanently painted pink and green on both the outside and the inside. Caroline knew this personally because she'd helped her mother paint the place.

She hadn't been home for the Watermelon Festival in years and years. But once, a long time ago, it had been a magical time of year. Her nostalgia grabbed her by the throat. She may have made herself over into a serious city girl, but she'd never managed to lose this deep-seated attachment to Last Chance. Caroline pushed a raft of syrupy emotions back where they belonged. "If you hang a right up there at the stoplight, on Baruch, I'll show you Miz Miriam's place."

Hugh pulled the Mustang onto a drive that led to Miriam Randall's home, which turned out to be a large wooden house decorated with vast quantities of Victorian-era ornaments.

The house wasn't in very good nick, but it stood in the midst of an amazing and slightly wild garden. A pair of old live oaks, trailing long beards of Spanish moss, dominated the yard, while a perennial border with drifts of orange and lavender bloomed in a sunny patch along the front side of the wraparound porch. A neatly trimmed boxwood hedge perfumed the air with its tangy scent.

Garden magic, of the kind his aunts believed in, enveloped this place. Were Aunt Petal ever to visit, Hugh had no doubt that she would find a veritable army of sprites and pixies living here.

The cherry red 1970s vintage Cadillac Eldorado convertible parked in the drive was also a thing of beauty. A shirtless man wearing a baseball cap, a sheen of perspiration, and a pair of holey blue jeans was bent over the car's long bonnet applying wax. The man looked up as Hugh cut the Mustang's motor.

"Hey, little gal," the man said. He approached the car in a limping gait, opened the Mustang's passenger side door, and then pulled Caroline into a big, sweaty hug that was...well...quite friendly.

A wave of resentment prickled over Hugh's skin as he got out of the car. He had been telling himself all morning that the dishy Miss Rhodes was off limits. Unfortunately, his libido had not been listening.

"Okay, Dash, that's enough."

The man let go and turned in Hugh's direction. "So I reckon you must be Lord deBracy. I'm Dash Randall, Miriam's nephew."

"It's nice to meet you. Thanks for allowing me to stay at your home." Hugh ignored the mistake in the form of address and smiled.

"He's Lord Woolham, not Lord deBracy," Caroline said. "I looked it up last night online. DeBracy is his last name, but his title is Woolham because that's where he's from. I don't expect you to understand how it works, but I know that his Lordship is really picky about his title."

Hugh heard the tone in Caroline's voice. Apparently all that pretending to be Granddad was having some impact.

Good. People always took Granddad seriously. Right now Hugh needed everyone in Last Chance to take him very seriously—maybe fear him a little. One couldn't underestimate the power of fear.

Randall pushed the brim of his cap up, revealing a pair of cool blue eyes. "Boy, I'm sure glad I'm an American," he said.

"So is Miriam around?" Caroline asked quickly, clearly changing the subject.

Randall shook his head. "No, Aunt Mim is getting a manicure down at the Cut 'n Curl. She told me that if you showed up while she was gone, I was supposed to show his Lordship to his room and tell you to get your tail down to the beauty shop right away. Is it true you're going to ride on the seventy-fifth anniversary float in one of those Watermelon Queen dresses?"

"Uh…" An unmistakable and utterly charming glow crept up Caroline's cheeks. "No. I am not. Where did you hear that?"

"Well, Aunt Mim got a phone call from Millie Polk, who heard from Thelma Hanks, who ran into your momma at the dry cleaners. Your momma was taking two dresses to be cleaned."

"Two dresses?"

"Yep. Hers and yours is what I heard, but hey, you know I don't really listen to the ladies' gossip all that much."

"Right, tell me another one."

Caroline turned around and gave Hugh a polite but disingenuous smile. "So, I guess I'll leave you here then, if it's okay. I have a few errands to run, and Dash will show you to your room. I'm sure he'll be happy to fill you in on where the local hot spots are." She rolled her eyes in Dash's direction.

"Honey, I'm in recovery."

"Yes, I know that, dear, and I'm proud of you. But I'm sure Baron Woolham would like to get himself some supper down at the Kountry Kitchen or barbecue out at the Pig Place. Would you be sweet and show him around? I've got to go tell Momma a second time that I'm not putting on that dress or having my hair poufed out. I have made a solemn vow never again to wear any kind of rhinestone tiara."

"Rocky, honey," Dash said, "the single men in Last Chance will be drowning their sorrows tonight when they learn you're going to ditch the seventy-fifth anniversary float. You coming home and riding on that float has been the hot topic of discussion most of the day. We're all wondering whose heart you're gonna break this time."

Caroline gave Randall an exaggerated punch in the biceps. "Shut your mouth, Dash. I'm in town to work, not ride on any parade floats. And I have no intention of ever breaking any hearts ever again. The fallout isn't any fun."

Caroline turned and strode around the Mustang's boot. She opened it and pulled out her small rolling suitcase. "I'm going now. Ya'll have fun."

"Um, can I drop you someplace?" Hugh asked,

wondering about the provenance of the nickname Randall had just used. Rocky Rhodes—it was rather amusing, wasn't it? But in some strange way, that nickname seemed to fit Caroline. Maybe even better than her real name.

"No, thanks." She shook her head, and her ponytail swayed. "The Cut 'n Curl is just down the block a ways and around the corner. You have my cell number if you need to reach me. I'll check in later with our schedule for tomorrow. I'm going to see if Daddy will give you a tour of the golf course. And I think my mother's got it all fixed so you can have a place on the reviewing stand with Senator Warren, his daughter, and the rest of the local VIPs. But I have to confirm all that."

She turned and strode down the drive toward the sidewalk.

"Hey, Rocky, good luck with that whole dress avoidance thing. Because I also heard through the grapevine that Dale Pontius has insisted that you ride his Watermelon Queen float," Dash called after her, "or else."

Caroline stopped and looked back. "What?"

Randall shrugged. "Just giving you the heads-up." He glanced toward Hugh and then back. "I heard something about Dale Pontius driving a hard bargain."

Caroline muttered an oath, turned, and stalked down the driveway, her shoulders straight. Hugh couldn't help admiring the swing of her hips and the nice shape of her derriere.

It was really too bad that her father owned the land he needed. Caroline—or Rocky—might be a very nice diversion.

· · ·

Caroline opened the front door of the Cut 'n Curl. The pungent mélange of permanent solution, shampoo, and hairspray invited her into her own private reverie.

The beauty shop was a world of its own, papered in pink-striped wallpaper and shuttered with green moiré curtains. Caroline remembered helping Momma pick out the paper and hang it. She'd learned to sew a straight seam by helping to make the curtains. Momma had done a real nice job of decorating the place. It was classy and homey all at the same time.

The Cut 'n Curl had three workstations covered in pink marble-patterned Formica, a bank of hair dryers with pink vinyl seats, and a two-seat shampoo area near the back with two-toned, lime green chairs.

As usual, a near-quorum of the Christ Church Ladies Auxiliary was present and accounted for.

Lessie Anderson was in Momma's chair with her hair up in permanent rollers. Thelma Hanks was under the dryer. Millie Polk, Rachel's mother, was sitting on a side chair waiting on her highlights to set. She was reading a much-thumbed copy of *Destiny*, June Morlan's latest bodice ripper that featured a snotty hero who was much like Hugh deBracy.

Jane, Caroline's sister-in-law, had Miriam Randall's hand in hers as she worked on painting the octogenarian's nails alternate shades of pink and green. Miriam's white hair was arranged in crown braids, and she was wearing a bright green pantsuit with a pair of pink Keds slip-ons.

Momma looked up as Caroline entered. Ruby Rhodes wore her dark hair in a short style that allowed it to curl freely around her head. As usual, she was well put together and looked way younger than her fifty-eight years. Her dark denim jeans hugged her still-youthful contours. A bright pink blazer over a green scoop-necked shell accentuated her tiny waist. A pair of pink ballet shoes and a tiny diamond pendant completed the ensemble.

Momma gave Caroline her maternal look—one part sappy smile and another steel magnolia. "Sugar," she said, "don't you ever wear anything that has color in it? I declare, you look like you're going to a meeting of Quakers in that suit."

Caroline looked down at her Jones of New York microfiber all-season gray pantsuit and the white August Silk shell. She looked professional and in charge. That was really all that mattered. "Momma, folks aren't going to take me seriously if I dress in pink and green. Which reminds me, I just heard from Dash that the whole town is expecting me to put on my old Watermelon Queen dress and make a spectacle of myself in front of my boss. But I told you that I wouldn't do that when we talked last night."

"Yes, I know, dear, but I'm afraid there's been a change in plans."

"A change in plans?"

"Yes. Dale said that he won't let that Englishman on the reviewing stand unless you ride on the float."

Caroline stared at Momma for a full thirty seconds as the implications of this settled in her brain.

"Shall I call Dale and tell him you refuse?" Momma asked, an unmistakable note of glee in her voice.

Caroline collapsed, defeated, into the stylist chair next to Lessie. "I can't ride on that float. The senator is going to be there on the reviewing stand."

"What difference does that make?"

She shrugged. "He's my boss. And, well, he doesn't know about my history as a Watermelon Queen. And besides, I'm supposed to be working. And when I work, he's supposed to be the center of attention, not me."

"Well, that's admirable, sweetie, but if you want to get his Lordship on the reviewing stand, you're going to have to put on your dress and ride on that float."

Caroline groaned. "I am never going to live this down."

"I'm sure the senator will understand. I don't see what's so embarrassing about being a Watermelon Queen, myself."

Caroline rolled her eyes. Momma had no idea about how politics worked. It was best, all the way around, for Caroline to be as plain and vanilla as possible. The more she worked in the background, the better it was for Senator Warren. In fact, that was her job description.

"Don't roll your eyes like that, Rocky. It's annoying."

"I'm sorry. But really, this is a disaster. I don't want to ride that float."

"I know. But if you don't, then the senator is going to be angry. So you've got a problem either way. That being the case, my advice is that you just relax and enjoy it. Riding on the float will be a lot of fun. You remember that, don't you—the fun of the Watermelon Festival?"

Caroline closed her eyes and sucked in a deep breath redolent with the aroma of the almond-scented shampoo that Momma always used. "I never wanted to ever wear that dress again," she muttered.

"Aw, sweetie, don't you remember how excited you were when you were named Watermelon Queen?"

"I do. But the excitement was replaced by embarrassment. I don't want to relive the experience."

"Honey, maybe putting on the dress and riding on the float will help you get over what happened twelve years ago," Momma said.

"I doubt it." Caroline crossed her arms.

"You know," Millie said into the silence that descended between mother and daughter, "my husband says we should be nice to this Englishman. We need his investment on account of the economy being so bad around here. Just last night he said that we needed a factory more than a putt-putt dedicated to the Lord."

Everyone looked at Millie like she'd lost her mind. Loyalty ran deep among the members of the Committee to Resurrect Golfing for God.

"Thanks, Mrs. Polk," Caroline said, "but to be clear with y'all, I'm not here to convince Daddy to sell his land. I'm here to convince the baron to take his factory someplace else."

"Oh, I'm not sure my husband is going to like hearing that," Mrs. Polk said.

Momma stepped in before a political discussion broke out. Momma might have political views, but she disapproved of them in her beauty shop.

"Rocky, you really don't have much of a choice. I certainly wish he hadn't come to town. But it seems to me that it will be worse for your career if he's denied the chance to sit up there with the VIPs because you refuse to put on a pretty pink and green dress."

Momma had, of course, put her finger right on the crux of the problem. "I'm stuck, aren't I?" Caroline said on a long sigh.

"I'm afraid so. So let's get your hair trimmed. And Jane can give you a manicure, too. It looks like you've been biting your nails again."

"Momma, I am not going to pouf out my hair and wear a tiara. I'll ride on the float, but do I have to wear my dress?"

"Yes. It's at the cleaners, and I'm sure it still fits you."

"It hardly fit me when I was eighteen."

"Oh, piffle, Rocky. It fit you just fine. I know you are a little sensitive about your bustline, but honey, you looked gorgeous in that dress twelve years ago."

"Cheer up, Rocky, it's not so bad," Jane said from her place at the manicure station.

Caroline braced for one of Jane's Pollyanna observations. "How do you figure that? I don't think my boss will ever take me seriously again if he sees me exposed in that dress with my hair poufed out and a tiara on my head."

"Oh, it can't be that bad. I mean, riding on the float has to be way more fun than standing around with a lot of self-important dignitaries. And besides, I've seen those dresses. They are way cool. And you don't have to pouf out your hair or wear a tiara."

Caroline turned her gaze on Momma, who was in the process of taking the permanent rollers out of Lessie's hair. "Did you hear that, Momma?"

"I did. No one said you had to have poufy hair," Momma said.

"You know," Jane said, "if you didn't try to fight the curl in your hair, it would look pretty just left down and kind of natural. And I have some pink and green ribbons left over from a dress I made for Haley. You could wear them like a garland instead of a tiara. If you like, I'll do your hair. We could make it simple. It could be done on Saturday morning. No fuss, no muss."

Caroline felt just a tiny wave of jealousy. She knew it was wrong to feel jealous of Jane. After all, Jane had made Caroline's older brother, Clay, a happy man. But sometimes Caroline envied the relationship Jane and Ruby had developed. Jane had taken up knitting and sewing and cooking and was turning herself into a real domestic goddess. Momma seemed to approve of that. But then Momma could cook and sew and knit—in addition to running a business.

Caroline could just about manage to heat up a Lean Cuisine. And she had never had any interest in sewing or knitting. Maybe God had given Jane to Momma as compensation.

"Thanks, Jane, you're on," Caroline said, then settled back in the chair and studied the members of the Ladies Auxiliary for a moment. "So, what's new in Last Chance these days?"

"We were just discussing the marital state of William Ellis when you came in." Thelma gave Caroline a furtive look out of the corner of her eye. "He needs a wife, preferably an Episcopalian, and that's a fact."

Well, that wasn't exactly new news in Last Chance. The girls had been trying to find a mate for Bill Ellis for at least a year. "Is he still being lured by Jenny Carpenter's pies?" Caroline asked.

"He is," Lessie said, "and everyone is in an uproar because he's judging the pie contest again this year, and we all reckon Jenny's peach pie is going to win again. Really, we need to find some unbiased judges for that contest."

"We do," the ladies chorused.

"And we need to find a good woman for Bill."

"Sounds like he needs a woman who knows her way around a rolling pin," Caroline said.

"Do not joke about this, Rocky. Besides, you could do a whole lot worse for yourself than Reverend Ellis. After all, Bill is gainfully employed and close to the Lord," Lessie replied with a little sniff.

"Reverend Ellis is not for Rocky."

This pronouncement, coming from Miriam Randall, brought all activity at the Cut 'n Curl to a screeching halt. Lessie got halfway out of her chair. Momma turned around at her station and stared at the little old lady. Thelma ducked down out of the hair dryer, and Millie closed *Destiny* with her finger inside the paperback to mark her place.

"No?" Ruby asked. "Then who?"

Miriam blinked in Caroline's direction from behind her 1950s-style rhinestone trifocals. "I'm not sure, but not Reverend Ellis. He belongs to someone else."

Caroline's stomach clutched. Everyone in town thought Miriam Randall had a pipeline to the Lord that allowed her to make perfect matches by helping to identify a person's soulmate. Caroline didn't need a soulmate right at the moment, so she hoped Miz Miriam would keep her thoughts to herself.

Apparently Miz Miriam had other plans. Because she gave Caroline one of her sweet little ol' lady grins and said, "Oh, Rocky, you should be looking for a salt of the earth."

"Salt of the earth?" Caroline's voice cracked.

"Honey, I've known for some time that you're destined

to be with a man who is...well, it's really hard to explain." Miriam paused a moment, her brown eyes twinkling. "See, your soulmate is going to be someone practical and down to earth and, well, just a regular sort of guy. And I've been getting the feeling that he's about to make an appearance in your life. Any day now."

"Really?" Her hands went clammy, and white spots invaded her field of vision. Finding a regular sort of guy sounded okay, so long as it happened after the election. Before the election was no good. And whoever he was, he had to be ready to drop everything and move to Washington. That was nonnegotiable.

"Well, isn't that a surprise," Momma said with a little frown folding her brow. "Oh, well, not as surprising as that time you predicted that Tulane would marry a minister's daughter. But Caroline with just a regular Joe is very reassuring, Miriam, thank you so much. I've been worried lately that she'd end up with one of those lawyers or politicians up in Columbia, you know?"

"Well," Miriam said in her chipper voice, "I can't say what his occupation might be, but it stands to reason that a man like that would probably work with his hands." The old lady cocked her head sideways and blinked her deep brown eyes at Caroline as if she were studying tea leaves in the bottom of a cup.

"Uh, thanks, Miz Miriam," Caroline said, "but I'm not actually looking for a soulmate, or even a steady boyfriend, right at the moment. I'm really trying to help Senator Warren get reelected. And then I'm hoping that he'll give me a job in his DC office. So all in all, I could wait to find true love. I could wait a long time."

"Yes, but can your true love wait for you?" Miriam said.

Lessie giggled like a schoolgirl. "You know," she said, "you don't want to wait too long, dear. The biological clock just keeps ticking, and if you don't pay it any mind, you might find yourself an old maid. And besides, everyone knows it's a blessing to be one of Miriam's matches. Those marriages never fail. Ever. So you listen to her advice, you hear?"

CHAPTER
4

Caroline guided her oldest brother's Ford pickup into the parking lot at the Red Hot Pig Place, a low cinder block structure out on the two-lane state road that stretched between the towns of Last Chance and Allenberg.

The Pig Place served real barbecue, not that tomato-based garbage that most suburban barbecue places served. The pork hash at the Pig Place was made with vinegar and pepper sauce, the hush puppies were guaranteed to clog your arteries, and the slaw was creamy and delicious.

For all that, Caroline, who was constantly watching her weight, would have preferred a restaurant closer to Orangeburg where she and Rachel could get a decent salad. But Caroline knew how much Rachel loved barbecue. And Rachel never had to worry about her weight.

Rachel was acting kind of weird tonight. She insisted that they take the back corner booth, and once they were seated, she kept looking around and jumping every time someone came through the door.

"Hey, Rache," Caroline asked once their platters of hash had arrived, "what's up?"

Rachel looked down at the checkered tablecloth, her shoulders slumped, her hair down around her face in a way that hid her beautiful peaches-and-cream skin, her incredible topaz eyes, and her amazing bone structure.

Rachel didn't think she was pretty. Caroline had been trying to argue her out of that belief ever since she could remember. But then Caroline knew the treachery of looking into mirrors. Somehow they always managed to reflect back every fault.

She reached forward and patted Rachel's hand. "Honey, what's happened? What's wrong?"

Rachel pulled her hand back, picked up her fork, and played with the hush puppies on her plate. "They're cutting corners at the chicken plant," she finally said.

"Cutting corners?"

She nodded and finally looked up with a truly tortured look on her face. "On safety. And I've been worried sick about it. I shouldn't even tell you. You'll probably tell someone in Columbia, and the whole thing will come crashing down on me. I don't want to be responsible. I just want my job. But I want things to be right at the plant."

"Are you talking about OSHA or food safety?"

"A little bit of both."

"Holy smokes."

"Yeah, exactly. What should I do?"

"You have to call the authorities."

"But, Rocky, Mr. Marshall seems really preoccupied these days, and I hate to say it, but he hardly ever shows up for work. I never really thought Hettie Marshall was married to a lazy man but..." Rachel let her voice fade out and popped a hush puppy into her mouth. She closed her eyes and chewed.

There was nothing like hush puppies from the Pig Place to provide immediate comfort, and about two thousand calories each.

"You have to tell the authorities. Lives might be at stake."

Rachel swallowed her food and took a sip of her sweet tea. "But if I call the authorities, they'll close us down, and I'm not sure we'll ever reopen. And if we don't reopen, I don't even want to think about what will happen to Last Chance."

The hush puppies in Caroline's stomach turned to lead. "Of course you'll reopen."

"I wouldn't be so sure. I don't think Mr. Marshall is in a very good financial position. I think he took a big hit during the economic downturn a couple of years ago, and the plant is hanging on by its fingernails. To make things worse, Mr. Marshall doesn't seem to be working very hard at keeping us afloat."

"That's not good."

"No, it's not." Rachel leaned in and spoke in a near whisper that just carried over the twangy sound of Brad Paisley singing on the radio. "I know how important Golfing for God is to your family. Heck, Momma's even joined the committee to resurrect it. But Daddy has been talking nonstop about how having a new factory in town would be a good thing. And he should know. He's a banker."

"Yeah, so your momma said this afternoon at the Cut 'n Curl. Boy, this could get really ugly."

Rachel nodded. "Look, Rocky, the point is that Golfing for God, even if it becomes a real tourist attraction, will never employ as many people as the chicken plant. And that's a fact no one can dispute."

Caroline's appetite for unhealthy food evaporated. She was conflicted six ways to Sunday, wasn't she?

"Oh, crap," Rachel said. "We've got trouble."

Caroline followed Rachel's gaze to the front door, and wouldn't you know it, there stood a trio of ridiculously good-looking men: Dash Randall, Bubba Lockheart, and his Lordship, Baron Woolham. Dash in his Wranglers, and Bubba in his mechanic's uniform, fit right in with the roadhouse décor. But Baron Woolham, dressed in a pair of gray worsted slacks, a Cutter & Buck golf shirt, and tasseled loafers that might have come from Cole Haan, looked a little like Queen Elizabeth at Wrestlemania.

The hostess led the three men to a table not far away. Boy and howdy, those three guys had sex appeal. In spades.

Even Bubba, who looked like he'd come from his job at Bill's Grease Pit via a stop at Dot's Spot for a beer or two. He wore his dark blue work shirt with his name—Bubba, not Francis or Frank Jr. or any other iteration of his true Christian name—embroidered in bright red thread right above his shirt pocket. The shirt stretched across his broad shoulders and chest. He'd rolled up the sleeves to expose forearms covered with sun-bleached blond hair and a heart-shaped tattoo that said "Rocky."

Rachel leaned forward. "Is that guy with Bubba and Dash the baron?"

"Yeah."

"Oh, boy."

"Yeah, I know. Look, Rache. Maybe we should go

now." Caroline looked around for their waitress, who had taken that moment to disappear.

"Uh-oh," Rachel said, her whisper even more urgent.

Caroline returned her gaze to the table where the men were sitting just in time to see Baron Woolham unfold all six feet and some inches of his ramrod-straight body from his chair and begin walking—in a stately manner— in their direction.

Caroline watched him advance and couldn't help herself. She gave him the once-over gaze, from the tips of his loafers, up his long legs, over his flat stomach and broad shoulders and right up into those incredible whiskey-colored eyes.

In short, she ogled his Lordship. And she knew better, really. Because Bubba was right there in the room, and Bubba didn't like her ogling other guys. Not that Bubba had any say in the matter, but that never stopped him from thinking he had a say in the matter.

So it came as no surprise when Rachel hissed, "Oh, crap, look at Bubba."

Caroline tried to do just that, but Baron Woolham had come to a stop right in front of Caroline, blocking her view. His eyes crinkled up at the corners so handsomely. "I've been trying to reach you," he said in his ever-so-polite accent.

Every atom in Caroline's system went nuclear. The man was a walking fantasy. He was, in every respect, the complete antithesis of Bubba and Dash. He was not a regular Joe, and Caroline needed to stop letting her hormones run rampant every time he showed up on the scene. It was just plain stupid not to listen to Miriam Randall's advice about things like this.

And besides, he was an English aristocrat—completely out of her league.

"I didn't hear from you," his Lordship continued. "Do we have an appointment with your father tomorrow?"

"I'm working on it. Believe me when I say that he's not really interested in talking to you."

"I see."

"I'll call you in the morning if I have any success." She managed a little smile, even though she didn't feel like smiling. What she felt was an odd mixture of sexual attraction for deBracy, irritation at him for being so demanding, and pure panic that Bubba was about to do something Bubba-like.

Hugh took that moment to study her chest in a rather salacious fashion. She was wearing a perfectly ordinary white golf shirt, buttoned all the way up. There wasn't even a hint of cleavage. But he looked anyway.

And for once, she kind of enjoyed being looked at.

Bubba finally erupted. "Rocky!" he shouted in a too-loud voice that everyone in the restaurant heard. The rest of the patrons stopped eating and turned to watch the latest episode in the Rocky and Bubba Show. Oh great, the last thing she wanted was to make a scene of any kind in a public place.

Hugh turned around. And Caroline could finally see Bubba again. His face was red, and he was advancing on them in a way that spelled trouble.

Rachel was practically hyperventilating at this point. Caroline felt like hyperventilating, too.

"Hey, Bubba," Caroline said in her calm, cool, professional voice. "How are you? It's really nice to see you again. Rachel and I were just having our supper."

"Hey, Rachel," Bubba said, giving Caroline's friend a little nod. Then he turned his sad, moony face on Caroline. "Rocky, you need any help? Because I saw the way this guy was looking at you, and I know how you don't like that sort of thing."

Caroline's face burned. She'd been caught red-handed. And Bubba was right. She hated guys who leered at her bustline. But Hugh hadn't actually leered. And besides, Hugh's look made her tingle from head to foot.

She took a deep breath. "No, Bubba, I'm fine, really. Why don't ya'll—"

"I need to get home," Rachel announced in a firm voice. "And Rocky is driving. Come on, Rocky, we need to go." Rachel stood up and headed across the room toward the cashier, leaving two plates of half-eaten hash on the table.

God bless Rachel. She knew how to make an exit when it was required. Caroline gave Bubba a big, phony grin. "Well, Bubba, it was nice seeing you. But I gotta get Rachel home." Caroline took a step forward in the direction of the cashier.

"Don't go, please." Bubba's words were practically a whine. He grabbed Caroline by her left wrist and yanked her back.

Caroline didn't think about avoiding a scene or being careful when hot pain radiated from her shoulder joint. Instead, she reacted on pure instinct. She swung with her right fist, aiming for Bubba's nose, just like she had learned in the self-defense classes she'd taken last year down at the Columbia YMCA.

Thank goodness she missed her target. Bubba got the message, though. He staggered back and let go of her wrist.

So everything was good. All she had to do was talk Bubba down, and she and Rachel could make an escape without making a big scene.

And then Lord Woolham decided to play hero.

It happened so fast, Caroline was powerless to stop it. His Lordship assumed a fighting stance, and when Bubba took a step forward, Hugh threw a withering, left-handed punch that put Bubba on the floor. No muss, no fuss, no heavy breathing, or sweaty brows. No broken tables.

Nothing like that.

Just a James Bond move, and Bubba, the big line-backer and one-time NFL hopeful, was left lying on the floor whimpering. His mouth a big, bloody mess.

Caroline stood there stunned.

So it was a good thing that Rachel took charge. She hurried back across the room, fetching one of the patron's iced tea glasses off a table. She strained the liquid through her fingers onto the floor, got down on her knees, and packed the two teeth Hugh had knocked out of Bubba's jaw into the ice left in the glass.

You just had to love Rachel. She always had your back in every life-and-death situation, and she traveled with a first-aid kit in her purse.

Just then, Earl Williams, the proprietor of the Pig Place, arrived on the scene, shotgun in hand. He took aim at Lord Woolham's chest. "Don't move," he said. "The local law is on its way."

CHAPTER 5

Caroline probably should have let Stone arrest Lord Woolham. After all, the man had completely overreacted to Bubba's little power play. And of course, Stone wanted to arrest him, just because Stone was like that. He hated any outsider coming into his town and causing trouble. He'd even arrested Jane that time she showed up with a fake ID.

But Caroline sweet-talked her policeman brother out of it. She pointed out that Hugh had been trying to protect her, and that arresting him would needlessly complicate an already complicated situation.

And she promised to drive Hugh back to Miriam's.

In the meantime, Rachel had continued to play Florence Nightingale with a cold compress, while Dash drove Bubba over to the clinic, where Doc Cooper had put in an emergency call to an oral surgeon.

It had been another truly sordid scene in the Bubba and Rocky Horror Show. And usually, whenever something like this happened, Bubba's bad behavior was given a pass, while Caroline got blamed for everything.

Why couldn't she manage the Bubba situation in a calm and rational manner? After all, she managed difficult and sensitive situations all the time. But every time her path crossed Bubba's, something awful happened.

Well, at least this time, it wasn't entirely her fault. His Lordship was the one who had thrown the punch. It certainly gave her another excuse to be annoyed with him. But of course, she would keep her snotty comments to herself. That was her job.

"I suppose I ought to apologize. I do hope that prat isn't your boyfriend," his Lordship finally said from the passenger seat as Caroline drove him back to town.

"Bubba is not my boyfriend. But I do think you owe *him* an apology, not me. I had taken care of the situation. Bubba is harmless, really."

"You think so? Seems to me he overstepped his welcome, even if he *is* your boyfriend."

"I told you, he's not my boyfriend. We were together a long time ago. In high school. But it's over. Bubba thinks we're going to get back together, but he's delusional."

"He's got a tattoo of that nickname of yours on his arm."

She tried not to cringe. She didn't know why she felt humiliated by this arrogant man discovering her name. But she did.

"So you heard about that, huh?" she said.

"The tattoo or your nickname?"

She gripped the steering wheel a little harder. "My full name is Sirocco Caroline Rhodes," she said. "Everyone's always called me Rocky because I have brothers named Stone, Clay, and Tulane."

Silence beat for a moment while his Lordship figured

out the joke. He chuckled. "Tulane, huh? Like the one we're driving on."

Well, if she had to endure humiliation for the sake of her job, at least maybe she could use it to some good purpose. "You know, the whole family name thing should give you pause. My kin are eccentric."

"Is that why you changed your name?"

He was kidding, right? Like he didn't get why she changed her name? Or was he just ridiculing her? She swallowed down her annoyance and spoke in a calm voice. "Lord Woolham, no one takes a person named Rocky Rhodes seriously. Rocky Rhodes is the name of an ice cream flavor, and I work for a senator who might one day run for president."

"So why not use Sirocco? It's a lovely name. Mysterious and foreign. You look rather like a Sirocco."

"Mysterious and foreign? Really?"

"Yes, quite."

Wow! In all her born days, no one had ever called her mysterious and foreign. She was a country girl, no matter how hard she tried to hide all that with her business suits. "Uh, well, that's nice, but no one knows how to spell Sirocco, probably because it's mysterious and foreign."

"I see."

"Besides, Sirocco sounds a little self-important, don't you think? On the other hand, Caroline is a nice, middle-of-the-road, domestic-sounding name. It's perfect for my career."

"And I rather think your career is important to you, isn't it? Otherwise, you would never have agreed to help me with my factory."

She glanced over at him. It wasn't yet fully dark, and the golden glow of the setting sun caught in the highlights of his curls and lined his profile. He was incredibly handsome.

She really needed to clear the air, before she did something dumb. "You're right," she said in her best senatorial aide voice, "my career is important to me. But I love my family, too. So I will do my best to introduce you to all the important people in Allenberg County, just as you've asked me to do. But the thing is, I'm not on your side if it means trying to force my father to sell his land. And besides, Daddy will never sell out. So maybe it's time for you to rethink the location of your factory."

"And I told you I was not willing to do that."

She gritted her teeth. The man was used to getting his way, wasn't he? "Okay, I understand. But you're not going to win on this point. You can't convince Daddy to sell, and if you try to push the issue, the church ladies of the Committee to Resurrect Golfing for God are going to tar and feather you."

"I can handle churchwomen."

She stifled a snort of laughter. Hugh deBracy had no idea what he was up against. It might be fun to watch Hettie and her minions take him apart piece by piece.

Caroline pulled into Miriam Randall's driveway, just as the daylight had faded to dusk. "Here we are, Lord Woolham. I'll give you a call in the morning when I get a better sense of our schedule. I don't think we'll have anything on the agenda until midmorning at the earliest." She set the parking brake.

"Are you going to schedule a meeting with these church ladies who want to save the golf course?"

"Absolutely. The Committee to Resurrect Golfing for God always meets on Friday at noontime at the Cut 'n Curl. I have no doubt they'll want to meet you. They are all pretty curious."

"Curious about me?"

"Yes. You see, they read a lot of regency romances. And they all watched the royal wedding together over at Thelma Hanks's house. They're still talking about the breakfast kippers she served that morning."

"I see."

"I'm sure I can get you on the agenda for tomorrow's meeting. Momma owns the Cut 'n Curl. I have an in." She gave Hugh one of her best professional smiles.

It was as phony as a three-dollar bill.

He turned in his seat and studied her for a long, breathless moment. No doubt he was thinking about her lowly station in life, the daughter of a hairdresser and a putt-putt owner. Well, he could just fry in hell for all she cared. She kept her grin steady.

After a long moment, he said, "I get the distinct feeling that you are trying to deliver me to the lions, Miss Rhodes."

"I'm doing no such thing. Meeting with the members of the Committee to Resurrect Golfing for God is one way to get your opposition in a single room. After all, didn't you just say that you knew how to handle churchwomen?"

"I suppose I did say that."

"And I pointed out that it was hopeless. And I'm trying, with great professional patience, to show you the error in your thinking. You aren't going to build that factory on my daddy's land."

"I suppose you wouldn't appreciate it if I told Senator Warren that you weren't being helpful."

The bottom of her stomach dropped a couple of inches. This was her biggest fear—that Lord Woolham would say something to Senator Warren, and her boss would suddenly realize that Caroline wasn't up to the task of being his main administrative assistant in Washington.

"No, Lord Woolham, I wouldn't appreciate you calling the senator and saying things like that. The fact is, I've been very helpful. I'm introducing you around. I'm helping you to see the facts. And I talked my brother out of arresting you tonight."

"Yes, you did, didn't you?" He said the words in his stuffy accent as if he didn't really appreciate the fact that she'd pulled out all the stops for him. Her brother could be kind of serious-minded.

She held her tongue. There were any number of choice things she could think of saying, but none of them would be acceptable. He was going to really screw up her life, wasn't he?

Lord Woolham opened the passenger side door and stepped out into the hot and humid night. The porch light burned brightly, silhouetting him as he walked toward the old house. He was tall and well built, and arrogant as the day was long.

She hated him.

Hugh strolled down the walk toward Miriam Randall's boardinghouse, trying not to be amused by the gravel Caroline had kicked up with her sudden, ferocious departure.

Granddad certainly wouldn't have been amused. Granddad had been grumpy and unpleasant and often quite mean to people. Granddad would have called the senator by now and demanded that Caroline be removed from her job.

But of course, Hugh had no intention of calling the senator and complaining. A complaint might just unsettle things further. The pixie-like Miss Rhodes would definitely fight for her job, and in the process, she might discover how flimsy his financing was. And then where would he be?

No, it was best to let things lie and see what the senator's dishy aide could come up with as a solution. He was getting the feeling she was actually quite competent at her job.

She had done a marvelous job of sweet-talking that copper out of arresting him. And really, he had seriously overreacted this evening. Given all of that, Caroline had been remarkably civil and helpful. That wouldn't have mattered to Granddad, of course. Granddad was a terrible snob—he would have looked right through a working-class girl like Caroline and steamrollered over her and her father's golf course.

And that, in a nutshell, was the difference between Hugh and his granddad.

He stepped up on a creaky porch step. The old Victorian home was just a little shabby—kind of like Woolham House, although on a much smaller scale. He reached the top step and realized that he wasn't alone.

A little white-haired lady sat rocking patiently on the porch. "Good evening," he said in his best public school voice. "You must be Miriam Randall. I've heard a great deal about you."

"Sit down and visit a spell. It's Hugh, isn't it?" She gestured toward an adjoining rocker.

Granddad would have sniffed at this woman using his first name. But Hugh kind of liked the fact that she'd been so familiar.

And besides, he was in a different land, with different mores, and he'd gotten into quite a bit of mischief. So he sat in the rocker and rested his head against its back. His companion kept up her steady motion, an old floorboard protesting with each transit of the rocker. The sound of the squeaky board provided a counterpoint to the buzz of insects and the deeper song of the frogs.

Boxwood and summer perennials perfumed the balmy night. "Your garden is quite lovely," he remarked in a bald-faced attempt to get on her good side. Gardeners, he knew from long experience, could be easily wooed into long, benign conversations.

"Well, thank you, son, but it's not my garden. I have a brown thumb when it comes to plants. Lord knows what will happen when Harry leaves me."

"Harry?"

"My husband of fifty-one years. I'm afraid the Lord means to take him from me soon." She gazed out toward the screen of pines that hid her home from the street. She seemed melancholy, and Hugh decided to remain silent until he could politely get away to his room, where a great deal of work awaited him. His prototype had been built, of course, but he and his handpicked team of engineers (basically a bunch of classmates from university who were moonlighting on the project) were still working out some of the kinks in the planned manufacturing process. There would be dozens of e-mails to read.

Miriam lifted her old hands from the rocker's arms, and Hugh noted the swellings at each joint. His old Great-

Aunt Maude had suffered terrible arthritis in her hands, and often the pain would drive her from her bed and down into the ladies' parlor, where old Sam would set a fire for her in the stone fireplace. Sometimes, when Hugh had come home from school on holiday, he'd sit up with her well into the wee hours, telling stories over tea, just to help ease her pain.

Great-Aunt Maude had been gone for almost fifteen years. He relaxed into the movement of the rocker and let the nostalgia settle in. It was a lovely, star-filled night—perfect for reverie.

Miriam took another deep breath and let it out. "You know I keep praying that the Lord will send Dash a gardener, but that's a selfish kind of prayer. The Lord will send Dash what Dash needs, and Lord knows that boy needs a great deal. I reckon I'll have to be happy if He sends a strong woman, even if she does have a brown thumb like me."

"Well, I suppose Dash could always hire a gardener if push came to shove."

"Ah, so you've been in town long enough to know the state of my nephew's bank account."

"Well, I had heard something along the lines that he was well off." Which begged the question as to why Miriam Randall's house looked as if it might tumble down around her ears. Was Dash one of those selfish bastards?

"Hiring a gardener would break Harry's heart. Harry loves this garden, and the house, too. He used to work on things all day long. Kept him fit until the last year. Now he can't breathe well enough to walk across the room. Dash hired a man to do some weeding, and Harry nearly 'bout had a fit."

She let go of a long breath. "Well, I don't have much to complain about. Fifty-one years of happiness is more than most of us get, I reckon."

Perhaps Dash wasn't selfish at all. And the old lady didn't need or want any kind of affirmation of what was, after all, a platitude. Fifty-one years of happiness were more than many got, but if one was left behind, it would still never be enough.

She rocked a long moment in silence. "I do like a man who knows when to keep his mouth shut."

"I'll take that as a compliment."

"It was intended as such. And more so, given what you've been up to this evening."

"Ah, I was wondering when you'd get to that. Shall I pack my bags and take myself off to the Peach Blossom Motor Court?"

Miriam laughed and turned her head. The yellow porch light caught a glimmer in her dark, myopic stare. Her eyeglasses were perched on the top of her head, and the twin indentations on either side of her nose told him that she was probably blind without them.

He knew the feeling. He was utterly blind without his contact lenses. But there were times when leaving them out and letting the world blur would give him a moment of inner peace.

"No, I don't think I'll send you off to the Peach Blossom. That would put you at Lillian Bray's mercy."

"Lillian Bray?"

"Hmm. She's the chair of the Christ Church Ladies Auxiliary, a member of the town council, and the chair of the Garden Club. Now *there* is a woman who takes gardening seriously. Her gladioli are legendary."

"Really?" he said politely, as if he were sitting down to tea with Great-Aunt Maude.

"Yes. And she's on your side, if you must know."

"Well then, I will have to seek her out and enlist her work on my behalf."

"You do that." There was a sour note in Miriam's voice.

"I take it you're not keen on my building a factory here in Last Chance. Would it change your mind if I told you it would employ two hundred people?"

"Not if it means disturbing the angels who've been watching over this town for a hundred and fifty years." She stopped rocking. "You know about the angels, don't you?"

"Oh, yes, Caroline was very thorough with her briefing. I told her we needed to get the angels on our side."

Miriam huffed a laugh. "Lord a'mercy, you are a funny man. But honey, that may be harder than you think."

"Why not? The factory will create jobs. If the angels are interested in protecting the town, wouldn't they see that?"

"Hmmm. Good point. But you see, the angels are probably on the side of the environmentalists. And even if they aren't, I'm thinking Elbert's angels are more interested in having people learn their Bible by playing golf than helping with the unemployment situation. And that's why we formed our committee. The golf course could easily save the town. It is a marvel, and well, there is only one Golfing for God, and there are factories everywhere."

"That's a very good point. I wonder if it would be possible to move the golf course."

"Move it?"

"Hmm. Yes, all the statues and whatnot."

The old woman leaned forward. "Hugh, honey, have you seen the golf course?"

"No. I gather Caroline is trying to schedule something for tomorrow."

Miriam chuckled. "You know, I wouldn't count on Rocky being entirely on your side on this."

"Oh, don't worry, I'm not counting on her."

"No?"

He shook his head. "She's conflicted, of course. I'm certainly not above using her local knowledge. But I'm not foolish enough to trust her."

"If you don't mind my saying so, I think you had better count on the fact that you aren't going to get that land. You'd have to convince God, and He's on Elbert's side, I believe."

"That's too bad for the people of Last Chance, isn't it? Because I'm very close to losing my patience. I could very easily return home to the UK, marry Lady Ashton, and forget about this project altogether."

Miriam turned and pulled her glasses down and rested them on her nose. They were thick trifocals, upturned at their corners and decorated with rhinestones. They reminded Hugh of Aunt Petal's eyeglasses, although Miriam's frames were a steely blue and Aunt Petal wore frames the color of a male gnome's hat—holly berry red.

Miriam eyed him through the glasses as if seeing him for the first time, which was probably the case given the thickness of the lenses. He braced himself for the well-worn suggestion that he should find another site for his factory.

But Miriam surprised him when she said, "Lady Ashton? Really? Is she rich?"

"Well, yes."

"So did someone tell you that you should be looking for a woman who will bring you a fortune?"

"Well, to be honest, Mrs. Randall, my forebears have made a science of doing that sort of thing. You know, I come from a long line of aristocrats, who were not a particularly talented bunch, unless you count picking the right brides."

"Right brides? All of you? Do you have the sight then?"

"The sight? No, we're just a practical bunch. Every one of my forebears going back ten generations or more has picked a bride who has brought wealth to the family." He hesitated for a moment. "Except my father, poor sot. His marriage was a disaster and then he died quite young. My father, I'm afraid, was a failure."

"Oh, I'm sorry, honey."

Hugh shrugged. "Well, I was only three at the time. I don't remember my parents. Before I went off to school, I was raised by my grandfather and my Aunts Maude, Petunia, and Petal. I am well aware that marrying the right woman is important for a person such as myself. Lord knows Granddad drilled that point into my head relentlessly. Marrying well is practically a duty in my family."

She reached over and squeezed his arm. "Hugh, honey, listen to me. You should be looking for a wife who will help you find your fortune. Just remember that, and you'll do just fine."

He cleared his throat. "Um, can I ask you something?"

"How do I know?"

"Well, no, that's not what I was going to ask. I was

going to ask why you aren't concerned about losing the factory."

She snickered like an old lady enjoying herself. "Oh, I reckon the factory will work its way out. My main concern in life is to make sure people find their soulmates."

"What? I'm sure my forebears were more interested in money than love."

"All the more reason you should listen to me."

She turned and started to rock again, pushing her glasses up to the top of her head and closing her eyes. "Sometimes I can just see how two people fit together. Folks around here say I'm a matchmaker, but that's not really what I do. God makes the matches, but sometimes He clues me in."

"Really?"

"You're humoring me."

"Maybe a little." He was skeptical of fortune-tellers. And of course, he was trying very hard to break out of the deBracy mold. He didn't want to marry for money, as Granddad had done. He wanted to be a success on his own merits. Maybe if he could make a go of this factory, he could finally lay Granddad to rest.

"You know," the old woman said, "folks around here say that I've never missed with one of my predictions."

"Quite impressive, I must say." And just a little bit depressing, given what she'd predicted for him.

She continued to rock. "I see you aren't convinced."

"Well, I haven't ever heard of a matchmaker quite like you. But I will keep your advice in mind. Thank you," he said very politely.

But of course, he wasn't going to take her advice seriously, even though he had a deep romantic streak and sometimes wanted to believe in fairies, and angels, and all things supernatural.

But Miriam had simply parroted back his own history, which is exactly what charlatans and fortune-tellers did. The fact that her forecast was likely to come true meant nothing. All the family had ever expected of him was to marry well. And Lady Ashton had almost been handpicked for him. Victoria had been waiting for a long time. But it appeared as if her wait was about to come to an end.

If he had to marry Victoria to save Woolham House and keep a roof over Petal and Petunia's heads, he would do it. He knew his duty.

He stood up. "It's been a pleasure, Mrs. Randall, but tomorrow is going to be a busy day."

"Honey, you have no idea."

The next morning, after she'd confirmed the schedule for the day with Lord Woolham, Caroline donned one of her gray business suits, and drove down to the Allenberg County courthouse. She arrived just as the place opened its doors, and spent more than two hours poring over land records. By the time she had finished, she had a good idea of who owned what property and what they'd paid for it.

Something fishy was going on in Last Chance, South Carolina, and it didn't involve cane poles, night crawlers, or the Edisto River.

Her morning's research had turned up a big surprise: Jimmy Marshall didn't own nearly as much land in Allenberg County as Caroline had thought. In fact, Dash Randall had been snapping up land faster than anyone, and he'd bought most of it from Jimmy over the last year. Dash had paid somewhat inflated prices for the land, too.

But not nearly as inflated as the price paid for the land adjacent to Golfing for God. Jimmy had made a killing on that real estate—selling the parcels for ten times their assessed value.

Why would Hugh's partner do a thing like that? Of course, it was common for land prices to rise on rumors of a big development. But as far as she knew, no one in Allenberg was aware of the factory proposal prior to the sale.

And then there was the problem that the land Hugh's partner had purchased had swamp on it. Not a lot of swamp, but just enough to make developing it expensive.

Caroline knew a lot about wetland abatement issues. You couldn't live in South Carolina without being aware of something like that. And putting industrial development near any swamp was sure to bring out the environmentalists and the snake lovers, not to mention the government with a whole passel of red tape.

Hugh really *was* up the swamp without a paddle.

But there was something else going on—something way more ominous.

Why the heck was Jimmy Marshall selling off the family land like that? Caroline wondered if his daddy knew what Jimmy was up to. Of course, Lee Marshall was about eighty-five years old, but last she'd heard, he was still pretty sharp. Lee would never have sold the family land like that.

The plant was cutting corners, but Jimmy was still selling land for top dollar. Where the heck was the money going, if not into the business? Maybe the chicken plant was in worse trouble than Rachel had made it sound.

Or maybe Jimmy was getting ready to sell out.

Either way, the town of Last Chance was in deep trouble.

The plan to convince Lord Woolham to build a factory upstate didn't seem like such a good plan after all. Last Chance might actually *need* his high and mightiness.

She was climbing into Stone's truck for the drive back to town when her cell phone rang. She checked the ID. It was Rachel.

"Hey, what happened after I left you last night?" Caroline asked her friend. "How's Bubba?"

"It's awful, Rocky. The doctor couldn't save his teeth."

"Oh, no."

"And he's got stitches all over his upper lip, and his nose is broken."

"Great."

"The oral surgeon told him he should sue Lord Woolham. I'm thinking maybe the doctor is right."

"Come on, Rachel, Lord Woolham was just protecting me. Bubba is the one who started the fight."

"I know. But that man didn't have to break his face, did he? I mean we were going. It would have been okay, and besides, there is the whole Miriam Randall prediction, which, by the way, you didn't say a word about last night."

"Uh, okay, you mean that stuff about how I should be looking for the salt of the earth, a regular Joe, a guy who works with his hands?"

"Right. Exactly."

"Okay. First of all, what does that have to do with Bubba's broken face? And second of all, I didn't get a chance to tell you about Miriam's prediction because we were busy talking about the problems at the chicken plant, and then Bubba arrived, and the rest is history."

"Don't you see, Rocky? Miriam is talking about Bubba."

"What? No."

"Of course she is."

"No, Rachel, Miriam is not talking about Bubba."

"But she described him to a T. And this morning everyone in town is saying that you and Bubba are going to get back together. Momma even said at breakfast that you and Bubba are a match made in Heaven, and that the fistfight down at the Pig Place was just a confirmation of everything. Really, Rocky, you ought to consider it. Bubba is always looking after you, you know? He practically worships the ground you walk on." Rachel's voice sounded wobbly.

"Uh, Rache, this makes no sense. I dumped Bubba twelve years ago. Remember? And Bubba's face was smashed last night because he decided to come after me. How is that a sign of anything except his infernal stubbornness?"

"I know, but everyone is saying it's proof that he loves you in spite of everything, and you will come around to understanding it eventually."

"Oh, great. Look, I don't love Bubba."

"But you will. Miriam said so."

"Honey, it's not going to happen, okay? There are plenty of regular Joes out there. I'm sure I'll stumble on one of them someday. But in the meantime, I've got bigger problems. I need to figure out this factory mess. I spent the morning at the courthouse and you won't believe who sold Lord Woolham the land adjacent to the golf course."

"Who?"

"Your boss man. And Jimmy ratcheted up the price, land shark that he is. Do you think he really expected my daddy to sell out? Or was he just playing a flimflam game with his Lordship?"

"Oh, no. Do you think Hettie knows Jimmy did that?"

"I have no idea. Probably not. But that's not the important thing—there's something off about the whole situation. Jimmy's been selling off a lot of land lately, Rache. Like he's either in deep financial trouble or...I don't know."

"Shoot. This is bad. I heard something else this morning in the break room."

"What?"

"Roy Burdett was complaining, like he always does. But this time Harlan Gregory said Mr. Marshall was paying off the state OSHA inspector to look the other way."

"Well, that might explain where some of this money is going. Rachel, if Jimmy is bribing inspectors, we've got to say something about it to the authorities."

"We don't have proof. We just have something I overheard."

"Even so, we might want to make a couple of calls to the authorities."

"No. I can't. If I blow the whistle and the factory closes, everyone will blame me."

"Not if you do it anonymously."

"There is no such thing in Last Chance. My life is utter crap, you know that?"

"It could be worse, honey. Your career might hinge on convincing a bunch of church ladies to give up on saving a putt-putt place dedicated to the Lord. And also you could be the focus of one of Miriam's matrimonial forecasts."

"Uh, Rocky, I wouldn't mind being included in one of

Miriam's forecasts. It's you who wants to go off and have a career. Me, I'd like to settle down with a nice guy and maybe raise a few kids."

Caroline gritted her teeth. Rachel could be maddening sometimes. She'd gone to college and had worked in Columbia for a bank until an unhappy love affair had sent her home three years ago. Now she seemed to think being an administrative assistant at the chicken plant was the pinnacle of achievement.

She just didn't seem to understand her own worth.

"Look," Caroline said, "call me if you hear any more rumors at the chicken plant. I'll be at the meeting of the Committee to Resurrect Golfing for God."

Caroline ended the call and drove from Allenberg to Last Chance. She parked her brother's truck in the parking lot behind the Cut 'n Curl. It was still early so she strolled into the doughnut shop that shared the alleyway. She inhaled the scents of powdered sugar and frying oil like an addict. Despite the state of her waistline, she ordered a Boston cream and a cup of coffee.

Her plan was to hide out for a few minutes while she ate the doughnut and checked e-mail on her smart phone. Caroline needed the sugar fix before she met up with Lord Woolham. There were just too many things going wrong with her life at the moment for her to face him—or a meeting of the Committee to Resurrect—completely cold turkey.

But as so often happens to the best-laid plans, hers fell apart a minute later when Dash Randall sauntered into the shop and ordered a cup of coffee to go.

He was dressed in full-out western mode. His Wranglers were cowboy worn, his alligator boots had pointy toes and stacked heels, and his hat was a dusty gray Stetson.

He looked like he'd been born in the saddle, which wasn't too far from the truth, seeing as Dash had started his life in Texas. He'd moved to Last Chance to live with his great-aunt and -uncle after his granddaddy died. The whereabouts of Dash's parents had always been a mystery—one he never spoke about.

He ambled over and dropped into the molded plastic seat at the little round table where Caroline was devouring her doughnut.

"Sneaking junk food again, huh?" he asked, taking a noisy sip of his coffee.

"Did I ask you to sit down and insult me?"

The corner of his mouth turned up. "I reckon you're allowed to be nasty this morning. And I can fully understand the need to fortify yourself before your Englishman makes a fool of himself in front of the ladies of the committee."

"You can go away now."

"Did I miss something? Are you mad at me?"

"Yes, I am."

"Why?" His big blue eyes opened wide, and he gave her an innocent "who-me?" look. Dash was way too cute for his own good.

Luckily Caroline had learned how to ignore his antics a long, long time ago. She stared up into his face, making eye-to-eye contact while she explained his most recent transgression. "You did nothing to stop that whole scene at the Pig Place last evening. I mean really. I could have used your help before it came to blows."

"I didn't think it was going to come to blows. You and Rachel looked like you had things under control."

Caroline took a long sip of coffee and considered her next words carefully. "Look, Dash," she said, "I just talked to Rachel, and I know what everyone in town is saying about last night. And they're all crazy. I'm not in love with Bubba. In fact, Bubba needs to realize that his behavior last night triggered that fight. And the town needs to quit enabling him."

Dash's eyes lost their spark of humor. "For once, Rocky, I agree with you. But what can I do about it? You know how it works in this town when Aunt Mim makes a prediction. And you combine that with Bubba being a football hero and you being a Watermelon Queen and you're dealing with the power of myth."

"Could you please get your aunt to clarify her forecast for me? I'm sure Miriam knows that Bubba is not my soulmate."

"Right. That's like asking the Edisto to stop flowing to the sea. And besides, even if you and I try to clarify things, no one will listen. The last time Aunt Mim got up to her tricks, Thelma and Millie were convinced she intended to match up Sarah Murray with Bill Ellis, and all the while it turned out she was talking about Tulane. You know how this stuff goes. I think gossip is like the national pastime in this town. It doesn't matter whether it makes sense or not, it's just something to do."

Caroline let go of a deep breath. "Well, right now I wish your aunt had kept her mouth shut. Why couldn't she just find some kind of matrimonial forecast for you? I mean you're just like Bubba, carrying a torch for someone you loved in high school. When are you going to put that torch down, Dash?"

Everyone in town knew about Dash and Hettie's high

school fling. Hettie, the daughter of a judge, had selected Dash, the son of no one in particular, to have her one rebellious moment. Hettie had gotten over it. Dash had not.

Dash glowered at Caroline. "I don't want to talk about Hettie. And the idea of Aunt Mim trying to match me up with anyone makes my skin crawl."

She held his stare for a moment—just enough to make him feel uncomfortable. Then she popped the last bite of doughnut in her mouth and closed her eyes, savoring every calorie-laden moment. She let go of a little groan of pleasure.

"That good, huh?"

She opened her eyes. "Dash, I mean it. If you care about Bubba—and I think you do—I need your help. We need something big to shake up his world. The stuff folks are saying this morning about Miriam's marital forecast is only going to encourage him. It has to stop, for his sake as much as mine."

Dash took a thoughtful sip of his coffee. "I reckon you have a point."

"You know I do. You have any ideas?"

He shook his head. "Nothing that comes immediately to mind. But let me think on it for a while." He nodded toward the front window of the shop. "Here comes the champ. That was some kind of punch he laid on Bubba. I thought he was a sissy until he took that swing."

Caroline looked out the front window just in time to see Lord Woolham coming up the sidewalk, his shoulders back, his stride confident, his suit impeccable, and his hair an unruly mess.

God. He looked as sweet as the doughnut she'd just ingested. And about as bad for her, too.

"Guess you gotta go back to work, huh?" Dash said.

"Yeah. This should be fun. Maybe the ladies will scare some sense into him." But she wasn't sure she wanted to scare Lord Woolham away anymore.

The churchwomen of Last Chance wore flowered dresses, drank tea, and brought chicken salad sandwiches to their meeting.

This made them practically identical to their sisters across the Atlantic in Woolham. Although, to be fair, the women of Woolham drank their tea hot and used flowered china cups and saucers instead of tumblers with ice.

But aside from that minor difference, the women of Last Chance and Woolham were identical in every respect. And Hugh had always been very good at charming church ladies.

He put on his best Sunday manners and handed out several flyers about his factory project, which contained information about the jobs he would be creating and the employment benefits and the multiplier effect that his business would have on their community. He also handed out technical sheets with information about his loom.

No one was very interested in those, unfortunately. If they had been, he'd have probably talked for an hour about the revolutionary design that had won Hugh several patents. Instead, he kept it almost entirely nontechnical and spoke for twenty minutes before opening it up for question time.

A middle-aged woman named Millie, wearing a pink sundress, kicked things off. "So, Lord Woolham, do you personally know Prince William?" she asked.

His face prickled with heat. "Uh, no, I don't."

"Have you ever been presented to the Queen?" another lady wanted to know.

"Um, no, I haven't, I'm afraid."

"Have you ever gone to Ascot?" came another.

"I'm afraid not. I'm not much of a horse lover, you see."

A pall of silence fell over the ladies. "Really?" one of them asked in a hushed tone. "Don't all English gentlemen love horses?"

"Uh, well, you see, I'm rather allergic. I much prefer motorcars, to be honest."

Behind him, Caroline snorted a laugh.

He turned to glare at her. A pixie light danced in her green eyes. She really was quite lovely. And she had a very good sense of humor, all things considered.

"Does anyone have any questions about the factory or the loom?" Hugh asked.

"Not really." This came from the blond woman named Hettie Marshall, who was the chairwoman.

"Nothing at all?" he asked.

Mrs. Marshall gave him a cool smile. "Well, Lord Woolham, it's really very simple. We'd love to have your factory. Just not where you want to build it." She turned to the rest of the assembled ladies. "Is that a fair representation of everyone's view?" she asked.

"Yes," they chorused.

The chairwoman turned back toward Hugh. "Thank you so much for your presentation. We were all quite excited to have a real English baron come and talk to us, although, bless your heart, we're all a bit disappointed that you don't know the Duke of Cambridge. We think he's very handsome."

"I'm sure the Queen would be happy to know that you approve of her grandson," Hugh managed between his clenched teeth. What a bloody waste of time this had been.

"Well," Mrs. Marshall continued, "if you knew the Queen, you could convey our message. Now, if ya'll don't mind, we have plans to make for our booth at the Watermelon Festival. Be sure to stop by. We'll be selling pies, preserves, and kisses."

"You know, Hettie, I'm not really sure about the whole kiss thing," Miriam Randall said, her eyes twinkling behind her upturned glasses. "I mean who's going to spend money to kiss any of us? Except maybe our husbands."

"Oh, I don't know, Jane might sell a few kisses," Caroline's mother said. Ruby Rhodes looked like an older version of her daughter, right down to the mischievous green eyes.

"Uh, um, I'm having a little trouble with Clay on that score," a young woman in the front row said. She had spent the entirety of Hugh's speech knitting something in dark green yarn.

"I've got an idea," Miriam said.

"Oh, no," Caroline said, taking a step back toward the door. "I'm not selling kisses. Not for this cause. It would be unprofessional and—"

"I think that's a great idea," the woman named Millie said. "I figure Bubba will buy a few."

"Bubba's mouth is broken," Caroline said.

Hugh turned around. "Oh, dear. Broken?"

"Well, you knocked out his front teeth, and he needed a plastic surgeon to stitch up his lip. Which, thank goodness, puts him on the disabled list when it comes to kisses."

"Oh, dear. I didn't mean to hit him that hard," Hugh said. His face got hot.

"Well, you did."

"Yeah, you did," Jane said. "We ought to make you pay for that damage by having you sell kisses, Lord Woolham. I'm thinking we could really make a killing on that."

The ladies tittered, and he turned toward Caroline and gave her one of Granddad's "we're not amused" looks.

Caroline looked unimpressed.

In fact, none of the ladies seemed impressed.

He cleared his throat. "Well, ladies, thanks for the offer. I'm sure there are many lovely women in Allenberg County that I would enjoy kissing. But I would rather give my kisses away than sell them."

"Ooooh," the ladies said in unison, just as Hugh realized that his comment had come out all twisted and wrong. His face got hotter still. "Um, well, what I meant to say was that I don't sell myself to the highest bidder. I mean I..."

"I think we got the message, Lord Woolham," Caroline said. Ire sparked in her eyes. No doubt she thought he was a snob. That was good. He had her right where he wanted her. Didn't he?

CHAPTER 7

Caroline sat in the passenger seat of the rented Mustang as Hugh drove it at a sedate pace down Palmetto Avenue, past the Kountry Kitchen on the right and The Kismet, the derelict movie theater, on the left. They reached the southern edge of town and left the fifteen-mile-an-hour speed limit behind. With each passing mile, Caroline got more worried.

His Lordship had just been teased and practically humiliated by the committee, and aside from a really cute blush when the subject of selling kisses had come up, the guy had kept his cool, remained polite, and continued to believe in his factory.

Heck, after listening to him talk—especially the ten minutes he spent on the technology he was putting into his looms—even Caroline believed in his factory. It was precisely what Last Chance needed. Especially if Jimmy Marshall was fiddling while the chicken plant failed.

But Hugh needed her help.

Even if he convinced Daddy to sell out, he was going to need help negotiating the wetlands permits. He would need additional financing to do the wetlands reclamation. It would take months. It would be expensive. Maybe more expensive than walking away from this overpriced land and starting over somewhere else. She would pull together some numbers for him. Maybe numbers would speak louder than her daddy would.

She stuffed all these thoughts into the back of her mind as Hugh guided his rental car to a stop in the parking lot of Golfing for God. First things first, she needed to convince him that Daddy wouldn't sell out.

Then they could attack the other problems one by one.

Caroline smoothed her windblown hair back into its ponytail, turned in her seat, and gave his Lordship a long stare. "You were good with the ladies at lunch, I'll give you that. They can be rough on outsiders, you know. But, um, Daddy is a whole different animal. So please, don't confront him or anything, okay?"

"I wasn't planning on any confrontations. I rather thought I'd talk with him." He gave her a stiff smile and opened his door.

She did likewise, and followed him to the remains of a twenty-foot fiberglass statue of Jesus that lay on its side. Jesus had been pretty much totaled by a Country Pride Chicken truck. But at one time, he had presided over the parking lot with a sign in his holy hands saying, "Golfing for God." His halo had included an additional sign telling the world that this particular mini-golf place featured a life-sized Noah's Ark.

Hugh stared at the wreckage with the oddest expression on his face. By the way the corners of his mouth curled up, he seemed amused. That wasn't the reaction Caroline had been looking for.

Shocked, awed, appalled—any of those she could have worked with. But amused was a big problem.

"You think it's funny?" she asked, her words coming out just a tad sharp.

The words missed their mark. "It's rather charming, actually."

"Charming?" Boy, she hadn't seen that one coming. "No one has ever called Golfing for God charming."

"Well, it is, quite." He turned on his heel and strode off toward the pathway that led to Noah's Ark and the golf course. The truck accident was only one of the calamities that had befallen Golfing for God last October. A freak lightning storm had triggered an explosion that had taken out the propane tank that fed the tiki torches. The tikis had been blown to smithereens and ignited the woods that surrounded the golf course. The charred remnants of pine trees still lined the path, and it looked as if Daddy and members of the Committee to Resurrect Golfing for God had been out here trimming back the kudzu that had taken over the last few months.

Caroline traipsed after Baron Woolham as he strode down the ruined path toward Noah's Ark. The Ark wasn't actually life-sized, no matter what the sign out front said. Caroline had realized this truth when she was about nine or ten and had figured out that the real Noah's Ark would have had to be ginormous in order to carry all the species of life on earth. The Ark at the golf course was about the size of a modest horse barn. Two elephants would have been a tight squeeze, which made it kind of puny by Ark standards.

Of course, Daddy always argued that since the Ark at Golfing for God was big enough to house a petting zoo comprised of a longhorn steer, a llama, a goat, a sheep, and a bunny, it was, therefore, life-sized. Caroline had eventually conceded that point, but continued to feel a certain level of disappointment that the Ark was so small. To make matters worse, the older she got, the smaller the Ark seemed.

The Ark also housed Daddy's office and the check-in where customers paid their greens fees and got their little colored balls and putters. The check-in counter was buttoned up with a shutter that needed painting, as did the Ark itself. Hugh stopped, put his hands on his hips, and looked up at the building, which towered about fifty feet above them. Caroline stood behind him and searched the grounds for Daddy.

She found her father over in the back nine pruning azaleas. Daddy turned toward them, as if sensing their arrival. "Hey, darlin'," he said, then leaned his lopping shears against the rock that sealed Jesus's tomb. He headed in their direction—a path that took him through the hole representing the resurrection.

Caroline wondered what his Lordship was thinking about Daddy's black T-shirt, which boasted the slogan "God is. Any questions?" across the chest in huge white letters. Daddy's salt-and-pepper hair was pulled back into a long braid that reached halfway down his back. His goatee, beer belly, biker boots, and earring gave him the appearance of a motorcycle gang member, but not exactly a member of Hell's Angels. Daddy's angels were probably serious hallucinations, born of the time he'd spent in Vietnam.

Daddy walked up to her and pulled her into one of his big bear hugs. "Mmmm, how's my littlest angel?"

It always felt safe inside his big arms. Try as she might to run away from Daddy and his eccentricities, every time he gave her a big hug and called her his "littlest angel," she wanted to burrow down into his shoulder and never come up for air. When she was a little girl, before she realized that the Ark was not life-sized, she had believed that her daddy hung the moon.

The truth had hurt. A lot.

"Uh, Daddy," Caroline said, "I want to introduce you to Hugh deBracy, Baron Woolham. Baron Woolham, this is my father, Elbert Rhodes."

The two men stared at each other. Daddy looked at his Lordship as if he had just flown in from some alien land, which was not really too far from the truth. Hugh studied Daddy as if he really wanted to get to know the man, which made no sense at all.

Daddy narrowed his gaze in a way that made him look semicrazy. Daddy's eyes were really pale, and they could be pretty scary when he wanted them to be. Hugh seemed impervious to Daddy's put-on eccentric routine.

"So," Daddy drawled, "you figure you're going to make me an offer I can't refuse?"

"Well, Mr. Rhodes, the truth is I've already offered as much money as I can afford. So I don't think money is going to get you to give up your land."

"I reckon that's why you got my daughter involved."

"Now Daddy, don't—" Caroline started, but was unable to finish.

"Well," Hugh interrupted, "it did occur to me when I learned of the connection between Senator Warren's aide and this property that getting your daughter involved might be helpful."

Indignation stiffened Caroline's spine. "Daddy, I never said that I was going to help him—"

Elbert waved her words away. "Daughter, you should know better than to try to walk a line as fine as this one. But I'm going to forgive you for it because I know your boss is a hard man. And besides, just this morning your momma reminded me that the Lord has a plan, and this embarrassing and difficult situation might be something He thinks is necessary."

"Daddy, I..." Her throat closed up, and she couldn't go on. This was so typical of Daddy. Just when she was about at her limit, he would say something like this, and she'd be reduced to a puddle of butter. Daddy's ability to forgive almost anything was something Caroline loved about him. Lots of people talked about forgiveness, but Daddy lived it every day of his life.

Daddy turned toward his Lordship with one of his patented good-ol'-boy grins. "Would you like a tour, so you'll know exactly what you're trying to destroy?"

Once again, the corners of Hugh's mouth quirked. Was he laughing at Daddy? Caroline felt her hackles rise. Daddy was eccentric, but she hated people who laughed at him. Up to now, Hugh had been pretty polite and really nice to everyone in Last Chance. With the possible exception of Bubba Lockheart. And that had been a big misunderstanding.

"A tour would be lovely, thank you," Hugh said.

Elbert headed toward Adam and Eve, the first hole on the course, talking over his shoulder as he walked. "We have eighteen holes here, the front nine are dedicated to the Old Testament and the back nine are all New Testament..." Daddy droned on about the fiberglass and the water circulation system and half a dozen other issues.

Hugh surprised Caroline by clucking in admiration in all the right places. The man even asked a number of intelligent questions about the damage the lightning storm had done.

When they got to the plague of frogs, which at one time had frolicked on fiberglass lily pads while spitting water in synchronized bursts over the fairway, the two men stopped for a long moment. The lightning storm and subsequent problems with the water circulation system had shattered the frogs' fiberglass bodies. Now only a few shredded frog's legs and the guts of their spitting mechanisms remained.

Daddy and Hugh hunkered down to inspect the damage and began to talk to each other in a language so filled with engineering terms that Caroline couldn't follow. The eccentric and the Englishman seemed to be completely copacetic despite the differences in their ages and backgrounds. She was suddenly tempted to ask his Lordship what he wanted more—to fix the frogs or buy the land. At the moment, she would have bet he was all for fixing the frogs.

That thought arrowed right through her. She liked Lord Woolham when he behaved like this. He wasn't being bombastic or arrogant. He wasn't appalled by Golfing for God. He was *interested*. And he was treating her father with respect.

Outsiders rarely did that on a first meeting.

Maybe this was a good thing, given what she'd learned that morning at the courthouse. She didn't want to scare him. She needed to reason with him.

Eventually Hugh stood up and leaned back against the sign that bore the verse from Exodus 8:6 about Aaron calling the frogs out of the Nile. "Elbert, I'd be most interested in learning more about your business plan. I have just the spot for a small putting-only golf course like this at the nature center on my family's land near Woolham House. I'm thinking maybe a course dedicated to garden gnomes."

"Because everyone knows that gnomes are really a part of nature—as opposed to say snakes or frogs," Caroline snarked out loud and then immediately regretted it. She should know better than to open her mouth and say something like that.

Hugh turned and arched his eyebrow. He might have looked snotty and arrogant were it not for the fact that the corner of his lips were quivering. Like maybe he thought her joke was funny.

"Well," he said, his voice rich and warm, "my aunt has amassed a very large collection of garden gnome statues, and I'm thinking a golf course like this might be a good way to get them out of the vegetable garden."

Daddy laughed right out loud.

Hugh gave him an imperious stare, but now his eyes were smiling, too.

"So tell me," his Lordship continued in that stuffy accent of his, "where did you acquire all these statues?"

"We didn't purchase them, if that's what you're asking," Daddy said. "Rocky's grandfather was a fiberglass artist. He made most of them, and I don't think I could rival his talents."

Hugh turned away and made a great show of inspecting the statues. "Well," he said at last, "the fiberglass art is really quite amazing."

"Which is one of the reasons I don't want to sell the land," Daddy said.

"Oh, but the statues could be saved, couldn't they? I mean wouldn't it make more sense to have the golf course someplace where there are more people? Like"—his Lordship shrugged—"I don't know, the guidebook I have indicates that Hilton Head and Myrtle Beach are very big on golf."

"I don't live in Hilton Head or Myrtle Beach."

"Oh, right."

"And besides, there are the angels who live here." Daddy stood his ground and folded his arms across his chest. He looked pretty badass when he did that.

Caroline crossed her own arms and hugged herself. She really hated it when Daddy started talking about the angels. She hadn't always felt that way, but about the time she had figured out that the Ark was not life-sized (the same year her older brothers clued her in to the whole Santa Claus myth), she also realized there weren't any angels. That had been extremely painful.

Hugh rubbed his chin with his right forefinger and thumb as if he were thinking deeply. "I was wondering if I might have a word with the angels? How many are there?"

This line was delivered utterly deadpan. It surprised Daddy almost as much as it surprised Caroline. "You want to talk to *my* angels?" Daddy tilted his head and studied Hugh more closely. In all of Caroline's memory, no one had ever asked to speak with Daddy's angels. Ever.

"Well, of course I do. I understand they aren't happy about my factory. I'd like to find out why."

Daddy's bushy brows lowered, and he gave Hugh his scary Daddy face. "You think I'm crazy, don't you? You reckon I'm going to turn around and start talking to the air?" He shook his head. "And I almost liked you there, for a minute."

Daddy turned toward Caroline with a killing look in his pale eyes. "Girl," he said, "I'm going to forgive you for this, on account of the fact that I can see that Baron Woolham is as stubborn as a mule. So do us all a favor and explain to him how the angels don't talk to everyone, won't you? And then, in real slow words, you tell him I ain't never gonna sell this land."

Daddy turned on his heel and strode back toward the azaleas that lined Jesus's tomb, shaking his head the whole way.

"Well," Caroline said up into the frowning face of Hugh deBracy, "that went well, don't you think?"

"I expected him to let me talk to the angels."

Caroline gave him a funny look. "You're kidding, right?"

"That tack always works with my Aunt Petal, the one with the gnomes and fairies. She speaks with them regularly."

A giggle bubbled right out of Caroline's chest. And once that giggle started, it developed a mind of its own, until it had grown from a chortle right into a bona fide belly laugh. Before she knew it, she was having trouble breathing, and tears were leaking from her eyes.

Hugh caught her sillies when that happened, and his laugh softened everything about him. It took a good minute before either of them managed to reexert control.

When Hugh had finally quit chuckling, he said, "Aunt Petal enjoys her daily chats with Woolham House's gnomes and fairies. And in her case, she's always been willing to invite me in for tea and conversation."

His gaze shifted toward Daddy, who had gone back to pruning azaleas. "It would appear that your father is not nearly as dotty as Aunt Petal. That's a shame, really."

"I'm glad you realize that. And I hope you can see now why it's going to be impossible to change my father's mind. And not to be the bearer of bad news, but there are a lot of other reasons why you should think about another location."

"What reasons?"

"I was down at the courthouse this morning looking at land platts, and I discovered that there is swampland right over there." She pointed in a southeasterly direction. "It's located on the land you now own. If you build on that land, the state and federal government will be all over you for wetlands permits."

Hugh's face turned pale. "Swampland? Really? You're not just saying that?"

"Would you like me to take you for a canoe ride? I'm sure one of my brothers would be happy to take you upstream right into that swamp. When they were kids, they used to go gator hunting up there."

He blanched. "Do you think George knew this when he bought the land?"

"I don't know, but I do know you and your partner paid way too much for that land given the development issues it poses."

"I see. Any chance of getting my money back?"

"I don't know. We could always appeal to Hettie Marshall's honor."

"Hettie Marshall? Chairwoman of the Committee to Resurrect Golfing for God? She's the one who sold the land?"

"No. Hettie probably doesn't know a thing about it. But her husband does. He's the one who took you to the cleaners."

"I see." He frowned and managed to look just a little forlorn.

"Look, not all is lost. Tomorrow morning, during the Watermelon Festival parade, you may have a chance to chat with Hettie about things. Her husband is a member of the town council, and I'm sure they'll be on the reviewing stand during the parade. Maybe you can talk her into getting her husband to give you your money back."

Of course, Lord Woolham had no chance of getting his money back. Jimmy was either bribing officials, or propping up the chicken plant, or God knew what else. It didn't really matter. All that mattered was that Jimmy was clearly hurting for cash and getting his money back was going to be difficult.

She didn't tell his Lordship this, of course. He wouldn't have believed her. He was going to have to figure this out for himself.

Then, maybe, she could work with him to find a solution to his problem.

At around eight-thirty that evening, Caroline headed down to Dot's Spot, Last Chance's main watering hole. She told Momma and Daddy she was going to hear Clay and Jane's band, the Wild Horses, but her ulterior motive was to hang out at the bar and talk to Roy Burdett.

She figured by eight-thirty Roy would be on his fourth or fifth beer. That meant she might get something out of him about those safety issues down at the chicken plant. Not that the safety issues were directly related to her reason for being in town. But still, in her experience, finding solutions to insoluble problems usually hinged on having more, not less, information.

She pushed open the door. All the regulars were there tonight, and Hugh deBracy was slumming with them. *Bam,* one glance in his direction, and the entire room faded out, leaving his Lordship in sharp relief.

He didn't look like an English baron tonight. Oh, no. Tonight he was wearing a pair of faded blue jeans and a black T-shirt that showed off his seriously cut muscles. He was sitting at the bar listening in rapt attention as Roy regaled him with one of his fishing stories. This particular whopper involved a twenty-pound largemouth bass that got away.

Hugh actually appeared interested, in addition to looking really, really hot and sexy. And not at all like a character out of one of Momma's regency romances.

The man would have fit in anywhere in those blue jeans. They looked soft, and there was a little worn spot on the left back pocket where he kept his wallet.

This was a disaster.

As long as Hugh was there listening, Roy was going to talk fishing. So any plan to get Roy to gossip about the plant went right up in smoke.

Aw hell. She was here now. She had to stay and have at least one drink or everyone would want to know why she had turned around and walked out.

Speculation would rage on and on and center on her relationship with Lord Woolham. Not that she had a relationship with the baron. But people would talk. And she couldn't afford that, especially seeing as Senator Warren was going to be in town tomorrow and might hear something stupid.

So she marched across the floor and up to the bar, where she nodded at Hugh and Roy, and then, in an attempt to appear cool and sophisticated, she ordered a dirty vodka martini.

This earned her a glare from Dottie Cox, the proprietor and chief bartender. Dottie was pushing sixty hard, but didn't look a day over forty-five, at least not in the dim neon glow that passed for light in the establishment.

Tonight, Dottie wore a watermelon pink western shirt with green fringe along its yoke and down its arms. Her ears were adorned with a pair of dangly watermelon earrings.

Dottie leaned on the bar, earrings swaying. "Rocky, since when are you drinking vodka martinis?"

"Since right now." Caroline was painfully aware of Hugh standing right on the other side of Roy. Hugh was watching every move while nodding at Roy like he was actually listening to the fishing story.

Hugh was drinking something whiskey colored in a glass without ice. It looked like a manly and sophisticated drink. No long-neck Buds for him, even if he did look like a regular guy in that T-shirt and jeans.

"I'm not sure I have any olives," Dottie said.

"No olives? In a bar?"

Dottie shrugged, her fringes swaying. "I know. It's pitiful. But ain't no one ever comes in here and orders martinis."

"I used to drink appletinis."

"That's not a true martini. That's a sweet excuse of a girly drink." Dottie smiled like a sage.

"Do you have vodka and vermouth?" Caroline asked.

Dottie didn't answer the question. She continued in a sagacious voice. "Course if you wanted an appletini, I could get it for you. I have a whole batch of apple vodka and schnapps that I laid in just for when you come to town."

Dottie reached out at that point in her oration and patted Caroline's hand. "Rocky, sugar, I know youth is a time for experimentation with alcohol. But don't you think it's time to settle down to one favorite drink? That way I could stock the ingredients. To tell you the truth, honey, I'm having a hard time keeping up with your drink choices."

"Experimenting? With alcohol? Really? Can I help?" Hugh's voice was smooth and sophisticated. But this was not exactly what she expected an English aristocrat to say out loud in a honky-tonk. Heck, she didn't expect an English aristocrat to ever set foot in a honky-tonk.

Dottie snorted a laugh. "Ain't he cute? I could listen to him talk all day. And, honey, any man who comes into my place and orders a single malt scotch straight up is swoon worthy, if you ask me."

"Right." Caroline turned and nodded at Hugh. "Glad to see you're getting on the right side of the locals."

"So glad you approve. So, what are you experimenting with this evening?" he asked, launching one of his charming, boyish smiles—the one where his dimple came out. Darn him.

Dottie leaned in and batted her eyes. "She ordered a dirty vodka martini. I'm not sure I have any olives, though. If you want my opinion, the girl is just being uppity. A month ago, she came in here and ordered a Broken Down Golf Cart."

"A what?"

Dottie nodded, and her earrings bounced happily. "It's a shot made with Midori and almond liqueur. It's disgustingly sweet, but on the other hand, a drink by that name might be just right for Caroline, given her family's business. Know what I mean?"

Hugh had the audacity to nod in agreement. Then he sort of smirked in Caroline's direction. "So vodka martinis are new for you, then?"

"I don't think it's your business."

"No, it's probably not. But you know I'm rather an expert in helping people find the alcoholic beverage that fits them. Sort of like your Miriam Randall only with booze, not soulmates." He said this in a voice so loud it carried across the room.

The rednecks and good ol' boys who were Dot's regulars turned to watch the show. Even Caroline's brother Clay, who was up on stage tuning his fiddle, turned and looked. Clay had one of those "watching out for little sister" expressions on his face. Thank goodness Hugh was semipolite, and Clay was averse to picking fights without good cause; otherwise Caroline might just find herself in the second fistfight in so many days.

"I would like a dirty vodka martini, *please*."

"All right, honey, it's your funeral. Let me go see if I can find some olives." Dottie turned away and headed into the storage area behind the bar.

"Hey, you wanna trade places?" Roy said.

"Well, that would be quite nice, if you don't mind," Hugh replied.

"No problem. One day you and me have a date in my bass boat, you hear?" Roy picked up his long-neck Bud and moved down the bar. Caroline watched him go.

"Right-o, Roy. It's a date."

She watched Roy slide into a seat and start talking to Avery Anderson. Just great. She wasn't going to get any info out of Roy tonight, was she? Those two boys could talk fishing from sundown to sunup.

Hugh moved over a stool and immediately invaded her space. Not intentionally, of course, but just being near him was kind of unsettling.

"You know," he said, "when I was a young man at university, I supplemented my living by serving as a part-time barman. There is a huge gulf between a sweet shot and a dirty vodka martini, although technically they both have vodka in them."

"Well, I'm a woman of wide-ranging tastes."

"Yes. I can see that."

"Good. And for the record, I don't let men select my drinks. I can think for myself."

He shrugged. "I'm not selecting anything. I'm helping you explore. Now, tell me, do you like sour things or sweet things?"

"I like both."

He grimaced. "I'm sure you do, but if you're like most people, you like one just a little bit more than the other."

"No."

He seemed annoyed. A warm and intoxicating flush hit her blood. She liked fighting with him.

"Are you always like this?" he asked.

"Like what?"

"Afraid to make a choice?"

"I'm not afraid." Caroline straightened her spine and set her shoulders as if to prove the point.

"No, of course not," he said, his eyes twinkling in that superior manner of his. "I must have been mistaken then."

Dottie returned. "Sorry, sugar, I can't find any olives. Why don't I get you a Budweiser?"

Like she was going to drink a Bud when his Lordship was over there sipping scotch and being superior about his knowledge of mixology. Not bloody likely. "Okay," she said, "I'll have what he's drinking."

Dottie rolled her eyes. "You sure about that, sugar?"

"What do I have to do to order a drink in this place?"

Dottie nodded. "Okeydokey, we aim to please." She turned and started pouring scotch.

"Might I inquire—have you ever been a scotch drinker before tonight?" Hugh asked.

Dottie put the drink in front of Caroline. She wasn't about to admit anything to his Lordship or Dottie Cox so she picked up the glass and knocked it back like a tequila shot. She had tried tequila shots with Tulane once. They made her lips numb. And of course, she had ended that particular evening hung over a toilet bowl.

Never again.

But scotch was not tequila. And she was trying to make a point. So she dumped that liquor into the back of her throat and promptly choked on it. She ended up coughing like some little girl who didn't know any better.

Across the room, she heard Clay's brotherly voice of concern, "Little gal, are you all right?"

Hugh gave her a thwack between the shoulder blades, and Dottie replied to Clay, "Oh, I think she's in capable hands. But someone needs to tell her that you don't shoot single malt scotch."

The men at the bar laughed.

And that, more or less, did it for Caroline.

She caught her breath, slid off the seat, and started toward the door without paying her bill. But Hugh followed her. He touched her arm and stopped her midstride. He didn't need to grab her, or haul on her, or twist her arm like Bubba had done last night at the Pig Place.

Nope. He merely touched her and it was like some kind of electrical charge. She couldn't move.

"Caroline," he whispered into her ear. "Stop trying to be something you aren't."

She wanted to turn and spit in his eye. Not for insulting her, but for being so astute as to recognize the truth of her most recent behavior. She had seen him at the bar, looking debonair and aristocratic even in blue jeans, and she'd tried to prove she was some kind of sophisticated person.

But she wasn't. She was a country girl. That's what she saw every day in the mirror, and her business suits and professional haircuts could never hide that.

Shame crawled right through Caroline. She was acting like an idiot. She should get out of here, now, and remember to keep a lid on her libido whenever Hugh was around. "I should go," she said as she turned back toward the door and took a step.

Hugh wasn't about to let her go. He grabbed her by the arm in a move that was similar to what Bubba had done last night. But instead of pain, Hugh's touch made electricity run right up her arm. "Come back to the bar. Let's start over, shall we?" His voice made her insides quiver.

She sucked up her pride (and her sanity) and let him lead her back to the bar. He helped her up onto a stool, just like a real gentleman, and then he did the unthinkable in Dottie's establishment.

He stepped behind the bar.

No one stepped behind Dottie's bar, ever.

Dottie made to protest, but Hugh waggled his eyebrows and then pulled out his wallet. He produced a fifty-dollar bill and tucked it, with great savoir faire, in the

V of Dottie's western shirt. "I assure you, madam, I know my way around a bar."

Dottie batted her false eyelashes. "Honey, I have a feeling you know your way around more than that."

Hugh inclined his head, and Caroline could actually imagine him in one of those Masterpiece Theatre productions where everyone is always bowing and curtseying.

"So," he said, leaning on the inner edge of the bar, "since you've started the evening with whiskey, we'll need to stay there."

"Why?"

"Because it's never a good idea to drink different kinds of alcohol in one go. Didn't your brothers teach you that?"

She glanced over her shoulder to where Clay and the rest of the Wild Horses were fixing to start their first set of the evening. Clay was, mercifully, not paying attention to her right at the moment.

She let go of a big sigh. "No. My brothers tried to keep me from learning about alcohol and anything else that was even remotely interesting. Southern brothers are brought up to protect their sisters that way. Of course, they are not above teaching their friends' sisters all the important things. Most of the naughty things I learned came from Dash Randall."

Hugh's eyes widened a bit. "So you and Dash were..."

She shook her head. "No. Nothing like that. But Dash got around and taught a lot of girls a lot of stuff. And the girls passed on what they learned. I avoided Dash like the plague when I was younger. He was one of my brothers' friends, and that made him automatically gross and annoying."

She glanced over her shoulder again. This time Clay was watching her out of his silver eyes.

Hugh followed her gaze. "I gather that bloke over there tuning his violin is another one of the aforementioned brothers? He looks rather like your father."

She nodded. "Yeah, he's the big one. You've already met Stone."

"Right, I have. He's the one who frightens me the most. So I promise to be on my best behavior."

She snickered but didn't otherwise comment that, compared to the average good ol' boy in Allenberg County, Hugh was always on his best behavior, even when he was punching Bubba in the mouth.

"It's time to find the right alcoholic beverage for you," Hugh said. "But since you refuse to tell me if you like sweet more than sour, I'll have to use my imagination." He turned and pulled down an old-fashioned glass, then he grabbed a bottle of blended whiskey, which he proceeded to toss into the air so that it flipped over, spout down. He caught it as it tumbled, like a juggler, without spilling a drop, until he poured a shot's worth into the glass. Then he tossed the bottle up and behind him before he pirouetted and caught the bottle in its flight and returned it to its place. He repeated the entire move, adding a few additional embellishments, with a slightly dusty bottle of Drambuie.

By the time he tossed some ice in the glass and placed the glass on his bent elbow, Dottie's mouth had sagged open, while half the patrons were watching in utter fascination. He levered his elbow up—tossing the drink, ice cubes and all, up in the air. He caught the drink on its way down, not sloshing a single drop as he placed it, with a flourish, in front of Caroline.

The men at the bar clapped.

"Honey, if you ever decide you need a job, I'm sure I could find a place for you," Dottie said to him.

Hugh bowed to one and all, then scooted around the bar and took a seat beside Caroline, retrieving his own scotch. He raised it in salute. "To the novice drinkers we all were at one time."

Roy Burdett lifted his long-neck Bud and said, "Hear, hear."

Caroline picked up the cocktail. "I'm not a novice drinker."

Hugh's lips quivered. "All right, then here's to the journeyman drinkers we've all become."

"Hear, hear." Roy lifted his Bud again.

"What is this?" Caroline asked before she brought the glass to her lips.

"That, my dear, is a Rusty Nail, the classic cocktail of the rich and famous."

"Really?"

"It was popular in the 1960s in Hollywood."

"And how do you know that?"

"Because I was a barman near a university and studied mixology rather seriously at one time. Believe me, I have helped many a novice drinker discover their inner drunk. Go on then, try it."

She sipped. It was strong. And not sweet. It burned on the way down and made her body flush.

"Hmmm," he said, studying her closely. "By that wrinkle in your nose, I'm thinking that the Rusty Nail is not exactly the right fit. We'll have to explore other options."

"Now?"

"Oh, no, you have to finish the Rusty Nail first." He smiled and sipped his drink.

She sipped hers as the band began their first set, which made talking a lot more difficult. So they sat and listened to Clay play fiddle while Caroline finished her Rusty Nail. Then Hugh made her a whiskey sour, which she liked a little better, but it still made her mouth pucker.

She finished that one, too, and started in on the whiskey Collins, which she actually liked the taste of, but maybe because she was getting seriously buzzed by this time.

Then Clay's band, with Jane singing lead, struck up the old standard "Can I Have This Dance." And damned if Hugh didn't lean in and ask her to dance. It didn't really occur to Caroline until she reached the dance floor that "Can I Have This Dance" was a slow song. A waltz, in fact.

The folks who had been line dancing had all left the floor, and there Hugh and Caroline stood, just the two of them.

She found herself looking up into Hugh deBracy's incredible brown eyes, knowing that she was more than a little drunk and way out of her league. But, oh, her hormones were enjoying this moment.

"Well, it appears to be a waltz, doesn't it?" he said, his eyes smiling but his mouth remaining quite serious. "Now you will see just how badly I managed in cotillion classes."

Cotillion classes? He had to be joking.

Fear swept through her. "Um, ah, I didn't go to cotillion classes. The truth is I don't know how to waltz, and I'm just a little…" She let her voice trail off. No sense telling him she was heading toward serious inebriation.

But Hugh, the ex-bartender and English baron, seemed to know everything without being told. He placed his hand at the small of her back, lower than she expected, his palm pressing over her spine in a move that was utterly possessive, even though he was not very close to her. He adjusted her left hand down from his shoulder onto his upper arm, where her palm connected with the skin, just below the edge of his shirtsleeve. The warmth of it jolted through her, just as he took her right hand in his left.

His hand caught her by surprise. An aristocrat's hand should be soft, but Hugh's hand was dry and rough and seemed to have more than a few calluses on it. It enveloped hers, and her pulse climbed right into the stratosphere.

They stood almost eighteen inches apart. And yet she had never been more aware of a man in all her life. God help her, she had the hots for this guy, and that was a ginormous problem.

"Just start on your right foot and let me lead." He arched his eyebrow. And then…

Well, then he created magic. He accomplished this feat despite her lack of skill, the slightly seedy dance floor, and the copious quantities of whiskey she had imbibed.

Every little girl who has ever seen *Cinderella* or *Beauty and the Beast* has a moment when she longs to transcend the story and become the heroine in the arms of the hero, wearing some wonderful dress, moving lightly and gracefully on her feet as he waltzes her around the dance floor. Caroline might have devoted her life to career advancement, but down deep, she wanted romance in her life even if she knew it was a silly desire for a working girl like her.

But for one shining moment, Hugh deBracy gave her romance. Never mind that it took place in a honky-tonk bar, or that she was wearing a white sleeveless golf shirt and a pair of khaki capri slacks, instead of some fabulous gown.

It didn't matter.

The moment was utterly magic.

Hugh glided her across the floor, his left hand aiming her in the proper direction, while his right hand connected them in a carnal way that took her breath away. He never lost the beat of the music. He made her feel completely beautiful despite her casual clothing. He twirled her until she became dizzy with more than the alcohol.

And all the while, he never once broke eye contact. He sucked her into the fantasy with his dark eyes. As the music died, she knew she would never, in all her life, forget this moment.

God help her. She suddenly wanted to rush headlong into what was clearly a fantasy of her own making. And that was just plain stupid. She had crossed a line, and she needed to get safely back on the other side of it. She was Senator Warren's aide, and she had no business dancing with Baron Woolham.

So she did the only sensible thing she could think of. She turned on her heel and ran from Dot's Spot like a raccoon with a hillbilly dog on her tail.

• • •

Caroline concentrated really hard on walking without stumbling and made it safely across Palmetto Avenue without being run over—which was no great big thing seeing as it was midnight, and there wasn't any traffic on Palmetto this time of night.

She was halfway down the main block before she became aware of the headlights behind her. She turned just as her brother Stone pulled up in his police cruiser.

He stopped the car and rolled down the passenger side window. "Girl, you're drunk as a skunk, aren't you?"

"Go 'way." She turned and kept walking down the street, trying to pretend that Stone wasn't following her in his big ol' impressive police car.

"Honey, quit being stubborn and get in. I'll take you home."

"Clay called you, didn't he?" she said over her shoulder.

"Uh-huh." Stone pulled ahead, stopped the cruiser, and unfolded himself from the driver side. He strode up the sidewalk in her direction. "Don't make me arrest you. After what happened at the Pig Place last night, I'm starting to wonder what's going on with you."

"Look, you can't pin anything on me about last night." She stood there bobbing and weaving for a moment. "*I* had the whole thing under control until Lord Woolham smashed Bubba's face. I didn't do anything wrong."

"C'mon, little gal, I'll get you home safe."

She stood there for a moment weighing her options. But there were no options. So she let Stone guide her firmly to the cruiser and help her into the front passenger seat.

"From what I've heard, you've been dancing with

that Englishman. You know Momma and Daddy won't approve. I know I don't," he said when he got behind the wheel.

She slid down into the seat and closed her eyes. The world spun, and her stomach gave a little lurch.

Stone fired up the engine. "What in the world were you thinking?"

"About what?"

"About going into Dot's and getting drunk with that man."

"That man. You mean Hugh."

"Yeah, him."

She thought for a moment. "Um, I don't think he was drunk. And it was not my plan to get drunk with him. My plan was to pump Roy Burdett for information."

"What? What information?"

Stone pulled the car from the curb and headed toward Momma's house.

Caroline let go of a sigh. "I wasn't supposed to tell you that."

"Right. What information?"

Caroline leaned her dizzy head back on the headrest. "It's not important," she lied. "Just something to do with Lord Woolham's land purchases."

It wasn't long before Stone pulled the cruiser to the curb in front of Momma's house. The lights were ablaze even though it was past midnight. "Honey, you need to listen to me," Stone said as he killed the engine. "It's not a good idea to be seen taking sides with the man who wants to force Daddy off his land. You already have a reputation in this town."

"Was that a reference to Bubba?"

"It was."

"That's not fair. You know good and well that—"

"It doesn't matter if it's fair or not. This is a tiny town, honey. Folks talk, and they have long memories. I may not like Golfing for God, but I know good and well that the Rhodes family needs to hang together when it comes to things like this."

"I'm not trying to force Daddy off his land. I'm trying to convince Lord Woolham to find another place to build."

"Well, that might be true, but your actions are saying something else. You need to think about how all this is going to reflect on Momma and Daddy, and on me, too. I'm a public servant in this town, and that scene yesterday at the Pig Place was ugly. I should have put that guy's butt right in jail."

Caroline was sobering up fast. "Stone, you couldn't arrest him without Big Bob and a bunch of other council members getting annoyed. Yesterday I even heard Millie Polk talking about how the town needs a factory more than it needs Golfing for God. This is a political reality."

"Politics don't matter, Rocky. We Rhodes have always hung together. You know that."

Yes, she did.

He picked up his cell phone and placed a call to Clay to let him know that she'd gotten home in one piece.

When he'd finished, he turned toward her and said, "You stay away from Dot's and you keep it clean with that Englishman, you hear? If you're worried about politics, what you did tonight was just plain stupid."

"You're right." Stone had a way of cutting right to the chase.

She got out of the car, and Stone drove away. She turned and headed unsteadily up the walk to the house. Momma was waiting for her, rocking patiently on the front porch, taking in the balmy summer night.

One look at Momma's face and Caroline knew she was officially in trouble. But then again, what else was new in Last Chance, South Carolina?

CHAPTER 9

Hugh stood on the dance floor in something of a fog as he watched Caroline's retreating derriere. She was running away, like Cinderella masquerading at the ball. Only in this case, Cinderella was wearing pants and was, not to put too fine a point on it, pissing drunk.

He really ought to see that she got home safely.

He took two steps in pursuit and fetched up against the broad and immovable person of Caroline's brother Clay. It was only then that Hugh noticed the sudden absence of music and the fact that most of the pub's patrons were watching the two of them square off against one another. He was outmatched. Clay Rhodes was, as the adage goes, a mountain of a man.

"You can stay right where you are. Stone'll make sure Rocky gets home. No thanks to you."

"Ah, the local law."

"That's right. And based on what you've been up to tonight, I would say Rocky probably needs police protection. And by the way, I heard all about what happened last night at the Pig Place. For the record, I don't like fighting. But if I have to, I will. And you really don't want to mess with me."

"You know, I don't really like fighting either. I have a reputation back in Woolham as being rather a mild-mannered sort of man."

Clay frowned in obvious confusion.

"Woolham is my home in the UK. It's a village about the same size as Last Chance. In fact, I would say the two places are quite similar."

"Really?"

Hugh shrugged. "Well, we do speak a better brand of English, but aside from that..." He plastered a friendly smile on his face. The kind he had perfected during the three years he had served as a part-time barman at the Royal Arms—a job that Granddad would have disapproved of, if Granddad had still been alive.

Clay returned the smile. The man was sober as a judge, and his smile was not in the least bit friendly.

The big man put a finger into Hugh's chest. "You can just quit trying to seduce Rocky. And while I'm at it, I ought to tell you that you aren't ever going to convince my father to sell his golf course. So maybe you should just hightail it back to Woolham."

Hugh straightened his spine at that. Had he been trying to seduce Caroline? Well, not intentionally, but that hardly mattered, did it? He'd been having a great deal more fun with her than he ought. He probably deserved a thrashing from her male kin, given the circumstances.

He was making himself quite the villain, wasn't he? Aunt Petal would be so disappointed in him, but he supposed Granddad would have been encouraged. Granddad was a prat. But he had been a success, and Hugh should remember that.

Hugh raised his hands, palms outward in a gesture of compliance and submission. "Look, I'm terribly sorry. I'll just pop back to Miriam Randall's now and—"

"No, you sit right there." Clay pointed to a table near the stage. "And you stay there until I get the all-clear from Stone."

Hugh sat. Everyone watched. Clay paced.

The phone eventually rang about five minutes later. Clay took the call, nodded, then turned toward Hugh with arms akimbo. "She's home safe. You can get out of here now."

Hugh stood up and headed for the door. He had almost reached it when Dottie Cox called out, "Honey, don't let Clay intimidate you. I saw those drinks you made, and I know they weren't very strong. You can come tend my bar anytime."

He turned and gave her a little nod. "Thank you very much, Dorothy. I'll remember that should my plan for the factory fall through."

But of course, if his plan for the factory fell through, he'd be going back to the UK and doing what was expected of him. He might as well have the words of the deBracy motto tattooed on his chest. *Honneur dans le devoir.* Honor in duty.

He would certainly find honor in marrying Lady Ashton. But he would have to give up his factory. Victoria was not very keen on spending her money on bits and pieces of machinery.

He turned north and strolled down Palmetto Avenue past darkened storefronts, many of them permanently empty.

Last Chance appeared to be in the grip of an economic downturn. The place needed his factory. But it didn't look as if his factory would ever be built. He was not smart enough, or mean enough, or wily enough to make a success in business.

No doubt this was why he'd been such an easy mark for George Penn. It seemed just a little too convenient that his erstwhile, "late" business partner had disappeared in a private plane accident somewhere in South America, only a few weeks after concluding the disastrous land deal here in the States.

Hugh had a feeling bad luck had nothing to do with it. He wondered if perhaps Jimmy Marshall had given George some kind of kickback for agreeing to the land sale at such a high price.

George could have come away with a significant amount of cash. Not enough to live on for the rest of his life, of course, but then if George was a con man, he probably did this sort of thing all the time.

Hugh could almost hear Granddad's cold, emotionless voice telling him that he needed to quit trusting people. How many times had Granddad said that a successful man was one who did unto others before the others could do him in?

Trusting George had been a mistake. And now Hugh would have to "hightail it" back to Woolham and do his duty.

Granddad wouldn't have felt any remorse marrying a woman he didn't love. Granddad would say that a man could find plenty of love with lower-class girls. Girls you tumbled behind your wife's back. But a deBracy always picked his bride with two things in mind—her pedigree and the size of her fortune.

And Lady Ashton was loaded on both accounts.

• • •

"Aunt Rocky, it's time to get up and get your hair done and put on your beautiful dress." Haley stood in the middle of her aunt's room and bellowed. Granny had given her permission to use her outside voice even though it was inside, and Aunt Rocky was still asleep, and it was still dark outside.

But there was a lot to get done before the parade even started. And Haley had been awake for a while anyway, on account of the fact that the Sorrowful Angel had been especially sorrowful this morning. The darned angel was still bawling her eyes out.

The angel had been hovering around Daddy since they all got up. Haley had halfway hoped the angel would leave the house with Daddy when he went to help the other policemen set up the parade route. But the angel had stayed behind, all the more sorrowful because Daddy hadn't seen her even though she had tried so hard to make him notice.

The angel had caterwauled to beat the band once Daddy left. It was a wonder, really, that Aunt Rocky had slept through the angel's noise.

Aunt Rocky cracked an eye that looked kind of red. "Go 'way." She waved at Haley but not at the angel, who also had on her outside voice, even if she wasn't exactly talking at the moment.

"Granny says it's time to get up."

"I'm sick." Aunt Rocky squeezed her eyes closed and rolled on her side.

Haley gave her aunt a once-over. She looked a little pale, but she wasn't coughing or sneezing or barfing or anything. Haley stood there a moment trying to decide if she should go get Granny, who also seemed to be grumpy this morning. Haley wasn't exactly sure about what.

The Sorrowful Angel decided to be helpful, for once. She floated across the room and settled on Aunt Rocky's bed, where she took hold of Caroline's comforter and yanked.

"Hey, let go." Caroline played tug-of-war for a moment with the angel, but the angel won.

"Hey, kid, quit it." Aunt Rocky opened her eyes again. Yup, they were definitely red. Aunt Rocky didn't look too happy either. "Go someplace and play with your Barbies or something, okay? I'm not getting up, and I'm not putting on any dress. And you can quit trying to take my covers." Aunt Rocky pulled the comforter back over her shoulders and closed her eyes.

"I didn't take your covers. It was the angel."

Aunt Rocky's eyes flew open, and she lifted her head off the pillow and looked around the room. "Haley, there's no one here but you and me, so quit fibbing, okay?"

Aunt Rocky's eyes closed, and she turned on her side again, this time with her back to Haley.

The Sorrowful Angel managed to look even more sorry than usual and let go of a big loud wail that almost broke Haley's ears.

"Stop it," Haley said.

"Stop what?" Aunt Rocky said, raising her head and looking over her shoulder. "Are you talking to me or the angel?"

Haley's face got hot. She had forgotten to be careful about speaking directly to the angel. Most folks—even Granddaddy, who said he sometimes spoke with angels—couldn't see the Sorrowful Angel. And every time the angel did something like move the covers or knock something off a table, Haley got blamed.

"I wasn't talking to anyone," Haley fibbed.

"Well, stop talking altogether. I'm trying to sleep."

"But Granny wants you to wake up."

"Well then, Granny can come in here and haul me out of bed, okay?"

The Sorrowful Angel must not have liked what Aunt Rocky said because the next thing Haley knew, Aunt Rocky's bed frame broke in two. The broken bed left Aunt Rocky with her butt on the floor and her legs and head up in the air.

Aunt Rocky said a bunch of bad words. But no one heard them except Haley and the angel. The angel didn't seem at all surprised by those words. Haley wasn't surprised, so much as curious. There were a few words in there that she had never heard before. And just then, Granny came rushing into the room. Granny had half a head full of curlers in her hair and a worried look on her face.

"Good Lord, Rocky, are you all right? What in the world happened?" Granny said.

Granny turned on Haley. "Honey, you haven't been jumping on this bed, have you?"

Haley's face got hot again. She knew it was a sin to tell a lie. "Well, maybe a little, but it was—"

Granny's mouth turned down. "Young lady, if you tell me that this bed was broken by an angel, I declare I will ground you today, and you'll miss the parade."

A lump lodged in Haley's throat. It was time to put on her very bestest behavior even if that required telling a lie. Sometimes life with an angel was really unfair.

When Haley told the truth about the angel, well, it usually resulted in worse trouble than if she just fibbed.

She pulled in a shaky breath. "No, ma'am, it wasn't the angel. I reckon the bed was broken the last time I jumped on it. And so when Aunt Rocky rolled over, it just broke in two."

Aunt Rocky unfolded herself from the bed and gave her a funny look. "I didn't roll over."

"You didn't?" Haley asked, her heart suddenly pounding in her ears. She really didn't want to be grounded on the first day of the Watermelon Festival. Tears filled her eyes.

"No. It just broke. Kind of sudden," Aunt Rocky said. She stared down at the bed, with its split wooden bed rails. "Momma, there was nothing wrong with this bed last night."

Granny let go of a sound that wasn't really a laugh. Haley knew that when Granny made a sound like that, it was probably best to go hide somewhere. "Honey," Granny said. "You were so pie-eyed last night I doubt you would have noticed if the bed was on fire. Now get your butt in the shower and be ready for Jane to do her magic on you in the next ten minutes, you hear?"

Haley braced herself because sometimes Aunt Rocky and Granny got to arguing about stuff. But the angel drifted between them, and that seemed to take all the starch out of both of them.

Aunt Rocky closed her mouth, turned on her heel, and headed toward the bathroom at the end of the hall. Granny turned in the other direction toward the kitchen, where Aunt Jane had been working on her hair.

"Haley," Granny said as they walked back to the

kitchen, "I'm glad you didn't fib about the angel this time."

"Does that mean I can go to the parade?" Her voice wavered. "I'll help clean up the room after?"

Granny chuckled warmly. "Honey, you can go to the parade. I think I'll make Aunt Rocky clean up the mess in her room. It would do her good after the way she's behaved the last few nights."

Granny sat back down at the table, and Jane started back to working on her hairdo. The angel drifted in and took her usual place by the broom closet. Haley sank down into the pink rocking chair that Granddaddy had made for her. Prissy, the cat, jumped in her lap.

She gave Prissy a hug, but it didn't make her feel any better.

What was she going to do about the Sorrowful Angel? Something wasn't right if an angel was making her lie. She was going to have to ask Reverend Ellis about this. She had a feeling he might have better answers than Dr. Newsome.

Dr. Newsome didn't really believe in angels, but the preacher had to. And the angel broke that bed. Even worse, the angel didn't seem to be very sorry about it either.

"Goodness, sugar, I think you've grown some since you were eighteen." Momma stared at Caroline over her shoulder as the two of them looked into the full-length mirror on the back of Momma's bedroom door.

As usual, this mirror wasn't telling any lies. Momma looked fabulous in her green and pink dress. Jane had done up Momma's hair in short sausage curls down the back with her rhinestone tiara holding her bangs back off her face. She looked twenty years younger than her actual age. Her dress fit her exactly the way it had fit her forty years before. Momma had a really nice hourglass shape that she had managed to maintain even after four children.

In contrast, the dress that had made Caroline infamous as an eighteen-year-old might just humiliate her twelve years later. Her boobs, always just a little too large for her comfort, were poured into that tight bodice, and the girls were not all that happy about it. One or both of them looked like they might make an escape at any moment.

She wanted to throw a first-class, Watermelon Queen hissy fit. But her head was hammering so hard that any loud noise might cause it to split wide open. Her stomach was queasy, too, and she wondered if she could manage to hang on to the float for the duration of the five-mile parade without hurling. She decided that if she had to hurl, she would do it on the dress, thereby getting her out of this ridiculous situation.

At least her hair was good.

Not only could Jane sing like an angel, but the woman had taken Caroline's unruly mop of hair and transformed it into something amazing. She wore a crown of woven pink and green ribbons that cascaded down her back. Instead of trying to blow-dry the curl out of her hair, Jane had coaxed it into a mane of wavy darkness that made her look like something out of one of Haley's fairy-tale books.

And—good news—she could use the long hair in Lady Godiva fashion if the seams on her dress gave way or she encountered a sudden wardrobe malfunction.

"I declare, Rocky, all my life I've wanted to have a bustline like that. I wouldn't be surprised if someone noticed."

"Momma, I think the entire county of Allenberg is going to notice. And for the record, I don't want people to notice my boobs. They could notice my eyes, or my hair, or something else. To be honest, I don't want to be noticed at all. I'd like to be sitting along the parade route wearing sunglasses and a big floppy hat."

Momma chuckled. "Well, I'm sure your soulmate will notice all of you, sweetie, including your bustline."

"Honestly, Momma, I didn't feel comfortable with this low neckline when I was eighteen. I feel even less comfortable now. And to think my boss is going to see me dressed like this."

Not to mention Hugh deBracy, whose opinion she suddenly valued as much as Senator Warren's.

And valuing his opinion of her wardrobe was simply insane. Hugh was an English baron—an aristocrat. He was so far out of her league that it didn't matter what she wore. In fact, in a strange sort of way, she should be thankful she was dressed like a fluffy watermelon today. Hugh would take one look at this dress and know the truth about her. There would be no more waltzing with Hugh when he saw the real Rocky Rhodes.

"Think of all the eligible bachelors out there," Momma said, breaking into her thoughts, as if Momma knew that Caroline was thinking about one particular bachelor— the one she needed to treat professionally.

"Right, Momma," she said unenthusiastically.

"Oh, come on, honey, the parade route will be lined with hardworking, regular Joes. One of them is going to be your true love. You know when Miriam starts with her forecasts, love is usually right around the corner." She gave Caroline a little hug. "Now won't that be fun?"

"No. Especially not if the only thing that attracts this regular Joe is my bustline." She wanted to be valued for more than that. She wanted to be taken seriously.

And, well, back in her twisted female mind, she wanted to be taken seriously by the one guy she'd recently met who was most definitely not the salt of the earth and a regular Joe. Just thinking about the warmth of Hugh deBracy's hands on her made her all quivery inside.

"Sirocco Caroline Rhodes, you listen up now," Momma said, putting her hands on her hips. "Love is never anything to sneer at. It's likely to knock you right off your feet when you're least expecting it, and you have the advantage because Miriam has told you that love is coming your way. The kind of true love that Miriam predicts is a blessing. You hear me?"

"Yes, ma'am." Caroline gave her bodice another upward tug.

Clay called from the front room. He'd brought his minivan to take them over to the parade staging area. It was time to go. She followed Momma out to Clay's car feeling exposed, sour, and grumpy.

Three hours later, Caroline's head had finally stopped throbbing. Her feet, on the other hand, were killing her.

What had possessed her to wear these high heels? She had been standing all that time on the seventy-fifth anniversary float, holding on to a metal bar that was all that passed for safety on this moving contraption. Her arches were throbbing, and the small of her back was in agony.

Of course, if she'd been one of the older ladies, they would have given her a throne to sit in. Miz Miriam was sitting up on the highest level of the float, which looked like an elongated wedding cake with big numerals 7 and 5 at its top.

Caroline, being one of the younger ex-queens, had to stand on the lowest level of the float and wave and smile and endure an endless stream of salacious comments from the rednecks and good ol' boys lining the parade route. Her station was on the front side of the float so at least she could see where they were going.

This vantage point also gave her a horse's ass view of the Last Chance Gang, an equestrian group composed mostly of middle-school kids, including her niece, Lizzy. The kids wore white Stetsons and rode ponies. A couple of the older kids did some trick riding and lasso twirling. The kids were cute. But one of their adult supervisors turned out to be Dash Randall himself, looking surprisingly fit for a man who had undergone baseball-career-ending knee surgery a year ago.

Dash was getting his share of attention from the good ol' girls and their mothers. To be honest, Dash had impressed a lot of kids, too, since he was doing some seriously cool tricks with a lasso. But then Dash had always been a show-off.

Thank goodness it was almost over. The float saluting seventy-five years of Watermelon Queens turned onto Court Street in Allenberg, heading toward the square where the county courthouse and reviewing stand were located.

Caroline tugged up her bodice and fixed her beauty queen smile on her face. Up ahead, the dignitaries had gathered under the bunting-draped plywood of the reviewing stand. Senator Warren sat in the first row surrounded by U.S. and state representatives. A row of local dignitaries occupied the seats behind him. Caroline finally found Hugh, seated in the last row, wearing an impeccably tailored light gray suit with a crisp white shirt and a narrow light blue tie. He sat right next to Cissy Warren, who was dressed, as always, in the most expensive designer fashion money could buy. Hugh and Cissy looked good together—like refugees from Ascot, slumming today with the simple folk.

Her heart gave a little lurch in her chest, and her skin flushed hot with a wave of emotion she had trouble pinpointing. She was embarrassed to have her boss see her wearing this dress. And she was angry at herself for the stupid things she'd done last night. And she was consumed by a very unhealthy fascination with Lord Woolham.

Caroline was so busy trying to figure out these feelings that she didn't see disaster coming in the form of Dash Randall, cowboy extraordinaire.

Just as the seventy-fifth anniversary float arrived at the reviewing stand, Dash turned his painted pony and aimed his lasso at Caroline. One minute she was tottering on her inappropriate shoes, and the next she was roped and tied.

Then Dash literally swept her off her feet and right over the edge of the float. Good thing the cowboy wannabe was right there on his horse grinning like some kind of movie star as she toppled into his waiting arms. He eased her landing right into his lap.

Dash turned his pony in a direction opposite to the flow of the parade. A little tightening of his thighs, and his horse responded by trotting off through the ranks of the Davis High marching band and past the float bearing the current Watermelon Queen and her court.

It wasn't until she spied the Allenberg Fire Department, bringing up the rear of the parade, that Caroline managed to catch her breath and her senses enough for fear to set in.

She'd never liked horses much, and the feeling of losing control scared the crap out of her.

"Put me down," she said, but her voice came out in a rasp. "You know I don't like horses."

"I know, but bear with me. I won't let you fall, and this is all for a good cause."

Good cause? What good cause? All she could think about was the fleeting glimpse she'd gotten of Senator Warren's face as she tumbled into Dash's arms. Oh, God. She was never going to live this down. Her chance at that promotion had just evaporated.

"Dash, what in the Sam Hill are you doing?"

"Getting Bubba to move on."

"What?"

Dash looked down at her from under his ten-gallon hat. "Remember? Yesterday you said we needed to hit Bubba upside the head so he'd move on with his life. This is it. See, the way I figure is that I match Aunt Mim's prediction for you just about as good as anyone else in town. I'm about as regular a guy as you can get, and I actually earn my living working with my hands. So I figured that if I roped and tied you in front of everyone, folks would naturally start gossiping. We just have to play along for a while. We'll pretend to be falling madly in love, and in the meantime, we'll figure ways to introduce Bubba to some other single ladies. I figure we got several who might work. There's Jenny Carpenter and your friend, Rachel."

"Rachel? Are you kidding? I wouldn't wish Bubba on Rachel even if he were the last man on earth." Caroline started to hyperventilate.

"Calm down now. I got you, and I'm real good with horses. And we don't have to try to match up Bubba and Rachel. We can concentrate on Jenny Carpenter. I'm sure the church ladies would love to get Jenny married off to someone other than Bill Ellis, her being a Methodist and all."

"You're insane. And you've just made me a laughing-stock. My boss and everyone in Allenberg County just saw you rope and tie me. Bubba is going to be furious with you. And the church ladies are going to try to match us up as soulmates from now until the rapture happens."

"Yeah, I thought it was a pretty brilliant plan on my part. Honey, we're now officially the talk of the town."

CHAPTER
10

Hugh shook off Cissy Warren's clingy hand and stood up in order to get a better view of Dash making off with Caroline. "Good God, are they going to let him get away with that?"

Hugh's fists balled up of their own accord. Where were Caroline's brothers now? He looked around, searching for a means of exit. If he could appropriate one of those horses, he could—

No, wait. That would be crazy. He was allergic to horses, and he was not very good in the saddle—not any kind of match for Dash Randall with his rope tricks. He felt suddenly quite queasy. He'd been looking forward to seeing Caroline all morning. This was not what he'd had in mind.

"Don't worry about her," Cissy said. "That cowboy making off with her is Dash Randall. He used to catch for the Houston Astros. He's worth millions. Besides, you have to admire the man's direct approach."

No, Hugh most definitely didn't admire Dash's

approach. In Hugh's estimation, lassoing a former Water-melon Queen off a parade float was rather lowbrow.

He forced a smile to his face as he sat down in the hard folding chair. The heiress to the Warren Fabrics fortune studied him with a pair of Alice blue eyes. Her ash blond hair fell straight to just above her jawline, the bangs drooping down to partially obscure one eye. A narrow nose, sharp cheekbones, and a pointed chin gave her a thin, predatory look. She reeked posh. She was precisely the sort of woman his grandfather had married—on several occasions.

"Caroline can rescue herself if she needs to. Honestly, if I were her, I'd relax and enjoy the ride." Cissy leaned in and draped herself over Hugh's arm, where she remained for the rest of the parade.

When the festivities concluded, Cissy led Hugh through the crowd toward her father, Senator Rupert Warren, who was standing with a very large man wearing a tan suit and a pink and green bow tie. Warren turned as they approached, his face lighting up when he spied his daughter. He gestured toward Cissy and Hugh, then said, "Big Bob, let me introduce you to Hugh deBracy, Baron Woolham. Hugh, this here is Big Bob Thomas, mayor of Last Chance."

Big Bob, who had to weigh more than twenty stone, gave Hugh a ham-handed shake. His big easy smile conveyed the feeling that he was a regular sort of bloke who got things done by being practical and honest.

"Well," Big Bob said, "I reckon I'm the mayor until November. I'm going fishing after that." Bob loosened his watermelon-themed tie.

"I do hope I can get my problem sorted before November.

I'd love to drop by sometime and talk to you about the factory," Hugh said.

Big Bob nodded but he didn't look terribly enthusiastic. "That would be fine. After the festival."

Before Hugh could press the mayor for an earlier appointment, a high-pitched voice sounded through the reviewing stand like a herald with a slightly off-key trumpet.

"Lord Woolham, oh, Lord Woolham."

A moment later, a zaftig woman with a helmet of gray hair came toward Hugh like the *Titanic* advancing on the iceberg.

"Ah, Lillian, there you are," Big Bob said as he shifted his bulk aside to make room. "Lord Woolham, may I introduce Lillian Bray, the secretary of the Last Chance Town Council. Lillian, meet Lord Woolham."

"Oh, your grace, I'm just so *honored* to meet you." The woman took Hugh's hand and pumped it as if she were trying to bring forth water from a well.

Hugh clamped down on his tongue and refrained from pointing out that he was not of a high-enough rank to be called "your grace."

"Well," huffed Lillian as she turned toward Big Bob. "I think we need to tackle the Bert Rhodes problem as quickly as possible. We should schedule an emergency meeting of the town council this week to discuss what we can do to help his grace."

"Well now, Lillian, I don't—" Bob began.

"That might not be a bad idea," Cissy said. "Couldn't the town council condemn that old golf course, or something?"

Big Bob scowled. "Now, Miz Warren, we don't exactly have the money to—"

"Well, that's an idea," Lillian said.

Bob took out a handkerchief and mopped his brow. "Lillian, I think we should wait and think on this a little bit. I don't want to go up against a bunch of church ladies."

"Piffle," Lillian said, "I already talked to Jimmy Marshall. He thinks an emergency meeting of the council is a good idea. I'm sure he can control his wife."

"I wouldn't count on it," Bob said, tucking his handkerchief into his pocket.

"Well, Kamaria isn't opposed to an emergency meeting. I talked with her last night about it. And we all know she's going to win next November's mayoral election." Lillian turned and waved at an African-American woman who stood at the other end of the reviewing stand having a conversation with a group of women of various sizes, ages, and ethnic backgrounds. Despite their differences, all of those ladies looked like churchwomen.

Hugh suddenly wished that Caroline were beside him whispering in his ear about all these tangled relationships. Caroline had tried to brief him about all this, but he wasn't very good at names and faces and politicking.

"What's this about church ladies?" Senator Warren asked.

Big Bob hitched up his trousers so that his belt buckle rested above his paunch. "Rupert, we got us a group of crusading women, led by the wife of our leading citizen. They want to protect that miniature golf course on the land Baron Woolham needs for his factory. They say Golfing for God is a wonderful family place that can teach kids their Bible stories."

"Oh, that's not good," the senator said.

Bob nodded and turned toward Lillian. "Lillian, you're in the minority of churchwomen in this county. Hettie's done a remarkable job of organizing the Committee to Resurrect Golfing for God. And I don't want to go up against Hettie Marshall and her current cause."

"Hettie Marshall? Really?" Cissy said in a surprisingly chipper tone. "Would that be the daughter of Judge Gregory Johnson who married Lee Marshall's boy?"

"It is, ma'am," Bob said.

Cissy turned toward her father. "Daddy, you know her. Remember? Greg and Roberta's daughter? I went to summer camp with her. And we were sorority sisters at Clemson. Maybe I can help." Cissy turned and gave Hugh a big, brassy smile full of beautifully straight white teeth.

"Hmmm," Senator Warren said. "I didn't know anything about this committee of churchwomen. Hugh, in this state it's real bad politics to get crosswise with any churchwomen."

"I am aware of that, sir. We have churchwomen in Woolham."

"Really, Daddy, this situation has disaster written all over it," Cissy said. "I don't think you should entrust it to Caroline. I'm surprised you even asked her to help, given her obvious conflict of interest."

"I sure do wish ya'll would quit calling her Caroline. Her name's Rocky. Rocky Rhodes," Lillian said.

"I believe she legally changed her name," Hugh said.

"Well, thank God for that. Can you imagine going through life with a name like Rocky Rhodes?" Cissy's laugh sounded like a braying jackass, with an unmistakable note of cruelty in it.

"No, I can't," the senator said, "but I don't think less

of Caroline because her parents gave her an unfortunate name, or that man lassoed her. The fact is, Lord Woolham, I asked Caroline to help because she has a knack for untangling difficult situations. Especially those that require a certain amount of political delicacy, if you catch my drift. I knew her father owned the land, so I figured she'd be even more motivated to find a unique solution to your problems. If you trust Caroline, she'll find a solution for you. She hasn't failed me yet."

"Daddy," Cissy said, her voice sounding brittle. "I *know* Hettie. I mean we're on the same social standing. I'm sure I can help." Cissy's arm tightened again, and Hugh got the feeling he was in the embrace of a very large and deadly boa constrictor.

"Sweetie, Caroline has a real knack for untangling things."

Cissy's grasp spasmed on Hugh's arm. She was furious with her father, but managed to keep a lid on it. Instead she gave the senator a phony smile and then looked up at Hugh. "I can get you that land. You trust me, and everything will work out fine."

Hugh didn't trust Cissy very far. He was learning not to trust anyone. Besides, he halfway understood Cissy—she was brassy and hard and a lot like Granddad. She saw what she wanted, and she went after it.

Granddad would have approved of her. Not just her approach to life, but the fact that she fit all the requirements of a deBracy bride—she had both a pedigree and a fortune.

Dash let the horse walk its way down an unpaved road, heading toward the Painted Corner Stables. Caroline clutched the saddle pommel and tried to get her heartbeat under control. She didn't know where the fear ended and the anger started. "This is exactly like that time you blew up my Barbie dolls."

"No, it's not," Dash said from his place behind her. "That was all about my getting back at your little friend, Savannah, and the mean things she said about my daddy. You and the Barbies were collateral damage. I've been meaning to apologize to you for that."

"Well, this is a weird way of apologizing. Honestly, this is the worst idea you've ever had."

"You asked me for something big and outrageous. This is what came to mind."

She gave him an elbow to the ribs. "You're incorrigible. Couldn't you have told me about this? We could have discussed it. My boss was on that reviewing stand, Dash. Did you give one moment's thought to how this might affect my career?"

"Well, no, to tell you the truth. But the fact is, you were busy getting drunk and dancing with that Brit, which probably wasn't such a smart career move either. And besides, I reckoned that it would be better and more believable if you didn't know what I planned. That way it could look just like I was staking my claim on you."

Dash guided the horse into the main corral. "You weren't really staking your claim on me, were you?" Caroline asked.

He laughed. "No, ma'am, that's for sure."

He stood up in the stirrups and swung his leg over the saddle. When his foot hit the ground, he winced. "Damn, that knee ain't never gonna be the same," he muttered, bending down to rub it.

Caroline found herself sitting atop the horse all by her lonesome. "Get me down from here."

"Yes, ma'am." Dash called one of his stable hands over to help hold the horse's reins. He untied the lasso around Caroline's middle. Then, in a manly display of strength, he lifted her free of the saddle, turned, and set her on her feet.

Her stiletto heels immediately sank right into something soft.

"Uh, Dash, you didn't just put me in horse poop, did you?" She lifted up her skirts.

"Uh-oh, did I? I'm sorry. We got a lot of that stuff around here, you know."

"You did this on purpose."

"I didn't. But you know, this situation provides you with a real opportunity to trash that old dress. You let the skirt get soiled, you might have a good excuse for taking the dress off." His crooked smile made an appearance. "That would make you feel better, wouldn't it? You could dress in a shirt buttoned up to here." He gestured to his neck.

"You're obnoxious."

"I know."

"My shoes are ruined."

"Aw, poor baby. And they were such sensible shoes, too."

"Dash, you come right here and get me out of this pile of manure."

Dash followed orders. He snatched her up so fast that her pumps were left behind, mired forever in the muck. He threw her over his shoulder like a sack of potatoes. Caroline got a head-jarring, upside-down view of the world as Dash strode across the corral and into the parking lot beside the stable. When they reached the blacktop, he stopped and returned her to her bare feet.

"I'm going to murder you," she said as she put her hands on her tulle-swathed hips.

"I'm not worried. But you need to play like you're all hot and bothered by me. Otherwise Bubba will never get the message." He turned and headed toward his car, which was parked in the shade of a big oak tree.

Caroline trailed after him. "What about my shoes?"

Dash looked over his shoulder. "Honey, those shoes are toast. A country girl like you should be okay in bare feet. Besides, think of the great stories we could tell everyone about how you lost them." He kept walking, but she heard the laughter in his voice.

She minced her way after him, feeling every pebble under her soles. Those pebbles reminded her that she *had* traveled a long way from home. There had been a time when no one could *make* her wear shoes.

Life had been so much simpler then.

"Dash. This is crazy."

He turned around. "Yeah, it is, kind of. But you gotta admit it's also brilliant."

She stood there on her suddenly liberated feet and thought things through. It was much easier to think on solid ground. The genius of Dash's plan began to creep up on her.

"I hate to admit it, but this might work. I only wish it hadn't involved my being lassoed off a float. That was incredibly embarrassing, actually."

"You're looking at this all wrong. I didn't embarrass you today. I made you a legend. Name one other Watermelon Queen who broke two hearts twelve years apart while wearing the same darn dress. They're going to be talking about this for years."

"Right. That's what I'm worried about. And besides, I'm not really going to break your heart, because I think Hettie already beat me to it."

His smile cooled just a little. Caroline had touched Dash's sore spot.

"All the better, because you won't do any more damage than has already been done," he said, then opened the car door. "Get in, honey, let's go have us some fun at the barbecue."

CHAPTER 11

Every year, right after the watermelon parade, folks had a big barbecue out at the river. Granddaddy always helped cook the pigs, and all the ladies in the county brought cakes and pies and put them on long tables and the kids could pick whatever they wanted.

The eating was pretty fun, but as far as Haley was concerned, the best part of the barbecue was swimming in the river. Her folks didn't have a regular membership to the country club, and they weren't one of the rich families who had summerhouses down here either. So this was the only time she got to swim in the river. The rest of the time, she had to make do with the public swimming pool.

But this year, Haley was so worried about her angel problem that she didn't feel like swimming. So she sat with Granddaddy for a while, watching him carve up the pigs. And then she went off to play by herself on the swings near the baby swimming area.

The playground wasn't that far from the parking lot,

so she had a good viewpoint to watch people come and go. A big black car came up the drive, and Mayor Bob and Miz Bray got out with some other people Haley didn't know. They all went up to the picnic pavilion built on the lawn.

Then along came Dash Randall in his big red car, with Aunt Rocky sitting right beside him in the middle of the seat.

Suddenly the angel took note and stopped whimpering. And then she did the strangest thing. She drifted away from the playground and hovered right over Aunt Rocky as she and Dash headed up to the pavilion to join the other grown-ups who were gathering there for the barbecue.

For once, Haley was left all by her lonesome. Haley waited for the angel to come back, but she was gone. It was really kind of weird. Haley thought maybe the angel might decide to move in with Aunt Rocky. That would be good if it happened.

Finally Reverend Ellis and Pastor Mike from the Methodist Church each gave a blessing. And after that, everyone started in to eating.

Haley got up and helped herself to some barbecue and a piece of Miss Carpenter's peach cobbler. Then she found a place on the back step of the pavilion where she could eat it. It was nice to be alone.

The angel was still hovering over Aunt Rocky, like maybe she needed some protection or something. Haley sure hoped the angel didn't break anything today. That would be bad.

So Haley kept half an eye on the angel and another half on Reverend Ellis, who had taken his plate over to

Miz Bray's summer place after he'd said the blessing. Miz Bray was one of the rich and important people who actually had a house down here.

Uncle Tulane was talking about buying a house here at the river so she and Lizzy could swim. That would be pretty cool.

Haley licked the sticky cobbler off her fingers, put her paper plate and napkin in the trash, and then headed on over to Miz Bray's house. She stepped up and knocked on the frame of the screen door.

"I declare, is that Haley Rhodes?" Miz Bray came out of the house onto the porch wiping her hands on a checkered dishtowel. She opened the screen door and looked down at Haley.

Haley suddenly wished she hadn't knocked. Her legs started shaking. She was scareder of Miz Bray than just about anyone else in the whole wide world.

"Uh, yes'm, it's me. I was wondering..." Haley stepped a little to one side and peered around Miz Bray. "Uh, I was..." She twisted her fingers together as words and breath failed her. The barbecue she'd just eaten sat in her stomach like a big lump. "Uh, I was—"

"Well, speak up, child. I don't have all day. The preacher is here and—"

"Can I talk to him?" Haley said really fast on one breath.

Miz Bray gave her a really mean look. "You want to speak to the preacher? Now?"

"Yes'm."

"About what?"

"Well, I—"

"Oh, for goodness' sake, let the child in." This came from Reverend Ellis himself.

Haley let go of a deep breath as Miz Bray opened the door a little wider and stepped back. Haley edged her way through the narrow opening. She came forward until she was standing in front of the preacher.

He smiled at her, and a little of her fear eased. The preacher was easy to talk to. He had big hands like Uncle Tulane, and a deep soft voice that put her at ease.

"So what brings you here, darlin'?"

She clasped her hands behind her back and tried not to fidget. She knew that fidgeting wasn't allowed anywhere near the preacher or the church.

"Well, um…"

"Oh, for goodness' sake, girl, spit it out. Reverend Ellis doesn't have all day, you know." Miz Bray lowered her fat body into a rocking chair beside the preacher. It looked like Miz Bray aimed to hear what Haley had to say. Haley didn't really like the idea, but this was an emergency situation.

"Um, see, it's about the angel."

Miz Bray made a rude noise. The preacher held up his hand to hush up Miz Bray. That was good.

"What about the angel?" he asked.

"She's starting to do things."

"Do things? What kind of things? Miracles?"

Haley shook her head. "No, not miracles, but she did smite those bad men that time down at the golf course. I know nobody believes that, but it's the God's honest truth."

"Young lady, don't you use that kind of language in

my house." Miz Bray had leaned forward in her seat and was giving Haley her mean look.

"Lillian, maybe you could leave us here on the porch for a minute and go inside," the preacher said. He turned and gave Miz Lillian a really scary look of his own.

Miz Bray got up and went into the house. The preacher leaned forward in his rocking chair. "So what's the angel doing?"

"She's breaking things."

"What things?"

"Well, this morning she broke the bed Aunt Rocky was sleeping in on account of the fact that Aunt Rocky didn't want to get up." The preacher gazed down at Haley with the same look on his face that grown-ups always got when she started talking about the angel.

He took a deep breath. "Now Haley, we both know that angels don't come to earth to break things."

"No, sir. I know that. But she did it just the same. And the angels broke Golfing for God, too. So I reckon that sometimes, if there's a good reason, an angel might break something."

"Haley, you know angels had nothing to do with what happened at Golfing for God, don't you? It was a thunderstorm."

All the grownups said this, even Aunt Jane, who was at Golfing for God with Haley the day the angels broke stuff. But just 'cause Jane hadn't seen the angels didn't mean they hadn't come when Haley needed them the most.

"I know you think I'm fibbing," Haley said, "but that's the problem, see."

"No, I don't see."

"Well, the angel does things, and then I get in trouble for them. But I get in worse trouble if I tell the truth. So I have to lie."

"What do you mean you have to lie?"

"Well, like this morning, the angel broke the bed, but I told Granny that I broke it. That was a fib, and I'm really worried about that. Do you think Jesus will mind if I lie in order to avoid getting punished?"

The preacher blinked down at her for a few long uncomfortable moments. "Haley, I know for certain that Jesus expects us to tell the truth, even when it means we get punished for it. However, Jesus will forgive us for our lies, just so long as we put our faith in Him. That's not permission to lie with impunity, but it's something to keep in mind. Nevertheless, I think it's time for you to start telling the truth."

Haley nodded her head even though she had no idea what the word "impunity" meant. Or for that matter, anything the preacher had just said. He seemed to indicate that Jesus would forgive her lies, which was something of a relief. But his tone said that he was as tired of her angel stories as everyone else.

She tried to keep a knot from forming in her throat. "I was afraid of that," she said, her voice shaking.

"Sweetie, an angel that breaks things can't be an angel. Do you think maybe this is something you made up to get attention?" The preacher gave her a little squeeze on her shoulder. His words were soft and kind and not scary at all. Haley had a feeling he was trying to be helpful, but he was like every other grown-up. He didn't believe in the angel to begin with.

"No, that's not right. The angel is real, and she's the one who broke the bed. I just told Granny that it was me because I didn't want Granny to ground me."

"You mean your granny was going to ground you if you told her the angel did it?"

"Yes, sir. So I lied. I told her that I did it. But I didn't do it. Honest. And it's worse than that. Daddy makes me go to see Dr. Newsome two times a week, and I know that the only way I'm going to get out of going to see her is to fib about the angel. You know, tell her that the angel isn't there. But the angel is there. And she wants to get back to Heaven in the worst way, but I don't know how to get her there."

The minister looked down at her out of his bright blue eyes. Haley didn't feel any better now that she'd explained her problem, though. In fact, she had this feeling she'd made a really big mistake.

Before the minister could say anything else, Miz Bray came out of the house, where she had been listening, even though the preacher had told her not to. "Young lady," Miz Bray said, stepping onto the porch and standing over Haley, her finger pointing. "This nonsense has got to stop. Either you're lying or you need to be put away someplace where they keep crazy people. Is that what you want? To be a crazy person like your granddaddy?"

"Now Lillian—" the minister started.

"You get out of here right this minute and stop wasting Reverend Ellis's time. You and your granddaddy may think this is funny, but it's not."

"Lillian, I think you had better..."

Haley didn't wait to hear what the preacher had to say.

It didn't matter anyway. The preacher didn't believe her, any more than Granny did. And if no one believed her, then she would have to be crazy.

And she didn't want to be crazy. Although being like Granddaddy didn't seem like such a bad thing. It had never occurred to her until right this minute that seeing angels was a pretty big burden.

She turned and ran for the door, just as her throat closed up and tears filled her eyes. She ran from Miz Bray's house, down the hill toward the barbecue area.

Since the cooking was done, Granddaddy was resting in a lawn chair talking with old Mr. Jessup when she found him.

Granddaddy saw her coming even before she got there. He stood up, and she ran right into his legs and hugged him. Granddaddy's arms came around her. He pulled her up into his lap and sat the both of them down in the lawn chair. "Now, little gal, what's the matter?"

She let go of a sob onto the soft fabric of Granddaddy's T-shirt just as the preacher showed up.

"Is she all right?" the preacher asked.

Granddaddy squeezed Haley's shoulders a little tighter. "What in the Sam Hill did you do to her to make her cry like this?"

"It wasn't me. Lillian said a few unchristian things. Haley came to ask me some questions about her angel. Apparently the angel is quite destructive."

Haley felt Granddaddy go still. "Well, obviously, you didn't give her any advice about dealing with a destructive angel, did you, Bill?"

"Well I—"

"I can just imagine what Lillian said to her."

Haley sniffled back her tears. "Miz Bray said I should be locked up someplace where crazy people go." Another wave of tears flooded her eyes. "I don't want to go to a place like that." The sob broke over her, and she buried herself in the safe haven of Granddaddy's T-shirt.

"Elbert, I'm very sorry. Lillian didn't give me a chance to speak with the child. Haley is very troubled. She needs guidance."

"Right. I got it," Granddaddy said.

"Elbert, I—"

"Look, we'll talk later. It would be best if you left us alone. Now."

The preacher turned to go, but Granddaddy called him back. "Bill," he said, "I'm disappointed in you. After all the help you and Hettie have given me these last few weeks with the golf course, I would have thought you still had faith in angels. Lillian is a lost cause, I know. But I had high hopes for you."

Hugh spent most of the afternoon in the company of Senator Warren and his daughter. Both of them were keen on schmoozing the other political VIPs in attendance at the barbecue.

Hugh wanted nothing of that sort of thing. He wanted to enjoy himself, and politicking was like torture, especially since Senator Warren was quite fond of cigars, and the smoke always reminded Hugh of his grandfather.

Hugh might have made an escape but Cissy had anchored him to her side. He bided his time until Cissy excused herself for a visit to the washroom. Then Hugh headed up to the second floor of the picnic pavilion, where Clay Rhodes's band was playing and people had gathered to dance.

He stood like a wallflower, watching the dancers move about on the floor. He didn't know the dance. It was one of those American line dances with intricate steps and moves. He was less interested in the dance moves than he was in watching the utterly fetching Caroline Rhodes, who was dancing barefooted with Dash Randall.

After her pony ride and an afternoon of dancing, her hair looked like a wild mane around her pale face. Her crown of ribbons had tangled down her back, and she moved like a sprite in the afternoon light. She was a vision from a storybook: round in all the right places; her amazing bosom displayed by the bodice of that dress; her porcelain cheeks blushing pink. He wanted to possess her. He wanted to collect her and walk off with her into the piney woods and see what magic she really commanded.

And he wanted to put his fist right through Dash Randall's handsome face.

The man had kept her right by his side all afternoon. He had thoroughly staked his claim, and Caroline seemed to be completely besotted with the bloke.

Well, he could hardly blame her. Randall was supposedly quite well heeled and handsome as the devil.

He was also an appallingly bad dancer.

Not that Hugh was particularly good on his feet. But Randall was downright clumsy.

"It sucks, don't it?"

Hugh turned to find Bubba Lockheart standing right beside him. The poor man's nose was in a splint, his eyes were black, his lip swollen, and there was a noticeable gap in his smile where his front teeth had once been. He was sipping what looked like a Coke through a soda straw.

Shame washed through Hugh. "I say, I'm terribly sorry about Thursday night. I probably overreacted."

Bubba nodded. "Yeah, I know, I probably did, too."

"No hard feelings."

"Nah. The surgeon said I should sue you, but the way I see it, I probably started the fight. I shouldn't have grabbed Rocky the way I did. I just lost my head there for a minute. And I'd already had a couple of beers."

"Well, that might be true, but I probably should have given you warning before I swung."

They lapsed into silence for a few moments, both of them watching Caroline dance. Finally Bubba said, "I'm thinking the two of us might be able to take him, what with him being gimpy and all."

"Him? You mean Randall?"

"Yeah. Him." Bubba sounded miserable.

"You know, I rather think that would be poor form right here in the middle of the party."

"Right. We could sneak up on him later and open up a can of whup ass on him."

"Hm, yes, I suppose he deserves it for lassoing Caroline off that float."

"He manhandled her. I don't like it when people do that to Rocky."

Hugh refrained from pointing out that Bubba had manhandled Caroline, or that Hugh had not liked it either. Instead he said, "I think Caroline would be quite annoyed at us if we picked a fight with Randall. She was quite angry with me on Thursday for what happened. I don't think she approves of fighting."

"That's probably right. But she's ignoring me."

"Well, there is more than one way to get a woman to notice you."

Bubba turned to give him a long, hard stare. Bubba was a very large man. Hugh doubted he could take him a second time, especially since he appeared to be stone sober at the moment.

"I think she's noticed *you* plenty, from what I've heard around town," Bubba said, his voice taking on an edge.

"Well, last night doesn't count. I got her drunk, which I realize was reprehensible. But let's face it, she's noticing Randall right at the moment, and she looks to be completely sober."

"Right."

"So I've got an idea."

"You do?"

Hugh nodded. "If we want her to notice us, we can't stand here on the sidelines. We have to join the battle, right there on the football pitch, as they say."

Bubba frowned. "You know, you sound real pretty when you talk, but I don't understand half of what you say."

"Bubba, old man, we need to get into the game."

"Right. But how? Besides knocking his block off."

Hugh scanned the crowd looking for wallflowers. He found two: the pretty girl with long brown hair and a curvy figure who had been dining with Caroline on Thursday night, and Cissy Warren, who was scanning the crowd, no doubt looking for Hugh so she could drag him back downstairs.

"Perfect. You see that young lady over there? The one who came to your rescue on Thursday?"

"You mean Rachel? She's Rocky's friend. She's real pretty."

"Yes, she's quite dishy. Which is the point. Go ask her to dance."

"Me? Ask Rachel Polk? Uh, she isn't ever going to dance with me. Especially after what happened to my face. She's too pretty for me."

"She is not. She cares about you. She tried to save your teeth."

"Yeah, she did. Then she disappeared after the doc told her it was a hopeless case. I'm sure she isn't interested in a guy who looks like a hillbilly."

"Nonsense. I'm sure she likes you quite a bit. And besides, your smile can be fixed. You're an American, and all Americans have fabulous smiles. The number of dentists per capita in your country is completely amazing."

"The doc said they could fix my teeth with implants."

"So, see? You should go right over there and thank her for trying to save your teeth. And then dance with her. Dance a slow dance with her."

"Why?"

"Because it will send Caroline the message that you don't care if she's off dancing the night away with that cowboy."

"But that's not the message I want to send."

"I know. It's reverse psychology. See, if she doesn't think you care, then she's going to care more."

"Uh-huh. It kind of makes sense, I guess. Sort of."

"Trust me. This works all the time."

Bubba frowned. "What are you going to do?"

"I'm going to dance with Cissy Warren. She's rich. I'm not entirely sure I like her very much, but she certainly fits the bill when it comes to Miriam Randall's forecast for me."

"Miriam gave you a forecast?"

"Yes, she told me to marry a rich woman, which is, more or less, what my grandfather used to tell me when I was a lad."

"Well, that kind of leaves Rocky out of the running, don't it?" Bubba grinned. It wasn't a pretty sight.

"Well, I suppose so, more's the pity. But we can still carry on. Are you game?"

Bubba shrugged. "Yeah, sure. Let's go get 'em."

"I'm a freaking genius," Dash said. "Look."

Caroline turned her head and saw two things. Bubba and Rachel dancing together, and beyond them, Lord Woolham guiding the model-thin and naturally blond Cissy Warren around the dance floor with his undeniable grace and aplomb.

A whole raft of conflicted feelings raced through her. Seeing Bubba dancing was a positive sign. Seeing him dance with her best friend was, on the other hand, deeply distressing. The last thing Rachel needed was clingy Bubba screwing up her life.

And then there was the whole Hugh and Cissy thing. She didn't like them dancing. Not even a teeny bit.

But there wasn't a thing she could do about it. Cissy and Hugh matched. They were both rich and came from blue-blooded families. She was the country girl who needed to be looking for a regular Joe.

"What? Aren't you happy?" Dash asked.

Caroline turned back toward him and studied his craggy face for a long moment. He was handsome, and funny, and a pain in the backside most of the time. They had known each other since she was a little girl. He was her brothers' friend.

He was rich. He owned almost all the land in the general vicinity. He'd worked with his hands most of his life. He was a regular guy. People liked him, now that he was working through his problems. He'd gotten sober. Cleaned up his act.

There was a lot a girl could like in a man like Dash. But Caroline wasn't the girl.

"What? Why are you looking at me that way?"

"You're sweet, you know."

"Don't get any ideas."

"I'm not. You're sweet but you're also a terrible dancer. And my poor bare feet need a break."

"Okay. Want to take a walk down to the first pier? That should get everyone talking."

"No. I don't need any more talk. And besides, while I want Bubba to move on, I'm not sure I want him to move on to Rachel."

Dash frowned. "What? Are you jealous?"

She rolled her eyes. "C'mon, Dash, I wouldn't wish Bubba on my worst enemy, let alone my best friend."

He gave her a sober look. "You know, Bubba is an all-right guy when he's sober. Rachel could do worse."

"I don't think Rachel and Bubba are a match made in Heaven."

"Well, maybe not, but look at him. He's enjoying

himself for once. So, see, I'm a genius. You should be grateful to me."

"Yeah, I guess, but right now I'm just exhausted. And you need to rest that leg. So let's drop the charade, okay? I need some alone time."

"Okay. I need to wet my whistle anyways."

He leaned in and gave her a peck on the cheek. He played it up and lingered over it, but it was still a brotherly kiss.

Caroline left him at the pavilion with a bunch of local guys discussing Carolina football like the only teams in the universe were Clemson and the University of South Carolina. She wandered down to the river's edge, where she collapsed onto a wooden bench. She sucked in the warm summer air, filled with the coppery scent of black water. Out beyond the riverbank, a gaggle of teenagers were trying to sink the float that rode the current between the first pier and the baby pool. They would pile on, get the float under water, and then the current would take over and knock people off. The activity came with its share of girls shrieking and boys laughing.

Caroline had been one of those kids once. The first day of the Watermelon Festival used to be the best day of the year. School was out, the weather was warm, the food was delicious, and her family got to come swimming out here.

All of that had changed twelve years ago, the last time she'd put on this dress.

And now, thanks to Dash's admittedly brilliant plan, she might never be able to live down the legend.

She'd heard folks whispering all day. They halfway

expected her to ride off in Dash's Cadillac tonight and come back two days from now as his blushing bride.

Such was the legacy that Stone and Sharon had left in their wake. Everyone wanted a happy ending to that story. Unfortunately Stone's happy ending had been cut short. So now everyone kept looking for another, substitute, Watermelon Festival romance.

She was doomed. She would have to play this charade for a while. And then when folks realized it was a hoax, she'd get blamed. Dash was right, his lasso had made her a living legend, and not in a good way either.

Her throat knotted up at that thought. She had no reason to cry, except that sometimes when she thought about Sharon and Stone, she'd get all weepy. Sharon had treated her like a grown-up, even when she'd been a teenager. Her sister-in-law had encouraged her to go to college, to be her own woman.

Sharon had loved Caroline's brother, but Sharon had given up a lot to be with him. Sometimes Caroline wondered if Stone understood all that Sharon had sacrificed in the name of love.

And now Sharon was gone, and Caroline missed her. For a little instant, it almost felt as if Sharon was right there with her, enjoying the day as she always had. Sharon had loved the Watermelon Festival. Caroline's eyes watered up, just thinking about Stone and Sharon.

Great. She needed to have a crying jag in front of everyone like she needed a hole in the head. She gathered up the yards of tulle in her skirt and raced on her bare feet down the path that ran beside the river's edge.

The tears overwhelmed her as she made her way past the first pier and on into the overgrown area upstream. A narrow dirt track led along the riverbank to a second pier, where people used to fish all the time.

She walked out onto the pier, the wooden slats smooth and cool under her feet. She sank down onto one of the benches and wrestled her tears under control. She had no reason to cry.

She was alive, and it was a beautiful day. She sat on the pier for a long while as the sun sank in the sky and the light turned golden. It was peaceful here, watching the river run, listening to it burble underneath the pier's planking as it rolled its way to the sea. She let her thoughts run free, and of course, her mind went back to last night and the touch of Hugh's hand, and the feel of his skin, and the way she had floated across the dance floor in his arms.

And then, as if she'd conjured him up with her thoughts, Baron Woolham strolled down the pier and sat himself right down next to her.

He said nothing. Instead, like one of those English lords in one of Momma's books, he handed her a fine cotton handkerchief with his initials embroidered on it. "Your mascara has run a little bit," he said.

She took the handkerchief and dabbed at her eyes. The soft cotton came away black. She didn't even want to think about how she looked at this moment—poured into a too-tight dress, her hair all windblown from her wild ride on Dash's pony, and eye makeup destroyed by a PMS-laden moment.

And then there were her dirty, bare feet, and her close encounter with a pile of horse pucky.

So much for her carefully groomed professionalism.

"In case you're wondering," Hugh said in his clipped

accent and deep, sexy voice, "I wanted to put my fist through that buggar's face. I might have done, too, except I worried that it might have added to your problems. And of course, I didn't want to damage any more faces in Last Chance. I've been rather a prat in that regard."

She straightened up and turned in his direction. He had cocked his head and was giving her the oddest smile. It didn't quite touch his lips, but his eyes were full of kindness.

Something eased inside her chest. "Buggar? You mean Dash, right? You already punched Bubba."

He nodded. "I really think that lassoing someone off a parade float is rather an immature way of showing one's affection."

"You do?"

"Yes. Apparently I'm seriously out of step with you Yanks in this regard. And up to now, I was thinking that Last Chance and Woolham were quite alike, actually."

She laughed. "You're being droll or something, aren't you?"

"Or something," he muttered. "Look, Caroline, I know it's really not my place, but um...well, you see, I know everyone says Miriam Randall never gets it wrong, but that prat is not the right man for you."

She let go of a sudden and unexpected laugh. "What makes you say that?"

"He's a terrible dancer."

His gaze seemed more avid than it should be. He leaned in a little bit, close enough for Caroline to see the texture of his closely shaved whiskers and to feel his body heat. She suddenly wanted to snuggle up to him and rest her head on his shoulder. He had very broad shoulders, like every good English hero ought. But she couldn't do that. Snuggling up to him would be very unprofessional. She needed to start thinking with her brains and not her hormones.

"Well," she said, "dancing isn't everything."

"No. I suppose not. But you danced with Dash, and then ran away and came down here for a cry?" Hugh's mouth finally quirked into a funny, uneven line. "I thought that was rather interesting, so I escaped from Cissy and came down to see if it was his dancing or something else."

She looked away.

"So, what is it?"

She lifted a shoulder. "It's really stupid. You wouldn't understand."

"Try me."

"Well, it's just that every time I put on this dress, it's like I have to live up to something that isn't true."

"What?"

"My brother Stone ran off with a Watermelon Queen when he was eighteen. He and Sharon found a justice of the peace and got married and didn't come back for two days."

"So what does that have to do with you?"

"It's complicated. See, my sister-in-law died in a car wreck a few years ago, and if that hadn't happened, she and Stone would probably be here together today, and everyone would be joking and laughing and retelling their story. But instead, no one can talk about it because it makes everyone so sad."

"I see. So you were crying about Sharon?"

She nodded. "Yeah, and the expectations that Sharon's behavior has imposed on every Watermelon Queen since. It's like the town wants us all to run off and have a romance. When the truth is, Sharon, probably more than anyone else, is the person who encouraged me to avoid romance, go to college, and find a career instead."

"Right. I think I'm getting it. But I must admit that I do sometimes have rather a problem with female logic." He said it with humor in his voice; otherwise she might have punched him herself.

"See, Bubba asked me to marry him in front of everyone that summer I was Watermelon Queen. He had a full ride to Clemson, and I had a scholarship that I worked hard for at the University of South Carolina. He wanted me to give up my scholarship and come to Clemson, where I couldn't afford to go to school. But he just wanted me to be his wife. He practically expected it, because that's what Sharon did.

"I'll never understand why Sharon gave up her chance to go to college. I've never asked my brother because it's too sensitive a subject. But I knew I wanted to go to college. So I told Bubba no.

"The first time I said it privately.

"The second time, he forced the issue and asked me in front of a big crowd of people. And I got angry and said a few things I'm not proud of. I've paid the price. Not only because I was ugly to Bubba, but because small towns are places where myths are invented on a daily basis. And the myth in this town is that I treated Bubba so bad that I broke his heart. He fell apart and ended up flunking out of college, thereby messing up a bright

NCAA college football career that was going to land him in the NFL.

"Sharon was proud of me for sticking to my guns. She might have been the only one. And I miss her."

Caroline pressed the handkerchief to her cheeks. "I'm sorry. You didn't need to know all that, did you?"

Hugh reached out and patted her hand. His skin was warm and his hands conveyed a sense of gentle strength. "Darling, small villages can be trying sometimes. People must have their heroes, and when the heroes fall, someone has to be blamed."

"What do you know about small towns?"

"I've lived my entire life in Woolham, which is about the same size as Last Chance. And being the lord there, everyone in the village expects me to live up to a standard set by my grandfather. I'm afraid I've been a terrible disappointment to them at times, and they've blamed my aunts for it."

"Your aunts?"

"Yes, they raised me after Granddad got sick. And my aunts are a bit, well, peculiar. They get blamed for everything I do that isn't exactly like what my grandfather did. It's not quite fair to them because I'm the one who's a failure."

Somewhere close by, a cicada turned on its motor. The sounds of children laughing and country music floated on the summer air. And suddenly it seemed hotter and more humid than it had been a moment before. Everything seemed clearer, louder, larger than life. Even the texture of her tulle skirt against her legs seemed to affirm that she was alive. She could feel the life in everything around her.

"How are you a failure?" she asked. "You seem very successful to me. You went to college. You've invented a new kind of loom. You're going to build a factory and employ people."

He smiled with his eyes. "Well, the jury is still out on the factory, isn't it?"

"Yes but—"

"You are so lovely," Hugh said, halting her arguments. He raised his hand and adjusted the ribbon garland in her hair. His stiff upper lip softened. "Like the queen of the American fairies. You look like you belong right here, among the palmettos and Spanish moss."

Caroline closed her eyes and swallowed hard, but neither of those things did anything to stop the shivery feeling overtaking her middle or the prickling of her scalp where Hugh touched her hair. He thought she was lovely? She'd just shown him the worst parts of Rocky Rhodes and he'd taken them all in stride.

She opened her eyes, expecting him to have vanished like a magical fantasy lover. But he remained, looking down at her. His eyes were soft and warm. There was a little smile on his lips now. His hair was all-over curls. He was like some dream come true, only he was better. There were depths to him.

So she didn't resist when he cocked his head and moved in. She didn't stop when his not-so-stiff-upper-lip hit hers.

His mouth took her to some other world of heat and desire and wonderful sensation. He kissed like he waltzed. Closer than the air, but still farther away than she might like. Her body sang in reaction.

Holy smokes, this kiss was like something from out

of a romance book. The fact that it was happening on the second pier at the country club in Last Chance, South Carolina, didn't diminish it in any way. She relaxed into the heat of his kiss and was just beginning to really enjoy the whole experience when a voice wafted down to them from the path.

CHAPTER
12

Hugh, where are you?" The sandpapery voice tugged Hugh right out of the moment.

Damn. It hadn't taken the bloody heiress long to find him, had it? He pulled away from the incredible woman in his arms.

Caroline's kiss had been like the river, carrying him off to some new, but remarkably familiar place. Her scent made him dizzy. She looked up at him with those pixie eyes. She was amazing, despite her runny makeup and her wild, untamed hair. His chest felt heavy in a way that was new and strange.

That kiss had been...otherworldly.

He wanted to get back to it and discover what secret doors it might open to strange and lovely places.

"Hugh?" Cissy's voice sounded louder.

He stood up and put several paces between himself and Caroline.

"Oh, there you are." Cissy emerged from the undergrowth and stepped onto the pier. Her high heels rang hollowly against the boards. She reached for his arm and took complete possession of it, just like William the Bastard conquering England.

It was only after she had staked her claim that she turned and pretended to notice Caroline for the first time. There was nothing genuine about this show. Hugh had no doubt Cissy knew exactly what he and Caroline had been doing.

What *had* they been doing?

Had he been dallying with her, like Granddad used to dally with young, common girls? The thought made him slightly sick.

Maybe he should thank Cissy for rescuing him from his own libido. But one look at the tousled and buxom Miss Rhodes and his libido was not feeling thankful at all.

Perhaps he was more like his grandfather than he had imagined. His chest constricted at the thought.

"Oh, Caroline, Daddy was looking for you," Cissy said, then paused for a moment before continuing. "Honey, your mascara is a mess. You really need to go put yourself back together." Hugh heard the disdain in Cissy's voice. He didn't like it very much.

Caroline dabbed her cheeks with his handkerchief. "Where is the senator?"

"Oh, he's up at the pavilion but he's fixing to go. That's why I came to get Hugh." Cissy turned her blue-eyed gaze on him. "You've been invited up to Columbia to our city house for the next few days. Daddy has suggested that we just let Caroline get the job done while you come and visit with us. Come along now. We'll take you over to collect your luggage. Daddy figures nothing much is going to happen down here until the town council meeting that's scheduled for Tuesday. Might as well enjoy what the city has to offer."

Cissy turned and gave Caroline an icy smile. "Daddy wants you to stay here and lobby the town council on Hugh's behalf. I hope you have something a bit more professional to wear."

A muscle ticked in Caroline's cheek, and her shoulders tensed. But she kept whatever she wanted to say to herself. She stood up, stepped forward, and pushed the balled-up handkerchief into Hugh's chest. "Thanks for listening," she said, then turned on one bare foot and made her way with the grace of a queen toward the pathway leading up to the pavilion.

He tucked the cloth into his trouser pocket.

"Really, Hugh, I'm surprised at you," Cissy said. "Caroline has a nice shape, even if she's a tad top-heavy, but beyond that there really isn't much there." She reached out and took Hugh by the arm.

"You need me," she said. She ran her fingers up his arms and over his shoulder and tipped up on her toes to give him a kiss.

The woman certainly knew her way around a French kiss, but for all that experience, there wasn't much magic in it. The kiss was competent and almost interesting. But in comparison to what had just happened with Caroline, Cissy's kiss fell utterly flat.

She pulled back, her blue eyes sparking in the late afternoon sun. Her index finger played over his chin.

If he wanted to do his duty to the deBracy legacy, he should be considering the size of Cissy Warren's bank account right now. That was how Granddad took care of things.

That was how every deBracy took care of things, except for Hugh's failure of a father. And given that Hugh had allowed himself to be swindled, and the land in Last Chance was swamp, and Elbert Rhodes was never, ever going to give up that marvelous golf course, Hugh looked to be following in his father's footsteps.

Hugh could still salvage his situation by doing the one thing Granddad would approve of—marrying Victoria.

Granddad would also approve of his doing business with Cissy Warren, who, in addition to being a senator's daughter with a trust fund, was also the chairwoman of the largest textile manufacturing company in the United States. Granddad would point out that Cissy was perfect for him, and Caroline was utterly unacceptable.

Just like Elisa.

Just thinking about Elisa made Hugh's hands tremble. An old and deep-seated anger percolated through him. He gritted his teeth and sucked in air.

No, he wasn't going to give in. Not this time.

"I do appreciate the invitation to Columbia," he said in his most polite voice, "but I think I'll stay here with Caroline and see what happens next."

Cissy's eyes grew round. "You honestly want to stay here?"

"Why not?"

"Because it's in the middle of nowhere, populated by rednecks, and their chief form of entertainment is spitting watermelon seeds."

This was exactly the kind of thing his granddad used

to say about the people of Woolham. It was the kind of thing that brought out Hugh's rebellious schoolboy every time.

He gave Cissy a polite smile. "Well, Cissy, the people in Last Chance *are* ordinary working people, it's true. I hope, one day, they will be the people who work in my factory. That being the case, I plan to stay."

Caroline ducked into the bathhouse down near the baby pool. She gazed at herself in an ancient mirror whose silvering had begun to deteriorate. The hazy image gave her a start.

Like every mirror, this one was brutal with the truth. She looked exactly like she'd been crying. In addition, the woman staring back at her had lost any pretense of being professional. It was like all her hard work had been swept away by Dash's Lasso Fiasco—not to mention the forbidden kiss Hugh had just laid on her.

Her stomach flip-flopped, and she got that shivery feeling again. She was in trouble, wasn't she? That kiss had been amazing. It was going to be hard to forget.

She dampened a paper towel with cold water and pressed it against her cheeks. She couldn't seriously entertain kissing him again, could she?

No, absolutely not. She had a job to do, and kissing Hugh would get in the way of it.

"Hey, Rocky." The voice carried an unmistakable note of derision. Caroline turned to find Cissy Warren leaning in the doorway with a smirk on her face that seemed to confirm every single one of Caroline's self-doubts.

She should thank Cissy for her sudden appearance

down on the pier. Really, the senator's daughter had probably saved Caroline from making an utter fool of herself. She hadn't expected to have anything in common with Lord Woolham.

"I told Hugh I would go make sure you were okay," Cissy said. "You look okay to me. A little windblown and tacky in that dress. But still, okay."

"Thanks," Caroline said between clenched teeth as she continued to dab away the ruined mascara on her cheeks.

"You need to keep your mitts off Hugh."

Caroline said nothing. Cissy was Senator Warren's daughter, a big mucky-muck in the textile industry, and everyone knew that whatever Cissy wanted, Cissy got. And besides, Cissy and Hugh were both playing in the same league.

"You hear me?"

"I hear you."

"Good, because I'm telling you that the idea of becoming a baroness has some attraction for me, and according to Daddy's research, his Lordship is just the kind of man who might be looking for a rich wife." She let go of a little gravelly laugh and reached into her purse and pulled out a pack of cigarettes and a lighter. She lit up and blew out a plume of smoke.

"And so I'm here to let you know that if you want to follow a Cinderella dream, you should aim for Dash Randall. A poor girl like you should always go for the money. A rich girl like me can go for the impoverished Englishman with the fancy title."

Caroline turned around. "Impoverished?"

"Oh, yes. I've seen his Dunn and Bradstreet rating,

honey, and the man is mortgaged up to here. According to my sources—and they are good ones—he's planning to marry some rich English aristocrat named Lady Ashton just to get his mitts on her money."

Caroline stood there thunderstruck. "He's engaged?"

"Well, no, not officially. But he *is* strapped for cash. That much I know." Cissy took a drag on her cigarette. "So, you see, he's not the Cinderella fantasy you think he is. He really does need my help if he's ever going to build that factory. And trust me, I've seen the technical details on his loom. I want that technology." She stopped and carefully blew out a few smoke rings.

Caroline knew better than to rise to Cissy's bait. But even so, every muscle in Caroline's body felt over-wound, like a clockwork toy ready to explode into action. Hugh had kissed her like that and he was practically engaged?

He was mortgaged?

He was broke?

Oh boy, she hadn't seen that one coming.

Cissy and her father finally departed from the barbecue. Hugh declined their offer of a lift back to the boardinghouse. Instead, he turned back toward the pavilion, intent on finding Caroline and taking up that kiss where they had left off.

This plan was, he knew, completely dastardly, seeing as her father owned the land he wanted. But he couldn't help himself. He wanted to spend some more time with her. She had magicked him, like one of Petal's little people. He was practically obsessed with her. He wanted to get to know her better.

His search for her didn't get him very far before Bubba accosted him.

"You lied to me," Bubba said.

"I did? About what?"

"You said Rocky would come crawling back to me if I danced with Rachel, but instead she took off."

"She's gone?"

"Yeah, I heard she left with her momma and daddy. They all took off kind of quick. And I couldn't just take off after her, you know? I was dancing with Rachel Polk. You can't just ditch Rachel."

"I see, and why is that?"

"Because she's drop-dead gorgeous, and also my truck loan is at the First National Bank, where her daddy is the manager and main loan officer. And besides, a guy missing his front teeth needs to show some respect. To be honest, I'm still amazed she danced with me." Bubba blushed.

"So," Hugh asked, "how was it, dancing with Rachel?"

"Oh, she's real nice. We even talked some, which is amazing since she's gorgeous, a college girl, and her daddy has money. She's completely out of my league." Bubba looked quite forlorn, which wasn't all that difficult given the state of his face.

"So, you fancy her then?"

"Fancy her?"

"You like her."

"Well, sure, everyone likes Rachel. She's sweet and cute and, well…"

"So why don't you ask her out, to the cinema or something?"

"Rachel Polk? I don't think so."

"Why not?"

Bubba looked down at his feet.

"She was quite attentive to you on Thursday when I... uh—"

"Busted up my face?"

"Yes."

"Well, that's a good reason not to ask her out. I mean look at me. I lisp now."

"Look, about that, I am terribly sorry. I suppose I ought to pay for the dentist's bill, and once the dentist fixes you up, I'm sure Rachel will be happy to go out with you some evening. You should ask her."

"Right. I'll get my teeth fixed first."

"I'll help. Is there anything else I can do for you? I feel very bad about what happened."

"Well, I need a good mechanic, but I don't guess you fit that bill. Dash was going to help me with my demolition derby car, but I told him I didn't want his help. I told him I was really pissed at him. He took it surprisingly well." Bubba sounded confused and demoralized.

"I can help. I've mended my share of cars and tractors over the years."

"No shit? Really? A guy like you with a fancy title and all?"

"I'm an engineer. And to be honest, I much prefer cocking about in the workroom than spending time being a businessman behind a desk."

"I hope what you just said don't mean what it sounds like."

Hugh's cheeks got redder. "Uh, um, I think you Yanks would say *fooling around* instead."

"Well, hell, if you know how to weld, I could sure use your help. C'mon, I'll give you a ride back to town. You can change your clothes and meet me at the Grease Pit."

Hugh stood in one of the bays at Bill's Grease Pit staring down at the dilapidated 1977 Dodge Aspen that was to become Bubba's chariot for Monday night's demolition derby. The car didn't look in very good nick, but then it was about to be smashed to bits, so its appearance didn't matter, did it?

The headlamps and passenger seats had already been removed, and a spray can paint job consisting of neon pink and green watermelons had been applied. The bonnet was up, exposing a very dirty, large block V-8 motor.

"You know, you don't really have to help me. I was just trying to make you feel guilty about my teeth," Bubba said as he strode across the garage bay toward the MIG welder and reached for a welder's mask. "Besides, when it comes to cars, I'll bet you're about as useful as tits on a bull."

"You'd be surprised what I know about motorcars."

Bubba turned. "I'll be surprised if you know your backside from a hole in the ground. And for the record, all that reverse psychology crap is a load of bull, too."

"Might I ask a question?"

"I'm sure you will have many."

"Caroline told me about the stunt you pulled twelve years ago."

"Stunt?"

"You know, the time you asked for her hand in front of the entire town, and she said no. Did you think before you did that? Because, Bubba, if you want to succeed in wooing a woman, embarrassing her is not the way to go about doing it. Have you ever apologized to her for that blunder?"

"Apologize? To Rocky? Hey, look, she called me a stupid hillbilly. She had nerve doing that, seeing as her folks are not so high and mighty, you know?"

Hugh frowned. "Well, you were stupid if you asked her in front of the whole town."

"Yeah, I guess that wasn't my swiftest moment."

"Well, I'm sorry she spoke her mind to you, but you probably deserved it. After all, you surprised her. I found her crying about the episode this evening."

Bubba's eyes got wide. "You did? Boy, I didn't want her to cry. I love her." He leaned against the wall. "But I guess I'm going to have to let her go. She's in love with Dash." He gave Hugh an assessing look. "And I heard all about how you were dancing with her last night."

"Yes, I was. She's a pretty good dancer."

"Yeah, I know, but see, you're not the one for her. So you shouldn't be flirting and buying her drinks, you know?"

"What makes you so sure I'm not the one for her?"

"Because Miriam told her she should be looking for a regular guy, and you're not a regular guy. That's the only reason I'm being nice to you. I mean, you and Rocky together is about as silly as me and Rachel Polk." He pushed off the wall. "So, you wanna help or what?"

"Sure, what can I do?"

"Take a look at the engine and tell me why it's misfiring on one cylinder. I'm going to concentrate on the safety cage."

Bubba headed to the steel tubing already laid out for the roll cage. He donned the mask, made a few adjustments to the MIG, and pulled the trigger, igniting a bright blue arc that forced Hugh to look away.

Well, Bubba certainly had a very good point about Caroline, didn't he? Not that Hugh believed any of that rubbish about Miriam Randall, but Hugh couldn't escape the fact that he was Lord Woolham, and he had duties and obligations.

Dallying with Caroline was not the same as doing his duty to his aunts or Woolham House. It was exciting to think about kissing her, dancing with her, and maybe doing more—but it was impossible, even if he and Caroline were more alike than they were different.

They came from two different worlds. And he had so many obligations. Letting go of the fantasy was rather depressing, really. But he had to let it go.

Hugh strolled over to the car's bonnet and started taking off the air filter. He soon lost himself in the job at hand, checking sparkplugs, compression, and carburetion. Nothing cured a lonely heart better than messing about with bits and pieces of machinery.

Hugh's mobile phone vibrated as he was shucking out of his trousers. It was after two in the morning, local time, and he stank of motor oil and grease.

He checked the caller ID: Aunt Petunia. He weighed whether to answer and decided that avoiding her would be futile. She would likely ring again in a few hours, completely oblivious to the time difference between America and the UK.

He pressed the talk button. "Hello, Aunt Petunia."

"Hugh, darling." Petunia's voice came through over Hugh's mobile phone so clearly she might have been just down the street, instead of five thousand miles away. He could imagine her sitting at the breakfast table at Woolham House, wearing one of her colorful and slightly ratty hand-knit sweaters and passing bits of bacon off to Dr. Jekyll and Mr. Hyde, her much-loved Yorkies.

He relaxed back into the feather pillows on the slightly squeaky bed. "Aunt Petunia, have you any idea what time it is over here?"

"Oh, dear, I forgot about that. Did I wake you?"

"No."

"Good heavens, Hugh, you aren't suffering from insomnia, are you? An infusion of valerian in chamomile tea is just what you need. I don't suppose there is anyone there who—"

"I'm not suffering from insomnia, Aunt Petunia. I'm just up late. I was helping a bloke with his car."

"Oh, that explains it. Hugh, you can't really expect to impress people if you're constantly getting yourself all greasy playing with motorcars. Really, dear, you should remember what your grandfather used to say about things like that."

Hugh didn't want to be reminded about Granddad. "It's my own business," he said in rather a surly voice. "And besides, I owed this fellow some help."

A little beat of silence on the line told Hugh that Petunia had noted his foul mood. "Well," she said. "I think someone needs to get some rest."

"Yes, and I would be in bed were it not for your phone call."

"I'm sorry, Hugh, dear. But really, we have a problem."

As if Hugh needed more problems. "What is it?"

"Bascomb has lost the engagement diary for the house." Bascomb, the steward at Woolham House, was nearly eighty-five and had a bad hip and a wandering mind. Petunia kept him on even though he was entirely useless in keeping the place up. Granddad would have fired him years ago.

Hugh should have fired him years ago, but he hadn't.

"And why is this a problem?" he asked.

"Well, we're all in a dither because we're not sure if we have a wedding here next weekend or not."

"You don't. There aren't any weddings scheduled until September."

"Oh, good, how did you remember?"

He didn't want to be unkind, but they booked only three or four weddings a year at Woolham House. Unfortunately, Woolham House's dated kitchen precluded them from booking any more than that. Weddings were a source of much-needed income for the estate. He would have booked one every weekend, if he could have afforded to fix up the kitchen and hire a staff.

"Well," Petunia said, nattering on as she often did, "now that worry has been laid to rest. How is your business trip, dear? Have you bought the land you needed?"

"There are complications."

"Oh, goody, I do like complications. They are so much fun."

He gripped the phone a little tighter. "I beg to differ. These complications are not fun. And this is not like one of those murder mysteries you love so much."

"Well, of course it isn't, unless there's a dead body. You haven't found one of those, have you?"

"No. Only a rather eccentric gentleman with a miniature golf course, who is refusing to sell me his land." He left out the part about Elbert's dishy daughter.

"A mini-golf course?" Petunia said after a moment. "How utterly unexpected."

"Yes, exactly. George seriously underestimated the difficulties involved in buying this piece of land."

Petunia cleared her throat. "Pardon me, dear, but there was something a little dodgy about George. I'm terribly sorry that he bought it in that plane crash, but I think you may be well rid of him in the end."

"Yes, well, he's certainly created a problem for me here. I don't think I can make a go of things unless I can convince Elbert Rhodes to sell me Golfing for God."

"What?"

"Golfing for God. I'm afraid the mini-golf is themed on the Bible. The fiberglass statues are brilliant. Aunt Petal would love the Tower of Babel. For some inexplicable reason, the tower has balconies populated by an entire tribe of sprites, fairies, elves, and gnomes."

"How delightful."

"Yes, well it is rather," Hugh said. "The place is currently out of business because of storm damage, but I asked Elbert to show me his business plan. I doubt he will. But it did occur to me that a mini-golf down at the nature center near Woolham House might be an additional source of income for us."

"Hugh, that's a marvelous idea."

"Do you think Petal would allow us to move some of her little people from the garden?"

"Hmmm. Perhaps. If we asked her to help with the landscaping."

"Well, it's something to think about if things fall through here."

"You sound worried."

He sank back against the pillows. "I *am* worried," he admitted.

"Just as I thought," Petunia said in what Hugh always thought of as her no-nonsense voice. "I knew I needed to call you. The spirits were definitely telling me that you were in trouble."

Hugh knew better than to say one word of challenge to Petunia's spirit guides. The woman fancied herself some kind of witch or Druid or some such irrational nonsense. When Granddad had been alive, he'd kept Petunia in check. But after Granddad died, she'd come out, so to speak, telling the vicar that she was the lead witch in a Wiccan coven. That had not gone over very well in the village.

People had expected him to put Petunia in her place.

But how could he? He was only fourteen, and he loved Petunia. She had been the only real mother figure he'd known.

"So did your spirits give you any idea of how to get me out of my current predicament?" he asked. He didn't really believe in her spirit guides, but out of kindness, he humored her.

"No. You know it doesn't work that way. If you're in trouble, it's because you need to learn something. Tell me, what precisely is the matter?"

He took a deep breath. He would have to tell her

something or she would nag him to death. So he gave her an abridged version of the truth that included Elbert Rhodes and his angels, and Cissy Warren and her billions. He mentioned Caroline and her difficult situation, but omitted the bit about the swampland he had unwittingly purchased, as well as his moment of weakness when he'd kissed the dishy Miss Rhodes down by the river.

"Oh, dear, it is a muddle, isn't it? Just like an Oscar Wilde play," Petunia said when he was done.

"No, it isn't."

Petunia ignored his petulance and cut right to the chase. "So this Cissy person, you say she is wealthy?"

"Yes, very. Richer than Lady Ashton and not nearly as horsey."

"Well, that *is* something, isn't it?" Petunia paused for a long moment. It was, in every respect, a pregnant pause. Hugh tried to read this little hesitation and failed utterly. He wasn't sure whether Petunia was suggesting he should pursue the cool and rich Cissy Warren, come home and marry Victoria, or continue on with his quest to build a loom factory.

"Yes, I suppose it is," he said into the silence.

"And this Caroline? She sounds a sensible sort of girl, doesn't she?" Petunia countered unexpectedly.

There was no mistaking the tone in Petunia's voice. She had entered the nosy zone. He said nothing. He wouldn't give up anything about Caroline or the way she looked like some otherworldly goddess and tasted like something from the land of fairies.

"And haven't you put the poor girl in a bit of a situation?" Petunia said into the silence. Hugh heard the censure in Petunia's voice. She had lived with Granddad and knew all about his dalliances, too.

"I reckon I have," he said.

"Hugh, dear, you need to be careful."

As if he hadn't already figured that out.

CHAPTER 13

Caroline uttered a filthy swear word as she hobbled up the walkway to Christ Church. Two hundred bucks she'd shelled out for these gently used Christian Louboutin numbers in an auction on eBay, and the heel on the left shoe hadn't lasted the short walk from Momma's house.

So much for her plan to appear strong, professional, and well put together for the confrontation she intended to have with Baron Woolham after services.

Caroline was angry at more than the shoe. She was furious with herself. Nothing rankled more than making a stupid mistake. She should have investigated Hugh's financial situation before even embarking on this mission for Senator Warren. She had made an assumption, and she knew good and well that making assumptions was stupid.

Almost as stupid as allowing his Lordship to kiss her yesterday.

What had she been thinking?

Not anything rational, that was for sure.

Muffled organ music drifted on the warm summer wind when she finally pushed through the doors and into the vestibule at the back of the sanctuary. The air-conditioning hit her perspiration-damp blouse with the force of a blizzard. Holy smokes, someone had really cranked that thing up, hadn't they?

The place was packed. Momma was there already, having left early to get Haley to Sunday School. She sat in a pew way up at the front with Lizzy beside her. There wasn't any space for Caroline.

Dash was sitting on the other side of the aisle with his aunt. There wasn't any space there either.

A quick scan of the congregation told her that Bubba was missing in action. That was probably good. She wouldn't have to obviously cuddle up to Dash after services.

Rachel was there, sitting with her momma and daddy. She looked tired and hollow-eyed. The trouble at the chicken plant was really taking a toll on her, wasn't it? And the poor thing had had to put up with Bubba last night. Caroline felt bad about leaving Rachel to deal with that problem on her own. No wonder she looked worn out this morning.

Boy, it was a good thing it was Sunday.

Because between the mistakes she'd made and the lies she'd told, Caroline needed all the forgiveness and divine guidance she could get.

Eugene Hanks, standing in the back and looking like the very definition of an usher in his blue suit, handed her the printed program for the day's services. He gestured toward an open seat in the last pew. She took the program and slipped into place.

"Morning." The greeting was whispered into her ear by a deep, masculine voice with an unmistakable accent. His breath simultaneously feathered across her face and torched her insides.

The Right Honorable Hugh deBracy, Baron Woolham, was turned out in his most impeccable tropical weight worsted. All that sartorial excellence made last night's lust suddenly reappear.

Her face flashed red hot despite the subzero setting on the air-conditioning. She snuck a glance at him.

He was sneaking his own glance at her.

Uh-oh. Not good.

His eyes sparked with mischief as he handed her the hymnal, which was turned to the proper page for the first hymn of the morning: "Songs of Praise the Angels Sing."

Oh, the irony. Clearly Hugh was enjoying the joke, judging by the semismirk on his lips. Caroline was not amused—at him or herself. She needed to get a grip on her hormones.

She took her side of the book and stood ramrod straight, looking ahead. They stood side by side, shoulders almost touching. She glanced down at the book and couldn't keep her eyes off his long-fingered hands.

They were well shaped and sexy as hell.

But wait a minute, they didn't look very aristocratic. His nails were cut to the quick, and his right thumbnail bore an unmistakable blood blister right in the middle, as if he'd banged it with a hammer or mashed it in something. That little imperfection was almost perfect. It made his hands look well used and competent.

Caroline battled an untimely case of dry mouth just as the organ music swelled and the time came to sing.

Songs of praise the angels sang,
heaven with alleluias rang…

The congregation broke into song. And Hugh sang along with them in the most amazing baritone. He didn't swallow up the words either, but sang them out beautifully as if he was completely familiar with them. Which, on reflection, shouldn't have surprised her. He was English, which probably made him an Anglican. And Anglicans were practically like Episcopalians. He certainly knew this hymn, that was for sure.

The hymn ended, and Reverend Ellis said the collect, and finally everyone was allowed to sit. The pews at Christ Church were not built for comfort, but this morning, Caroline's discomfort had nothing to do with the hard oak under her backside.

Hugh deBracy sat slightly too close. His leg pressed against her skirt, and his shoulders took up too much space. He smelled good enough to eat, and as usual, Caroline had skipped breakfast and was ravenously hungry.

Reverend Ellis began to read the Gospel passage for the day from Mark 12:38–44, where Jesus tells his disciples to beware of the scribes who dress up in long robes and make a pretense of long prayers. Reverend Ellis got to the punch line of the story, where Jesus points out that the poor widow's small gift was larger than the rich man's, and Caroline's empty stomach decided to make a comment. It emitted the deepest, most ferocious, and hugely embarrassing growl ever heard from the back pew at Christ Church. Heads turned. Lillian Bray glowered. Eugene Hanks cleared his throat.

Hugh came to her rescue. Darn him.

He reached into his pocket and pulled out a partially

consumed packet of cheese crackers. He handed her one and took another for himself.

Lillian's glare morphed into something more predatory. As if she had just nosed out a juicy bit of gossip—or perhaps some blasphemous activity—right there in the back pew of Christ Church.

Caroline downed the cracker and then tried to move away from Hugh a little bit. But the edge of the pew gave her limited space, and he kind of inched over in her direction.

She folded her hands in her lap and concentrated on Reverend Ellis, which was no mean feat. The minister was droning on in his aw-shucks manner when suddenly his words crept up on Caroline and bopped her one on the forehead.

"We are all a little bit like those scribes that Jesus warned us about," he said. "We all work hard to keep up appearances. We dress up for church. We exercise for our health but we want to look good, too. We buy the best brands and work hard to make sure our houses show our best sides. Most of us, down deep, are fearful, uncertain, and imperfect."

Uh-oh.

Caroline clasped her hands together and tried to breathe deeply as a strange sensation crept through her. She was fearful and uncertain and imperfect. That's why she wore demure suits and designer shoes and made sure she never made stupid mistakes.

The walls closed in and a strange sense of panic made her shiver. And then, out of the blue, Hugh reached over and took her hand. The touch of his warm and rough fingers settled her right down in a strange and sexy way.

Hugh kept hold of her hand and ran his thumb over her skin, making heat out of the subzero temperature in the church.

She ought to pull away from him before anyone noticed that they were holding hands in church. She was supposed to be pretending to be in love with Dash. And besides, holding hands with him was not exactly in her job description.

Boy, she was in morally ambiguous territory all the way around. She squeezed Hugh's hand. He squeezed back. And the sermon finally ended.

Everyone got up to say the Nicene Creed, and after that everyone had to kneel and pray for a while.

Caroline had a whole lot of things to pray about, most especially the future of Last Chance. She tried, very hard, to ignore the man kneeling next to her.

It was impossible. Her prayers had to include helping him find a source of cash so he could build his factory in some nonswampy location near Last Chance. In fact, Hugh deBracy was the centerpiece of her prayers that morning.

Before she knew it, she and Hugh were standing again, facing each other during the time where everyone greets everyone else. Hugh wished her God's Peace.

She looked up at him, and it almost seemed as if she were seeing him for the first time. He said he came from a small town. He said he understood what it was like to live up to expectations. The gentle and kind gleam in his eye was nothing like the arrogant man he sometimes appeared to be.

He looked deep into her eyes. Not anywhere else, just her eyes, and Caroline knew he saw her. Not just the size of her bust, or the fact that she was a country girl, or anything else. He really saw her.

Boy, that was refreshing.

But it was also a little bit frightening.

Her concentration was completely destroyed after that encounter. She went through communion, the prayer of thanksgiving, and the recessional hymn in a completely dazed and confused state.

Caroline managed to lose Dash about halfway through the fellowship hour. They'd had coffee, and he'd even given her a kiss on the cheek, right there in front of the entire congregation.

His kiss did not put a charge into any of her girl parts, though. It did make her blush, but only because the congregation was eating it up and she hated to think what was going to happen when she let them know it was all an act.

When she disappointed them again.

Dash finally headed off to the men's room, giving her the opportunity to seek out Lord Woolham, who stood across the room, charming Thelma Hanks and Millie Polk. The man really did have a way of disarming people, didn't he?

"Excuse me, I need his Lordship a moment," Caroline said, breaking into his conversation with Thelma and Millie. "Do ya'll mind? I know it's the Lord's day, but I still need to talk a little business."

The two ladies made a quick exit, but not before telling Caroline they expected to see her at the kissing booth later in the day. Caroline promised that she'd stop by. The two ladies tittered as they left.

"You're going to sell kisses?" Hugh said, his eyebrow waggling.

"I didn't say that. I said I was going to go by the booth."

"So I see you and Dash are getting pretty cozy." His eyes sparked, and the electricity flowed right to the tips of her toes. Obviously he knew she was faking it with Dash; after all, she'd kissed him last night.

Idiot.

She gulped down a breath. She really needed to put a stop to this. "Look, Lord Woolham, you can quit flirting now. I know the truth."

He blinked. "The truth? About what?"

She leaned in, speaking in a low whisper. "Cissy told me all about how you're strapped for cash. How you're cruising for a wealthy wife and all that."

He paled. "She told you that?"

"Yes, and you should know that Cissy's private investigators are the best money can buy. I have no doubt she got it right."

His whole body stiffened. "I *am* strapped for financing. But it's not true that I'm, how did you put it, cruising for a wealthy wife."

"No? What about Lady Ashton?"

He blushed. "You know about Victoria?"

"Well, I don't know much about her, just that she's loaded and Cissy said you were practically engaged to marry her."

"Look, Caroline, the truth is that for years everyone has expected me to marry Lady Ashton. And she's quite amenable to the arrangement. But I've always wanted to make a go of it on my own. I want to see my loom revolutionize textiles manufacturing."

He looked away. "But of course, that's a rather selfish goal. And I *do* know my duty. But still, I don't really want Victoria to swoop in and rescue me with her checkbook, although, God knows, that's what your Miriam Randall predicted for me."

Surprise jolted through Caroline. "Miriam gave you a matrimonial prediction? Really?"

"Yes, she did. I can't remember it exactly. Something about a woman giving me a fortune. It sounded precisely like Lady Ashton, and believe me, it didn't make my heart go pitty-pat."

"So you don't love Lady Ashton?"

He turned his gaze on her. "How should I know? I'm fond of her. But I've never really been in love. Have you?"

"No. Can't help you in that department."

"But you have one of Miriam's predictions, too, don't you?"

"Yes, he's going to be the salt of the earth and a regular Joe."

"So I heard. Everyone was thinking Bubba on Saturday morning. But since Dash lassoed you, everyone has changed their minds. Is it always like this in Last Chance?"

"Yup. You should have seen the mayhem that ensued that time all of Clay's ex-girlfriends showed up on the nine-thirty bus from Atlanta after Miriam said they would."

"Her prediction was that specific? Because, quite honestly, it seems to me that a prediction that you will settle down with an average sort of man, and I will settle down with an heiress, is not particularly startling."

A vague sense of disappointment stabbed at her chest. What had she been thinking in church earlier? She and Hugh were not similar at all. They were worlds apart.

"You know," she said, "the fact that you and I come from different worlds is a good reason that we should avoid any repeats of what happened yesterday on the pier. I'm not an heiress, and besides that slip was very unprofessional on my part."

He frowned. "You really *do* believe Miriam Randall's predictions are ironclad, don't you? How completely remarkable. You know, I'm rather a skeptic about fortune-tellers."

"And not angels?"

His eyebrow arched. "Just because I asked to speak with your father's angels does not mean I actually believe they are out there. I was humoring him."

"Right. I figured that out. But you should know that Miriam's predictions always come true." She straightened her shoulders in irritation.

"Well, your problems would be solved if I went home and married Victoria, wouldn't they? That would certainly keep your father's land safe."

"No, please don't misunderstand. The fact is, Lord Woolham, that I need to find a way to get that factory built, right here in Allenberg County."

"Oh, that's rather a change, isn't it? I thought you wanted me to build elsewhere."

"I did, but that was before I discovered that Last Chance's main employer may be in trouble."

"I see. Well, the truth is, unless I can build on your father's land, or Jimmy Marshall buys back his swampland, I *will* have to return to England and marry Victoria."

"Is it that bad?"

"I'm afraid it's worse than bad. You see, my business partner was dishonest with me. He had fewer resources than I believed. And then he made this spectacularly bad investment here in the States and promptly disappeared in a small plane somewhere near Rio."

"Holy smokes. Are you saying he stole the money?"

"Well, no. There is, after all, a record of the land sale where the price is listed, and the plane officially disappeared. But it's all rather dodgy, isn't it?"

"Wow. Jimmy could have given him a kickback."

He shrugged. "You have no proof of that. However, I do believe that someone swindled me. I just cannot believe that George was the kind of trainspotter who would unwittingly buy swampland for a factory."

"Train what?"

"Trainspotter. It means crazy. And George wasn't crazy, or stupid. He was rather smooth. He could well have been a con man."

"This keeps getting worse by the minute. Why didn't you tell me the truth?" She turned around and sank into a hard metal folding chair. Hugh sat down beside her.

"Because I didn't realize the dimensions of the problem until the last few days. You, dear Caroline, have been the bearer of much discouraging news, I'm afraid."

"I wonder if Hettie knows her husband is a crook?" Caroline looked across the room to where Hettie was talking with the minister.

Caroline would have to talk with Hettie. The fallout might be nasty, so she decided she would do it on her own and keep her mouth shut so the gossips of Last Chance didn't have a field day.

Poor Hettie. She was in for a shock.

"So what's next then?" Hugh asked.

"I'm not sure," Caroline said. "Tomorrow, I'll call the state and see if there might be some development funds available. But short of that, I'm stumped. And more than that, I'm worried."

She nodded to the people in the fellowship hall. "Probably a quarter of this congregation works at Country Pride Chicken. The plant is in trouble. I think Jimmy jacked up the price on your land because he needed cash. Your partner may have seen that as an opportunity. So his problem became your problem. And now it's everyone's problem."

"I see. Well, the senator told me you could work miracles."

"You know, Hugh, if you were smart, you would ask Lady Ashton for money. Or barring that, you might take Cissy up on her offer and drive up to Columbia and spend some time with her. When I spoke with her yesterday, she seemed very interested in your loom technology. It makes sense that she might want to invest in it."

"She'd want something exclusive. That would tie my hands and probably take the factory away from Last Chance."

Caroline let go of a big breath. "Yes, it would. But it may be the only way out for you. You would be crazy not to pursue it. You don't owe these people anything. I'm the one who loves them."

"You love them?" His voice sounded warm.

"Yeah. They're weird and crazy and definitely country through and through, but I have this soft place in my heart for them. And for the town, if you must know. If we lose the chicken plant, Last Chance will die like a lot of other American small towns."

Before Caroline could continue, Lillian Bray interrupted. "Oh, Lord Woolham," she cried, waving her hand as she came across the room, her tent dress flowing in her wake, "I'm so glad you joined us this morning. I have a huge, huge favor to ask."

Caroline watched as Hugh stood up and put on his peer-of-the-realm mask. The transformation was subtle but unmistakable. He stood up straighter, he clasped his hands behind his back, and his mouth turned down just a little.

And of course, his eyebrow arched.

"How can I be of service, Lillian," he said, not fumbling for her name or missing a beat.

"Well, you see, I just convinced Dale Pontius that it would be a huge mistake not to invite you to come judge the pie contest. You do like pie, don't you, your grace?"

Hugh's mouth twitched ever so slightly, and Caroline almost laughed out loud. Lillian amused him in some way. That little twitch of his mouth made him all the more adorable. He didn't have to be so nice.

But he was. Even when he was playacting at being a stereotype.

"I do like pie," he said in his oh-so-perfect accent. "I'm particularly partial to berry pies, if you must know."

"Oh, we have all kinds. And I'm sure Jenny Carpenter made one of her peach pies, too, darn her hide."

"Is peach pie a problem?"

"Oh, no, it's just that Jenny has a small grove of her own peaches right there on her daddy's land. Her peach pies win every year."

Hugh's eyes sparkled. "Do they?"

"Yes, as a matter of fact." Lillian glanced over toward Reverend Ellis. She looked worried. "There are people in this county who lust after Jenny's pies, and I take a dim view of lust."

The corners of Hugh's mouth turned up, but he didn't laugh or blush or anything like that. He wasn't laughing at Lillian. It was like his reaction to Golfing for God, when he'd said that the golf course was charming.

"I'm sure I can be an impartial judge, Lillian, even if I am partial to peach pie." Hugh's gaze turned toward Caroline and practically burned a hole right in her middle. "To be honest, I'm partial to quite a few things here in Last Chance."

"Momma, I don't have time right now. I'm behind on my e-mail, and I have to meet Rachel at three, and—"

"Honestly, Rocky, it's Sunday. Take a break." Momma pulled her Ford van into the parking lot behind the Cut 'n Curl. Caroline had accepted Momma's offer of a ride, because of her broken shoe. She'd finally given up trying to wear it and found herself barefoot again.

"This won't take a minute," Momma said. "C'mon."

"You want me to come in? But my shoe."

"Yes. I do. I need your help with something inside."

Caroline opened the passenger door and minced her way across the parking lot on her bare feet. Her soles were toughening up. Any more shoe disasters and she'd be back in full country-girl form.

She followed Momma into the beauty shop and stopped dead in her tracks. Jane, wearing a flowered sundress, was waiting for her. Jane had no problems displaying her cleavage.

"We've declared a fashion emergency," Jane announced.

"Uh, wait. What?"

Momma blocked the door. "Rocky, you are going to help sell kisses at the kissing booth today. And you're not going to do it wearing a charcoal gray suit and a white silk blouse. For one thing, you'll cook out there at the fairground. And for another—well—those clothes are drab, and if you keep wearing things like that, you'll never…"

"What Ruby is trying to say," Jane said when Ruby's voice faded out, "is that if you want to catch Dash Randall, you'll have to put a little color in your wardrobe. You know what they say about honey and vinegar."

"Uh, wait, I'm not trying to catch Dash Randall. And I'm not selling kisses. That would be real tacky, Momma, and I—"

"We need your help. We don't have many single girls to do this. Rachel's helping."

"She is? Really?"

"Well, maybe not entirely willingly, but her momma laid down the law, and besides, that girl needs to build a little confidence, and selling kisses is sure to help her out."

"But I can't. It would be embarrassing to sell kisses. And I've already been in too many embarrassing situations over the last couple of days. I'm here on business, Momma, not to help out at any kissing booth."

"It's Sunday. You can take a day off from your business and help out with the cause. I'm sure your daddy would appreciate any help you could give," Momma said.

Boy, Momma had just brought out the big artillery, hadn't she?

"Momma, please, I—"

"And besides, we've fixed it so Dash is going to buy most of your kisses anyway," Jane said. "I think it's kind of cute, you know?"

Caroline stared at her sister-in-law in stark panic.

"You're kidding, right?"

"No," Momma and Jane said in unison, and then they both kind of giggled.

Oh, brother. This was her worst nightmare.

She looked at Jane and Momma and thought about telling them the truth about Dash. She wanted to unburden herself. After all, Dash had kind of tricked her into this charade.

But on the other hand, if she told them that she and Dash were just faking it in order to send a message to Bubba, she would be in trouble. Momma always expected her children to be honest. And besides, telling the truth might have no impact on the situation, given Miriam's prediction. The church ladies loved matchmaking. They were probably not going to let go of this idea that Caroline and Dash were a match made in Heaven.

Jane headed into the storage room and came back with a garment bag. She unzipped it, and there in all its pink and green glory was a little seersucker sundress with appliquéd watermelons on the skirt.

It was girlishly cute. This was not the sort of thing a senator's aide wore in public.

"You want me to wear that?" Caroline asked, her voice cracking in alarm.

"I'm sure Dash will like it," Momma said.

Probably not. She had a feeling Dash liked his woman wearing something a little more mature.

But she was stuck. She was going to have to put on that dress and go kiss Dash, or run the risk of infuriating her mother and undoing any progress Bubba might have made as a result of the Lasso Fiasco.

CHAPTER 14

It was stifling in the Exhibit Hall that afternoon when Caroline, Jane, and Momma finally arrived for the big kiss-off. Apparently the Committee to Resurrect Golfing for God had photocopied a whole bunch of handbills advertising the fact that the single girls of Allenberg County would be selling their kisses between 3:00 and 5:00 p.m. The handbill made it clear that anyone with a deep enough pocket could participate in the kiss auction at the beginning of the event.

In the hours between church and the kiss-off, Jane and Momma had polished Caroline's nails, given her a pedicure, trimmed and coiffed her hair, and let out the top of that stupid watermelon sundress.

Rachel was waiting for them at the kissing booth by the time they all arrived. She was wearing her own little pink and green dress and looked way cuter than Caroline, in a deeply tanned, beautifully straight-haired, and uneasy way.

Caroline took a seat next to her friend at a long table

where six other young ladies were sitting. Most of these women were college kids, the daughters of members of the Committee to Resurrect Golfing for God. "I was sandbagged and hoodwinked and all but roped into doing this. What's your excuse?"

Rachel managed a little smile. "I, quote, volunteered, unquote, after Momma twisted my arm. I'm sorry I didn't give you fair warning. But I reckon it's okay because Dash is going to buy up all your kisses. You better be prepared to give everyone a real big show on the first one, though."

Caroline had already figured out that she was going to have to tongue kiss Dash Randall—in public. Just thinking about it made Caroline's throat close up right to her tonsils.

She scanned the growing crowd, made up mostly of younger, college-aged men. "This is unseemly, you know. I think I'd rather be the victim in one of those dunking machines."

"You don't mean that. Just think about it for a minute. If you get dunked in one of those machines, you end up in a wet T-shirt," Rachel said.

"Oh. Yeah. I forgot. Maybe this is better. Not much better, but better."

"Quit whining. I'm sure those young guys are not here to kiss an old maid like me. And I don't have someone like Dash in the wings to buy up my kisses. I'm going to get all the frogs. I'm hoping one of them will turn into Prince Charming. At least that was what Momma said when she was twisting my arm."

Caroline scanned the crowd. "Well, you could always hope." And then she saw him, a head taller than most of the other men and wearing another one of his Cutter & Buck golf shirts. Hugh deBracy did not fit in with this crowd. An ordinary man he was not.

But one glance at him and Caroline's hormones started waltzing.

"What's *he* doing here?" Rachel asked, nodding toward his Lordship.

"Maybe he fancies you."

Rachel started laughing and then stopped abruptly. "He's with Bubba. Oh, bless his heart, his face is a mess."

Bubba looked a little better today. The splint was off his nose and his shiners were fading from dark blue to various shades of green and yellow. His lip still looked puffy. And the stitches were pretty obvious.

"I don't think he's going to be doing much kissing," Caroline said. "But what in the Sam Hill is he doing with Hugh?"

Rachel blinked. "You don't know?"

"Uh, no. Is there something I should know?"

"Last night, Lord Woolham apologized to Bubba and then offered to help him with his derby car on account of the fact that Bubba is really ticked off at Dash over the lasso incident, not to mention the way the two of you were dancing last night. I'm a little worried that Bubba is not going to be happy with Dash buying up all your kisses."

"Hugh helped him with his derby car? Really?"

"Yeah, I heard he's a real good mechanic. And since when are you calling him Hugh?"

Caroline's face got hot as she flashed on an image of that tiny blood blister under Hugh's thumbnail. Maybe he'd gotten it last night working on Bubba's car. That blister made him seem so normal and ordinary. Like the kind of man she could actually call by first name.

Boy, she really needed to watch herself. She needed to remember that Hugh was practically engaged to an heiress named Lady Ashton.

Just then, Hettie Marshall clapped her hands and assumed her position as the mistress of ceremonies. "All right, ya'll," she said. "Welcome to the first annual kiss-off. I want to thank the single girls of Last Chance for volunteering their puckers." Whistles and catcalls greeted this announcement.

Caroline leaned toward Rachel. "And we went to college for this."

"Hush, Rocky, I'm almost looking forward to this."

"You are? Really?"

She shrugged. "It's better than worrying about the chicken plant."

Hettie continued with her discussion of the rules. "It's five dollars a kiss," she said. "So if you want to buy up the attention of any of these young ladies for the next two hours, you'll have to spend at least two hundred dollars."

A number of college-age boys looked disappointed by this news.

Hettie did not let their disappointment deter her. "We will begin the auction shortly, but before we do, I have to warn you that, just because you've bought a young lady's attention does not mean you can manhandle her. If any of ya'll start any funny business, you'll have to answer to me. And Stone, of course."

Hettie nodded toward the Last Chance chief of police, who stood to one side, arms across his chest, a Stetson on his head and a real badass expression on his face.

Caroline wanted to duck under the table and hide until it was over. Nothing good was going to happen here. She could feel it in her bones.

Hettie opened the bidding. Not too surprisingly, Bubba's hand immediately shot up. "I'll bid two hundred and five dollars on Rocky."

Caroline's stomach clutched. The crowd hushed.

"I bid two hundred and five dollars for Rachel," Hugh said. A little smile on his face.

Huh? Where the hell did that come from? Everyone turned and stared at him. He smiled back. "What?" he said aloud. "She's dishy."

"Dishy?" Drew Polk, Rachel's younger brother, asked.

"Well, I think you chaps would say she's hot. Either way, she's a very beautiful woman."

Rachel beamed at Hugh.

Oh, great. Caroline didn't want to think about the fallout when Rachel discovered that Hugh was about to go back to the UK and marry Lady Whatshername's checkbook. The last time Rachel broke up with someone was three years ago. Her split with Justin had been legendary. Six years that jerk led her on and then finally told her he needed some space.

And Rachel was the marrying kind. She'd been so devastated she'd given up her job in Columbia and come running home to her momma. Where she'd been ever since.

Maybe this whole kissing thing would be okay for Rachel. Although Caroline didn't really like the idea of Rachel kissing Lord Woolham.

"I'll bid two hundred and ten for Rachel." This came from Dash.

What the hell?

"I'll raise you ten," Hugh said.

"I'll bid two-ten for Jessie Cooper." This came from Roy Burdett, who was a married man and old enough to be Jessie's father.

Hettie scowled at him. "Roy, you'll do no such thing."

"But—"

Hettie gave him the evil eye, and Roy shut his trap.

"Put me in for two-fifty for the lovely Ms. Polk," Dash said.

A murmur went through the crowd. Caroline's face started to burn. God was punishing her. No question about it.

"In that case, I'll bid two-ten for Rocky," Hugh said.

Caroline turned and stared at him. He looked deadly serious standing there, like a cardsharp with an addiction for gambling. And he'd called her Rocky. The sound of her name seemed to awaken her girl parts.

"You can't do that. You're bidding on Rachel." Bubba turned around and glared at Hugh.

"I most certainly can, old boy. And besides it's for a good cause."

"You're just jacking up the price, aren't you?" Bubba grumbled.

"I might be."

Bubba turned back to Hettie. "I'll bid two-fifteen for Rocky."

"Well, I'll just put an end to this competition and bid five hundred for the lovely Miss Rocky Rhodes," Hugh said, and somehow hearing her name in his accent was okay. Her name didn't sound like a joke when he said it. It sounded sexy as all get-out.

"Hey, you can't do that," Bubba whined.

"Of course I can. It's an auction. Get in there and bid. If you can't afford Rocky, there are at least half a dozen other lovely young ladies available. Although given what you told me last night about Rachel, I'd say this was your golden opportunity. And besides, remember what I said about reverse psychology."

Bubba nodded. "Oh, yeah, I forgot about that." Bubba looked up. "I'll bid two-fifty-five on Rachel."

The crowed ooohed and aaahed.

Caroline clutched Rachel's arm. "Oh, God. I'm so sorry."

"It's okay. Better I should kiss Bubba than we should have to endure another episode in the Rocky and Bubba Show."

"You'd do that for me?"

"Honey, Bubba's okay. He's handsome and skilled at his job."

"Of course, the missing front teeth are kind of a problem."

"Those can be fixed."

The bidding on Jessie Cooper heated up. Randy Kent finally went over the top with his bid of three hundred dollars.

The bidding seemed to be at its end, with only Rachel, Rocky, and Jessie going up for auction. Finally, Hettie turned toward Dash. "We're waiting, Dash. You aren't going to let his Lordship get away with Rocky now, are you?"

Dash shrugged. "You know, Hettie, I've got this feeling that no matter what I bid, his Lordship is going to raise it. I could jack up the price a little bit, but that would probably demoralize Bubba. So I figure maybe the best thing all around is to snooker the outsider into giving us five hundred dollars cash money for the resurrection of the very thing he's trying to destroy. I'd say that was a good afternoon's work."

He smiled his cowboy smile at Hettie and then turned toward Caroline. "I'm sure you know how to handle a dude like this if he gets uppity, don't you?" Dash asked.

Hettie laughed out loud, and Caroline figured it may have been the first time she'd ever heard the Queen Bee of Last Chance laugh like that.

"Dash Randall, you have a devious mind," Hettie said. She turned back toward the assembled crowd. "Do I hear any more bids? I believe Bubba has bid two hundred and fifty-five dollars for Rachel, and his Lordship has bid five hundred for Rocky, and Randy has bid three hundred for Jessie. Going once, twice, all right then.

"Come on down here, gentlemen, and make your payments. We accept checks and credit cards. In the meantime, the rest of ya'll can line up. All kisses are five dollars."

It took a few moments for the transactions to be completed, but the crowd was waiting in anticipation.

"Kiss, kiss, kiss, kiss, kiss," the chant went up.

Oh great, Caroline was never going to live this one down. What was it about the Watermelon Festival anyway? It was guaranteed to cause one embarrassing moment after another.

Randy Kent, who was the son of one of Allenberg's contractors, pulled Jessie up from her seat, took her into his young, ripped arms, and kissed the dickens out of her. It was a good thing Doc Cooper wasn't there to see that boy give his daughter's backside the tiniest of squeezes.

"That's enough, Randy," Hettie said. Randy pulled away, and Jessie looked a little thunderstruck. He took her by the hand, and they walked away, heading in the direction of the Tilt-A-Whirl. Randy and Jessie were both juniors at Clemson. There was already talk about a wedding next June after graduation.

Ah, young love.

Now it was Bubba's turn. He came over to where Caroline and Rachel were sitting. He gave Caroline a look that started out moony and then transformed into something else—a studied disregard. He turned toward Rachel and ducked his head in a bashful sort of way. He swallowed hard, like he was really nervous.

"Hey, Rachel," he said. "I don't think I can kiss too good."

And Rachel, bless her heart, came to Bubba's rescue. She stood up, looking as cute as a button in her girlish sundress, and took Bubba by the shoulders. She laid a big sloppy wet one right on the uninjured corner of his mouth.

The crowd went wild.

Bubba blushed. Rachel took him by the arm and half dragged him off in the direction of the fun house.

Wow! Maybe Dash had consulted with Rachel on the whole help-Bubba-move-on-with-his-life plan.

The crowd was hooting and hollering as Caroline turned back and looked right into the smoldering eyes of his Lordship, who was patiently awaiting his turn.

"May I?" he asked, just like a man asking for a dance.

He leaned in, and he captured her mouth in a tender and half-chaste kiss that rapidly morphed into a raging inferno.

His lips devoured, his tongue plundered, his arms captured her around her middle and pulled her up into his chest so that her bosom had no place else to go. Then he bent her backward in one of those clenches that were always prominently featured on the cover of romance books.

The Watermelon Festival faded into the background. The cheers and catcalls of the audience were drowned out by the roaring in Caroline's ears. He tasted like every sweet, forbidden thing she'd ever eaten. She wanted to devour him, and damn the calories.

Something—probably the sound of her brother's voice saying, "That's enough now"—broke the spell. She pushed back. Hugh made sure she was semisteady on her feet before he let her go.

"Dash," Hettie said as Hugh withdrew, "I think you may have seriously miscalculated."

Caroline blinked a few times, taking in the suddenly quiet crowd, the stern look on Stone's face, the open mouths of Millie Polk and Thelma Hanks, and the perpetual twinkle in Miriam Randall's eye.

"I'm not worried," Dash said. "I figure his Lordship is about as far from a regular guy who works with his hands as a man can get." He glanced at his aunt. "And I have complete faith in Aunt Mim."

Rachel squinted in the semidarkness trying to read Bubba's battered features. It was impossible. The lighting in the fun house was supposed to be dark and murky. There were couples stashed in several corners.

"Gee, Rachel, you're really taking this whole kiss-off thing to heart, aren't you?" Bubba said in a husky voice.

Yes, she was. The fun house was the perfect place to indulge the fantasy of a lifetime. She'd been wanting to kiss Bubba Lockheart since she was fourteen. But of course, Bubba was sweet on Rocky, and Rocky was her best friend so she'd stayed away.

And after Rocky dumped Bubba, there had never been a moment like this one, where Bubba had been interested in kissing anyone else.

She pressed her lips gently to the corner of his mouth one more time, then she let her hands roam through his spiky hair and touch the texture of his beard and squeeze his totally ripped biceps.

He was a god among men.

He let go of a little groan and then, to her utter astonishment, Bubba reversed their directions and kind of pressed her up against the wall.

His mouth didn't seem to be all that damaged, it turned out. And time kind of ran away with them.

"Uh, Rachel," Bubba finally said against her cheek.

"Uh-huh."

"Why are you kissing me like this? Is it only because I bought them?" He sounded a little forlorn.

"Um. Well." Her voice stuck in her throat.

"It is, isn't it?"

"No." She said the word so fast she didn't even think about it before it left her lips. She pulled back so she could look at him. In the black light, his T-shirt glowed purple, but his face was dark. "No, Bubba, it's not because you bought them."

"But that's just weird. I mean, you and me together. We're not exactly made for each other, you know?"

"Why do you say that?"

He shrugged. "Your daddy is a banker and you finished college, and I'm just a mechanic."

"Yeah, but you're the best mechanic in the county. And Daddy says that a good mechanic is worth his weight in gold."

Bubba chuckled. "Well, you tell him thanks when you see him."

"Anyways, you went to college, Bubba."

"I flunked out. Besides I only went to college so I could play football. And you know..."

"Yeah. You shouldn't have let Rocky break your heart like that."

His shoulders tensed. "You know, it really wasn't like that," he said.

"What wasn't like what?"

"I mean folks always say that I flunked out of college because of what Rocky did, but that's not what really happened."

"What happened?"

"I partied. I messed up. I'm not real smart, and I wasn't really big enough to be first string up in Clemson. I mean, I got up there and I hated it. I just wanted to come home and be me, you know?"

She laughed. "Yeah, I know. I felt the same way when I was living in Columbia. Everyone thinks it was my breakup with Justin that sent me home. But the truth is, I told Justin I wanted to go home before we broke up. I didn't like living in the city."

"You didn't?"

"Nope. I like living here, where everyone knows me."

"Yeah, me, too."

He pushed away from the wall where they'd been

leaning. "You know it's kind of dark in here for a conversation. You want to go get some funnel cakes?"

"Yeah, sure."

Bubba took her by the hand and half dragged her out of the dark. They stumbled through the rotating drum at the end of the fun house and back out into the light of day.

They blinked at each other in the late afternoon sunshine. He looked battered but handsome, and somehow not nearly as unapproachable as he'd been an hour ago. She smiled at him, and he smiled right back, gap-toothed and all.

The funnel cake stand was way down the curving midway, and Bubba took a shortcut to the left and down a row of trees along the stock pens and exhibition area. They got about halfway there before they encountered a few men in cowboy hats watching a group of 4-H foals.

The men were talking and laughing together, and their voices carried on the wind, along with the unmistakable scent of barn animals.

"I swear, Allen," one of the men said, "she lit into me with every four-letter word in the book until I explained that the whole lasso scenario was merely a ruse to get Bubba to rethink his life."

Bubba stopped in his tracks and stared at the men across the small patch of scraggly summer grass that separated him from them. Rachel recognized the voice, and the men. It was Dash Randall with the Canaday twins.

"C'mon, Bubba, let's go." Rachel tugged at his hand. He didn't budge.

"You don't want to get into another fight. Not with Dash," Rachel pleaded.

Bubba stalked up to Dash, who suddenly realized that

his words had been overheard. "You lassoed Rocky off that float because you wanted me to move on with my life?" he asked.

"Uh, well, see, Bubba, it's not so simple." Dash looked just like a little kid who'd gotten caught sneaking his daddy's cigarettes.

"Yeah, so, explain?"

"Well, it's just that Rocky said that you needed something really big to rattle your cage, and I just figured that with Aunt Mim's forecast for her and all, that if I lassoed her, well...Shoot, Bubba, you know how this town is. They gossip about everything."

Bubba frowned, and Rachel knew things were going to get out of hand. "C'mon, Bubba, how about some funnel cake?"

Bubba ignored her. "Yeah, I know all about this town. And it seems to me you just let that fancy English dude pay five hundred dollars for Rocky, and you didn't do a damn thing to stop him. How you think folks are going to take that?"

"Well, I don't know. I reckon there will be talk. Bubba, there's always talk."

"Yeah, I know. And it's always wrong." Bubba pulled on the brim of his ball cap and stalked away, heading in the opposite direction of the funnel cake stand.

A lump the size of a pecan lodged in Rachel's throat. "Rocky had no idea you were going to lasso her, did she?" she said to Dash. "And she had no idea you were going to let that Englishman buy her."

Dash shrugged. "Nope, I reckon not. But Rocky's tough. She can take care of herself."

"Right. You're a jerk, Dash Randall, you know that?"

And Rachel stalked off heading for the funnel cake stand. Maybe a big, heaping plate of the stuff would be enough to fill the suddenly gaping hole in her heart.

Caroline sat in one of the Ferris wheel chairs grabbing the safety bar with all her might as the wheel moved back and upward one place and then rocked in the summer air.

"Don't tell me you're afraid of heights," Hugh said.

She gave him a wild stare. He was going to seek payment for every one of those kisses he'd bought. And what better place for kissing than the Ferris wheel. The setup was corny and classic, and she had a horrible feeling she knew how it would end.

She looked down. It wasn't that far to fall...yet.

"Uh, no, not really afraid of heights. I..." Her voice pinched with her confusion. "Look, I'm just not sure this is a good idea."

He looked around at the structure of the ride. "I don't see any obvious structural defects."

She laughed in spite of herself. He was being adorable. "That's not what I meant, and you know it. I was told that Dash had arranged to buy up my kisses. You weren't supposed to bid for them at all. And you weren't supposed to kiss me like that in front of everyone either. People don't like to be surprised. Surprised people talk, and this time the gossip is going to be vicious. I'm so tired of being the talk of the town."

The car lurched back, then the wheel stopped again as they loaded more passengers. The drop was getting bigger all the time. A girl could fall and get hurt. Bad.

"I know you're tired of the gossip. But what's done is done. Let's...enjoy the magic of the moment." He pulled her away from the safety bar and snuggled her right beside him, resting his arm along her shoulders. His warm hand found the skin of her upper arm.

Her pulse surged.

"You're an engineer. You don't believe in magic."

"Did I ever say that?"

"You said you were a skeptic this morning."

"Oh, that was about fortune-tellers. And you have to admit that most fortune-tellers are charlatans. Just because I'm skeptical of people like that doesn't mean I don't believe in magic. I'm a man who has been known to live in a fantasy world at times. And look around you, all those twinkling lights, the barkers on the midway, the smell of the sweet cakes. This is not the real world, Caroline. This is a world laden with summer magic."

"Wow, for an engineer you have a way with words."

"Look, darling, just for this afternoon, can't we leave the real world aside? Ride this Ferris wheel and see what happens next?"

"I told you this morning at church that we needed to make sure nothing happened."

"Because Miriam Randall says we're wrong for one another?"

"No, that's not the only reason. Getting involved with you isn't a good idea. I have a conflict of interest."

"Because of your father?"

"Among other things."

"Well, we both know I'm not going to build my factory on that land George bought. So let's dispense with that excuse, shall we?" He pulled her closer still and slanted another kiss across her lips. She didn't stop him. She was powerless to stop him. She loved every minute of kissing him. He was amazing and warm and charming and sweet, and tasted like...Well, something so sinful it was better than a jelly-filled doughnut.

The car rocked backward, but this time it didn't stop. She went weightless, but whether from the kiss or the ride, she didn't know. She tilted her head back and looked up at the deep, endless blue of the afternoon sky. And started to laugh.

And Hugh laughed with her. She snuggled a little closer. Her curves fit perfectly against the hard planes of his chest. She rested her head on his shoulder.

She should let go of her worries and her plans—just for a moment. This was the Watermelon Festival. Once, a long time ago, she hadn't worried about things like gossip or careers or land deals or economic recovery. Once, she'd just been a kid, drawn by the lights and sweet food and the thrill of it all.

She and Hugh rode the Ferris wheel five times, and by the time they finally gave it up, Caroline was light-headed and breathless from the fun and the kisses and the promise of more.

They made their way down the midway. Hugh excelled at games of skill, winning her a plush tiger that was as ugly as it was huge.

He made her eat funnel cake and a corn dog. They drank lemonade and ate peach cobbler. They spent a long time in the fun house in one of the dark corners doing something that Hugh called "snogging."

And when dusk finally came, they headed to the dance pavilion, where she taught him how to do the boot scoot and the two-step. He was real good at two-stepping. He said it was a lot like the fox trot, which reminded her that he was a fantasy. No good ol' boy, salt of the earth, regular Joe knew how to dance the fox trot.

By the time the band struck up a waltz, she was ready for it. He took her into his arms and moved her across the dance floor like Prince Charming.

She wanted to fall in love with him, just like Cinderella. But she wasn't going to. She was way too smart to fall for the twinkly lights and the midsummer magic.

He must have known what she was thinking because he stopped dancing and put his mouth over hers again, knowing good and well that she stopped thinking when he kissed her. Her whole body wanted more than these kisses. Her body felt taut with pent-up sexual need. All this kissing and not a lot of touching had left her breathless with want.

He broke the kiss and linked a string of little nips across her cheek to her ear. "We need to get out of here," he said.

She pushed back and looked up at him. His eyes were darker than normal. His lips looked soft. His hair was a complete mess of curls. She wanted him.

Sharon's words came back to her. *You don't run off with some man unless you can't live without him.*

She could live without Hugh deBracy. In fact, she was very good at living without men in her life. She loved her job. She liked her life. She wasn't looking for a fling. She wasn't even looking for love, except in the pages of a romance novel.

He held her closer and whispered in her ear, "You want this as much as I do." She laid her head on his shoulder.

"You do," he insisted.

She took his hand and led him from the dance floor.

She stopped to put on her shoes and pick up the big ugly tiger that he'd won for her. Then she headed toward the exit and back out onto the midway, where the food vendors and games of chance were closing up for the night.

She turned toward him. "We can't," she said.

"We can't what?"

"Go to the Peach Blossom Motor Court."

"The place that sells the rooms by the hour?"

"The very same."

"Why not?"

"For one thing, Lillian Bray keeps a telescope trained on the parking lot at the Peach Blossom. For another, my brother patrols over there. And for a third, it would be a big mistake."

She leaned into him, wrapping her arms around his middle and resting her head on his chest. She could hear his heart beating.

"I want to go there," he said, his voice rumbling in her ear.

"I know," she replied, letting herself get a fraction closer. "But we can't."

"Why ever not?"

"Because you're you and I'm me." She pulled back and looked him straight in the eye. "It's a wonderful fantasy, but it's not real. It's just watermelon magic. You know? And tonight, because we're both sober, we should act soberly. You know as well as I do that we would regret it in the morning." Her voice sounded thick. It cost her dearly to say those words.

He didn't say anything for the longest time. But his eyes, which she had once thought were cool and remote, didn't look anything like that as he gazed down at her. "Can I take you home?" he asked.

She shook her head. "No, I've got my brother's truck. I'm okay."

She didn't want to risk any further contact with him. If she let him walk her to the truck, she might succumb to that look in his eyes. So she turned and ran away on bare feet.

Thank goodness he didn't follow.

CHAPTER 15

Hugh's mobile phone rang just as he was pulling the hired Mustang up the driveway to Miriam Randall's boardinghouse. He put the car in park, set the brake, and checked the caller ID. With a call arriving at almost two in the morning, it had to be one of the aunts. He couldn't duck either of them without causing them to worry.

And truth be told, he was halfway glad of the call. Hearing from Petunia would remind him that having a dalliance with Rocky Rhodes was something he should be trying to avoid.

He pushed the talk button. "Aunt Petunia?"

"Huey, is that you?" came the querulous voice on the end of the line.

"Petal?"

"Yes, dear. It's me."

"Where's Petunia?"

"Oh, out and about, I guess. I'm not sure."

"Why are you calling, Aunt Petal?"

There was an ominous silence on the other end of the line.

"Petal?"

"Huey, are you all right?"

"I'm fine," he lied. "It's just very late—or early here in America. Aunt Petal, you see there is—"

"Oh, for heaven's sake, Huey, I do know the difference in time between here and there. But I got the very distinct feeling just a little while ago that you were in trouble. And of course, Aeval told me you were in some difficulty."

"Aeval?" His voice broke. In fairy lore, Aeval was supposed to have been a fairy queen reigning in some obscure place in Ireland who held court to judge whether husbands were satisfying their wives. Petal had a four-foot concrete statue of a fairy that she insisted was the resting place of Aeval's ghost. Not too surprisingly, when Petal had been speaking with Aeval, she had the annoying habit of getting the vicar up in arms—the vicar being a man who had probably never satisfied his wife.

Granddad had been the object of Aeval's scorn. And given what Hugh had been up to, it was probably not a surprise that Aeval was in a snit.

Hugh felt an ominous twitch in his middle. He didn't believe in Petal's ghosts. But it was truly uncanny the way Petal seemed to be able to predict divorces in the village. Petal, like Miriam Randall, had a knack for making it all seem logical.

But of course, it wasn't logical. And Petal had probably heard from Petunia that he was having difficulties. So Aeval was not really to blame for this call. Nevertheless, he humored his dotty aunt. There wasn't much else he could do. "What exactly did Aeval tell you?" he asked.

"She told me you were about to make a terrible mistake. She says I need to stop you."

Well, he could rest easy on that score. He'd been a gentleman this evening. He'd avoided the mistake of taking Caroline to a place called the Peach Blossom Motor Court.

"Look, Aunt Petal, I'm fine, really. I've behaved in a gentlemanly fashion in everything I've done here. You don't need to worry about me. Now it's almost two in the morning, and I need to get to bed."

He was unlikely to sleep, but it was a good ruse to get the old girl off the telephone.

"Petunia told me about this woman. This heiress you've met," Petal said.

"Who? Oh you mean Cissy Warren."

"I didn't get her name. Tell me about her."

"She's quite...wealthy," he said, not able really to get much enthusiasm going for Cissy Warren when his whole body was aching for Rocky.

"Well, that's something, I suppose. But—"

"Look, Aunt Petal, it's very late here. And I promise you that I haven't forgotten the family motto. I'll do what's expected of me. You needn't worry about that. Tell Aeval when you next speak with her that I've got things under control here, and I'm likely to be back in the UK in a few days."

"All right, Huey. I will. Good night then."

"Good night, dear."

He rang off the phone and then slumped forward to rest his head on the steering wheel. Petal wasn't in touch with reality. But sometimes he got the feeling her little people were.

• • •

Caroline set the parking brake on Stone's truck and sat in the dark for a long moment. Her heart beat in her chest. She sucked breath in and out. Nothing seemed outwardly different.

But everything had changed.

She'd been forced into the kiss-off contest, but she couldn't say she was sorry for it. If not for that, she would have run away from Hugh and missed all that two-stepping, not to mention the snogging in the fun house.

She wanted more. But she couldn't have it. It was insane to go chasing after a fantasy. And besides, tomorrow morning she'd be paying the piper for what happened today. She was glad she'd bypassed the Peach Blossom Motor Court.

The folks in town wanted a love story, not an erotic encounter that wasn't going to lead to anything but gossip.

Folks in Last Chance just wanted happy endings. And to them, her happy ending would involve some local boy. They didn't care if it was Bubba or Dash. Just so long as it was familiar and had Miriam Randall's blessing.

She sank her head down on the steering wheel as a knot the size of a peach stone clogged her throat. Why couldn't she have a guy like Hugh? Cinderella got Prince Charming, didn't she? Why did she have to settle for the salt of the earth?

Caroline didn't want an ordinary soulmate. She wanted an extraordinary one. She wanted someone who was good enough to run off with the way Sharon and Stone had.

Right now Caroline couldn't think of anyone she had

ever wanted to run off with—until tonight. She had really wanted to go someplace with Hugh.

But she had stopped herself. She'd done the right thing. But it made her feel crappy. But she had a job to do and Miriam's ironclad predictions to guide her.

She opened the car door. It let go of a loud squeal that advertised its ancient state. It broke the quiet of the night.

Caroline tiptoed through the front door and realized that Momma was waiting up for her, just like she'd done when Caroline was a teenager.

"Hey, Momma," she said as she closed the door behind her.

"Honey, I was all prepared to give you a deep down apology for what happened at today's kiss-off. I mean Dash was supposed to buy up your kisses, and I'm furious at him for letting that Englishman get the better of him."

"But?" Caroline added at the end of Momma's speech.

"Honey, that foreigner only bought two hours of your time."

"I know. But he was a real good kisser."

"Oh, honey, no. He's not for you."

"You think I don't know that?" The words came out wobbly, and Caroline turned and headed down the hallway toward her room. She was being so silly about this. Really. She hardly knew the guy, and kisses were not everything in life. And Cinderella was an old, worn-out myth. Really she needed to be patient and wait for her regular guy to arrive.

Momma followed her down the hall. "Honey, everyone's talking about this. You danced every dance with him. You were...well, I'm not going to repeat the ugly things Lillian said even though Lillian thinks this

Englishman walks on water. Apparently his being a lord only takes him so far."

"Momma, I kissed him a few times, and you can argue that he bought those kisses. As for the dancing, well, he went to cotillion classes as a kid, and let's face it, Dash is a terrible dancer."

"So you still like Dash."

Caroline gritted her teeth. This was not a good time to clue Momma into the whole Lasso Fiasco. "I've known Dash all my life," she said.

"Good. I'm so relieved. Tomorrow you and Dash need to be seen around town together, maybe go to the demolition derby together, you know. This talk about you and the Englishman, well, I don't think your daddy or your brothers like it much."

"Momma, you don't have to worry about me and the Englishman. We just danced is all."

"All right. I'm glad we had this talk, honey." Momma gathered Caroline into her warm embrace, filled with the scent of the lavender body lotion she always wore.

Caroline always felt safe in Momma's arms. She loved her parents deeply. She knew good and well that having any kind of fling with the Englishman who'd come to buy up Daddy's land was something she could never do, even if he were The One that Miriam had forecast for her.

Which he wasn't.

Too bad her libido didn't believe in Miriam Randall and her forecasts.

Senator Warren's phone call awakened Caroline at eight-thirty the next morning. Early phone calls from the senator were not unusual. On any given workday,

Caroline was likely to be up at five-thirty and heading to the gym. The senator often called her before breakfast.

But Caroline had gotten in really late the night before, and everyone had decided to let her sleep in.

Except her boss.

"Senator," she said in a rusty voice after she fumbled for her phone and pressed the talk button. "What can I do for you?"

"I've decided to let Cissy help Lord Woolham."

"What?" Caroline's brain kicked into gear.

He chuckled. "Don't sound so surprised. The truth is, she's come up with an excellent plan for salvaging the situation."

A strange, confusing emotion darted through her. She didn't quite like the idea of Cissy being the one to help Hugh with his quest. "What plan?" she asked, her voice sounding just a little too urgent.

"Oh, she's hooking up with Hugh for breakfast this morning, and the two of them are going to make the rounds of all the local officials. I think they were also going to visit with Cissy's sorority friend, whatshername—Hettie Johnson?"

"Hettie *Marshall*." Caroline sat up and threw her feet over the side of the bed, confusion resolving itself into serious concern. The last thing she wanted was Cissy Warren talking to Hettie.

Hettie had to be handled carefully. After all, it looked like her husband, the largest employer in the county, was up to no good. And a person like Cissy, who talked without thinking, could really upset the balance of things in Last Chance. "What time were they going to meet with her, do you know?"

"Um, no, I don't. Is there a problem?"

"Yes, Senator, there are multiple problems here. The land Hugh bought is a wetlands, and he's going to have to get permits to develop it, even if my father agrees to sell the golf course. And the woman he's going to meet with is the chair of the Committee to Resurrect Golfing for God, in addition to being the wife of the man who sold Hugh the wetlands in the first place. For an inflated price, I might add."

"I had no idea." He sounded concerned now, too.

"Senator, this could be a real touchy situation."

"I'm so sorry. I should have checked with you before giving Cissy the green light, but you know how she can be. She's got a real bee in her bonnet about this fellow. I didn't want to discourage her. I mean he's precisely the kind of man I'd like to see Cissy settle down with, if you know what I mean."

"Yes. I do." And of course, that was the difference between what Senator Warren expected of his daughter and what Caroline's parents expected of her.

Not to mention the whole Miriam Randall forecast.

"So," the senator said, "would you mind finding them and making sure Cissy doesn't put her foot in it? And while you're at it, if you could play matchmaker, that would be a huge help."

Yeah, it probably would. Cissy had enough money to fund just about any project Hugh could dream up. Which meant they were probably made for each other.

"Sure," she said, but her voice lacked enthusiasm.

The senator chuckled. "I know you're not a matchmaker. But you have been known to work miracles from time to time."

"I don't make miracles. Only God does that, Senator."

"Well, you could give Him a run for the money. Which is the other reason I'm calling—I need you to hurry up and get this problem with the factory taken care of because Andrea has tendered her resignation. It was waiting on my desk this morning when I got in. I guess she's decided to run off to Montana and marry that cowboy sooner rather than later. So it looks like I need an administrative assistant in Washington before the election. I know you've wanted that job for a long time."

Caroline's heart skipped around her chest. "Uh, yes, I have."

"Well, I'm about to make your dream come true, and I'm going to give you a ten percent raise to go along with the new responsibilities. But I need you in DC just as soon as you can get there. Andrea wants to be on a plane to Big Sky country in two weeks."

"Senator, I'm so—"

"Just say yes, Caroline."

"Yes. Yes, yes, yes." She was so relieved. Apparently getting pulled off a parade float by a demented cowboy had not wrecked her career. Now she just needed to be professional, handle Cissy and Hettie carefully, and she'd be in Washington before the month was out.

"Good," the senator said. "I need you in DC. Now you go fix that problem for that Englishman and see if you can give Cissy some help corralling him. Then get on back here to Columbia and start packing your bags."

After disconnecting with the senator, Caroline made one call to Miriam Randall that netted a wealth of information. Cissy had shown up early, roused Hugh out of bed, and taken him off to the Kountry Kitchen for breakfast. They had a meeting scheduled with Hettie Marshall at 9:00 a.m.

Caroline didn't have a minute to spare. She threw on one of her suits, pulled her hair back into a ponytail, and headed out to the home Jimmy and Hettie had built on a rise of rolling farmland just north of the town limits.

She pulled Stone's beat-up pickup onto the long, circular drive, took one look at the big antebellum monstrosity, and immediately felt out of her league. The shiny red Corvette parked in the drive didn't make her feel any more sure of herself.

Cissy Warren's car was primo-cool. Hugh was sure to lust after it, which was all for the good. He needed Cissy. Cissy wanted him. And Caroline needed her job.

Of course, how she was going to sort through that muddle to make sure that Last Chance got a factory remained to be seen. One thing was for certain—Hugh and Cissy could really screw things up for Hettie. The Queen Bee might not know what her husband was up to. And someone had to break that news gently.

Caroline killed the engine and set the brake. A gardener came running over just as she was getting out of the car. He opened his mouth, took one look at her business suit, and shut it. He gave Stone's pickup the once-over, then shook his head and went back to pruning the azaleas.

Good thing Caroline had dressed for success today. Otherwise she might have been forced to use the service entrance.

She hurried to the big double doors and rang the doorbell, feeling the chip on her shoulder swell. A few moments later, the maid ushered Caroline into a bright parlor upholstered in yellow damask, filled with Civil

War–era antiques, and occupied by Hettie Marshall wearing Carolina Herrera.

And next to her on the priceless sofa sat Cissy Warren, in a pale pink Armani ensemble. Lord Woolham stood by the fireplace dressed in one of his beautifully hand-tailored business suits.

His hair had tumbled down his forehead, his eyes looked sleepy, his mouth looked kissable, and his body looked hotter than a billy goat in a pepper patch. Caroline experienced an erotic rush that left her feeling completely flummoxed.

She needed to get over him. Right now. She concentrated on the fact that she was the only person in this room wearing ready-to-wear. It didn't help.

"Caroline," Cissy said from her place on the sofa, "whatever are you doing here?"

"Your father called me. I thought I would join the meeting."

Cissy gave Caroline the stink eye.

Meanwhile, a spark of humor reached Hettie's eyes as she glanced at Caroline and then at Hugh, who was standing there looking down at the Persian rug. "I gather you two had a pretty busy afternoon yesterday," she said.

Hugh coughed.

Caroline's face flamed. "Well, you know how it is come festival time."

"Yes, I do," Hettie said.

"Did I miss something?" Cissy asked.

"No," Hugh and Caroline said in unison. Their gazes collided and then went their separate ways.

"Did you know that Cissy and I were sorority sisters?" Hettie said into the sudden, awkward silence.

"No, ma'am, not until this morning. The senator mentioned something about it," Caroline said.

Hettie gestured toward Cissy and Hugh. "They've come to try to convince me to give up my chairmanship of the Committee to Resurrect Golfing for God. Are you here for the same thing?"

Caroline gave Hettie a bold, direct stare. "No, I'm not."

Cissy made a strange noise that sounded like she might be about to burst a blood vessel. Hettie merely smiled a deep and genuine smile. "No?" the Queen Bee said.

"No. I'm not going to convince anyone that building a factory over on the south side of town makes sense, because the land Hugh bought over that way is swampy and would require a boatload of wetlands permits and reclamation. It would cost a fortune to develop that land."

"Really?" Cissy and Hettie spoke in unison. Both of them stared at Caroline like she was from outer space.

"Yes, really."

Hettie's mild gaze sharpened. It snapped to Hugh. "Did you know this?"

"Caroline did mention it, yes."

Hettie paled and glanced over toward Cissy, who clearly had been left in the dust. "I see."

"I don't see at all," Cissy said. She looked up at Hugh. "If the land is worthless, why'd you buy it?"

Hugh shrugged. "It's not worthless. It's just going to be very expensive to develop. And it was my partner who purchased the land. So now I'm stuck with land I can't really sell and can't develop either. And of course, there is Elbert's golf course."

"Which you'll never get," Caroline said.

"Well, I guess that's that, then," Hettie said, getting up, and putting an end to the meeting. "I don't see how I can help you with swampland, Lord Woolham. I'm sorry." Hettie clasped her hands behind her back. She looked nervous suddenly.

Was it possible that Hettie knew more than she was letting on? Caroline would have to find a time to confront the Queen Bee, but not here with Cissy and Hugh looking on. Hettie was a powerful force in Last Chance, and she had to be handled with kid gloves.

"Well, thanks for the meeting, Hettie," Caroline said. "I really do appreciate the time you've taken with us."

Hettie gave her a long, sober look. In that instant, Caroline felt for Hettie. She was in between a rock and a hard place.

Time to get Cissy and Hugh the heck out of Dodge, so Caroline could circle back around later and find out what Hettie actually knew about the doings over at the chicken plant.

"Come on, you two, we've got things to do," Caroline said in a chipper voice as she headed toward the foyer, Hettie leading the way.

A minute later, they had said their good-byes and were out in the drive. Now came the hard part. Caroline was going to have to hand Hugh off to Cissy. The senator expected it of her, and besides, it was all for the best. If she spent any more time with Hugh, she was going to make a big mistake.

Better to focus on her new job and the chicken plant and what Hettie knew about those shady land deals.

"Okay, Rocky, what are you really doing here?" Cissy turned on Caroline. She put her beautifully manicured hands on her pink hips and gave her one serious ice queen look.

"I'm doing my job. There are things about this situation you don't know and don't understand. So back off, Cissy. I'm actually on your side." Caroline gave Hugh a meaningful look. "Hettie is an important person in this town. She needs to be shown the right kind of respect."

"You think I don't know that?"

"Well, apparently not. We already spoke to Hettie a couple of days ago, and she's not changing her mind about the golf course. And pulling your sorority connections will not help this situation. Hettie's got a bee in her bonnet about my daddy's golf place. I know you mean well."

"She's right," Hugh said. "I told you this at breakfast."

Cissy sniffed. "Well, maybe you did."

"So," Hugh said, turning toward Caroline. The smile at the corners of his eyes set off a wildfire in Caroline's middle. "What's next, then?"

"We need to meet with the members of the town council," Cissy said. "I have a list right here." She reached into her white Dooney & Bourke purse and pulled out a piece of paper bearing a list of names. "Come on, darling, I've got it covered." Cissy glared at Caroline.

"Isn't Caroline supposed to be helping me with these meetings?" He gazed at Caroline—from the tips of her shoes up her legs, over her off-the-rack suit, and up into her face. He smiled gently. Cissy couldn't see his face, thank goodness. That smile spoke like the most eloquent of poetry and darted right into the middle of Caroline's heart.

She wanted to shuck off her suit jacket and start a cat-fight with the boss's daughter. She wanted to soil Cissy's designer suit and maybe even yank some of her beautifully colored hair out.

But she couldn't do anything like that. She was a professional staffer. She always kept her cool. That was how she'd won the senator's trust and landed that job in Washington.

So she looked up into Hugh's warm brown eyes and tried not to feel anything as she said, "Uh, look, there's been a change in plans. The senator really wants you to work with Cissy on this. I've been given some new responsibilities and—"

Cissy interrupted. "Haven't you heard, Hugh? Daddy's sending Rocky to Washington."

His gaze widened and darkened. "You're leaving?"

"Oh, well, not until—"

"Yes, she is," Cissy said. "She'll be moving to DC in less than two weeks. So really, she doesn't have time to help you solve your problem here. And since her daddy's land is the problem, it's all for the good."

The light in Hugh's eyes dimmed a little bit. "Is this true?"

She nodded. "The senator called this morning."

"So you're off the case then?"

She shrugged. "Well, we both know it was a difficult situation. Just think about what I said after church yesterday, and maybe a solution will pop up. In the meantime, I have a few other things to do."

Caroline glanced at Cissy's red Vette. "Have fun driving the car." She managed to say those last words in a bright and careless tone, even though they wanted to stick in her throat. She didn't wait for any more chitchat. She climbed up into her brother's pickup and took off down the driveway.

She wasn't going to look back in the rearview mirror. No sir.

But she did.

CHAPTER
16

Caroline spent an hour and a half at the doughnut shop, where she consumed a cruller and two Boston creams along with two cups of coffee. She checked her e-mail, made a few phone calls to the DC office with questions about short- and long-term living arrangements in the nation's capital, and worried about what Hettie Marshall knew about the situation at the chicken plant.

When she'd consumed more calories than her hips could absorb, she circled back to the Painted Corner Stables, where she hoped to find Hettie for a more private conversation.

Hettie always took her Thoroughbred out for a ride in the mornings. Caroline had to wait thirty minutes before Hettie finally trotted her horse into the corral.

Hettie reined in and dismounted. The bay gelding whickered, and his coat looked as hot and sweaty as Caroline felt, standing there in a dark suit and a silk blouse.

Hettie looked way more casual than she had earlier that morning. Gone were the pearls and the designer clothes. She wore a sleeveless T-shirt, a pair of Wranglers, and some pretty expensive-looking boots. Her blond hair was pulled back, and she hid behind her Ray-Bans.

"Rocky?" she said as Caroline came to lean against the corral fence. "What are you doing here?"

"I need to talk with you," Caroline said.

Hettie ran up the horse's stirrups, loosened the saddle's girth, and began walking the animal around the corral to cool him down. "Twice in one day," she said. "What's so important?"

Caroline watched as Hettie turned the horse one way and another as she walked him. There was no mistaking the tension in Hettie's shoulders. Even the horse seemed to know that his mistress was worried about something.

"I wanted to talk in private."

Hettie turned the horse in the opposite direction. "About what?"

"About the land your husband sold Hugh deBracy for an inflated price."

Hettie stopped. The horse whickered and crow-hopped. "What about it?"

"So you know he sold Hugh that land? Did you know that Jimmy has been unloading his land a little bit at a time for the last year or so?"

Hettie said nothing. She resumed her walk around the corral.

"Look, Hettie, the thing is, Lord Woolham is under-capitalized, and if he can't sell the land back to Jimmy, then Last Chance is going to lose out on a factory that could become a significant contributor to Allenberg County's tax base. We need his factory."

Hettie turned and pushed her sunglasses up on her

head. "So, since Jimmy isn't going to buy back the land, you want me to get out of the way so your father will sell out. I get it, Caroline. Your parents must be so proud of you."

Hettie turned away and led the horse toward the stable. Caroline followed. The shade was a relief. The smell was not.

"That's not what I said, and that's not why I'm here," Caroline said.

"Then what do you want from me?" Hettie said as she slipped the reins back over the horse's head and started taking off his bridle.

"I want the truth as you know it. I wouldn't mind your help in trying to convince Jimmy to buy back the land."

"I'm sorry, Rocky." Hettie slipped the horse's halter over his ears and snapped the left and right cross ties onto it.

"You're sorry? Don't you realize the danger the town is facing? I mean—" Caroline bit off her words as the horse whickered. She took a deep breath. "Look, I've heard from completely reliable sources that things aren't so good down at the chicken plant."

Hettie started unbuckling the girth of the horse's saddle. She worked in a calm manner, but Caroline could see unshed tears gathering in her eyes.

"What's going on, Hettie?" Caroline asked.

Hettie took a deep breath. "Jimmy can't buy the land back."

"Why not?"

"Because he's already spent the money."

"What? It was hundreds of thousands of—"

"I know how much money there was. He's spent it

all. And before you ask—no, there isn't enough money remaining in my trust fund to bail him out this time."

Holy smokes. Hettie and Jimmy Marshall were supposed to be loaded.

"Close your mouth, Rocky." Hettie lifted the saddle off the horse's back. She turned and lowered it to a rack sitting outside one of the horse stalls. "I know it's shocking but it's the truth. I'm sorry. There isn't anything wrong with selling land for what you can get for it, is there?"

"Swampland, Hettie?"

"Until this morning I didn't know about that."

"No, but you know something. You're as nervous as a cat in a room full of rockers. What is it? Are you afraid I might figure out that there was a kickback involved? What would the town council say if they knew that their last, best hope for new investment was ruined by your husband's greed and shady dealings?"

"What?" Hettie looked like she'd been hit with a Taser. "I don't know a thing about kickbacks. What are you talking about?"

"Okay, how about bribing an inspector?" Caroline said, testing the waters. She had no proof that Jimmy had bribed anyone. She was just trying to see how much Hettie knew.

She was not expecting Hettie's face to blanch or the next words that came out of her mouth. "So you know about that? Who told you?"

Holy smokes. Roy Burdett had been telling the truth for once.

"No one," Caroline said. "I've been putting pieces of the puzzle together."

Hettie closed her eyes and leaned her forehead against her horse. For a moment, Caroline thought the Queen Bee was about to break down and weep. But Hettie was made of stronger steel than that.

She finally looked up, across the horse's back, all trace of tears gone from her eyes. "I can't help you. I'm sorry. There is no money to buy back the land. I'm not going to give up on Golfing for God either."

"I didn't ask you to."

"I know. I appreciate that."

"But either way our town loses."

Hettie shrugged. "I can't help you. I can't help anyone. I can hardly help myself."

"This gets out and your reputation is going to be ruined, you know that, don't you?" Caroline said.

"Are you planning an exposé?"

"Hettie, if your husband is bribing inspectors, I've got to blow the whistle."

Hettie's stare remained fixed. "Well, if that happens, my husband is going to jail."

Caroline took a seat at the counter of the Kountry Kitchen. Her stomach was feeling a little queasy, but she didn't know whether it was the result of too many doughnuts or the bombshell Hettie Marshall had just exploded.

In any event, she figured she needed some healthy food just to get her system back on track.

"So what can I get you?" Ricki asked.

"I'll have one of your garden salads and an iced tea."

Ricki scribbled the order in her pad, just as a much deeper voice said, "Rocky, darlin', don't you ever get tired of eating food fit only for rabbits?"

Caroline looked over her shoulder and up into the twinkle in Dash Randall's eyes. Dash sat himself down, dropping his cowboy hat on the counter beside him.

"I'm furious at you," Caroline said.

He laughed. "Honey, don't kid a kidder. I saw you kiss that guy. You enjoyed every minute. You should be thanking me that I let him buy your kisses. Otherwise you and me were going to have to get a whole lot friendlier than either of us really wanted to be."

"Are you here to annoy me or to keep the rumor mill working?"

"Neither, actually. I came to let you know that we got us a great big problem, right here in Last Chance."

"Tell me about it." She planted her elbow on the table and propped her head. She was exhausted, demoralized, and discouraged.

Which was so strange because this morning the senator had made all her dreams come true. She was headed for Washington. She should be ecstatic.

But instead, she was worried right down to her marrow.

"So," Dash said, "I guess you heard about what happened, huh? I'm really sorry. I should have my head examined."

Caroline straightened and turned. "For what, buying up Jimmy's land?"

His smile faded. "What in the Sam Hill does that have to do with what happened yesterday, and how did you know that?"

"I looked it up at the courthouse. What have you been trying to do—keep the chicken plant solvent all by your lonesome? Honestly, if you wanted to infuse the plant with cash, why didn't you do it directly instead of buying up Jimmy's land at inflated prices?"

He stared at her for a full minute. "I didn't buy the land to shore up the plant." His cheeks reddened ever so slightly.

"Then why?"

He shrugged. "Land is always a good investment."

"Oh, my God, you bought that land because of Hettie, didn't you? You're still in love with her, and you're trying to protect her from her jerk of a husband."

He turned away and stared out the plateglass window for a long moment, a muscle ticking in his jaw. Yeah, Dash Randall was kind of like Bubba. He was still carrying a torch for Hettie. Caroline wondered, given the state of Hettie's marriage, if Hettie was carrying a torch for Dash. Boy, that would be some seriously hot gossip, wouldn't it?

"So why were you researching land acquisitions?"

"Because I'm here to make sure Last Chance gets a spiffy new textile machinery factory. Right now that looks like a complete impossibility—and not because my daddy won't sell his golf course. Jimmy sold swamp to Hugh at a price that was at least ten times its worth, and Hugh doesn't have enough cash to handle the wetlands reclamation, and besides, Daddy won't sell. So we're pretty much up that swamp without either a canoe or a paddle."

"Wow, you've been busy, in addition to kissing Englishmen and getting yourself lassoed."

"You can joke about it, but this is serious. More serious than you think. So what's your problem—did Lillian Bray catch you with some lady of the evening down at the Peach Blossom?"

He let go of a big breath. "No. I have more class than that, honey. If I want to fool around, I go to the Magnolia Inn outside of Allenberg. I have no desire to get on Lillian Bray's bad side."

"Okay, Dash, what did you do?"

"Bubba overheard me last night talking with the Canaday brothers about the whole lasso scenario, you know? I'm afraid he knows the whole thing was a ruse."

"You told the Canaday brothers about the lasso scenario? Oh, crap."

"Yeah, and both Bubba and Rachel overheard. Which is a darn shame because the two of them looked like they were having a nice time. I guess I got overconfident after Rachel laid that kiss on Bubba, you know?"

"I doubt that Rachel was having a good time with Bubba."

"Why not?"

She shrugged. "Because."

Ricki came back with two iced teas and Caroline's salad. She placed one of the drinks in front of Dash and said, "How are you, honey?" while she shamelessly batted her eyes. She glanced at Caroline. "I heard that you two aren't as close as some folks thought."

"Well, you know, you can't always trust gossip, Ricki. How about a ham sandwich?" Dash said.

"Sure thing, Dash," Ricki gave him a sultry smile and headed back to the kitchen to deliver his order.

"That woman has a thing for you," Caroline said as Ricki hurried away to get his order.

"Uh-huh. Her and just about every other woman in the county except for you."

"And Hettie."

"Yeah, but Hettie is married. She doesn't count."

Caroline was just opening her mouth to dish out some snarky retort when the front door of the Kountry Kitchen banged open and Rachel came stalking in. For once, her hair was pulled back in a tight ponytail that did nothing for her long, chiseled face.

She stepped right up to Dash and Caroline, put her hands on her hips, and said, "You two should be ashamed of yourselves. Honestly, Dash, you're an immature idiot so I don't expect much more from you, but you." She turned to Caroline. "You are supposed to be my friend."

Rachel looked pale and hollowed eyed—like maybe she'd cried herself to sleep last night.

Caroline jumped up and pulled Rachel into a big ol' hug while she simultaneously gave Dash a chilling look. Dash picked up his hat and slunk from the Kountry Kitchen like the guilty rat that he was.

"I can explain," Caroline said. "Why don't you just sit down and have lunch with me."

Tears started to fill Rachel's eyes, and she shook her head. "You lied to me, Rocky. I don't know if I can forgive that." Rachel's voice went wobbly, and she pulled away. "I gotta get out of here before I say something ugly."

Rachel turned on her heel and marched out of the Kountry Kitchen before Caroline could say one word.

Damnit. Caroline needed to talk to that girl.

She laid a twenty-dollar bill on the counter, and followed Rachel up the street calling her name. The more she called, the faster Rachel walked, until Rocky had to jog after her. She finally caught up with her friend right in front of the Cut 'n Curl.

Necessity being the mother of invention, Caroline

grabbed Rachel's arms and dragged her forcibly into the cool, pink and green confines of Momma's beauty shop.

"C'mon, Rachel, you need to give me a minute to explain what really happened."

"You lied to me," Rachel said as she shrugged away from Caroline's grasp. "It doesn't require any further explanation."

"I didn't lie. I let everyone in town jump to conclusions that weren't true. There's a huge difference."

"What conclusions?" This question came from the proprietor of the Cut 'n Curl, who was in the middle of touching up Carrie Price's roots. Jane was across the room giving a manicure to Miz Latimer, a little old senile lady whose daughter brought her by the shop every Monday to get her hair done.

It occurred to Caroline that having a fight with Rachel at the Cut 'n Curl was pretty darn stupid. But on the other hand, this was her opportunity to come clean of the whole thing.

"The conclusions people drew when Dash lassoed me off the parade float."

"It was a hoax," Rachel said, crossing the room and settling down into one of the big pink hair dryer chairs. "You did it just to fool Bubba Lockheart."

"What?" Momma, Jane, and Carrie said in unison. Miz Latimer smiled.

Caroline took a deep breath and explained the entire Lasso Fiasco to her mother, sister-in-law, friend, and neighbor. "Honest, Rachel, I had no idea that Dash was going to lasso me off the parade float. He came up with that all by his lonesome. But I will confess that I told him that we needed to make some kind of intervention in

Bubba's life. That was a big mistake on my part because Dash is an idiot."

Rachel sat in her chair and listened. Big fat tears began falling down her cheeks.

"I know it wasn't exactly nice of Caroline and Dash to hoodwink us like that, but you gotta admit that their plan seemed to have some real positive results." This came from Jane, who always looked on the bright side of every disaster.

"Like what?" Caroline and Ruby asked in unison.

"Well, Rachel kissed Bubba yesterday, and he seemed to like it," Jane said.

That was all it took for Rachel to come apart at the seams. "And he's not the only one," she wailed. "And now... now he's n-never... g-g-gonna... ever look at me... a-g-g-gain."

Five seconds after this monumental confession, Caroline, Ruby, and Jane Rhodes descended on Rachel and gave her the biggest group hug in the history of Last Chance, South Carolina.

An application of hot coffee, some new highlights, and a pedicure were immediately called for.

Hugh dialed Caroline's number and got her answering service once again. He disconnected without leaving a message.

"Who are you calling now?" Cissy asked as they headed up the stairs of the Humanities Building at Voorhees College.

"Oh, just checking my messages," Hugh lied.

They left the midafternoon heat behind as they entered the building and rode the lift up to the third floor.

The institutional hallway that housed the faculty offices smelled of chalk and bookbinder's glue.

They found Kamaria LaFlore, professor of African studies and longtime member of the Last Chance Town Council, in her tiny office. She looked at home, surrounded by bookshelves, tribal masks, and a wall filled with advanced degrees from places like Princeton and Yale.

"Thank you for seeing us on short notice," Hugh began as he settled himself into a chair by the professor's cluttered desk. "I thought I would—"

Dr. LaFlore put up a hand. "I know what you want. I just got a phone call from Lillian Bray, and she explained it all. I think it's an interesting idea, but I don't believe it will fly."

Since Hugh had yet to meet formally with Lillian Bray, he was momentarily confused. "Um. What does Mrs. Bray think I'm looking for? Because to be quite frank, I haven't yet spoken with her. I met her for the first time on Saturday, of course, but that was a social affair."

"Oh." Dr. LaFlore leaned back in her chair, the springs squeaking. "She said you wanted the town council to condemn Golfing for God."

"Well, if ya'll had the gumption to do that, it would sure solve all of Hugh's problems," Cissy drawled.

"Not all of them, Dr. LaFlore," Hugh said. "The land adjacent to the golf course has swamp on it. I've been informed just recently that wetlands reclamation can be difficult in South Carolina."

"It can be. But there are ways to get around some of that regulation. And I don't think we'll have too many locals lining up to save water moccasin habitat, Lord knows we have enough of that in our state. What we don't have is a healthy tax base."

"I see, so you could help me get through the environmental red tape?" Hugh asked.

"I can't guarantee that, but I think I can be helpful. My biggest concern, quite frankly, is that committee of churchwomen that Hettie Marshall is chairing."

"Well, if you don't have the courage to stare down a bunch of churchwomen, then Lord Woolham will have to build his factory elsewhere," Cissy said.

Cissy's threat wasn't real, of course. If he didn't build his factory here, he would have to go back to square one and find some additional partners. And before he could get that kind of thing set up, he'd have to pay taxes on Woolham House.

Really, he was sunk. He felt as if he were rearranging the deck chairs on the *Titanic*.

Dr. LaFlore gave Cissy a sober stare. "I support your factory. And I wish Bert would sell his golf course. That old place makes our town look like a Bible Belt backwater. But for the town council to legally take Bert's land, we'd have to be building a road or something."

"Building a road would make a difference?" Hugh asked.

"Well, yes. If the state were building a road, then we could take the land using eminent domain because we needed the land for a public use. But to simply condemn the place, force him to sell it to the town, and then turn around and resell it to you would be highly illegal."

"But I only need that small parcel for road and rail access."

Dr. LaFlore studied him for a long, uncomfortable

moment. "Well, that changes things." She steepled her long fingers. "Of course, public financing for a road through that land would be impossible. Now, if you could come up with some private financing, perhaps we could figure out a public-private partnership. That might make it possible, and certainly worth thinking about. I sure would hate to see Last Chance lose out on this kind of economic development."

"But this approach would require the state to force Elbert Rhodes off his land, wouldn't it?" Hugh asked.

She nodded. "Yes, it would. Are you squeamish about that? You ought to be, you know. And the churchwomen will be very unhappy. That could be a problem for my election, but I'm betting that economic development and jobs will trump a putt-putt place every time. Do you really have the money to build a road through there?"

The hairs on the back of Hugh's neck prickled. He had enough money, barely, to build the factory, which included road and rail connections. But if he had to spend a farthing more for wetlands reclamation, he was sunk. He doubted, very much, that Victoria would be willing to loan him money for this venture. Vicky had already told him that if he were to marry her, he'd have to give up tinkering about with bits of machinery.

"Dr. LaFlore, I'm very tight on cash. I would have to seek additional financing, which I might need in any case because of the swampland. Additional financing is not easy to come by."

"No, it's not. But perhaps we can help find you some. I would like to help deliver your factory to my constituents." The future mayor of Last Chance gave him a big American smile filled with very white teeth.

• • •

Haley sat in the backseat of Granny's van as Grand-daddy pulled up to the curb outside Miz Bray's house. Granddaddy was supposed to be taking Haley to the fair-grounds, where they were going to get dinner and ride on the Tilt-A-Whirl, but Granddaddy said he needed to stop and take care of some business first.

Miz Bray's house stood on the edge of town and had a really big front yard. The pink and yellow and purple flowers in Miz Bray's yard were real pretty. Folks said she had the prettiest yard in all of Allenberg County.

Granddaddy stopped the car and then turned in his seat. "You stay put, punkin'. This won't take a minute, and then I'll take you twice on the Tilt-A-Whirl."

Granddaddy got out of the car, and the Sorrow-ful Angel got out with him. A shiver of something not good took hold of Haley. The Sorrowful Angel had been mad the last few days. She'd stopped crying, but she'd started grumbling. Every once in a while, the angel said a bad word or two.

Miz Bray came to the door, and Granddaddy started talking to her right there on the porch. Haley couldn't hear what Granddaddy was saying, but she got the feeling—mostly by the way he took off his hat and started slamming it into his hand—that he was not happy.

This made Haley feel kind of warm inside. Grand-daddy really loved her, in spite of the fact that she could see the Sorrowful Angel.

Miz Bray slammed her front door in Granddaddy's face. And then things got out of hand.

Haley should have known something bad would hap-pen the minute the Sorrowful Angel got out of the car and followed Granddaddy to the porch. The angel let go of a shriek that hurt Haley's ears, and then...

Well, then she took after Miz Bray's flowers. She started pulling them up—the tall spiky ones that grew along the porch. And after she pulled them out of the ground, the angel threw them, roots and all, at Miz Bray's front window. Granddaddy just stood there and let it happen.

When the Sorowful Angel had finished pulling up all of Miz Bray's flowers, the front door to the house opened again. Miz Bray came out with a broom that she took to Granddaddy's head. He fended it off and took the broom from her. Then he used it to give Miz Bray a swat across her broad behind. Granddaddy knocked Miz Bray right off her feet. She landed right in the middle of her messed-up flowerbed.

Granddaddy and the angel hightailed it back to the car before Miz Bray could get up. Granddaddy started the car up, and they got going. Then he tilted the rearview mirror and gave Haley a long, funny look. "Little gal, we're not going to tell a soul about what just happened, are we?"

"No, sir."

Haley was no dummy.

CHAPTER
17

Hugh studied Cissy Warren as she guided her cherry red Corvette down Palmetto Avenue, heading toward Miriam Randall's boardinghouse. She was thin and well dressed and definitely knew how to air-kiss.

Granddad would have adored her.

Hugh, not so much.

He was exhausted. His meetings with individual members of the town council had made him increasingly uncomfortable.

He wanted his factory. But he didn't want to be a villain. It wasn't fair to force Elbert Rhodes off his land.

Cissy turned into Miriam's drive. "Look, Hugh," Cissy said as she killed the engine, "if you don't want to go for it on this whole condemnation thing, then you should cut your losses and rethink."

"Rethink in what way?"

"Well," she said, reaching out and running her long fingernails across his cheek in a gesture that was supposed to be alluring, "first of all, I think you should go get your things. Then we should drive back to Columbia and find a nice restaurant and a good hotel for you."

"Are you propositioning me?"

She giggled. "In a way, yes."

"Well I—"

"No, listen." She pressed her finger against his lips. He didn't really like being silenced that way.

"You want to build this factory and make your loom, right?" she said. "But you don't have the money to get the job done. The fact is, even if they condemn that piece of land, you'd be hard pressed to find the money to build the road and deal with the swamp. You are undercapitalized. You are going to fail."

Anger bubbled down in his gut. He'd heard this before. So many times, on so many things. "How do you know I'm going to fail?" He bit off the words, momentarily losing his cool.

"Because I've taken a look at your personal balance sheet."

"Right. Caroline told me all about that. Did you put a private investigator on my trail?"

"Yes, I did. And don't look like that. A woman like me has to be careful. I know you're underfunded. And I know you're considering marriage to a woman whose only assets are her assets. But it's okay, because you're smart and classy. I like classy men. And I happen to be rich enough to afford you."

"I'm so glad I have your approval," he said, the sarcasm barely disguised.

"Don't be angry. I had a feeling we weren't going to get very far with these yokels today. Now you need to listen to me."

"Why should I?"

"Because, dear Baron, we're wasting our time here. Daddy's taken a look at the specs for your loom, and he thinks you're brilliant—as an inventor and engineer, not a businessman. Given that, it just makes sense for Warren Fabrics to buy your design. Then we would have exclusive rights to this technology, which is going to revolutionize textile manufacturing. We'd finance the production line. You could be in charge of that if you wanted. Or you could spend your time inventing the next big thing, which I imagine is what you'd rather do."

Hugh stared at her for a long, tense moment. Cissy had just offered him the perfect solution. She'd even offered him an opportunity to get out of the business end of things and concentrate on what he loved the most—tinkering around with bits of machinery.

So why was he hesitating?

One single thought came to his mind—Caroline on Sunday morning talking about how she loved Last Chance and all of its citizens. Her passion had touched him. She wanted to save the chicken plant and find a way to build Hugh's factory here, where it would matter to a bunch of ordinary people.

If he said yes to Cissy, the factory would go elsewhere. No doubt there would be people in the I-85 corridor who would welcome new jobs, but they wouldn't be Caroline's people.

He should say yes to Cissy. Caroline, herself, had suggested that Cissy was the solution to his problems.

But he couldn't. For some reason, the people of Last Chance had gotten under his skin. Especially one particular senatorial aide.

"So what do you think?" Cissy asked, pressing her advantage.

"Can I think about it?"

"What's to think about?"

"Well, I had set my heart on building an independent business. I would love to do business with Warren Fabrics, of course. And your offer is very generous, but I need to think it over."

Cissy was, no doubt, used to getting her way, and the look she gave Hugh underscored that point. She was spoilt rotten. "That took balls," she said.

"What? My wanting to do things on my own, or my wanting to think things over?"

"You have no money. You need me. You're dreaming if you think you can do this on your own."

"You are probably right about that. My grandfather always said I spent too much time with my head in the clouds. But that's who I am, Cissy." He opened the car door before she could vent any more anger at him.

"You'll be sorry about this."

Hugh ignored the venom in her words. "Thank you, Cissy. You're quite generous, and I haven't said no. I just want to think about it," he said as mildly as he could.

"I don't make offers like this twice."

"Well, then, I guess I'm rather out of luck."

Cissy's lip curled. It wasn't a very attractive look on her. "Have it your way." She turned the key and revved the Corvette's motor. She yanked the gear lever, ground the clutch, and spun the tires as she backed out of the drive. It was a shame the way Cissy treated that beautiful piece of machinery.

· · ·

"Well, don't ya'll look good enough to eat?" Aunt Arlene said as Caroline and Rachel reached the top row of the grandstand.

Arlene pulled off her oversized sunglasses and peered at them out of a pair of sherry-colored eyes that had been decorated with false eyelashes and green eye shadow.

Rachel looked much better after the intervention at the Cut 'n Curl. She wore a pair of daisy dukes that showed off her long-stemmed legs, a little red bandanna halter-top, and a brand-new, sassy layered hairdo.

Momma and Jane had really outdone themselves. Their flawless application of concealer hid all traces of Rachel's spectacular crying jag.

Caroline wore her usual preppy summer outfit—a pair of navy madras Bermuda shorts, a white golf shirt, and a pair of espadrilles.

"Well," Arlene said, zoning in on Caroline's clothes, "let me amend that last remark. Rachel looks great. But Rocky, honey, you look like a refugee from a Hilton Head sailing regatta. If you're going to wear madras like that, maybe you should think about pink. Pink is such a nice color on you."

Caroline let the comment roll right off her back. After all, Momma had told her the same thing, right before her lecture about how Baron Woolham was not exactly the man Miriam had predicted for her.

Caroline had listened and nodded. Then she'd dropped her bombshell about the new job in Washington. She assured Momma that she was not interested in any kind of liaisons with English barons or regular Joes. Her entire purpose for being at the demolition derby tonight was to get Rachel hooked up with Bubba.

And if she had to kiss a pig—or Dash Randall—to get it done, she was prepared to make the sacrifice. Rachel had a thing for Bubba. Caroline wasn't entirely comfortable with that, knowing Bubba as intimately as she did, but Caroline was not about to talk her best friend out of it.

Any woman who cried over Bubba Lockheart the way Rachel had was going to be good for him. And Bubba needed someone who cared enough to have a crying jag over him, because Caroline never had cared that much.

Caroline plopped down beside her aunt-by-marriage and studied the arena where the demolition derby was about to start. The fire department had brought in a couple of big pumpers and hosed the place down so that the entire area was now mired in a good six inches of red mud. The commingled scents of funnel cake and corn dogs filled the air.

"So, girls, I heard all about the Lasso Fiasco and its aftermath. Rachel, honey, I'd say you are dressed for action tonight. And let's all pray that Bubba is smart enough to get it."

Caroline turned toward her aunt. "You know, Arlene, it's amazing how gossip travels in this county."

Arlene put her sunglasses back on. "Faster than tweets on Twitter."

"Since when do you tweet?"

"Since Alex bought me a new smart phone. If the church ladies ever catch on to texting, we're all done for." She chuckled at her own joke and took a couple of long-neck Buds from the cooler at her feet. She twisted off the tops.

"Here you go, girls. The beer is on me."

Caroline took the Bud and pressed the cold bottle to her head.

"So speaking of gossip, everyone's been talking about how that big ol' strapping duke feller outbid Dash for you at the kissing booth. Course, depending on which version of the story you hear, the duke either got outsmarted by Dash, or Dash got outsmarted by the duke. Which way is it, sugar? I'm dying to know."

"He's only a baron, not a duke," Caroline said then took a slug of beer. It was cold and refreshing.

"Duke, baron, whatever. C'mon, baby, Aunt Arlene wants to know all."

"Well, there's nothing to tell. Momma and Jane put me in that humiliating position because Dash lassoed me off the parade float and everyone misinterpreted that."

"You know, Rocky, you could have explained the truth," Rachel said.

"Right. And if I did that, then Bubba would have bid for me, not you."

"And you would have avoided the gossip that's running around as a result of you dancing barefooted with Lord Woolham into the wee hours," Arlene said.

"We were just having fun. Since when can't I have fun at the Watermelon Festival?" Caroline's voice sounded really defensive, even to her own ears.

"Well, you have a point," Arlene said, "and I can hardly blame you, if what they say about his kiss is true."

She blushed.

"Uh-huh, it must be true," Arlene said.

"Look, he's a good kisser, okay?"

"You know, seeing as he's here to force your daddy off his land, enjoying his kisses might not be a good move," Arlene said.

"I know." Caroline took another swig of beer.

"And besides, he hardly matches what Miriam predicted for you, does he?" Rachel said, getting her digs in.

Caroline nodded, but her mind kept running over the things Hugh had done over the last few days. He'd been surprisingly accurate with a wooden hoop and a baseball, winning her that stupid stuffed animal that still sat on her bed at Momma's house. He'd won nearly every game he played.

And he'd talked to Daddy about the broken frogs down at Golfing for God like he actually knew how to fix them.

And he had a bunch of engineering degrees that he'd told her about.

And he had a blood blister on his thumb.

She thought about that blister and her insides melted. Damnit, he was not a regular guy.

He was just exceptionally talented at carnival games and juggling booze bottles. And he was kind and sweet to everyone he met. Even Lillian Bray loved him, despite the fact that he'd given another blue ribbon to Jenny Carpenter yesterday in the pie-baking contest.

He didn't match the forecast. Did he? Maybe.

That was scary. She pushed it aside. It didn't matter because Miriam had predicted that he'd end up with Victoria Ashton, heiress. Caroline just needed to remember that.

Assuming, of course, that Miriam really was infallible.

Where had that thought come from? Was it possible for Miriam Randall to be wrong? That possibility had never occurred to Caroline before.

"Hey, ya'll," she said to Rachel and Arlene, "do you believe in Miriam Randall?"

"You mean like a god?" Rachel asked.

"No, I mean about her ability to foretell matrimonial bliss."

"What is it, hon, are you worried? Do you really love Dash even though he thought that whole lasso thing was a joke?" Aunt Arlene asked.

"No. I don't love Dash. But I guess I'm a little bit worried. What if my true love isn't a regular guy, and I go around trying to find a regular guy and I miss my *real* soulmate because I'm not looking for him."

"Rocky," Rachel said, "quit obsessing. If Miriam said you're going to marry a regular guy, you're going to marry a regular guy. And from what I've heard, the minute you look at this guy, you'll know—down deep."

Down deep where? In her girl parts? Oh, yeah, she felt that sexual pull the first time she'd laid eyes on Hugh deBracy. She'd also been annoyed at him for being a snob.

But he wasn't a snob, was he? He was...

She wouldn't let her mind go there. Hugh was a decent human being.

"What's got you so worried?" Rachel asked.

Caroline put the empty bottle down beside her feet then turned on the bleacher seat so she faced her aunt and her best friend. "Suppose you found someone, and you could see that he might fit Miriam's advice, but he had a forecast of his own from Miriam that you knew you could never match? What then? Should you try to become the woman he's looking for?" Not that Caroline could become an heiress, of course, but she asked the question anyway.

Aunt Arlene pushed her sunglasses up onto her frosted hair and gave Caroline one of those meaningful looks that older women always give younger women when wisdom is about to be imparted. Caroline braced herself for the bad news. "Honey, I just don't understand why you're always thinking that you need to be somebody other than who you are. I think, in order to find your soulmate, or just to make a good marriage or relationship, you've got to be yourself. You can't go pretending to be someone else just to please a man. That's just dumb, and you're smarter than that."

"I *am* smarter than that. That's what Sharon told me a long, long time ago. And that's why I told Bubba no."

"Exactly. So don't go being dumb now, especially since I heard from your momma that you finally landed that job in Washington. When you find the right man, he'll be all right with you being who you are, working for the senator and all. Trust me on this. Miriam helped me find my match, and your Uncle Pete never tried to change me."

Caroline leaned over and dropped her arm across Arlene's shoulders to give her a squeeze. Uncle Pete had passed away only a few weeks ago, after a long battle with cancer. Arlene was living alone for the first time in her life. "You doing okay, Arlene?"

She managed a trembling smile. "Yeah, I'm okay. But I sure do miss your uncle."

"Me, too." Caroline leaned in and gave Arlene a little kiss on the cheek.

Arlene gathered up her composure and batted Caroline away. "Don't you get all syrupy on me now. Your uncle wouldn't be happy about that. He was the happiest man I ever knew. And I'm trying to be happy without him.

"Here, have another beer." Arlene leaned into her cooler and pressed another cold one into Caroline's hand. She took a deep swallow. It tasted yeasty and better than anything Hugh had made for her the other night at Dottie's. Maybe she should read the signs. Like she was a beer person, not a martini person.

The loudspeaker squawked, and engines roared to life. A string of dilapidated cars made their way onto the muddy rodeo arena. One of those cars—a beat-up Dodge—belonged to Bubba. Caroline could just see the ex-linebacker-turned-mechanic behind the wheel, wearing a crash helmet, the ends of his too-long hair coming out the back.

She swept her gaze around the crowd.

Her backside practically lifted right out of the chair the minute she saw Hugh. She hadn't expected to see an English aristocrat at something as hopelessly lowbrow as a demolition derby. But then, hadn't he told her that he'd helped Bubba work on the car?

The baron had climbed up to sit on one of the hay bales set up across the way. He and Dash were sitting together like they were a couple of old buddies. Hugh wore his faded jeans and a black T-shirt—an outfit that wasn't that much different from what Dash was wearing. Hugh was drinking beer from a long-neck bottle. Dash was drinking a Coca-Cola.

Arlene gave Caroline a little nudge in the ribs and leaned in to scream in her ear over the revving of the motors. "Honey, who is that beautiful man sitting with Dash?"

"That, Aunt Arlene, is Hugh deBracy, Baron Woolham."

Arlene leaned back, her eyes growing wide. "You

mean that man over there is the duke who knocked out Bubba's teeth, got you drunk at Dottie's, and then kissed you senseless at the kissing booth yesterday?"

"Wow, news does get around this town, doesn't it?"

Arlene leaned in. "Honey, it all makes sense now."

"What?"

"That man is cuter than a baby's butt. And he's... well, he must spend some of his time in the royal gym."

Rachel laughed. "Yeah, he's got some pretty impressive biceps there."

"So what did Miriam tell him he needed to be looking for?" Arlene asked.

"She said he should be looking for a woman with a really big checkbook. You see, he's undercapitalized, and if he can't get Daddy's land, he's going back to England to marry an heiress named Lady Ashton." She said the words and felt her throat close up. It was so unfair. Why couldn't a girl like her have a guy like him? Like Cinderella.

She took another gulp of beer and could almost hear Sharon's voice echoing through her head. Sharon had told her that a woman shouldn't ever believe in Cinderella.

It sort of suggested that Sharon hadn't been as happy in her marriage as Stone had been. And Caroline didn't want to think about that. Was it possible that the whole Sharon and Stone thing was a myth, too? Like the Bubba and Rocky Show?

It didn't matter. Sharon was right. A girl had to think with her head, not her private parts. And Hugh was not the one Miriam had forecast for her. Even if Hugh was kind of a regular guy in some respects, Caroline could never overcome the reality of what Miriam said Hugh needed.

He didn't need her. She had no fortune to give him.

Two hours later Bubba had once again won the day, smashing all comers with his hulking Dodge. The victor was celebrating down on pit row.

Caroline linked her arm through Rachel's and practically dragged her down to where the celebration was taking place.

"Uh, maybe this is a huge mistake," Rachel said.

"You cried over Bubba, Rachel. You said you thought you'd never get another chance. Well, I'm not about to let that happen."

She stopped and gave Rachel a big hug. "Really, I want Bubba to have a life that doesn't involve him mooning over me. So I would be so grateful to you and to God if it turns out that you and Bubba belong together, because honestly, I've been praying for him—a lot."

Rachel let go of a little laugh. "I had a thing for him in middle school, but I knew he liked you more. I always thought, you know…" She shrugged, and her cheeks flushed.

"You should have told me. We're friends. No secrets, right? And besides, you knew Bubba and I weren't meant for each other."

"Yeah. I knew it and you knew it, but Bubba didn't. He always looked right through me. Until…well, to be honest, until Dash lassoed you off the float. So I guess maybe the whole Lasso Fiasco wasn't such a fiasco after all."

"Right. Just don't tell Dash that, he'll get a swelled head." Caroline pulled her friend forward toward the place where the steaming and smelly wrecks had been lined up.

They found Bubba surrounded by a group of good ol' boys, including Dash, the Canaday brothers, two of Rachel's younger siblings, and a bunch of guys from the Allenberg Fire Department. The testosterone was really flowing as the guys backslapped their momentary hero and poured beer over his head.

Caroline figured it was probably a good thing that Rachel was strictly a beer drinker and had never experimented with anything else in her entire life. Because Bubba was going to smell like some strange amalgam of motor oil, burning rubber, and hops.

"Hey, ya'll," Bubba yelled, exposing his gap-toothed smile. "I want you to meet my new buddy, Hugh."

Bubba pulled Hugh forward and thumped him on the back like he was just another guy in the crowd. Then Bubba let go of what could only be described as a Rebel Yell.

"Ya'll, this man is the best dang mechanic I have ever met. You shoulda seen the way he rebuilt my car's engine. I mean I was stumped. Couldn't get decent compression, and he just walked right up to that sucker and did his magic. I'm telling you, this guy is like an engine whisperer or something."

Hugh managed to look right at home despite his fancy pedigree. He didn't even look like he was slumming or looking down his long patrician nose. He was genuinely enjoying the moment.

"You know," Rachel said, "it's amazing how forgiving guys are. I mean, one minute Lord Woolham is breaking Bubba's face, and the next, they are bosom pals and he's helping him with his derby car."

"Yeah," Caroline agreed, "although to be honest, the idea of Bubba and Hugh being BFFs kind of makes me nauseous."

Rachel turned toward Caroline. "Rocky, the time has come to act on our feelings, don't you think?"

"*Our* feelings?"

"Yes, ma'am. I'm going to go get my man, because if I wait for him to notice me, it won't happen. I think you should do the same thing. Because if you ask me, Hugh deBracy looks like a regular guy. And I can see that he's got your panties in a twist."

And with that, Rachel fearlessly stalked right through that knot of men, ignoring the way every single one of them (including Bubba) ogled her bare legs. She walked right up to Hugh, pointed a finger at him, and said, "You may be an engine whisperer, but you also broke Bubba's face."

The men kind of paused for a moment, not sure exactly how to react. But then Rachel did the amazing.

She turned, grabbed Bubba by the shoulders, and gave him a serious kiss right on the mouth that probably hurt his stitches. She pulled back and glowered at Hugh. "And that just pisses me off, your highness, because I got plans to kiss this boy silly."

Bubba looked like he'd just been hit upside the head with a frying pan, but Rachel didn't give him a moment to get his bearings. She went back to kissing him—with her entire body.

The good ol' boys all let go of whoops and catcalls.

Not Hugh, thank goodness. There was a limit, really, and Caroline was so glad he hadn't stepped over it. It was nice that he could hang with the boys, but it was equally sexy that he wasn't exactly one of them.

Instead of hooting and hollering, his Lordship turned and spied Caroline standing slightly behind one of the hay bales. A slow smile filled his face. Laugh lines crinkled up at the corners of his eyes, and his whole face lit up from the inside.

Holy smokes, he had a great smile.

Rachel was right. If she had any kind of courage, she would go after him—even if he wasn't exactly a regular guy. Because a fantasy like Hugh deBracy didn't come along in a girl's life very often.

She ought to run toward it. Live in the moment. Let it happen. In a few days, she'd be packing to go to Washington. She didn't need or want a forever kind of thing.

Hugh stepped away from Bubba and strolled toward her, the multicolored fairground lights shining in his curls. "Rocky," he said in that sexy accent, "you look lovely tonight."

But she didn't look lovely. She was dressed like a J.Crew junkie. She suddenly wished she had worn that pretty pink sundress that was still hanging in her closet. Right then, she wanted to be Rocky Rhodes in something summery and girly—maybe even something mysterious and foreign like her name.

But no, she was wearing a white polo shirt.

And he still thought she was lovely.

No one was watching them. Everyone was still paying attention to Rachel and Bubba. He knew it. She knew it.

So he leaned down and stole a kiss. It wasn't like the kiss he'd bought yesterday. This one was as soft as the summer night, and just as hot and humid.

It didn't last very long either. It was a perfect kiss—just deep enough and long enough to make her yearn for more. He took her arm and deftly guided her away from the boys. She and Hugh walked toward the midway, saying nothing.

Eventually he let go of her arm and took hold of her hand.

She let him.

His touch was as intimate as it got. He intertwined his fingers with hers and the pleasure she found in the slide of his fingers across hers was almost too much to bear.

"You don't mind if I call you Rocky, do you?" Hugh asked, giving her hand the slightest squeeze.

"No." Her voice came out hoarse as a tsunami of lust hit her chest, practically drowning her. This wasn't love. She knew the difference.

But she still wanted it. If she let herself go, she could live one of her romances for a couple of hours. But she could also crash and burn—badly. So she pushed the fantasy away. "How did it go today with Cissy?" she asked.

"She made me an offer."

Caroline stopped in her tracks. "An offer? Of money?"

Hugh dropped Caroline's hand and turned toward her, the twinkling lights dancing in his eyes. "In a way. She offered to buy my loom technology and set up a factory near the I-85 corridor."

The worry that had been nagging her all day made a sudden and sharp reappearance. "I thought you were lobbying the town council."

"We did that, too. You know, the council is unanimous in thinking that it would be best if your father sold his land."

"That doesn't surprise me. Did you tell them about the swamp?"

"I did. Some of them believe that wetlands reclamation is not as big a deal as you do."

"Most of them haven't dealt with it like I have. So are you going to try to fight Daddy for his land, or take Cissy up on her offer?"

"Rocky," he said in the gentlest voice. When he said her name, it sounded magical and powerful and feminine and a whole load of things she had never heard in it before. She didn't want to hear anything in the way he said her name. She had pushed this conversation into the safe zone so she could avoid stuff like that. She needed to forget the fantasy. She needed to be practical and wise.

And run like hell.

Instead, she looked up into his handsome, patrician face. "What, Hugh?" she said, using his first name.

His eyes darkened. "There's something I need to tell you. Come on." He took her hand again and guided her to a secluded area behind the 4-H barn, where a grassy bank sloped upward toward a stand of shade trees. The little hill provided a wonderful view of the midway lights.

They tumbled down onto the ground with the cool and dew-damp grass at their backs. Caroline stacked her hands behind her head and looked up into the night sky. Out here in the country, even with the lights from the midway, the sky seemed dark and velvety. The stars incredibly bright.

"So what is it that you want to tell me? I've got a feeling you just wanted to get me into a compromising position," she said.

Hugh rose up on his elbow and looked down at her, the stars silhouetting him. "Well, yes, I did. But I also need to tell you something about Cissy and her proposal."

"You agreed to it, didn't you?"

"No, I didn't. And before you lecture me on being a very poor businessman, I want to tell you a story about a little girl named Elisa."

"Hugh, what..."

He leaned down and kissed her so gently on the lips. Just one little kiss to shut her up. He accomplished his mission. "Just listen, love.

"When I was about six or so, I befriended the daughter of our chauffer. Her name was Elisa. And before you snicker at me, I know it's pretentious to have a chauffer, and you're quite correct. But Granddad was pretentious.

"Anyway, Elisa was like a garden sprite. She had dark hair and green eyes much like yours. She was a wild thing that loved to run in the meadows or wade barefoot in the stream. She told lovely stories about the little people. I was only six, but I loved her just the same. She was my best friend.

"I loved her father, too. He taught me about motorcars, and he let me help him keep the Bentley in good nick."

"What happened to them?" Caroline asked, even though she had a feeling she knew the ending of this story.

"My granddad fired Mr. Henson. Not because of anything he'd done wrong in his employment, but because I had made a friend of him and Elisa. Granddad discovered me with Mr. Henson, working on the Bentley. I was covered in motor oil. Granddad said I looked like a common workman. My punishment for this transgression was to watch Mr. Henson and Elisa pack their possessions and leave the servants' quarters. I was not allowed to cry."

"How awful."

"I know. I was devastated. But Granddad had made his point. Granddad had very old-fashioned notions about things, and he wanted me to know my place. He said that a deBracy was never to befriend servants, or to be familiar with them, or even to be kind to them."

"I'm so sorry."

"Yes, well Granddad was a complete prat. And from that moment on, I was nothing but rebellious. He died when I was fourteen, and I didn't cry at his funeral. And ever since, I've always gone out of my way to be kind to people. I've always told myself it was a way of paying back the damage Granddad did to Mr. Henson and his daughter."

"That's sweet."

"Yes, well, my trusting soul has gotten me into nothing but trouble. And I'm afraid my philosophy has gotten in the way of my dealings with Cissy. I refused her offer because I couldn't stop worrying about the people living in Last Chance. Your passion for them on Sunday struck a nerve. But the thing is, Granddad was right about some things. The guys with the kind hearts usually fail."

Caroline reached up and gave his shoulder a little reassuring squeeze. "You're not a failure. You've invented a loom that Cissy wants to get her hands on. She made you that offer because she thinks she can make money on your invention, and I'll bet she's going to rethink and up the ante. You should call her up tomorrow and start a negotiation. And don't sell yourself short."

"I have no intention of doing any such thing," he said in that stubborn voice of his—the one she'd mistaken for arrogance a few days ago. Now she recognized it as something more like gumption. He was hanging on to his dream with both hands, wasn't he? It was admirable.

But she couldn't let him give up a chance like the one Cissy had offered him.

"Hugh, I mean it. You've got no hope of building here. You should—"

"Stop, love," he said, his voice soft and sure, "I know all the arguments. But I want to give it a day or two. There's no rush. Maybe working together, we can fix things here, and I won't have to sell my technology to Cissy. And in the meantime, we can get to know each other better."

He dipped down and slid his mouth over hers, nibbling at her lower lip until she yielded to his sultry demands. His kisses were delicious. They melted on her tongue like cotton candy, leaving nothing but sweetness behind.

She ran her hands up over his shoulders and down his back, feeling the play of firm muscles there. Meanwhile, he undid her ponytail and combed his fingers through her hair, messing it up beyond redemption and creating shivers across her scalp.

His beard rasped against her cheek, his mouth devoured. He was hard and sturdy and male in all the right places. And he knew how to kiss. Holy smokes, the guy's kisses were more intoxicating than the drinks he mixed that night at Dot's Spot.

She explored the contours of his body, pushing aside all her cares and worries. She forgot about the gossip in town, the job in Washington, the trouble at the chicken plant—all of it faded into the background.

He kissed down to the nape of her neck, and she melted right into him. When he finally retreated, she was breathless with yearning.

"I've been thinking about doing that all day," he murmured against her ear. "I've been thinking about the things we didn't do last night. The things we wanted to do. I have a long list of those things, Rocky."

"Me, too," she whispered.

Hugh had no clue how long they spent snogging in the grass. He lost track of time and place. Everything narrowed down to Rocky, and her warm skin, her soft breasts, and her spicy, exotic scent.

He undid all the buttons down the front of her golf shirt. It hardly reached her amazing cleavage, but kissing the spot right below her collarbone was making all his dangly bits stand up and pay attention.

She let go of a deeply pensive sigh and said, "What are we going to do?"

He raised his head to look down at her. The midway lights twinkled in her pixie green eyes, and her hair was a wild tumble around her head, spread out against the grass. If she'd been wearing anything other than a golf shirt and shorts, he might have mistaken her for the Queen of Faerie.

He wanted this woman in ways he couldn't quite explain. He'd told her things about himself he'd never meant to tell a soul. She knew his problems. She knew his failures and his fears. She knew all his mistakes. And she wasn't very dazzled by his title or his background.

Being with her was so easy. It had been such a long, long time since he'd had a friend he could trust with his secrets. Elisa had been like that. And in a lot of ways, she reminded him of Elisa. They were both magical in some way he couldn't quite fathom.

He smiled down at her and said, "I believe this is the point where you suggest that we go off into the piney woods for an evening's frolic with your magical friends. I will never return to the real world, of course, having been utterly ensorcelled by your beauty."

She giggled. "Uh, wait, I don't think I'm in the same fantasy. In mine, this is when Prince Charming sweeps me up into his manly arms and carries me off to his castle."

"Darling, my castle is very drafty."

"You have a castle?"

"Well, it's more of a manor house."

"Wow."

"And to be honest, the woods sound ever so much more delightful and magical. Listen, the crickets have been serenading us."

"Uh, yeah, along with the frogs. And believe me, there are other critters out there in the piney woods."

"Are you about to bring up scary stories of snakes and alligators again?"

She giggled.

"Perhaps we should compromise."

"Compromise is good. What did you have in mind?"

"Well, you did tell me about that place that sells rooms by the hour."

She laughed again. "I'm not taking you to the Peach Blossom Motor Court." He heard the regret in her voice and desperately wanted to erase it.

"Was that a tawdry suggestion?" he asked.

She ran her hand up over his shoulders and let her fingers roam through his hair. Her touch made him shiver. He closed his eyes and let her touch him, savoring every moment.

"Love, if we don't go to a place like that, what do you suggest?"

She didn't say anything for the longest time.

"Blast it, Last Chance needs a decent hotel, you know that?" he muttered.

"Well, there's the Magnolia Inn over in Allenberg. It's not much better than the Peach Blossom, but it has the benefit of not being within spying distance of Lillian Bray and her high-powered telescope."

He opened his eyes. "Are you saying yes to my compromising suggestion?"

"I want to, Hugh. I really do. But we need to be clear. This is a fantasy, you know? A fling. In a few days, I'm going to be moving to Washington, and you're going to figure out that the best proposal you've got comes from Cissy Warren."

He stared down into her lovely pale face. He ought to argue with her. He knew he was in far deeper than she was. He didn't want a fling.

He wanted to find a place here, in her town, where he could be himself. And he had this feeling she could give that to him.

But he knew if he said this aloud, she'd run away like the wild thing she really was. He could see through that disguise she wore. The real Rocky let her hair down without him having to help her. The real Rocky spoke her mind and wore frothy dresses that showed off her unbelievable breasts. The real Rocky went about on bare feet.

He smiled. "Madam, I am pleased to provide any fantasy you want."

She giggled again. "Okay. But you have to remember it's just for one night."

"Right, I have it. Sort of like Cinderella."

• • •

The Magnolia Inn stood just beyond Allenberg's town limits with a rusty sign bearing a blinking neon magnolia blossom. It was truly an awful place to play out a Cinderella fantasy.

Hugh killed the engine and gave the place the once-over. He said nothing, but Caroline could almost read his thoughts.

"I know, it's kind of trashy, but…" Caroline started to say.

"Well, darling, I suspect it's better than going off into your woods and getting eaten alive by mosquitoes. I must have twenty bites just from that time we spent in the grass."

"I suppose. We grow 'em big here in South Carolina." Her voice sounded uncertain, and Hugh turned to look at her.

The flashing neon magnolia lit up his gentle smile. "If you're nervous and don't want to do this, that's fine. But I want to be with you."

He leaned across the console and laid another scorching kiss on her that made her toes curl right up. She lost her espadrilles, and then she lost her sanity as he ran his hands through her hair.

Breathing became difficult after a few moments of this.

"Blast this console," he said, finally pulling away. "Darling, I will procure a key. You stay here."

A few minutes later they stepped into a motel room that gave the word "common" a whole new meaning. As he surveyed the room, Hugh missed nothing, from the ersatz walnut of the TV stand to the Magic Fingers massage unit bolted to the wall. Then his gaze fixed upon hers. "You are lovely," he said.

What an utterly sweet thing to say at a low-rent moment like this. Caroline stood on tiptoes and kissed his mouth softly. One kiss led to another, and soon they were lost in the heat of the moment.

He found the hem of her golf shirt and pulled it over her head. She unbuttoned his shirt. Her blood heated the moment he enveloped her in his arms. The slide of skin on skin made her lose her mind. His hands got busy getting her out of her shorts and her bra and her panties. Then those same amazing gentle hands moved down her backbone, to her butt, over her hips, and finally to her breasts.

This was always the point where Caroline felt just a little bit awkward. Most guys made a beeline for them, and Hugh already got points for making her boobs his last stop. Usually guys groped them, or squeezed them too hard, or played with her nipples in a way that wasn't at all pleasurable.

Hugh's approach was completely different. Holy smokes, the man knew what he was doing with those engineer's hands. He brushed his fingers lightly over her, circling toward the most sensitive parts. By the time he actually touched her nipples, she was ready to beg for it.

He generated so much heat and pleasure with those hands of his that it eventually became impossible for Caroline to stay upright.

She tumbled backward onto the bed. He followed after her, his hands and then his mouth continuing the thorough and amazing exploration of her body.

And then the profanity hit the fan, along with a wave of pleasure that took her someplace beyond reality.

Caroline said that filthy word more than a dozen times, right in a row.

She screamed it, actually.

So loud, in fact, that the folks in the next room over (who were undoubtedly doing the same thing as Hugh and Caroline) started banging on the wall.

And that's when Baron Woolham let go of a truly depraved laugh. "You are not nearly as prim and proper as you appear, Miss Rhodes," he said.

"Are you going to tell my boss about this?"

"No. I am the very soul of discretion."

He laughed again, and she laughed with him. It felt so incredibly liberating to laugh like this. To simply throw caution to the wind and let herself go.

Hugh divested himself of his pants, then pulled Caroline into an embrace as their laughter died. She halfway expected him to move on with his own pleasure. After all, he'd given her one orgasm. How many did a girl need?

The answer to that question was definitely more than one. He went back to business and took his own sweet time with it, kissing her, cuddling her, touching her, finding her sensitive places, and making her feel like she was the center of his universe.

No one had ever made her feel like this. So relaxed and special and cared for. This was every fantasy she'd ever dreamed. This was beyond fantasy, really. The shabby motel room faded into the background, and it was just the two of them, touching with their hands and their bodies.

Touching souls.

How could anyone live without this?

Caroline tumbled down into her fantasy so deeply

that it ensnared her. She was falling for Hugh deBracy in a way that was utterly forbidden. He was speaking a language with his hands that her heart and soul seemed to know and understand.

She forgot that the Magnolia Inn was a long way from those fancy London town homes featured in Momma's romance books. She forgot that a girl like her and a baron like him were never going to find a happy ending. Because, darn it, he didn't seem like a baron, and she didn't seem like a poor country girl.

They seemed to fit together in some strange way she'd never felt before. He was a lot like her. He came from a small town. He cared for people. He was just a little bit unsure of himself, even though he was amazingly talented. He kept up appearances to hide all his doubts and his fears. She understood him in a way that definitely knocked her for a loop.

"Rocky, you are perfect." He whispered her name as they reached for something amazing and lovely. And in that instant, she was his, completely and forever.

Rocky dozed off, utterly satisfied, in the circle of Hugh's arms. She drifted somewhere warm, wonderful, and disconnected with time and place. She never wanted to leave.

But unfortunately, she came back to her senses and found herself between the rough sheets of a not very fine motel. Beyond the window, the neon magnolia sign flashed on and off, sending its pinkish glow through the draperies. Beneath her ear, Hugh's heart beat in steady rhythm and his chest rose and fell.

She cuddled closer and built a few fairy castles in her mind. Maybe it was possible for a girl like her and a baron like him to find something special. He was pretty talented with his hands. He'd looked kind of like one of the boys this evening. He might be a match.

She might know that Cinderella was a big myth, but right at that moment she would have denied it. This was her Cinderella moment. It was possible. Everything was possible.

"A penny?" he whispered against her temple where his lips rested.

She sighed.

"Ah, that good, then?"

She snuggled against him, trying to hold the magic of her fantasies. She wanted him so bad.

"Are you having regrets?" he asked. "Because, love, I have none. I want to pursue this."

She raised her head. Could he read minds, too? "Pursue what?"

He tucked a wayward strand of her hair behind her ear. His eyes shone with kindness and something else in the rising and falling light from the sign outside. "Everything, darling. I want to pursue everything."

"Everything?"

And wouldn't you know it, before Hugh could say another word, the clock struck midnight, and someone pounded on the door.

It was not Caroline's fairy godmother.

No sir. It was the Last Chance chief of police. "Rocky Rhodes, you answer this door," Stone bellowed.

Rocky and Hugh both bolted upright. "Bollocks," Hugh said, "is that your brother out there?"

"Uh, yeah. Look, don't worry, he's mostly harmless. You stay there. I'll find some clothes," Rocky said.

Then she shouted at the door. "Shut up, Stone. Give me a minute."

She slipped from the bed, found her panties and Hugh's shirt, and made herself semidecent before cracking the door and peeping through.

Stone looked all business in his uniform and bullet-proof vest. He had his service weapon on his belt and a stern look on his face.

"Since when are you the morality police?" Rocky said. "And don't you dare tell me you've never seen the insides of this place, because I happen to know that you have." She stomped on the urge to remind him that he and Sharon had spent their first night as husband and wife at the Magnolia Inn. Of course, the main difference between Stone and Sharon and Rocky and Hugh was a little thing called a marriage vow.

She'd come here for a one-night stand. But she wanted more.

"Get dressed." Stone's gaze rose to meet Hugh, who had pulled on his jeans and was now standing right behind her. Rocky glanced at Hugh, taken aback once again by his beautiful naked chest. She wanted Stone to leave now so she could go back to jumping Hugh's bones and talking about the pursuit of "everything."

"Daddy's been arrested for assaulting Lillian Bray," Stone said.

Rocky turned, her stomach suddenly heavy. "That's not possible. Daddy wouldn't—"

"But he did this time. And it gets worse. Lillian's using what Daddy did to hand your *boyfriend* every-thing he's asked for." Stone pointed a menacing finger in Hugh's direction.

"What?" Rocky's head felt like someone had just taken a tire iron to it.

"You heard me. And I'm pretty sure you know all about it. You probably dreamed the whole thing up, seeing as you're the one who majored in political science, and this mess has a big political power grab written all over it."

"What are you talking about?"

"You don't know?" Stone paused for a moment as he stared daggers at Hugh. His gaze shifted again. "Your lover there is working up a deal with the town council to have Golfing for God condemned. Lillian is the chief sponsor of the effort. And after the bone-headed move Daddy pulled this afternoon, she's managed to get a majority of the council to go along with her. There's going to be a vote tomorrow."

The heaviness in Rocky's stomach began to roil. She turned around and looked up into Hugh's eyes. He looked sober as a duke. "Is this true?"

"In part. I did discuss condemning the golf course, but I never agreed to do it."

"But you discussed it? And you decided to go forward with this plan instead of taking Cissy up on her proposal to put the factory up north? Is this what you meant about trying to help the town?"

"No, Rocky, you know better than—"

"Shut up." Her head was sobering up fast. Her heart was screaming in agony.

"Now, darling, just calm yourself for one—"

"No. Answer me. Did you let anyone on the town council think that you supported condemning Daddy's land?"

"Well, I suppose some of them may have gotten that impression, but..." His voice faded off, as if he suddenly understood the implications of what he'd done and where he'd ended up the evening.

Rocky clutched the doorframe as the adrenaline rushed through her body. Meanwhile Stone gave Hugh a look that would have turned Medusa into granite. And Hugh glowered right back, eye to eye.

Hugh looked like a man who was used to getting his way. There was nothing about that look that said "failure" to Caroline.

Stone looked like a real badass ex-Marine turned cop who didn't let anyone mess with the people he loved.

It was a complete showdown, and Rocky was caught right in the middle of it—exactly the place she always tried to avoid.

"Get dressed. I'm taking you home," Stone commanded.

"No, you're not," Hugh replied. His hand came down on Rocky's shoulder, and her body went into a confused and conflicted spasm. His hand felt warm and reassuring and kind. Her body craved that touch.

But her head. Oh boy, her head was sobering up really fast. A rational, smart career girl knew better than to do what she had done tonight.

"I'll see that Rocky gets home directly." Hugh's speech was delivered just like a line from out of Momma's romance novels.

"You heard me, Rocky. Get dressed, you're coming with me," Stone said in his no-nonsense voice.

She shrugged off Hugh's hand. "Why didn't you tell me the truth about what happened today?" she asked him.

"Darling, listen, I don't want to swindle your father. I

did discuss options for condemning the land, but surely you don't believe that I would—"

"I'll be right with you," Rocky said to Stone. Then she slammed the door and started looking for her clothes. She was an idiot. A fool.

Sharon was right. She needed to focus on her career, not her love life. She could live without Hugh deBracy. He was a fantasy. And if she wanted fantasy, she could read a book. But her career and her family were realities.

She should take a good look in the mirror and remember who the hell she was. She was Rocky Rhodes of Last Chance, South Carolina. And she loved her family, even if it was the weirdest, most eccentric family in the universe. And she was not going to be part of any scheme to steal Daddy's land. No matter what her boss wanted, or her heart yearned for, or what Last Chance needed for its tax base.

She studied Hugh for a long moment. He looked like a baron all right, with that regal bearing and that narrow nose and square chin.

"It was a nice fantasy," she said. "But it's over. I had a good time, but you know, I never would have come here if I'd known you were talking about condemning Daddy's land. That hurt, Hugh. I love my father, and you know good and well that I've never thought for one minute that building your factory down south of town was a good idea. You should have been honest with me."

She shucked out of his shirt and started putting herself back together.

Hugh stood with a completely unreadable look on his face as he watched her get dressed. He did nothing to stop her. He seemed to have forgotten those whispered words right before Stone came knocking, about wanting to pursue everything. Perhaps that's exactly what he'd meant—that he wanted her and Daddy's land, too.

Proving that a girl could never trust words whispered before, during, or right after incredible sex.

Yup, Sharon had been right. A girl shouldn't ever let lust carry her away. A girl needed to use her head.

Especially a girl with a career working for a U.S. senator.

CHAPTER 18

Fifteen minutes later, Rocky sat in the passenger seat of Stone's cruiser with her elbows on her knees and the heels of her hands pressed firmly into her eye sockets. Maybe if she applied enough direct pressure, she could keep from hemorrhaging tears. So far it was working.

"We're home," Stone finally said. A second later, his fingers massaged her tense shoulders.

"So are you going to tell Momma where you found me?"

"Of course not."

She finally dropped her hands and turned her head. "You're not?"

"No, but it hardly matters. Momma will learn the truth eventually. She might know it already, the way the gossip mill works in this town. And don't get any ideas about me covering for you. I'm not lying to Momma and Daddy. I plan to say nothing at all."

"I suppose I deserve that." Rocky choked on the words.

"No one deserves what he did to you," Stone said. "That was dishonest and unkind."

She wiped an errant tear from her cheek. "You're not blaming me?"

He shook his head. "I'm satisfied that you didn't know a thing about his plan to have Daddy's land condemned. But you should have. By the way, the next time I see that guy, I intend to whup his ass. I don't like foreigners taking advantage of my little sister. He's not the one for you."

Stone reached out and tucked a lock of her out-of-control hair behind her ear. "But one day, some guy is going to come along and he's going to be everything you ever wanted. He's going to look at you and you're not going to know what hit you."

Caroline felt the sobs knotting up in her throat. For an instant back there at the Magnolia Inn, she could have sworn that's what had happened. Obviously, lust had blinded her to the truth.

She swallowed back her tears. She refused to cry over this. She had no reason to cry. She had gone for a one-night thing, and she'd gotten exactly what she'd wanted out of it. So what did she have to complain about anyway?

"Well, let's hope I meet my soulmate after I move to Washington, okay?" Despite her resolve, her voice sounded wobbly.

Stone's usually sober mouth curled up sweetly on one side. "Honey, whether it happens sooner or later is not the point. The point is that Miriam Randall predicted it. I don't believe in much, but I believe in Miz Miriam. I've been on the receiving end of one of her predictions. And boy howdy, one of those predictions can mess you up for a while, but it's a good kind of mess."

Is that why Sharon had run away with him? It was a good question because every conversation Rocky had ever had with Sharon seemed to suggest that a girl should think before she took any kind of wild leaps into the unknown.

"Are you okay, little gal?"

"Yeah, I'm fine." She was not about to share the advice Sharon had given her twelve years ago. She didn't think it was something Stone wanted to hear. Instead, she changed the subject. "So what are we going to do about Daddy?"

"I've got to go bail him out."

"He's really in jail?"

"Going after Lillian with a broom is not exactly a felony. But the penalty for misdemeanor assault is three years and a fine. He might have to do time if he gets a hanging judge."

"You mean this wasn't just a figment of Lillian's overactive imagination?" A really ugly emotion churned in Rocky's middle.

"Unfortunately, Daddy went after Lillian's flowers, and I doubt the old biddy is in a forgiving mood."

"Oh, crap. Please tell me he didn't do that because Hugh was trying to condemn the golf course. My shame will know no bounds if that's what happened."

"Well, you can relax about that. The truth is the fight started over the stuff Lillian said to Haley on Saturday about how my daughter should be committed."

"Oh, no."

Stone hunched his shoulders and gave his head a roll.

"So, I'm the one feeling ashamed. If anyone should have said something to Lillian, it should have been me, not Daddy. I guess Daddy waited a whole day for me to do something, and I didn't. So he took matters into his own hands."

"Oh, c'mon, don't blame yourself for this. Lillian is a bully, and Daddy always says we should ignore bullies."

"I know," Stone said.

Rocky drew in a deep breath. "Let me come with you to bail out Daddy."

"No."

"I need to, Stone. Don't tell me no. I need to tell Daddy the truth before any of the gossips do."

"The truth?" Stone asked.

"Yeah, the truth. The whole truth and nothing but."

Rocky sat on the hard bench at the county jail and watched Stone work through the paperwork for Daddy's bail. It took about twenty minutes before Daddy emerged from the holding cell at the Allenberg County Jail. The slogan on Daddy's T-shirt today said, "God Allows U-Turns."

Elbert gave Stone a man-hug. "Thank you, son. I never did think I'd live to see the day that you bailed me out of jail."

Daddy turned toward Rocky. "Little gal, why are you here?" He cast a shamefaced glance Stone's way, as if to say that the last thing Daddy wanted was for his daughter to see him like this.

Rocky didn't wait for any more words, she simply flung herself at her father, and Daddy caught her. Daddy always caught her. Daddy caught her the first time she jumped off a diving board. Daddy picked her up every time she fell. Daddy chased after her when she first learned to ride a bike. And Daddy stood by her the night Bubba humiliated her—not with words, like Momma, but with his big strong shoulder. Rocky had shed a lot of tears on Daddy's shoulder over the years.

So she burrowed deep into his chest, the hot tears she'd been holding back making a sudden appearance. She wrapped her arms around him and wouldn't let go.

"Honey, it's all right. Lillian Bray is a big bully. I just lost my temper with her."

"Daddy, I just want you to know that I have never, ever tried to convince anyone that it would be better to bulldoze Golfing for God."

"What does that have to do with Lillian's gladioli?"

"Because Lillian is telling the town council that you're crazy and that it would be a good thing for them to condemn the golf course. And even though Hugh needs that land, I have never tried to help him get it. I've been trying to convince him to build someplace else. I don't want to see the golf course bulldozed. And I..." The tears ran down her cheeks.

Daddy brushed her tears away with his big, rough hands. "I know that. You were just doing your job. And you're good at that job. I don't blame you."

"Daddy, my job didn't include falling for that Englishman. It was stupid. He didn't tell me the truth. On several occasions. And now I feel like a real fool."

"You fell for the Englishman?"

She nodded and snuffled.

"Well, that's a problem right there. I don't think he matches what Miriam told you to be looking for."

"Don't you think I know that? But I fell for him anyway. And now I hear that he's teaming up with Lillian. I'm so ashamed."

She broke down into sobs. Daddy held her tight. After a long time, when she finally re-exerted control, she pushed back and said, "I love you, Daddy."

"I love you, too, angel face."

She wiped tears from her cheeks and said, "What on earth came over you to attack Lillian's flowers? Haven't I heard you say a million times that the best way to handle bullies is to ignore them? And don't tell me you were mad at Stone because he didn't protect Haley. Didn't it ever occur to you that Stone was just applying your philosophy?"

Daddy appeared vaguely sheepish. "Yeah. But honest, I didn't go over there to rip up Lillian's garden."

"Then why?"

"I went there to tell the old biddy that if she had a problem with me, she could take it up with me, instead of using Haley as a surrogate."

"So what happened?"

Daddy didn't say anything. He looked away, over Rocky's head, toward Stone.

"Daddy, are you really all right?" Stone asked.

"Yeah." He said it a little too quick.

Rocky cocked her head and frowned at her father. "Daddy, what is it?"

Daddy paused for a long moment before speaking. "I can say without a doubt that I hit Lillian Bray with the business end of a broom. On her fat backside. I clearly remember knocking her down, but I didn't really hurt her. And the only reason I did that was because she came after me with the handle end of that broom. She was swinging for my head, and I had to defend myself."

"Why did she come after you?"

"I'm not exactly sure. They say I tore up her flower-bed, but I don't rightly remember doing that. One minute I was there talking about Haley and then the world got kind of wonky. I didn't exactly black out, but I was kind of stuck. It was weird."

"You blacked out?" Rocky asked.

He shook his head. "No, but my memories are all kind of twisted. I sure don't remember tearing up any flowers. I would never do a thing like that. I admire Lillian's glads, and those flowers deserved better."

"Should we be taking you to Doc Cooper? You didn't have dizziness or trouble with your eyesight, did you?" Stone asked, his voice suddenly quite urgent.

"Not exactly," Daddy said.

"That's it, I'm taking you to see Doc Cooper," Stone said.

Daddy gave Stone a big-eyed stare. "Son, you don't think I'm coming down with Alzheimer's, do you?"

No one in the Rhodes family got much sleep that night. Rocky and Stone took Daddy to Doc Cooper's, where Momma met them. And then, on the doc's recommendation, Daddy was admitted to the hospital in Orangeburg for a battery of tests and evaluations.

Tulane, Rocky's youngest brother, drove over from his home in Florence and stayed with Momma and Clay at the hospital and made arrangements to get Daddy the best lawyer money could buy. Stone and Rocky came home, where Rocky fell into her bed and proceeded to cry her eyes out.

She was an unmitigated fool for losing her heart to Hugh deBracy. She needed to grow up, accept her fate, pack her bags, and head for Washington. And she never, ever wanted to hear another word about Miriam Randall and her matrimonial forecasts. She was swearing off men and love and relationships.

But before she did all that, she had to stop the town council from trying to condemn Daddy's land.

The next morning, everyone seemed to have a place to be and something productive to do. Stone dropped Haley at Miriam's and Lizzy at camp and went to work. Jane covered at the Cut 'n Curl because Momma was in Orangeburg with Daddy.

And Rocky, her eyes still swollen, her heart still dinged and battered, her reputation in tatters, hauled herself off to the doughnut shop for a sugar fix. Maybe a cruller would help her figure out this mess.

She'd just taken a delicious sugary bite when her cell phone rang. She checked the caller ID.

"Hey, Rachel," she said as she pressed the talk button.

"Rocky, are you okay? Honest to God, the gossip is running rampant this morning. Is your daddy really in Orangeburg in the hospital? Was he really arrested? And I know everyone is saying you're behind the scheme to condemn his land and bulldoze the golf course, but I don't believe that one for a minute."

Rocky groaned. "Yes, Daddy is in Orangeburg. He had a blackout, and Doc Cooper is worried about him. And yes, Lillian Bray, in addition to having him arrested for assault, is trying to get the town council to condemn his land. And no, I had nothing to do with that idea."

"Was that Lord Woolham's idea?"

Rocky squeezed her eyes shut. She wanted to believe what Hugh had said last night. But a little part of her doubted him. He hadn't done a thing, really, to defend the accusations Stone had thrown in his direction. And besides, he'd given her that line last night about caring for Last Chance and its people. He'd talked about the lower classes and how he was their friend.

Yeah, right. She was a complete sucker.

"I don't know if Hugh is responsible," Rocky said, her voice sounding miserable.

"Oh, crap. Honey, a whole lot of people saw you with him last night. And you were not behaving in a professional way."

"I know. I let the fantasy carry me away."

"Aw, honey, I'm sorry. But hey, he wasn't the one for you anyway. We both knew that."

Caroline ground her teeth together. She was getting really tired of everyone telling her that Hugh was not the one for her. Because last night the two of them together had felt so right. Like it was meant to be.

Maybe that was only lust. She could live without lust, right? She clutched the advice that Sharon had given her like a lifeline. She could live without Hugh deBracy. But she couldn't live with herself if she let Lillian Bray condemn Golfing for God.

She decided to change the subject. She needed to move on. "How'd it go with Bubba?" she asked.

Silence beat for a moment followed by a long, contented sigh.

"That good?"

"Oh, yeah. I'm going to the country music concert down at the fairgrounds with him tonight. I can't wait until his mouth heals."

"Well, that sounds real nice, Rachel," Rocky said as a pang of jealously hit her in the gut. Why couldn't she be sighing and looking forward to a date with Hugh?

Just then an unexpected burst of noise came through the cell phone. It sounded like people hollering at one another. "Uh, Rache, what's going on?"

"Holy cow, Hettie's here at work. She just walked right into Jimmy's office, and she's screaming at him. And he's screaming right back at—" Rachel broke off the conversation, and Rocky heard several rather colorful cuss words being shouted in the background.

"Rachel?"

The noise continued for a moment, followed by what sounded like slamming doors. Rachel came back on the line, her voice suddenly urgent and worried. "Hettie just slapped Jimmy's face and told him she wasn't going to bail him out anymore. She said he needed to fix things here at the plant. And she said that if he continued to support the effort to take away your daddy's land, she would divorce him without batting an eye."

Rocky swallowed down a sticky sweet bite of cruller. The sugar wrapped itself around her mouth and made its way right to her brain, where it kick-started her thought processes.

She wondered idly if Dash and Hettie would ever get together again. Because it sure did look like the Queen Bee was about to get a divorce.

And just like that, all the pieces of the impossible

puzzle she'd been working on for the last several days suddenly fit together in the perfect solution.

Why the hell hadn't she seen it before?

Haley Rhodes sat in the swing on Miz Miriam's porch. Daddy had dropped her off here early this morning for breakfast on account of the fact that everyone in the family was in a really, really bad mood, and everyone had someplace important to go today, except Haley and her angel.

Granny, Granddaddy, Uncle Clay, and Uncle Tulane were off in Orangeburg, where Granddaddy was in the hospital. Aunt Jane was working at the Cut 'n Curl. Daddy was at work.

And no one was talking about Aunt Rocky. Everyone seemed to be kind of mad at her for something Haley didn't really understand. She had a feeling everyone thought Aunt Rocky was responsible for getting Granddaddy into trouble.

But it wasn't Aunt Rocky who tore up Miz Bray's flowers.

Haley stared at the Sorrowful Angel, who was sitting on the porch railing. The angel looked kind of pitiful today.

"You shouldn't have tore up Miz Bray's garden like that," Haley said. Haley hadn't told anyone that it was the angel who messed up Miz Bray's flowers. She really wanted to tell people, but nobody would believe her. They all thought Granddaddy had done it, and for some reason, they thought Aunt Rocky had put him up to it or something. It was confusing.

"I wish you would go back to Heaven," she told the angel.

The angel nodded and wiped a tear away.

"I hate you. Everyone's mad at Granddaddy on account of you."

The angel hung her head.

Haley's eyes filled up and pretty soon she was bawling as hard as the angel. She drew her knees up and rested her head on them. Meanwhile, the angel came to sit beside her and put her arm around Haley's shoulders.

The angel was cold. But having her there was a comfort just the same. Without the angel, Haley would be all alone. And that thought made her cry a little harder. What would happen if the angel really did find a way back to Heaven?

She cried until she couldn't cry anymore.

Sometime later, a strange voice said, "I say, is that a ghost?"

Haley opened her eyes to find a little gray-haired lady standing on Miz Miriam's porch. She wore a pair of bright red eyeglasses and a purple dress. The lady sat down in one of Miz Miriam's rocking chairs and fanned her red face.

"Crikey, it's hot." She smiled. "I'm Petal deBracy, and who are you two?"

Haley blinked. "You can see the angel?"

Petal turned and looked really hard at the angel. You could tell when someone was faking it. This lady wasn't a faker.

"I don't think she's an angel, love," Petal said. "More like a spirit of one who's departed, in my opinion."

Haley wasn't sure what the lady meant, but it was sure interesting to find someone who could actually see the angel. "Hi, I'm Haley."

The lady put out her hand, and Haley shook it. Petal had warm, sweaty hands. "And you." She tilted her head toward the angel.

The angel didn't say a word, which was not too unusual.

"Not a big talker, then?"

"Nope. She just gets people into trouble. And she cries a lot. But she's my friend."

Petal nodded. "Yes, I can see that. You've been crying as well. Spirits can be quite helpful at times, but then again when they get to haunting, they are more nuisance than help, I've found. The trick is to figure out what unfinished business they are on about. If you can help them finish up their business, then they are easily gotten rid of."

"Really?"

"Oh, absolutely. There are dozens of stories about how one goes about helping a spirit to move on. I could tell them to you. But first, what seems to be her problem?"

Haley took a deep breath and started to talk. It was such a relief to find a grown-up who took what she had to say about the Sorrowful Angel seriously.

Hugh's mobile phone pulled him from his fitful sleep. He cracked an eye and read the time on the clock radio beside the cheap and lumpy bed. It was almost noon. His head hurt.

After Rocky had left him last night, he'd taken a long walk, right into a rather seedy roadhouse across the street from the Magnolia Inn.

His single beer turned into more than one, and before he knew it, he'd befriended a group of locals and got pulled into a game of eight-ball snooker. Luckily the tavern was within walking distance of his room at the Inn because he'd gotten himself pissing drunk.

It seemed the appropriate thing to do, seeing as his fantasy woman had left in a huff, and he had no earthly clue how to win her back.

He reached for his mobile phone and checked the caller ID.

"Petunia," he said as he pressed the talk button. He tried to sound bright and chipper, but he failed. "Is there a problem at home, love?"

"Is there a problem?" The timbre of Petunia's voice reminded him of the times when he'd disappointed his aunt. Disappointing Petunia was far worse than disappointing Granddad. Granddad was always disappointed. But disappointing Petunia was a rare thing and always made him feel very low indeed.

"Have I done something wrong?" he asked.

Silence beat at him for several long moments before she spoke again. "Everything is fine at home. But not here in South Carolina. I've just had the most amazing story from Mrs. Harry Randall. My word, Hugh, this is a very interesting village you've found for your factory. Petal quite approves of it."

Hugh sat up in bed. It was a big mistake. His head felt like someone was driving nails through it. "Are you here?"

"Where is here? I am in Last Chance, South Carolina. You, apparently, are not here. According to your landlady, you did not return home last night. That is, apparently, cause for much gossip and speculation, which is quite unseemly."

"You're in Last Chance? Why?"

"Simple, really. Petal insisted that we had to come. Something about Queen Aeval being very upset with you."

"Queen Aeval, the mythological goddess of Irish fishwives? Since when do you believe in Aeval?"

"When Aeval and my own spiritual guides are in agreement, that's when."

"Oh, Christ."

"Yes, well, perhaps He can help, but I'm not one to put much faith in Him. Is it true what they say here? That you're trying to force that man who owns the golf course off his property? My word, Hugh, I would expect something like that from Father, but not from you."

"Granddad *would* approve, wouldn't he?"

"Yes, well, he might. But I don't. Goodness, Hugh, couldn't you build your factory someplace not already occupied?"

"Yes, I can. In fact, I was made a very nice offer yesterday to do just that."

"Really?"

"Yes. A textile heiress wants to buy my loom technology."

"And you accepted this offer?"

"No, I didn't. I probably should have. That would have made everyone happy. I would have lived up to the family motto—*Honor in duty*—and all that."

"Really, there are more important things than duty and honor, Hugh."

"Not according to Granddad."

"Well, he was misguided."

"Maybe he was. But he was usually right. And if I'd been more like him, I wouldn't have made such a mess of things."

"I take it this textile heiress isn't named Rocky Rhodes." Petunia managed to put her finger right on the heart of the matter.

His face burned. "Aunt Petunia, please. I don't think—"

"Exactly, Hugh, you haven't been thinking. I'm quite appalled, really. You've been behaving like Father, with all this rot about duty and honor and heiresses. It's a very good thing Petal insisted we come before you made yourself a complete villain."

"Right. Look, Aunt Petunia, I—"

"We need to talk. Face-to-face. You will meet us here at Mrs. Randall's boardinghouse directly. And then we are all going down to City Hall for the meeting at two o'clock. You will stand up and you will tell the town council that you oppose the plan to force that man off his land."

Hugh was not about to go back to Miriam Randall's boardinghouse to be dressed down by his aunts. He would, however, go to the meeting of the town council. He owed Rocky that much.

"I'll be at the council meeting. I'll see you there." He pressed the disconnect button before she could say another word.

He would clear up this problem with the town council and make it clear that he had no intention of forcing Elbert Rhodes from his land. And then he had to make a choice: Cissy Warren or Lady Ashton.

He propped himself in his bed for a long, long moment, weighing his dream of a factory against his duty to his family.

There was no contest. Duty won out. He was, after all, a deBracy.

He would go home and marry Lady Ashton, which was, oddly, precisely what Miriam Randall had predicted he would do.

Rocky leaned against the fence at the Painted Corner Stables and watched as Lizzy made another circuit around the corral, controlling her horse's gait with nothing more than the pressure of her legs.

The horse was as big as a house, but Lizzy had complete control of that critter. The sight of Lizzy and the horse put an unexpected smile on Rocky's lips. The kid was turning into someone Sharon would have been so proud of.

Dash Randall watched from the corral fence, making the occasional comment on form and technique. He was completely focused on the girl and horse, and it was nice to see Dash at work, doing something useful that didn't involve a bat and a ball.

Not that Rocky had anything against baseball. And baseball had certainly been good for Dash. But baseball had been an addiction for Dash, sort of like Hettie Marshall and alcohol. Maybe he was making a new start.

She hoped so. In fact, she was depending on it.

She kept her distance until Lizzy finished her session and had dismounted. When Lizzy started walking the horse, Rocky moved down the fence line until she was standing right beside the big ex-jock.

"Your niece has talent," Dash said. "She might want to think about competing in dressage one day. She's got that horse doing things I thought he never would. That's Hettie's rescued Thoroughbred she's been helping me train.

And that horse was broken down when he came here. Lizzy's done a great job with him."

"You got a minute to talk?" Rocky asked.

He tipped the Stetson back on his head, and the sun sparked in those blue eyes of his. "I've heard that Rachel and Bubba are an item now, so I'm done with any and all masquerades. Although you gotta admit I'm a genius. Maybe I inherited some of Aunt Mim's magic."

"Miriam is related to you by marriage."

"Oh, yeah, well, there is that." He gave her a lopsided smile.

"I came to deliver some gossip and to ask you to do something that you're probably not going to want to do."

"Okay, that's pretty ominous. Sort of like bad news and more bad news." He leaned his body against the fence post, obviously shifting his weight to his good leg.

"Exactly. I'll start with the gossip, which I got from a firsthand source, so it's more like news than gossip."

"Yeah? And?"

"Hettie went into Jimmy's office about half an hour ago, slapped his face, and told him she wasn't going to bail him out anymore. She threatened divorce if Jimmy didn't get his act together, and she vowed to stand in the way of the effort to bulldoze Daddy's golf course."

Dash's smile faded. "From the talk around town, that makes her a better person than you."

Rocky put her hands on her hips. "Dash, you know good and well I would never try to have the council condemn Daddy's land."

"Yeah, I reckon. But that Englishman you've been so cozy with would."

She gritted her teeth. "Yes, I suppose he would, but that's not what I came here to talk about, okay?"

"Cried yourself to sleep last night, huh?"

She glared at him. "Would you please shut up for five minutes? This is really important."

"Okay, shoot."

"Hettie's trust fund isn't what it used to be. I know this because she told me. And I think you know it, too, because you've been paying top dollar for Jimmy's land. Obviously, Jimmy is strapped for cash. I don't know what Jimmy is into—gambling, bad investments, it's not important. Whatever it is, he's started cutting corners down at the plant. And sooner or later, he's going to get caught.

"I'm guessing that you offered to buy the plant from Jimmy, but he wouldn't sell because he's a rat bastard and he's always hated you."

The lopsided smile disappeared. "I'm impressed you figured that out," he said in a very sober voice.

"It didn't take a genius."

"So what's the favor?"

"Someone has to save this town or it's going to end up like most of the other small towns in America. And for that, we need a real tax base. We can't be a picturesque place with independent shopkeepers, unless we have some bigger businesses providing good manufacturing jobs. The chicken plant does that, but if the state swoops in and shuts it down, where the heck are we going to be?"

Dash's gaze became oddly focused. "Gee, Rocky, to hear you talk, I might think you cared."

"I do care. I don't want the chicken plant to fail. I love this town."

"Sometimes you have a strange way of showing it, girl. You couldn't wait to leave this place. And you stay away at Watermelon Festival time. And from what I hear, you're heading off to Washington any day now for a big career in politics."

A deep pang of regret darted through Rocky's chest. "Yeah, you're right. I ran away. I've been absent. But I still love my folks and I love this town. Every time I see the water tower on the horizon, I get all lumpy in the throat."

His smile returned. "Well, that's nice to know."

She put her hands on her hips. "Look, Dash, you can lose the smug tone. The town's in trouble, and I'm not in a position to save it."

Their gazes locked.

"But you are," she whispered.

"Me?" His baby blues got big and round. "Me, the messed-up bad boy drunk? I don't think so. I'm just about the last person on the face of the planet Jimmy Marshall wants to do business with. He only let me buy his land because there wasn't anyone else interested. Most of it's not worth much. So how, exactly, am I supposed to save the town?"

"You can give Lord Woolham land north of town. You could even invest in his factory. He's not proud. He'd take your money, and I've got a feeling he's going to be really successful. Cissy Warren's hot to have his technology. She's made him an offer, and if he accepts it, the factory is going to be built upstate. Do you want that to happen?"

He stood there staring at her. "Holy crap, you've fallen ass over tea kettle for him, haven't you?"

"Look, Dash, this isn't about Hugh. This is about you

and the town. You could be everyone's hero, Dash, the way Bubba once was. Only you'd be a real hero, instead of just a football hero. There isn't anyone else who can save this town. And think of how happy Hettie will be if you save Golfing for God."

CHAPTER 19

The air-conditioning at City Hall was taxed beyond its capacity. Sweat collected under Hugh's arms and dampened the back of his shirt. Arrayed before him on a small dais, behind a scarred and battered mahogany table, sat the members of the Last Chance Town Council. Big Bob presided, wearing a bow tie and a seersucker suit. Bob looked quite put out by this meeting.

Lillian Bray was turned out in a white dress that made her look like a Wagnerian opera singer without the long braids. Kamaria LaFlore wore a dress made of kente cloth. Dale Pontius looked a bit like Mr. Chips with his round glasses, mustache, and balding head. And Jimmy Marshall, dressed for the golf course, looked bored.

"All right, ya'll, we're here and it's hot, so let's get this over with as quickly as possible." Big Bob mopped his brow with a white handkerchief. "Lillian, I believe you have something to say?"

"Yes, I do." Lillian folded her hands in front of her and looked down her long narrow nose. "As ya'll know, I was brutally accosted last evening by Elbert Rhodes. And we all know that Doc Cooper thinks he may have finally lost his mind. Given that fact, and the fact that our town desperately needs new investment, I think we should consider using our town's power of eminent domain to condemn Golfing for God, so that Lord Woolham can build his factory on that land." Lillian stopped and gave Hugh a big smile that burned a hole right in the middle of his chest.

Big Bob took a breath and folded his handkerchief and returned it to his pocket. "Is there any discussion on this item?" he asked.

None of the other council members made a move to speak. So Hugh knew it was his time to stand up and stop this nonsense. He walked down to the microphone placed before the dais.

Before he could identify himself, or state his business, a commotion broke out in the hallway. The door to the chamber burst open, and a half-dozen women bearing hand-lettered signs marched up the aisle chanting, "Down with Lord deBracy." Hettie Marshall was in the lead, and it was almost as if her calm exterior had cracked a little between yesterday and today. She wore a blue suit and pearls, but her hair was askew, her eyes were big and a little wild, and she was chanting louder than all the others. It was almost as if she'd suddenly discovered her inner rebel.

"Good lord, Lavinia, what are you doing here?" Big Bob said to the woman right behind Hettie, who was carrying a sign that said, "God Bless Golfing for God."

The woman named Lavinia glowered at Big Bob. "I could be asking you the same thing. What makes you think you can just take away Bert Rhodes's land when he's never been anything but nice to you? And besides, we all love his wife."

"Lavinia, you get your butt back home, you hear?" Bob said.

"I will not. And if you think you're going to do this thing and have a blissful retirement with me, you have another think coming. Doesn't he, girls?" Lavinia turned around to her compatriots, her dark eyes sparking with her passion.

"Right on," the girls chorused with a few fist pumps. They renewed picketing up and down the aisle. All of them were wearing trainers on their feet, so it appeared they were ready to stay for quite a while.

Bob turned toward Stone Rhodes, who stood at the side of the room with one of his deputies. "You get these women out of here," Bob bellowed.

Stone hooked his thumbs in his belt, but he didn't move. "Your honor, are you sure you want me to arrest Miz Marshall?" Stone eyed Jimmy, whose boredom had vanished.

Jimmy Marshall sat there red faced, looking like he might stroke out at any moment.

Bob glanced at Last Chance's leading citizen and then back at Stone. "Belay that order," the mayor said.

Stone nodded and stayed put.

Bob banged his gavel. "All right, ya'll, you've made your point. Now sit down and behave like the ladies we know you are. We want to hear what Lord Woolham has to say."

Hettie scowled at her husband, who made a point of not looking at her. But Bob had made his point, and so had Hettie. She quietly directed the church ladies to line the back wall. They took their places, placards clutched in their hands.

Hugh turned back to the dais and the council members. "Thank you for this opportunity to speak. I—" he began.

The door at the back of the room burst open a second time. "Stop, right now, ya'll don't want to do this."

Hugh turned around to see Dash Randall stride up the aisle. Rocky followed behind him.

Rocky Rhodes seemed to trail magic wherever she went. Her presence left Hugh confused, dazed, and breathing very hard.

She wore one of her charcoal gray business suits, buttoned up all the way. Her hair was sleeked back. Her eyes were red, as if she'd had a really good cry. Her face looked pale and tired.

When their gazes connected, she stared at him, her green eyes hard and resolute. She'd put her mask back on, hadn't she? This was Caroline staring at him. Looking poised and polished and in control of herself and everything around her.

And yet, a little curl had escaped her hair clip. It dipped down over her forehead, and it seemed to represent everything Hugh knew about this amazing and beautiful woman.

Aunt Petal would say that he'd been bewitched. And maybe Aunt Petal had the right of it. Unfortunately, in all of those fairy stories, the besotted man didn't get his beautiful fairy princess. He had to return home and live out his drab, predictable life.

Hugh needed to quit woolgathering and get on with it.

He looked away from Rocky and said, "Mr. Mayor, may I speak, *please*."

"Not until I do," Dash said.

"Excuse me, but I believe I was here first."

"Yeah, you were, but what I have to say is more important." Dash turned toward the council. "You see, your honors, there is a way for the town to—"

"Hold on one minute." The door to the back of the council chamber slammed open one more time and in marched Cissy Warren and her father. Cissy looked quite fetching today in a classy yellow suit that matched her blond hair. She was the antithesis of Rocky—colorful in every way on the outside, but utterly lacking in any kind of magic.

The moment Cissy and the senator arrived, Rocky made herself seem smaller. She hunched her shoulders. She looked down. She tried to appear demure. All of that bothered Hugh a great deal. Rocky was far more interesting and vital than Cissy in all the important ways. Rocky was more interesting and vital than Victoria, too. If only Rocky would lose the gray suits, she wouldn't look like such a little wren, instead of the magnificent bird of paradise that she truly was.

"Senator, what can I do for you?" Bob stood up.

The senator cast his eye around the room, taking note of the church ladies lining the back wall. He frowned in Rocky's direction. "What in the Sam Hill are you doing?" he asked her.

"Uh, I was trying to help Lord Woolham," Rocky said.

"Help him? Good gravy, Caroline, do you see what's written on those signs?"

Rocky blushed. "Uh, yeah, I do, but, see . . . um."

"Look, just shut up," Dash said. "I have something monumental to say."

Rocky groaned. The senator's face got red. "Caroline, I really don't like your boyfriend talking to me that way. And I'm very disappointed in you. I distinctly told you to help Cissy, not to work against her. And, lord knows, the last thing any of us wanted to do was to rile up a bunch of churchwomen. Really, I thought you had more sense."

Rocky's face paled. "But—"

The senator turned toward the town council. "I'm taking charge of this situation. There is no reason for ya'll to condemn the land because—"

"Huey! What are you doing?" This comment came from Aunt Petal, who arrived on the scene wearing a purple dress and her red spectacles. She came striding into the room with Aunt Petunia, followed by Miriam Randall and a little girl with big brown eyes, a dirty T-shirt, and skinned knees.

"Hello, Aunt Petal. I'm here to do what Petunia asked me to do. I'm going to tell these good people that I don't want Elbert Rhodes's land. And when I'm finished, we'll go home to the UK, and I'll marry Lady Ashton, just as you want. I'm sure Aeval will be pleased to hear this news."

"What?" Petal, Petunia, Cissy, and Rocky said in unison.

Dash turned toward Rocky. "Shoot, Rocky, you didn't say he was engaged to be married to someone in England. Did you know that?"

The spectators began to speak at once. Big Bob banged his gavel but no one noticed. Hettie and her church ladies took that moment to renew their "Down with Lord deBracy" chant.

And into this fray strode Stone Rhodes, the chief of police. One might have expected him to impose order, but instead he walked right up to Hugh and asked, "Are you really engaged to be married to someone else?"

"Um, well, I—" Before Hugh could finish the sentence, Stone hauled back and punched Hugh right in the solar plexus.

Pain exploded, but he couldn't even whimper. The punch had taken away his ability to breathe. He went down on his hands and knees, stars circling his vision.

Somewhere, from a distance, he heard a child's voice saying, "Daddy, why did you hit that man? Don't you always say that it's better to talk than to fight?"

Rocky stared at the damage her big brother had just inflicted. She wanted to rush to Hugh's side. Help him. Hold him. Kiss him.

But she couldn't move. Her fingers, toes, and lips went numb with cold. Her eyes lost their focus. Her mind went fuzzy. Something strange and yet oddly familiar touched her and held her in place.

She watched as a bevy of little old ladies, including Miriam Randall, descended on Hugh. They went down on their knees and started tittering and stroking and comforting him.

He was in good hands. He seemed to be recovering.

But the situation in the council room still teetered on the brink of disaster. Caroline needed to do something.

But what?

The blood roared in her ears. Tears threatened to

spill over. And then, something down deep inside of her snapped.

And the unseen force that had pinned her in place released her. She yanked off her jacket, moved forward, and snatched the gavel from Bob Thomas's suddenly slack hand.

She pounded the gavel on the desk and shouted, "Ya'll, just shut up and listen to me!"

The room went quiet, more in shock than because of her gavel banging. The last time Rocky had lost her temper had been pretty darn memorable. But she really didn't care anymore. She was moved by this weird feeling she couldn't quite explain.

"Look," she said. "Let's get one thing straight. No one is going to bulldoze Golfing for God. So you ladies can just shut up. Now!"

The church ladies stopped and stared. A few mouths hung open.

Rocky continued, "Even if Lillian could condemn the land, the town has no money to buy my daddy out. And besides, you should all know that Lord Woolham is a fake and a phony."

A collective gasp went through the crowd.

"I say, young woman," one of the gray-haired ladies ministering to the recovering lord said, "I do take exception to that remark." The woman spoke with an English accent. Could this be one of Hugh's aunts?

Rocky cocked her head. "Are you Petal or Petunia?" she asked.

"Petunia."

Rocky nodded. "Well, it's true. He came in here all snotty and lord-like, but he's not at all like that." She gestured to the crowd in the council room. "And ya'll know that, too. He gave money to your committee, Hettie. And he helped Bubba with his car. And he even played matchmaker with Bubba and Rachel. Ya'll know this."

Everyone nodded.

"What you don't know is that someone"—she looked pointedly at Cissy—"made him an offer yesterday that would solve all of his financing and real estate problems. All he had to do was to build his factory upstate along the I-85 corridor. Building up that way would have been easier and cheaper for him. A wise businessman would have taken that chance and run with it. But Hugh deBracy didn't.

"And you want to know why? Because he didn't want to sell ya'll out. That's why. He knew you needed this factory more than the folks up north do. He didn't have to care about you, but he did. And if he were some snotty lord, he wouldn't have cared. He would have just taken his business elsewhere.

"So that's what I mean. He's not what you think he is. He's a good man. In fact, he's the kindest man I've ever met in my life. He's, well…he's a regular guy."

She spared a moment to look at Hugh, who had regained his feet and looked no worse for having been manhandled by her older brother. She almost lost herself in his gaze. He was staring at her, with just a hint of a smile on his face. The kindness she loved so much was evident there. How could she have ever doubted him?

She turned back to the people in the visitors' gallery before she broke down in tears. "If you want to be angry at someone, why not be angry at Jimmy Marshall? He's the one who sold Lord Woolham worthless swamp and then egged Lillian on with this whole notion of condemning the golf course. Jimmy should be tarred and feathered for selling that land to Hugh for the price he sold it."

More mouths dropped open. Behind her Jimmy Marshall stood up. "I'm not listening to this crap." He hurried from the room. Hettie watched him go. She didn't follow him.

Dash watched Hettie watch Jimmy. It was pathetic.

Caroline took another breath. "And you"—she pointed to Cissy—"you came into my hometown yesterday and got everyone all riled up, and then when Hugh didn't agree to your proposal to build the factory upstate, you told your daddy it was my fault. That was dishonest all the way around.

"And don't you ever say my name again the way you said it the other day at the barbecue. My name is Rocky Rhodes. You say it with respect, because I deserve respect. You'd get on a lot better if you were more like his Lordship. He's kind to people. You are not. And I've got news for you, I'm one of your daddy's constituents. And the plain, hardworking, slightly quirky folks who live here in Last Chance are his constituents, too. So you can take your red Corvette, and you can go on back to the city."

"Now Caroline," the senator said, his face getting red.

"I'm sorry, sir. But I haven't done anything wrong here. All I've done is to find the solution to Lord Woolham's problems."

"You have?"

Rocky didn't elaborate on her solution. That was for Dash to do. Instead, she looked out at the people in the visitors' gallery, who were watching as if this were a roller derby. "And the rest of you. Just because I love ya'll doesn't mean you can't improve on some things. You need to stop with the gossip. Before you open your mouths to pass on something unkind, you can also stop to figure out if it makes any sense. You've been blaming me for Bubba all these years, and you know what? I let you. But I'm not going to let you do that anymore.

"I never loved Bubba Lockheart. He asked me to marry him at the Davis High senior prom that year we graduated. The prom was in May, ya'll, not July when we have the Watermelon Festival. I told Bubba no in May. I told him I had a scholarship to USC, and I was too young to get married.

"And you know who supported me in that?"

"No," a few of the people said in unison.

"It was Stone's wife, Sharon."

"What?" Stone said.

"Yeah, it was Sharon." Caroline took a deep breath. She could almost feel Sharon right beside her, giving her courage. "Sharon told me I shouldn't run away and get married. Even though ya'll wanted that to happen in the worst way. You wanted me to be like Sharon. But Sharon told me I should be my own self. She told me that the only reason for running off with someone is because you can't live without them.

"Well, I could live without Bubba, all right. And I told him so privately. But he reckoned he would up the stakes, and he asked me to run off with him that night I wore my Watermelon Queen dress. Only unlike my brother, he asked me in front of everyone. What did you expect of me when he ambushed me that way?

"He humiliated me. I didn't break his heart—not

publicly anyway. I wanted to go to college. And he wasn't willing to wait for me. The fact that he messed up and flunked out is not my fault. He has to take some responsibility for his actions. Being a football player does not absolve him from responsibility for his own life.

"And one last thing—it's hard for a Watermelon Queen in this town. Girls may want romance in their lives, but an eighteen-year-old in the twenty-first century is not really interested in running off and getting married. Most of your daughters and sisters want to go to college. So quit trying to force us all into that outdated mold. I don't know why Sharon ran off with my brother, but she was the exception, not the rule. And she knew it, too."

Rocky glanced at her brother. He looked ashen. She felt a pang of remorse for telling her big secret out loud this way. But maybe it was for the best. People had a way of making Sharon out to be some kind of saint. And she hadn't been. She'd been a great friend and a good wife and a loving mother. Rocky missed her. But Sharon was a real person, and it was time to give up on the myth.

"All right. Now that we've cleared the air, I want ya'll to sit in your seats and listen to Dash. I know ya'll still think of Dash as the bad boy orphan who came to town with an attitude when he was twelve. But you know, he's moved on with his life, too. So y'all listen to him. He has something really important to say."

She handed the gavel back to Bob, then strode down the aisle and out the door and into the hot, humid day.

Haley and the little old ladies were on a mission to save the day and the town. Haley knew this because Miriam had told everyone that's what they were doing.

Haley wasn't sure exactly how the ladies intended to save the day and the town, but they had brought her here to the big government building on Palmetto Avenue just in time to see Daddy punch someone.

Haley didn't like that one bit, on account of the fact that the man Daddy punched hadn't been doing anything mean or nasty. He'd been talking about something.

And boy, the Sorrowful Angel wasn't happy with Daddy either. She was madder than a wet hen.

Just as soon as Daddy finished punching that man, the angel kind of moved over to stand next to Aunt Rocky. And then Aunt Rocky got mad and started talking about a bunch of stuff Haley didn't understand.

When Aunt Rocky stopped talking and everyone got real quiet, the Sorrowful Angel smiled.

Haley had never seen the angel smile before. It changed the angel's face. She looked way more like an angel when she smiled like that.

And then the angel's smile faded and Aunt Rocky got a funny look on her face. Aunt Rocky hightailed it out of the room and the angel followed her.

Dash Randall started talking, but Haley was way more interested in what the angel was up to. So was Miz Petal, because the old lady put out her hand toward Haley and said, "Shall we go, love. I think Aeval and your spirit friend want us to help." She winked.

Haley had no idea who Aeval was, but Miz Petal was really smart about angels. Haley put her hand in Miz Petal's and let the old lady lead her out of the building.

Hugh's chest ached with more than the blow Stone Rhodes had delivered.

Rocky thought he was kind. She believed in him. She thought he could make a success of himself.

No one had ever had faith in him before.

He was not about to let Rocky go. Not after that speech she'd just given. He couldn't imagine trying to find happiness with Victoria when he could be himself with Rocky.

He rushed down the aisle and out onto the small lawn in front of City Hall. He found Rocky there, standing with her back to the door, her hands balled up. She seemed to be about to scream or to cry. He wasn't sure.

Aunt Petal and the little girl were there. He glanced in his aunt's direction. Her smile was gentle and kind.

If he had learned kindness, then Petal had taught it to him. And perhaps that was why Granddad had been so hard on him all those years. Granddad had been ashamed of his daughter. Petal had never been exactly right in her mind.

But she had been the best aunt a boy could ever want.

She winked. It was as if she expected something of him. And it didn't have a thing to do with Lady Ashton.

Caroline turned and strode toward the sidewalk, her body strung tight and shaking with emotions Hugh could only guess at. When she reached the curb, she pulled off her high heels. She stood on bare feet, breathing hard. Then she said an extremely filthy curse word that sounded remarkably sexy coming out of her adorable mouth, before she heaved both shoes into the middle of the gutter. Then she tossed her little gray suit jacket into the street as well.

She stood there looking at her conservative shoes and that colorless jacket as if she had come to a serious decision about things. At just that moment a passing Ford pickup hit the shoes with an audible crunch.

"Good riddance," he said as he strolled toward her.

She turned, frowning. "You're supposed to be inside listening to Dash."

"I didn't want to listen to Dash. I'm so glad you got rid of that gray jacket and those shoes. Why did you throw them in the gutter?"

"I don't know. The jacket and shoes felt like they were strangling me somehow." She took a couple of deep breaths. "Jeez, I really lost my temper in there."

She frowned up at him. "I'm really, really sorry for blowing up at you last night, too. After I thought about it, I realized you weren't the kind of man who would cheat Daddy out of his land."

"You owe me nothing. Am I really the kindest man you've ever met?" His voice came out husky with emotions he was trying to hold in check.

A little twinkle lit up her pixie green eyes. "You are. You suck at business, but you're a really nice guy." She paused a moment. "I know I don't exactly meet Miriam's forecast for you, but I think I've fallen in love with you anyway," she said in a little husky voice.

"I think I've fallen in love with you, too."

The light in her eyes grew a little brighter and more intense. "I fixed it so you don't have to go marry Lady Whatshername. You can build your factory here."

"I can?"

She nodded. "Yeah, that's what Dash is in there talking about. He's got land out the wazoo that he'll lease to you for practically nothing. And if you treat him nice, he might even invest in the factory."

He laughed out loud. "Oh, my goodness, Senator Warren was right about you. You just managed a miracle."

She shook her head. "No. It wasn't a miracle. It took a lot of persuading. Dash is not nearly as sure of himself as he might appear. He doesn't realize that he's now, officially, the richest man in town, or how much good he could do. But I've got this feeling you'll help him learn. Also, I'm really sorry but I'm afraid you're going to have to do some fence mending with Cissy. I really got carried away with what I said to her. And I know better than that, really I do."

"I'm sure I can charm Cissy. Besides, she's going to want my looms. They're better than anyone else's. I'm not at all worried about her."

"You're not?"

"No. But there is one important thing I do need to say."

"Okay."

Her gaze met his. "Darling, will you marry me?"

A series of catcalls and hoots rose up from the steps of City Hall.

Rocky tore her gaze away from Hugh's serious brown eyes.

Holy smokes, the entire town was standing over there. Rocky flashed on that night twelve years ago when Bubba had pulled this same stunt. Everyone had hooted and hollered and catcalled that time, too.

She turned back toward Hugh. "You really want to marry me? Even though you're supposed to marry an heiress?"

"Poppy feathers," Miz Miriam said from the front row of the peanut gallery. "I didn't tell him to go looking for an heiress. I told him to go look for the woman who would find him a fortune."

"Yeah, and she failed to mention that the fortune belongs to me," Dash said.

Hugh grinned. "Darling, I do recall that you said something a moment ago about my being a regular sort of guy. I believe that fits the bill. We'd be idiotic not to let ourselves get caught up in Miriam's magic. In fact"—he turned and gazed at the little gray-haired lady holding Haley's hand—"I believe Aunt Petal came all this way to help me see the truth. I've changed my mind about fortune-tellers, spirit guides, and even angels."

Emotion clogged her throat. She stood there looking at him, wanting to simply fall into his arms and let him carry her away. But really, she hardly knew him. And besides, Sharon had set a very high standard.

Could she live without him? Rocky was pretty sure she could survive. She loved him, of course. But running off with him? That was a whole different kettle of fish.

"Aunt Rocky," Haley said. "You're making the angel really unhappy."

Rocky turned to look at Haley. "The angel is here?"

"Oh, yes, quite," Petal said.

Hugh stared at his aunt. "You can see the angel, too?"

"Oh, it's not an angel, Huey. It's a spirit of some kind. I think it's a ghost. Maybe someone Rocky knew in her past. She's quite agitated. Whatever you're thinking, my dear, the ghost knows, and she's quite displeased."

"What were you thinking?" Haley asked.

"I was thinking about your mother."

"Oh, good," Haley said. "Momma ran off with Daddy.

You should run off with Mr. Hugh. I think the angel wants you to."

Rocky turned back to Hugh. "Your aunt is kind of odd."

"So's your niece."

He smiled.

She smiled back.

She didn't give it another moment's thought. She just did what seemed like the logical thing to do at a moment like this. She threw caution to the wind, took a deep leap of genuine faith, and wrapped her arms around Hugh deBracy, Baron Woolham.

And Hugh, understanding his role in this fantasy as well as anyone there, did the expected. He picked her up and carried her off down Palmetto Avenue toward his silver Mustang convertible.

EPILOGUE

Rocky stared at herself in the mirror. It told the truth, as always. She looked radiant today, as any bride should. She was glad Hugh had convinced her not to elope with him. A wedding was so much more fun.

"Knock, knock. You wanted to talk to me?"

She turned. Stone had cracked the door to the little anteroom near the vestibule of Christ Church. She smoothed down the yards of tulle in her skirt. "Yes, I did. You can come in. I'm decent."

Stone strolled through the door. He looked incredibly handsome today, dressed in a gray suit and a dark tie and a pink rose in his lapel. He wasn't young. A few gray hairs had started to sprout at his temples. But he exuded a kind of raw masculine energy that made women turn and watch him.

He was a real hero. A war hero. A cop. And she loved him with all her heart, and she feared she had hurt him. Not only by telling her secret about Sharon, but by her choices on this day of days.

He took two steps and stopped. The look in his eyes made something hitch in Rocky's throat. "I wanted to give you warning before I marched down the aisle," she said.

He pressed his lips together and nodded. "Thanks." The tears that almost filled his eyes were gone in an instant. He straightened his shoulders and went back to being iron man. It was almost sad, really, that even after six years, he'd never really allowed himself to grieve.

Sharon wouldn't have approved of this. Rocky knew that, deep down in her soul. And even though she knew it was completely irrational, she couldn't help but feel that somehow Sharon had been with her that day when she'd lost her temper and told the town both how much she loved them and how much they annoyed her.

Thankfully the town had forgiven her—mostly because she'd given them another myth.

"You look beautiful," he said. He continued into the room and then leaned down and gave her a brotherly kiss on the cheek.

"Stone, I wanted to explain about the dress."

He shook his head. "There isn't any need." He turned around without another word and left the room, abridging all the things she wanted to say to him. All the sisterly advice about moving on and not being sad because of what she had chosen to wear today. But he wasn't ready to listen. He might never be.

She turned back to the mirror. Well, that was his problem, not hers. She wasn't going to let Stone's sadness ruin the happiest day of her life.

Haley came skipping in. She was dressed all in green and pink, and she looked like a little imp with flowers in her hair and carrying a wicker basket filled with pink rose petals. "We're all ready. And I promise I'll make my petals last until you get all the way to the altar."

Rocky leaned down and gave Haley a kiss. "Just like we practiced last night."

"I got it, Aunt Rocky. I won't mess up. The angel is happy today. Did you know that? She likes your dress."

"I'm glad. I like my dress, too."

Daddy entered the room then, dressed in a rented suit and looking pretty dapper, despite his earring and long braid. Rocky took his arm and let him give her away. He'd been sentenced to some community service because Lillian refused to back down. He'd helped her rebuild her garden.

Doc Cooper said all his tests came back negative, and as near as anyone could tell, Daddy was the same as he'd always been. But Caroline wondered. She'd had a strange, fuzzy moment, and so had Daddy.

Maybe they'd been touched by an angel. Or maybe they both had lost their tempers beyond all reason.

Either explanation worked.

Daddy took her arm and led her down the aisle to her groom. She loved the moment when she took that first step, and everyone in the congregation stood up in shocked silence. They had all expected her to wear white. They had expected something like the pageantry of William and Kate's wedding.

But this was Last Chance, South Carolina, not merry old England.

So she'd worn the dress that defined her. Pink and green with yards and yards of tulle. They said she had been the prettiest Watermelon Queen who had ever reigned. And it just seemed appropriate that she should wear it, along with her rhinestone tiara, especially since she was marrying an English lord.

And by the look in everyone's eyes that morning, especially Hugh's, Rocky knew she'd made the right choice.

She said her vows. Hugh spoke his.

And they sealed the union of the Watermelon Queen and the English baron with a kiss that the old church ladies of Last Chance would probably gossip about for the next twenty years.

READING GROUP GUIDE

Discussion Questions for
Last Chance Beauty Queen

1. Rocky's character has been shaped by the fact that Bubba Lockheart humiliated her when she was eighteen. What are some of the ways Rocky deals with that humiliation? Which ones are positive and help her to grow as a person? Which ones are destructive? Have you ever suffered a public humiliation? How did you handle it? How did it affect you?

2. In the scene where Rocky and Hugh are sitting together in church, the minister is giving a sermon based on Mark 12:38–40, the story where Jesus tells his disciples to beware of the scribes who go in long clothing and make a pretense of prayer. The minister's message in this sermon is that God can see through the pretense that we sometimes hide behind. How does this sermon affect Rocky's view of herself? How do you think Hugh was affected by this sermon?

Talk about how this passage relates to the love story between Rocky and Hugh.

3. Hugh worries that he can't be a success because he's too kindhearted. Do you think that kindhearted people are doomed to business failure? Can you think of a kindhearted person who has managed to be successful in his business dealings?

4. Rocky loves her town, but she's afraid to admit just how much. Discuss how Rocky's assignment to assist Hugh with his factory helps her to more fully appreciate the town where she grew up.

5. As a young woman, Rocky found a mentor in Sharon Rhodes, her sister-in-law. Discuss how Sharon's advice was helpful to Rocky. Discuss how Sharon's advice was potentially hurtful. Have you had a mentor? How did he or she change your life?

6. The book discusses how small communities make up myths. Besides the myth of Stone and Sharon, what other myths have the people of Last Chance developed through the retelling of community stories? How do these myths and stories form a collective culture for Last Chance? Why do you think it's so hard for people to live up to these expectations? Is this tendency for communities to make myths a good thing or a bad thing? Do you think this is limited to small towns?

7. Haley faces a serious dilemma with her angel. The Sorrowful Angel is misbehaving, and Haley is being

blamed for her actions. In Haley's mind, she's innocent. The rest of the world sees it a different way.
Have you ever been out of step with the rest of the
world? How does it feel? How did you cope? Did you
feel crazy?

8. Have you ever been blamed for something you didn't
   do, as Haley is? Have you ever had to confess to
   something you didn't do in order to avoid punishment
   or in order to protect someone from being punished?
   Do you think it's okay to lie in a situation like that? Or
   should you always be honest, even if you'll be blamed
   for something you didn't do?

9. How are Rocky's shoes a metaphor for the things
   that hold her back from being the person she really is
   and the person that Hugh will come to love? Contrast
   Rocky's lost, broken, and discarded shoes with Cinderella's lost slipper. How are Cinderella and Rocky
   the same? How are they different? Hugh prefers
   Rocky barefoot. How does that make him different
   from Prince Charming, who goes on a quest to find
   someone to fit an impossibly small shoe?

HEAD HOME FOR THE HOLIDAYS...

LAST CHANCE CHRISTMAS

Please turn this page
for a preview.

Jesus looked like he'd been hit by a Mack Truck. The statue of the Son of God lay on its side, its fiberglass infrastructure torn and ragged. Scattered on the gravel beside the bleaching carcass were the remnants of a sign that read "Golfing for God."

Well, I guess that's it. Lark Chaikin hugged her elbows and tried to keep warm against the December gust that blew her bangs into her eyes. Wasn't it supposed to be warm this time of year in South Carolina?

Apparently not.

She looked up at the tops of the pine trees, swaying in the wind. She shivered.

She had to be crazy to have driven all the way from New York on this fool's errand. Roadside America was littered with the corpses of mini-golf courses, their windmills suspended in time, their giant Paul Bunyons toppled. It only stood to reason that Golfing for God would have gone the way of all the fiberglass dinosaurs.

Pop should have checked before he made his last

request. But of course, Pop had been sick for a long time, and in the last few days, it was almost as if he'd come back to this place in his mind.

Lark turned back toward her late father's SUV, a giant silver thing that drove like an ocean liner and guzzled gas like one, too. She opened the back door and stared down at the cardboard box containing Pop's ashes. The box was eight inches square with the words "Chaikin, Leon" scrawled across its top.

She pressed a couple of fingers against the ache in her forehead that had been growing all day. "Why'd you make a big *megillah* about being buried here in the middle of nowhere on a closed-up mini-golf course?" She couldn't go on. Her throat closed up, and tears threatened her eyes. She swallowed back the grief that was too new and too raw to be endured or expressed. Pop had left her alone only two days ago.

Lark leaned on the tailgate, her gaze shifting from the box to the canvas camera bag sitting beside it. Her fingers itched to pick up the Nikon, maybe shoot a few photos of the broken statue. She might be able to capture the Picasso-like perspective of its smashed face. Maybe shooting a few photos would help her get her balance back.

But she couldn't find the courage to pick up the camera. She slammed the tailgate and turned toward a gravel path clearly posted with No Trespassing signs.

Something violent had damaged the stand of pines growing on the right side of the path. The trees looked as if they had been blasted by napalm at some point. A wave of nausea gripped her. Oh boy, she was losing it. The last photo assignment in Somalia had done her in.

Her feet crunched on the gravel, and the wind in the pines sounded like the rattling of dry bones. Lark searched the darkening sky. Clouds, heavy with rain, scudded across her view, and a lone hawk circled above, watching and waiting. Dizziness assailed her. She couldn't remember the last time she'd eaten, or slept.

She lowered her gaze. A medium-sized structure resembling Noah's Ark loomed ahead of her. Scaffolding had been set up around it, and it looked as if someone was giving it a fresh coat of paint. Still, for all that, the place seemed sad and worn and abandoned. A few dead leaves swirled across the path driven by the wind.

She turned right and made a circuit of the place, hole to hole, past Adam and Eve, the Tower of Babel, and David and Goliath. Most of the holes seemed in semigood repair, except for the Plague of Frogs. The fiberglass frogs were missing, their guts exposed to the elements. She remembered Pop talking about how the frogs used to spit water over the fairway. Now only mangled plumbing was left.

She turned and walked past the mostly undamaged Jonah and the Whale, then cut through the Wise Men with their bobbing camels and Jesus walking on water, until she reached the eighteenth hole.

She halfway expected this hole to be the much-laughed-about Tomb of Jesus. It would be just like Pop to want to have his ashes buried in the ersatz tomb of a Savior he didn't believe in. She could see him laughing his ass off as people putted golf balls across his grave. After all, Pop had a murderous short game.

But the eighteenth hole wasn't a tomb.

It was a celebration of the resurrection.

• • •

Stonewall Rhodes, the chief of police for the incorporated city of Last Chance, South Carolina, drove his cruiser south on Palmetto Avenue, taking his second-to-last circuit of the day. It was nearly five o'clock, and the light was fading quickly into dusk. It would be dark by the time he drove out to the edge of town and back.

He got about halfway to the Allenberg County line before he saw the silver Cadillac Escalade parked in the lot at Golfing for God. The New York tags caught his attention.

Cars with New York plates didn't come through this neck of the woods very often—unless the folks in them were lost tourists searching for the road to Hilton Head, or on a pilgrimage seeking out Golfing for God.

At one time, Golfing for God had attracted a fair number of pilgrims. The place was listed on roadsideamerica.com and had made it into a couple of tour guides. But the place had been closed up for more than a year—ever since its propane tank had been struck by lightning.

Of course, Hettie Marshall and the Committee to Resurrect Golfing for God had just hired a contractor to begin fixing the place up. They were aiming for a big reopening in the spring. In the meantime, though, the No Trespassing signs were designed to keep the pilgrims away.

Stone pulled his cruiser into the golf course's parking lot, the gravel crunching under its wheels. He eyeballed the Cadillac. It appeared to be unoccupied, but appearances could be deceiving. Before leaving his cruiser, he keyed the plate information into his in-car computer. An instant later, the Cadillac's history came back to him. There were no outstanding warrants involving the vehicle, which was registered to one Leon Chaikin of Kings Point, New York.

Stone stared at the name for a long moment as the little hairs on the back of his neck stood up on end.

The past had come back to haunt him.

He snagged his Stetson from the passenger seat and dropped it down on his head as he left the cruiser. He pulled his heavy-duty flashlight from his utility belt as he cautiously approached the vehicle. He shone the light through the driver's side window and confirmed that the car was unoccupied.

The SUV was a late model—clean and fully loaded, with a GPS system and satellite radio in the dashboard. A well-worn duffel bag in army green occupied the cargo area, loaded with what looked like expensive camera equipment. The SUV was locked.

He turned away from the car and walked up the charred remains of the main walkway. He saw the woman as soon as he turned the corner by the first hole. She sat on the wooden bench at the feet of the resurrected Jesus on hole eighteen, with her head bowed as if deep in prayer. For a brief moment, it appeared as if the Savior's hand moved outward toward the praying woman, as if He were trying to comfort her.

A shiver inched down Stone's spine, and he blinked a couple of times. Only then did he realize the deepening dusk had played a trick on him. A little sparrow sat in the hand of Jesus. It turned its head this way and that and gave the appearance of the statue's hand in motion.

The woman was as tiny as the bird, with short-cropped dark hair that spiked around her head. She wore jeans and a peacoat. A stiff wind might blow her away.

She looked up, turning a pair of dark, hollow eyes in his direction. All the breath left his lungs as he found himself caught up in her stare. For an instant, he felt as if he might be looking at a ghost from some forgotten past. Her face was oddly gray in the fading light, the skin beneath her eyes smudged with the purple of exhaustion.

She wasn't beautiful, but her looks stopped him in his tracks. She looked hopelessly lost, like a small waif or street urchin.

A hot, tight feeling slammed into his chest. The unexpected intensity of that feeling was tempered by the immediate clanging of alarm bells in his head. She was trouble.

She had arrived in a car registered to Leon Chaikin, a man who had upset the balance of things in Last Chance more than forty years ago.

Stone couldn't shake the feeling that the woman was here for the same purpose. This tiny woman was going to rend the daily fabric of life in his town, and he couldn't let that happen.

She looked up at him, and he recognized his doom right there in her hollow eyes, just as he recognized something about her that he couldn't even put words to. He had this odd feeling that he had known her for a long, long time.

"Ma'am," he said. "What part of 'No Trespassing' do you not understand? Golfing for God is not in business, and I'd be obliged if you would move on."

Lark gripped the edge of the bench and willed herself to stand up. It was difficult. The nausea and dizziness she had felt earlier had grown steadily worse.

She turned her attention to the policeman. He sure didn't look like the stereotype of a small town cop. He was big, well armed, and wore a bulletproof vest.

"Ma'am, are you all right?" he asked.

Well, no, she wasn't all right. Pop was dead. She was feeling like crap. She was scared of her camera. And her editor wanted her on a plane to Africa so she could take more photos of starving kids.

She focused on the cop's face. She recognized the green eyes, dimpled chin, and meandering nose. Crap. She was hallucinating.

"Carmine?" she asked. Her throat hurt.

"Excuse me?" The cop went on alert. His shoulders stiffened, and his body coiled in that ready-for-action pose she'd seen in the Marines patrolling the streets of Baghdad. "Ma'am?"

She blinked a couple of times, trying to clear her vision. He wasn't Carmine, of course. If she were seeing Carmine now, at the age of thirty-four, she really *was* losing it. Carmine wasn't real. He was a figment of her childhood imagination. He was long dead and buried, and he needed to stay that way.

"I'm all right, really," Lark said, coming to a decision. If Pop wanted us to scatter his ashes here, who the hell was she to say it couldn't be done. She needed to finish this chore and then go someplace warm for a couple of days where she could tackle her sudden fear of cameras.

She cleared her dry throat. "I was wondering if you could tell me where I might find Zeke Rhodes. I need to speak with him about something."

"Ma'am, Zeke Rhodes has been dead for more than forty years. I would have expected you to know that."

"Oh," Lark said as she fought another wave of dizziness and disappointment. "More than forty years? Really?"

"Yes, ma'am. He died the day Leon Chaikin left town. There are folks who say old Zeke died of a heart attack, but there are equally as many who think he was murdered."

Her head throbbed, and her face went hot and then cold. The world spun around her. "Murdered?"

"Yes, ma'am. Zeke died right where you're standing right now."

She took a reflexive step forward as if to avoid the long-dead body of Zeke Rhodes. "Murdered by whom?"

"Well, not everyone thinks he was murdered. There's a big debate on that topic."

"But you think he was, don't you?"

The cop's shoulders moved a little. "Maybe. It happened before I was born. Are you related to him?"

"Him? Who?"

"Leon Chaikin."

"Oh, yeah, I'm his daughter." The world started tilting sideways.

"Well, ma'am, Lee Marshall has always believed that your daddy murdered Zeke. That's not the official story, of course. If it *was* the official story, I'm pretty sure the old sheriff would have issued a warrant for Leon Chaikin's arrest back in 1968."

Lark's stomach clutched and darkness crowded her vision right before she passed out.

THE DISH

Where authors give you the inside scoop!

From the desk of Jennifer Haymore

Dear Reader,

When Olivia Donovan, the heroine of SECRETS OF AN ACCIDENTAL DUCHESS (on sale now), entered my office for the first time, she stared at the place (and me) wide-eyed, as if she'd never seen an office—or a romance writer—before.

Bemused, I offered her a chair and asked her why she'd come. I was surprised when she got straight to the point; honestly, from the way she looked, I'd expected her to be far more reluctant.

"I want you to write my story."

I leaned forward. "Well, just about everyone who comes through my door wants me to write their story. To get me to do it, however, requires...more."

She carried a reticule looped around her wrist, and at this point she began to riffle around in it. "How much more?" she asked. "I haven't got much, but whatever I have—"

"Oh, no. I didn't mean 'more' in the sense of payment."

She frowned. "Well then, it what sense *did* you mean?"

"Well, I write about love...the development of relationships, the ups and downs, the ultimate happily ever after."

She gave a wistful sigh. "That's exactly what I want.

But"—she clutched her reticule so hard, her knuckles went white—"I fear I shall never have it."

I raised my eyebrows at her. "Why not? You're a lovely young woman. Obviously well bred, and from the looks of that silk and those pearls you're wearing, you're not lacking in the dowry department."

She gave me a wry smile. "I believe there's more to it than that."

"Look, I'm pretty familiar with your time period, Miss Donovan. In the late Regency period in England, looks, breeding, and financial status were everything."

She shook her head. "It's partially him...well, the man I'm thinking about, the one I'm hoping..." She hesitated, then the words rushed out: "Well, he's going to be a *duke* someday."

I blew that off. "In one of my books, a duke married a *housemaid*." (And this lady was no housemaid, that was for sure!) "Honestly, I can't see why any future duke wouldn't want to pursue a lady like you. You'd make a lovely duchess."

She licked her lips, hesitated, then whispered, "There's where you're wrong. I fear I'd make a terrible duchess. You see, I'm...ill."

I looked at her up and down, then down and up. She was a little thin, and pale, but ladies of this era kept themselves pale on purpose, after all. Otherwise, she looked healthy to me.

She stared at me for a moment, blinking back tears, then stood up abruptly. "I think I should go. This is hopeless."

She wasn't lying. She really believed she'd never have a happy ending of her own. Poor woman.

"No, please stay, Miss Donovan. Please tell me your

story. I promise, if there's anyone who can give you a happy ending, I can."

"Really?" she whispered.

I raised three fingers. "Scout's honor."

She frowned, clearly having no idea what I was talking about, but she was too polite and gently bred to question me. Slowly, she lowered herself back into her seat, still clutching that little green silk reticule.

I flipped up my laptop and opened a new document. "Tell me everything, Miss Donovan. From the beginning."

I truly hope you enjoy reading Olivia Donovan's story! Please come visit me at my website, www.jenniferhaymore .com, where you can share your thoughts about my books, sign up for some fun freebies and contests, and read more about the characters from SECRETS OF AN ACCI-DENTAL DUCHESS.

Sincerely,

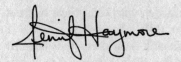

♥ ♥ ♥ ♥ ♥ ♥ ♥ ♥ ♥ ♥ ♥ ♥ ♥ ♥ ♥ ♥ ♥ ♥ ♥

From the desk of Kristen Callihan

Dear Reader,

I fell in love with classic movies at an early age. While other kids were watching MTV, I was sighing over Cary Grant or laughing at the antics of William Powell and Myrna Loy.

There was a fairytale aspect about these films—from the impeccable clothes and elegant manners to the gorgeous décor—that took me out of my own world and into a place of dreams. Much like a good romance novel, if you think about it.

Watching old Fred Astaire movies had me dreaming of living in New York City in an apartment done up in elegant shades of white. *It Happened One Night* had me yearning for a road caper with a handsome stranger. I coveted Marilyn Monroe's pink satin dress in *Gentlemen Prefer Blondes*...all right, her diamonds too! But hands down, my favorite aspect of classic movies was the dialogue.

Back in the 1930s and 40s, the tight rein of censorship turned scriptwriters into masters of innuendo. Dialogue back then wasn't merely conversation; it was banter, the double entendre, a back-and-forth duel of words and wit. It was foreplay.

Therefore, it wasn't any surprise to me that when I started writing my own stories, dialogue would play a key part in my characters' relationships. Before the touches, there are the words.

In my novel FIRELIGHT, the verbal foreplay between my hero, Lord Benjamin Archer, and my heroine, Miranda Ellis, is particularly important. Archer hides his appearance behind masks, determined not to let Miranda see what lies beneath. In turn, Miranda hides her true nature behind the mask of her beauty. With so much hidden, they must rely on verbal communication to slip past their physical walls.

And so we have a dance of words. Words that say one thing but mean another. Words that test and tease. Words that make the sexual tension between Archer and Miranda burn hotter and hotter, until it can do nothing less than combust.

Hope you enjoy the heat,

♥ ♥ ♥ ♥ ♥ ♥ ♥ ♥ ♥ ♥ ♥ ♥ ♥ ♥ ♥ ♥

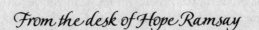

From the desk of Hope Ramsay

Dear Reader,

Among the things I love best about small, rural towns are the events they hold. Some of these events commemorate national holidays, others celebrate civic pride. And still others, like festivals and county fairs, seem to be mostly about having a real good time.

You can find small-town events everywhere. Even in the suburban landscape around Washington, DC, small towns maintain their sense of identity through their festivals, fairs, and special days. Alexandria, Virginia, where I currently live, throws an annual birthday party for its hometown hero, George Washington. Imagine parading through the streets in the February cold and snow. Seems strange, but it's a big annual event. It's fun. And my kids have fond memories of marching in that parade as members of their scout troops.

So it should come as no surprise that, when creating the world of Last Chance, I made sure to give it a festival complete with a parade, a barbecue, dancing, games of chance, and carnival rides. What better place to turn the matchmaking church ladies of Last Chance loose? The fact that they set up a kissing booth to raise money for a good cause should come as no surprise to anyone. Of course, I couldn't let the women have all the fun, so I also gave the local men a demolition derby where they could wreck cars to their hearts' content.

It was a lot of fun to send a member of the British aristocracy off to attend Last Chance's Watermelon Festival. Since my hero comes from a small village in the UK where they light bonfires on Samhain, Lord Woolham surprises the locals by taking to my county fair like a duck to water.

His Lordship enjoys his visit to Last Chance so much that he decides to stay. I hope you enjoy your visit too.

Hope Ramsay

From the desk of Cynthia Garner

Dear Reader,

I have been a fan of the paranormal since I was a kid. My teenaged years were spent watching re-runs of Christopher Lee and Peter Cushing in those wonderful Hammer horror films. When Frank Langella played Dracula and later on Gerard Butler...whoa! Tall, dark, and sexy won the day, except...those Draculas were evil. While I don't mind an evil vampire every now and again (they keep us on our toes, right?), I highly prefer them to be one of the good guys. Or at least a reforming bad guy who's struggling against his inner big bad.

When I first came up with the concept of an interdimensional rift being the origin of Earth's creatures of lore, excitement at the wonder and unlimited potential of such a world made me giddy. And it takes a lot to make me giddy. But a lonely, hot-bodied vampire named Tobias was my first indication that my gleefulness wasn't going to end anytime soon.

Add a feisty heroine who's part demon, part human, and full-on furious with this yummy vamp, and you have all sorts of fun as each of them fights their feelings for the other, determined to keep their relationship on a professional level while they investigate a string of murders.

Yeah. Like that ever works—in fiction, at least. We want our characters to be heroic, but flawed. And you can't get much more flawed than when you fall in love and completely complicate your life.

My website has some extras from KISS OF THE VAMPIRE: a deleted scene, a map showing where the bodies were found as well as an X-marks-the-spot where the final battle took place, a page of Nix's investigative notes, and a brief interview with Tobias Caine.

Look for Dante and Tori's story in my upcoming *Secret of the Wolf.*

Thanks for coming along for the ride!

Happy Reading!

Cynthia Garner

cynthiagarnerbooks@gmail.com

Find out more about Forever Romance!

Visit us at
www.hachettebookgroup.com/publishing_forever.aspx

Find us on Facebook
http://www.facebook.com/ForeverRomance

Follow us on Twitter
http://twitter.com/ForeverRomance

NEW AND UPCOMING TITLES

Each month we feature our new titles
and reader favorites.

CONTESTS AND GIVEAWAYS

We give away galleys, autographed copies,
and all kinds of exclusive items.

AUTHOR INFO

You'll find bios, articles, and links to personal websites
for all your favorite authors—and so much more.

GET SOCIAL

Connect with your favorite authors, editors, and
other Forever fans, and share what's important to you.

THE BUZZ

Sign up for our monthly romance newsletter,
and be the first to read all about it.

VISIT US ONLINE AT

WWW.HACHETTEBOOKGROUP.COM

FEATURES:

**OPENBOOK BROWSE AND
SEARCH EXCERPTS**

•

AUDIOBOOK EXCERPTS AND PODCASTS

•

AUTHOR ARTICLES AND INTERVIEWS

•

**BESTSELLER AND PUBLISHING
GROUP NEWS**

•

SIGN UP FOR E-NEWSLETTERS

•

**AUTHOR APPEARANCES AND TOUR
INFORMATION**

•

SOCIAL MEDIA FEEDS AND WIDGETS

•

DOWNLOAD FREE APPS

Bookmark Hachette Book Group
@ www.HachetteBookGroup.com